PERFECT IN EVERY WAY

MANORS AND MYSTERIES
BOOK II

KRISTEN ASHLEY

ROCK CHICK
PRESS

A MANORS AND MYSTERIES ROMANCE NOVEL

KRISTEN ASHLEY

NEW YORK TIMES BESTSELLING AUTHOR

DEDICATED IN MEMORY

To Mike and Gwyneth Ashley
I did the opposite of what Vivienne did.
I kept your name to honor both of you and Mark
on my books and in my life.
Thank you for gifting it—and many, many happy memories—to me.

AUTHORS NOTE

This novel tackles a variety of sensitive issues. In order not to spoil the story, I won't list those issues here.

However, if you're a sensitive reader, please be aware.

CHAPTER 1

THE DOWNS

I idled outside the ornate, twenty-foot-high gates, not thinking about the grand adventure that, for months, I'd been so excited to embark on, I could barely stand myself.

Instead, I was concentrating on the sudden bizarre feeling I had, which I'd never felt before.

A feeling that assaulted me (and that violent of a word was an apropos descriptor) the second I saw those gates.

It was a feeling so strong, I was idling in the road in front of the gates of a drive I was supposed to be turning into, a drive on a fortunately not very busy road, and yet for some reason, I was unable to turn in.

I didn't understand what I was feeling. It was, in my cadre of as yet experienced emotions, undefined.

I was exhilarated, yet alarmed.

Excited, yet terrified.

It was kind of like the sensation you get before you go into a haunted house.

You know it's going to be fun, but even so, you're facing the unexpected.

What you further know is, what's about to happen will be completely out of your control.

But in order to face that unexpected—though what you could expect was that you were going to have the pants frightened off you—you had to let go, put one foot in front of the other, trust, and know things are going to scare you, but in the end, you'll be laughing.

It took some effort to pocket this strange emotion so I could peer down the lane beyond the gates.

The lane was shaded with beautiful old trees and carpeted with vibrant green lawns.

It was then, out of nowhere, although this time predictably, I felt a strong pang of melancholy.

I did this even though I'd never met him. He was gone before I was alive.

Even so, I knew my great-grandfather had seen these gates. He'd been driven through them. He'd stayed in the massive house that lay beyond the intricate wrought iron and parkland.

In that house, he'd convalesced.

In that house, he'd fallen in love.

In the end, he'd left this extraordinary estate with a broken heart.

And I was there to tell his story.

On that thought, taking a bracing breath, I turned into the lane, stopped beside the security speaker and noted it had a camera.

I hit the button to roll down my window and was about to reach out and hit the one that would call to the house, but the speaker squawked at me before I could even raise my hand.

"Ms. Dupree?"

"Yes," I answered.

"Can you please hold your passport or some other official photo identification to the camera?" the speaker requested.

Unsurprised by this request, for I knew what lay beyond those gates, and thus I knew they wouldn't let anyone through them who shouldn't be going through them, I turned to my bag, pulled out my passport, opened it to the picture page and held it to the camera.

"One moment please," the speaker said.

Although I wasn't surprised they had security, and it was not just a couple of Ring cameras, I wondered what they could do with my passport information that would take a moment.

Could they check it?

And if they could, how did they get access to that kind of data?

As far as I knew, only government and law enforcement agencies could do something like that.

I mean, if they could, that would take this security to a new level.

I pocketed that emotion too as I slid my passport back into my tote and waited.

I waited some more.

And longer.

I was just about to say something when I heard a mechanism start churning, the gates started opening and the speaker squawked again.

"Thank you for waiting, Ms. Dupree. Please drive through."

"You're welcome. And thank you," I replied.

As the gates slowly opened, I took my foot off the brake.

I was a writer, but I'd been a researcher first.

Therefore, I didn't come here blind. I knew all about The Downs and the family that had lived there for more generations than my country had even been a country.

But as I drove through the opened gates, taking in the vast manicured lawns under the sprawling canopies of mature trees, I was blown away.

Everything was better in real life than in pictures.

However, this was something else, and "better" didn't cover it.

And when the trees gave way and I started to see the house...

"Holy crap," I whispered as more, and more, and *more* of it was unveiled.

I'd seen pictures of this too.

But...

Good God.

It was built of sandy-gold Bath stone. At the front middle, there was a dual staircase, each side leading up to a vast landing that was home to the fifteen-foot double doors of the main entrance. The house was three stories, one below stairs with half of the level rising above ground. It had a wide central section with two wings angling back at each end.

I drove my long-term rental to one side of the front steps, and I did it on autopilot, I was so entranced by the house.

No, not a house.

The Downs.

Home for twelve generations to the Duke of Burleigh.

Current home of said duke and his three sisters.

In order: Battle, Temperance, Prudence and Chastity.

Oh yes, those were their names.

And oh yes, considering Talyn Family lore, those names were far from surprising.

It was Prudence who I'd corresponded with for the last year after I'd come across my great-grandfather's letters in a box of stuff my sister and I found in our mom's house when we were going through it after she passed.

It was Prudence who'd been excited about my idea for my next book.

And it was Prudence who'd invited me to stay.

And stay I would, for two weeks, being offered unfettered (maybe) access to the pictures, papers, journals, photos, daguerreotypes, ledgers, and anything else they could dig out for me about the life and times of the Talyn Family: keepers of the Duchy of Burleigh and the jewel of The Downs.

Or, hopefully this would happen.

One not-so-minor blip in my excitement about my six-month sojourn to England that had put a pall over embarking on this journey…

A journey that included me moving on to a cottage by the sea after the two weeks I'd spend here. I'd stay at that cottage for six months, close to The Downs and anything I might need, and in the area where it all happened, so I could immerse myself, hit museums, libraries and church registries, and anything else I might need…

And that pall was about commencing this without Battle Talyn, the Duke of Burleigh, approving the contract my agent and her attorneys had been negotiating with his attorneys so that I could have access to Burleigh documents.

However, Prudence assured me, although this had not been sorted, I should feel free to come regardless, because in the end, again she assured me, vehemently, this would not be a problem.

Battie is just really careful about protecting our family, Prudence had written in one of our plethora of email exchanges. *He's being nitpicky. He knows how excited I am about this! And he's my big brother; he likes to give me what I so wish to have. But in the end, it's his job to protect The Downs. Though it's my opinion he takes it too seriously! Then again, in my opinion, Battie takes everything too seriously.*

This, I'd discovered, was true.

"Battie" took things very seriously.

Especially privacy.

Honest to God, regardless of this family's aristocratic lineage, their famous holdings, and their immeasurable wealth, it was hard to find a picture of any of them.

And trust me, I tried.

The one who the paparazzi attempted the hardest to capture was the duke, but he'd perfected the art of angling his head, or his umbrella, or the upturn of a lapel so all you saw was maybe his ear, his temple or a hint of his (chiseled, as far as I could tell) jaw.

Images or even presence of Temperance, Prudence and Chastity were nearly nonexistent on the internet, including social media. The only one of all the siblings who had an account was Chastity, on Instagram, and all she posted were pictures of flowers.

Okay, so maybe the sensation I had before turning into the lane to The Downs wasn't strange.

Any good researcher loved a good mystery, and there were four in this house I was about to meet.

I grabbed my tote and exited my white Peugeot 3008, continuing to stare up at the house, and therefore I saw a gentleman walk out of it.

Not Battle.

Too old, too short, too stocky, and this man was wearing a black suit, gray waistcoat and red tie that looked less of a suit and more of a uniform.

The butler?

I walked up the steps, pulling my coat closer around me as I did. It was April in the West Country of England, therefore damp, cold, dreary, gray and windy.

When I made it to the top, I noted there was a complicated crest embroidered on the man's red tie.

It was a study of flamboyant red and cerulean swirls surrounding a shield in the same stripes. This was topped with the helmet of a knight, adorned with gold, pearls and rubies, out of the top of which was a surfeit of fluffy, vibrant plume feathers (yes, they somehow got all of that embroidered on a tie).

This was the Duchy's crest, which was also on the flag, emblazoned on two stripes, one red, one cerulean, and the right edge of the flag cut out into the sharp points of a sideways V.

A flag I'd noted was flying under the Union Jack above The Downs right then.

"Miss Dupree. Welcome to The Downs," he said on a very slight bow.

He intended to say more, he just didn't get the chance.

Out from the front doors flew a petite woman with stick-straight auburn hair, which was cut in a severe style with a radically level edge across very high bangs at her forehead and the same at a length that hit her chin.

And she was wearing…

I didn't know what she was wearing.

I just knew Moira Rose would like it very much.

The top looked like an overlarge, stiff, stark-white piece of posterboard was slapped against her body on an angle, the edge by her neck slightly curled inward. This concoction had long sleeves, gave a tunic feel and went down to her knees. Beyond those knees was a pair of flowy, wide-leg, black pants.

On her feet she wore black leather Mary-Jane flats with a separation stitched in between the big toe and the rest of them. They were not attractive in the slightest (I never understood that toe thing in shoes). But my guess, they were comfy.

And they totally rocked with that wild outfit.

Her makeup was as severe as her hairstyle. Very pale skin, heavily drawn brows, and dramatically dark raspberry lipstick. And the expertly smoked black liner that lined her upper and lower lashes made her unusual light gray-green eyes seem incandescent.

This was as far as I got in my impression before Lady Prudence Talyn cried out, "You're here!" and immediately, as well as shockingly, threw herself at me.

After I avoided having my eye poked with that curled edge of her top, I rounded her with my arms, surprised by this greeting.

I'd been to England before and had met English folk back home. They didn't tend to be affectionately demonstrative.

At least not on first meeting.

That said, Prudence and I had struck up a friendship after I reached out to the steward of The Downs about the letters I found. He'd forwarded my email to Prudence.

And that friendship wasn't all about my books (books she'd already read before I reached out) and my desire to write one that historically, though fictitiously, involved her family.

Almost since the beginning, we emailed each other every day.

As such, she'd become a daily touchstone for me, and I could tell the same happened for her.

So perhaps this wasn't that strange.

On that thought, I settled into her embrace.

Almost the instant I did, she popped back with as much exuberance as she'd jumped me and tossed out an arm to the gentleman standing with us, nearly knocking him in the chest.

With practiced ease, he avoided the blow while Prudence introduced, "This is Fitzgibbons. Our butler. Fitzy, did you meet Vivienne?"

"We were just getting to that, Lady Prudence," Fitzgibbons replied.

As she regarded him, Prudence's face shifted to kindly severe, something I wasn't sure I'd ever seen anyone pull off with such aplomb, not even moms of two-year-olds.

"Vivienne doesn't live with staff," she informed the butler with more than necessary weight, not something I liked all that much.

Not the part about her sharing openly I was not of their class.

Not many were, and undoubtedly "Fitzy" knew that about me already.

It was the dire tone and what came next that seemed ominously weird to me.

And what came next was, "We're going to have to look out for her."

"Of course," Fitzgibbons murmured.

I had no chance to ask after what seemed like a warning.

Prudence turned to me and instructed, "This means they're going to get your luggage. And park your car. And unpack you. And all sorts."

Although I'd never "lived with staff," I could have guessed this.

I didn't share that, and not only because, at once, I found the keys in my fingers whisked away and offered to Fitzgibbons, who took them.

Prudence then hooked her arm in mine, and with strength I'd never guess someone of her stature could possess, she dragged me into the house.

It wasn't that I didn't want to go. I was dying to get inside The Downs. There were pictures of the outside, but not one to be found of the interior.

It was just that she dragged me there.

And she did this talking.

"Rest assured, like I promised, we're turning the house upside down. Anything we can find, we're putting out in great-*great*-grandmama's studio." She looked up at me as she continued to drag me into and through the entryway. "That's out in the north garden. It's a very nice space. I think you'll love it there. It'll also give you privacy."

I was listening. And even if I wanted to hear what she had to say, I also wanted to be in this moment where I was finally in the presence of someone who, until then, had been nothing but emails in my inbox: however, she was still a woman who'd become a friend, and then a good friend, and now, we were finally together.

However, I couldn't quite concentrate due to what was assailing my eyes.

The front hall was massive.

No, that didn't describe it correctly.

It was *colossal.*

The walls were beautifully creamy and only adorned with two massive portraits hanging on opposite sides of the floor-to-ceiling (and that ceiling was two stories up) windows at the back of the space.

The windows gave a view of the courtyard gardens. They were situated beyond a central stairwell. After the first grand sweep of it from the floor at the center of the hall, that stairwell split into flights that rose gracefully off to each side.

And above those flights were the portraits.

One was a man in a uniform, a sash across his chest, many medals pompously displayed, standing holding a hat with an ostentatious plume under his arm. He had a disapproving look on his aristocratic face.

Opposite him was a portrait of a seated woman in a filmy, white dress with cerulean satin ribbon detailing, swaths of crimson satin wrapped shawl-like around her arms, and she had auburn curls around her forehead and temples and very rosy cheeks. Her doe eyes were blue, and her lips formed a small smile.

He looked terrifying.

She looked hopeful.

They graced not only those creamy walls but also the acres of buttermilk marble floors that spanned the space, the two seating areas (left and right) in front of two fireplaces, the intricate white plaster moldings, and the stairway railings, finely wrought black iron topped with blindingly shining elm wood.

Last, there was an enormous crystal chandelier that hung like a threat from the middle of the ceiling. It dipped very close to a gleaming, circular table that had an unusual arrangement of delicate flowers and trailing greenery that didn't rise much from the low, wide bowl they were in. But the foliage did creep out along the wood of the table to drip over the edge in a manner it looked like the flora actually grew from the table.

It was supremely cool.

However, presently, we were around the table and going up the stairs as Prudence kept gabbing.

"We're set to have tea in about half an hour, all us girls. Tempie and Chassie cannot *wait* to meet you. After that, Battle wants to talk to you. He'd like to see you at three thirty, in the study."

That got my attention.

"The duke is here?" I asked.

We went left at the landing, and as we did, through that tall window, I got a swift gander at just how prolific and extraordinary the garden was.

It was already a riot of color and greenery, and it was only April.

"Yes," Prudence answered, waving her hand in front of her dismissively. "He wants to finalize the agreement."

Well, that would be good, since I had an advance from my publisher to write this very book, and a deadline, and if I had to pivot at this late date, I'd be screwed and I'd have a publisher who was none too happy, and an agent who would be unhappier.

Prudence yanked me closer so that she was veritably leaning on me as she said earnestly, "I cannot tell you how glad I am you're here. I almost went to London when you arrived so I could meet you live and in person…*finally*. But I thought that'd be too clingy."

Before arriving at The Downs, I'd spent three days in London managing jetlag, seeing the sights and doing some preliminary research into the Talyns.

It was necessarily only three days because I had my advance, and I'd published seven books— four romances (my firsts), three historical fictions (the genre I was obsessed with at the moment)—so I was earning royalties.

That said, neither were enough to hang in an expensive London hotel for very long (and they were all expensive, if you didn't just want a bed surrounded by an inch of floorspace—though you could get out of that bed and find yourself right in the bathroom, so they could be time savers, if you wanted to put a positive spin on it).

Sure, my sister and I had inherited a tidy sum from Mom and the sale of her house and car and stuff, but I wasn't allowing myself to dip into my portion of that, because I was hoping to buy a house when I got home from England, and that was going to be my downpayment.

"That wouldn't have been clingy. I would have loved it," I told her.

Her eyes lifted to mine and they were shining with…

Dear God.

Were they tears?

"You're so lovely," she declared.

"As are you," I replied quietly, taken aback by the strength of her emotion.

She beamed a smile at me and cried too loudly, "We're here!"

And we were, after walking the length of the front of the house and a little down the north wing, where she was taking me into a room.

And…

Well…

Wow.

Candy red walls. White plasterwork. Arenberg parquet floors. A comfortable sitting area in front of a fireplace. A big bed, four-poster, curtained. Exquisite silk rugs under the bed and seating area. An escritoire against a wall. Cushioned benches strewn with toss pillows built in the three tall wide windows.

But like the entry, minimalism was the key to this room.

It wasn't a showplace crammed full of antiques and priceless knickknacks picked up over the centuries, carelessly laid somewhere and forgotten.

The bold colors of the red juxtaposed with the white, just like the antique escritoire contrasted with the contemporary lines of the golden-yellow velvet couch in front of the fireplace, all this clashing exquisitely with petal-pink bedding heavily embroidered in magenta and gold.

But among these were a few bouquets of flowers, all much like the one in the foyer: unusually but gorgeously arranged.

And there was a portrait of a woman, surrounded by sky and clouds, wearing a straw hat brimmed with flowers and a feather (she also had very rosy cheeks) and another of a woman (again with the cheeks) wearing a blue dress festooned with flowers, dancing in a forest being watched by a man and a trio of musicians.

Other than a screened smart unit and some crystal-based laps on the nightstands, different lamps on the tables by the couch, that was it.

It was the biggest bedroom I'd ever been in.

And the prettiest by a mile.

Prudence let go of my arm only to grab my hand and pull me into an adjoining room. It was the bathroom.

Fully modern, shower big enough for two, streamlined soaking tub, double basin sink, with thick pink and rose towels and rugs a similar contrast to what was happening in the bedroom, albeit having a more forceful effect, because everything else was white.

After only what amounted to a glance, Prudence led me onward through the bathroom to a room that made me gasp out loud.

Fitted open rails, drawers, shelves, enough for the biggest clotheshorse in history to feel safe they had plenty of space for now *and* to expand, not to mention have all their onerous shopping efforts proudly on display.

Further to this beauty, there was a large, round tufted bench dead center upholstered in rose velvet.

And the pièce de résistance, every girlie girl's dream of a vanity sitting in front of a tall window at the back of the room.

"Grandfather started the modernizations," Prudence told me. "Father continued them. And Battie updated the modernizations by ridding the place of all the curios and pompous paintings. That's one of the reasons the attics are a mess. But mostly, five hundred years of cast-off stuff takes a lot of space. I think that's why we haven't been able to locate Great-Aunt Harmony's letters."

That pulled me out of my closet-happy trance.

"You haven't been able to locate her letters?" I asked.

Prudence had let my hand go and was wandering to the window as she shook her head and answered, "No. We're still looking." Gazing out the window, she gave a dramatic shudder. "Something must be done with the attics. I suppose on the errand of finding those for you, I'll have to take them in hand."

I wanted to say I could help, but I was already overstaying my visitor's visa by two weeks, so in order to get this book done, I needed to get to work.

Because, I would repeat, I had a deadline.

Also, I wasn't keen to experience being kicked out of a country.

Even so, I wanted to get into those attics just to see what the "five hundred years of cast-offs" of a dukedom looked like.

Prudence whirled so abruptly, I jumped.

And then she clapped.

"I hear your luggage coming," she announced.

She did?

I didn't hear a thing.

"I'll let you freshen up." She tipped her head. "Half an hour? Then I'll collect you and take you to the blue salon. That's where we're having tea."

I could use a second to get my bearings, so I replied, "Sounds good."

She came to me just as a door behind me opened.

A young man was coming in with all my luggage, and there was a lot of it (six months' worth).

"Oh, sorry," he murmured. "I didn't know you were in here."

"That's okay, Scotty," Prudence replied as she took my hand again and tugged me toward the bathroom. "This is Vivienne," she threw over her shoulder.

"Hello, Miss Dupree. Welcome to The Downs," Scotty greeted.

"Thank you," I said, unavoidably loudly, as we'd made it through the bathroom and into the bedroom.

Once Prudence got me there, she took my other hand so she had both, and she smiled up at me.

"This is just so lovely, having you here," she asserted.

I squeezed her hands and replied, "I was honored by the invitation, but mostly, it's about time we met, so I will firmly agree, it's lovely to be here." I shook her hands. "With you."

Another beam before, "Now, take a bit of time to yourself. I'll return. Cook makes *luscious* teas. I hope you're hungry."

And I hoped there were scones, jam and clotted cream.

Prudence left.

I heard someone else go into the dressing room, and on peeking through the bathroom, I saw Scotty leave and a woman head deeper into the room. Probably to unpack my stuff.

Instead of introducing myself, I dumped my tote on the couch, shrugged off my coat and tossed it over my tote, moved to the window and looked out.

Oh yes.

Holy hell.

The garden was amazing.

Lush and well kept, but in a wild way. Profuse. And it spanned the entirety of the space between the wings and beyond. There were a few fountains, some paths, some benches and...

A woman in a pale blue dress and light cardigan.

She was wearing a wide-brimmed straw hat even if there was no sun.

She had light-blonde hair, an abundance of it, all of it frizzy curls that poofed out under her hat, over her shoulders and down her back.

I couldn't see her face due to the hat, and she had her back to me.

What I could see was a tall, sandy-haired, well-built, good-looking man was also in the garden. He was wearing jeans, a chambray shirt, and appeared to be measuring something on a rosebush. I knew this because he had a clipboard where he'd jot things down after he did whatever he was doing.

Oh.

And he snuck peeks at the blonde who was a good twenty yards away, seemingly oblivious to him as she deadheaded into one basket and clipped healthy blooms for another.

That certainly wasn't Battle. I'd never seen a full-face photo of him, but I did know he had dark hair.

But I wondered if the woman was Temperance. Or Chastity.

"I'm sorry, madam?"

I turned at the voice to see the maid was in the room with me.

"Hi," I greeted.

She smiled and asked, "Do you prefer your night creams to be on the bedside table, or in the bathroom?"

"Bedside table, thank you," I answered then added, "I guess you know I'm Vivienne Dupree."

She nodded, still smiling, as she walked to the bed. "I do. And I'm Mary. I'm the maid who'll be taking care of your rooms."

"Nice to meet you, Mary. And thank you in advance for taking care of me."

Another nod from her, and she was going back across the room, saying, "We hope you enjoy your stay here."

"I'm sure I will."

And I *was* sure, in that moment.

I was hungry for tea. I couldn't wait to meet Chastity and

Temperance (though, Battle had been a bit of a pill before this excursion, so I was of two minds about meeting him). I was happy Prudence and I finally had the chance to get to know each other without a keyboard involved. And one of my favorite things was starting a book (also the writing of it, though, the finishing of it sucked since I'd miss it in that way you missed things you loved, but you knew you'd never get back).

So it was all good.

Very good.

I was on an adventure.

Another of my favorite things.

But I had no idea.

I had absolutely no idea all that was about to befall me in the seat of the Duke of Burleigh, The Inimitable Downs.

And all that was about to befall me would be *a lot*.

CHAPTER 2

THE SISTERS

The blue salon was, indeed, blue.

Ice blue.

This mingled with a continuation of the richly creamy creams of the entryway and was, as Prudence shared when she'd escorted me there, "Where we like to take tea because it's cozier than any of the other sitting rooms or parlors. Except, of course, for the one where we have cocktails before dinner. But you can't have tea and cocktails in the same place!"

After she said this, she'd giggled, like I knew this rule and the very thought of enjoying both beverages in the same room was a universal understanding of ridiculous.

However, once accosted by the room, I wasn't sure she had a handle on the meaning of the word cozy.

Set in the central section (not in a wing), on the hall off the south side of foyer, that room was like all the rest I'd encountered: huge.

And like all the rest, it was a study of contrasts. Old and new. Antique and modern. Formal and relaxed. Stiff yet comfortable.

But all of it expensive.

The sisters were a study of contrasts too.

There was Prudence with her avant-garde clothes and auburn hair.

And then there was the blonde I saw out in the garden.

Chastity.

She'd taken off the cardigan and hat to have tea, and her blue dress was a sundress—pretty and as ethereal and delicate as she was (no way I'd garden in that dress, but I was not Lady Chastity Talyn). Her hair was wild and thick and chaotic and amazing. Her face had that pinched but pretty Nicole Kidman look to it. And her eyes were a startling, almost-hard-to-witness sapphire blue.

She was soft-spoken to the point every word she said was a whisper, hard to hear, and she never made eye contact.

Not even close.

Temperance, on the other hand, was seriously something.

Shining ebony hair falling from a middle part in loose curls along the sides of her exquisitely beautiful face, her hair tumbling further down over her shoulders and chest. Her cold gray eyes were watchful and calculating. Her skin was so pale, you could see the blue of her veins. Her lips were perfectly slicked with a bright crimson lipstick. And her body was covered in a pair of casual black slacks, a complicated, edgy, short-sleeved black blouse, and a pair of black patent leather, four-inch Louboutin heels, with the lipstick sole that matched her lips.

She spoke in a sophisticated, catty, aristocratic drawl that reminded me of any of the actors who played the Royals on *The Crown*.

We sat around the low coffee table covered in a formal tea service and tiered trays filled with crustless sandwiches, pastries, biscuits (or to Americans, cookies), little cakes—and thank you, God (I'd had two) —scones filled with jam and clotted cream.

Chastity poured.

She also sat in one of the ice-blue Louis XV bergère chairs opposite the one Temperance sat in.

Prudence and I sat together in a curved-back settee that faced the fireplace.

I wasn't sure Chastity knew I was there.

I wasn't sure Temperance wanted me there.

But I was sure Prudence could talk for England.

"So I think Vivi's book will span from Reign to Saint, or Bishop," she was now saying after she'd pretty much outlined everything from my very first email to The Downs's steward, to now, a history it was clear both her sisters already knew.

Though, curiously through this, she'd sometimes suddenly go off on another tangent that had nothing to do with what she'd been saying. Or she'd trail off and stare into space for a second, like she was in a mini trance, before she'd shake herself and start right back up where she left off.

With the practiced way Temperance and Chastity reacted to this, that was to say, they didn't react at all, I got the sense this was just a thing for Prudence.

She and I had never been able to schedule a FaceTime, what with the time difference and both of us being busy, so I'd only ever known her in written conversations.

Truthfully?

It might be curious, but it was also kind of cute.

Fortunately, her talking meant I could scarf down four sandwich triangles (two coronation chicken, one egg, the last prawn and avocado), a little cake and two scones.

And she was correct about the time period during which my book would take place.

I would be starting it around the turn of the twentieth century, when Reign Talyn was duke, through World War II, when Saint Talyn held that title, and just beyond, when Bishop Talyn was duke.

Duke Saint Talyn being the one who flatly refused to allow his daughter, Harmony, to marry the man she'd fallen in love with: an American soldier convalescing at The Downs.

My great-grandfather.

"And I think, as I've told you, from what Ravenna told *me*, if Harmony and Charlie's story is shared, the curse will finally be broken," Prudence declared.

Chastity gave no indication she even heard these words.

Temperance rolled her eyes.

I said nothing.

Though, through our email correspondence, Prudence had shared at length about what she considered The Curse of The Downs.

This, according to Prudence (which was according to Ravenna), started with Harmony losing her beloved Charlie (my great granddad).

And it affected every generation since, according to Prudence (read: Ravenna).

Prudence's clairvoyant, the aforementioned Ravenna, I sensed, but only very carefully alluded to Prudence, had more of a bent toward charlatanism than being able to read the mystics.

And I'd just learned Temperance and I might be of the same mind about that.

"Don't roll your eyes," Prudence snapped at Temperance.

"Darling," Temperance drawled. "There is not a curse on this house."

"So how do you explain what happened to great-great-grandfather and great-great-grandmother?" Prudence demanded.

I sipped tea and listened hard, knowing she referred to Saint and his wife Marie.

Doing this wasn't entirely nosy (though it was also nosy).

Learning things like this was why I was there.

Prudence was referring to the fact that Saint and Marie, who had seemed at one with all things The Duchy of Burleigh, suddenly found themselves with such irreconcilable differences, she spent most of her time in the studio in the garden, which was a waste of a big, beautiful house, because he spent all of his in their home in London.

Or, that was, he did when he wasn't in his mistress's bed.

"Marie did her duty," Temperance replied. "She provided an heir, a spare, and a couple of girls they could use to advance their positions in society. In their case, lord those poor, wretched brood mares over others and grant permission for them to use our very blue blood to advance *their* positions. Once they were all raised and gone, Marie could stop pretending she liked her husband and spend her days painting and, I don't know"—she fluttered a regal, scarlet fingernail-tipped hand off to the side—"fornicate with stable boys or something."

"Tempie!" Prudence snapped.

I bit my lip to stop from laughing.

When I got control over that impulse, I took another sip of tea and kept listening.

Whisper-talk came from Chastity's direction. "That doesn't explain what happened to Bishop and Caroline."

Bishop was Saint's son and heir, Harmony's older brother, and Battle, Temperance, Prudence and Chastity's great-grandfather.

See what I mean about the names?

"Yes," Prudence jumped on that. "Is it just coincidence he fell off his horse…and broke his neck? And she fell down the stairs…and broke hers?"

"She *was* eighty-seven at the time," Temperance replied. "And it was twenty years after her husband met his untimely end by the same means, if in different places doing entirely different things. So yes, I would say it was a coincidence. An unfortunate one, but for her part, she'd lived a long life."

"A goodly amount of it without her husband," Chastity whisper-added.

Temperance made no reply.

"All right. Then explain grandpapa and grandmama," Prudence challenged.

In order to keep track, that was Cannon Talyn and his wife, Victoria.

Temperance, clearly having had enough of this topic, leaned forward and dropped her delicate china teacup and saucer with a clatter on the table, snapping, "For goodness' sake, Prue. They both got food poisoning from eating the same food. Three of the staff died too."

For once Chastity met someone's gaze.

And it was Temperance's.

"And Father and Mother?"

That would be Atlas and Rebecca.

Temperance appeared to be attempting to shoot laser beams out of her eyes at her youngest sister.

"Ah-ha!" Prudence crowed to Temperance who appeared to be stymied. "You don't have anything to explain that away."

Temperance sat back, aimed her chilly gaze at her second youngest sister and stated, "He was an ass. She was a spoiled brat. They were a match made in heaven, meaning they deserved each other. The problem was, they couldn't stand each other, so after she gave him the issue required of her, she buggered off to Corfu to live in a fabulous villa and fuck copious Greek men who were built like gods, something, as far as we know, she's still doing. As such, he was free to open his revolving door of whores anywhere he wanted on British soil, until he died of a heart attack *whilst* fucking one of those whores."

Again, all true.

Even that last part.

Regardless of how hard the Talyn line did their best, and mostly succeeded, to work to guard their privacy, that particular tidbit had been spread widely.

Though, what hadn't been, but what I'd learned from Prudence, was the fact that Rebecca had not that first thing to do with her children after she left for that Greek island, something I'd come to learn affected Prudence very much, as it would do.

I couldn't imagine not having a mom who loved and adored you, got frustrated by you acting like an idiot, but allowed you the freedom to do it so you could learn from it, shared her wisdom with you, and then when you finally got to a certain age, became the best friend you could ever have.

No, I couldn't imagine that at all.

Prudence turned to me. "Don't listen to Tempie. Although she has no excuse to be this way, she's as cynical as they come."

"Did I lie?" Temperance demanded. "Well?" she pressed in Prudence's and Chastity's directions when neither said anything.

"Not really," Chasitity finally whisper-admitted.

Temperance turned to me. "You write this kind of thing for a living. Therefore, you know, in our world, we don't marry for love. We marry for money. For status. For alliances."

"That's hardly been the case for the last sixty, seventy years, or even longer," Prudence contradicted.

"If you don't think Mother married Father for his title, his money and this damned house, you are a bigger dreamer than I thought," Temperance shot back.

"Tempie," Chastity whisper-admonished.

But if that was a hit to Prudence, she didn't show it.

Instead, she lifted her chin. "If it was for this house, why did she leave him?"

Temperance didn't miss a beat. "I've already answered that. Because he was an ass." She returned to me. "It's a thing, tonight, because you're here. It's a tradition we all enjoy. We're all going to dress up for dinner. Did Prue tell you?"

I nodded.

Prudence had warned me my first night there would be formal, and to be prepared, because if they had other guests, it might happen again.

Since I didn't have a closet full of evening dresses, this required me to hit some online designer resale sites, but that had been a blast, as it always tended to be, and score: I'd found some awesome things, and not just evening dresses.

Temperance continued, "But that's not a thing for us. At least not when we don't have visitors. Of course, Chassie doesn't sidle into the parlor for pre-dinner cocktails in mud-splattered wellies with dirt under her fingernails. And we are not normal. We're rich. People say the word 'lady' before our names. Someone cooks our food. Someone else serves it. I have never cooked a meal in my life, nor washed a dish. And I don't intend to do either."

Suddenly, I strived for yet another goal in my life, the dish thing.

Though, I liked to cook.

Temperance wasn't finished.

"But we're not weird. We eat dinner as a family, normally. But if we don't want to pitch up to the table, we have a tray in our room or wherever. Though, back before he died, under Father's edicts, you'd think it was still nineteen-oh-two."

"He was just traditional," Prudence said.

"A man had been on the moon," Temperance retorted. "The future king got a divorce and had his dirty talk with his mistress aired all over the globe. And that talk was *filthy*. You could call Bangladesh from your mobile in your car. *We had cars.* It was no longer required for me to wear white gloves and a hat to church, or a formal gown to dinner, for God's sake."

Neither of her sisters had a response.

I didn't either, and although I thought it'd be cute to see the Talyn sisters in hats and gloves, going to church, if I was a kid and that wasn't what I wanted to do, I had to admit, it would stink.

When the silence lengthened, I carefully waded into it.

"I intend to do a pretty thorough read through of all the things Prudence has gathered for me." I turned to Prudence. "And of course, I'm excited to meet Ravenna."

Not really, but Prudence liked her, and outside of her family, she didn't mention any other friends, except her bi-monthly readings with Ravenna, so I was (currently) withholding judgement.

And anyway, who was I to judge?

Even Elizabeth I hung out with and took counsel from Dr. John Dee.

I looked between the other two sisters. "And unless there's some note of it, or it fits into the narrative, I probably won't be mentioning the curse."

"Well, that will be good," Temperance murmured while she crossed her long, slender legs. "We don't need every lunatic who shops exclusively in Glastonbury poking around and doing rituals outside the front gate."

This made Prudence twist excitedly toward me and again with her clap.

"Oh yes, Vivi! It's a bit of a jaunt, but while you're here, we *have* to go to Glastonbury."

"I would bypass that and go straight to Cheltenham. Better shopping," Temperance drawled, but oddly, she did this watching Prudence closely, and, maybe I was wrong, but I could swear I read in her gaze it was hopefully.

That was strange.

Chastity nibbled at a biscuit while her bright-blue eyes darted everywhere but to a human being.

A throat was cleared.

We all looked to the doorway to see Fitzgibbons standing there.

"I hate to intrude. But Miss Dupree has a meeting with His Grace."

"Oh,"—another clap from Prudence—"right. Be sure to tell him not to keep her too long. She'll want to have time to change for dinner."

Once Fitzgibbons nodded, she latched onto my arm, therefore I turned to her.

"We start cocktails around six thirty-ish, most everyone's there by seven," she told me. "We wander into dinner whenever Cook sends word it's ready. Once you've changed, just go to your smart screen and hit the icon to call a member of staff. Someone will escort you to the parlor." She gave me a big smile. "We'll do the full house tour tomorrow."

I got the sense from this that she wasn't going to take me to her brother, Fitzgibbons was.

And the duke was calling.

Thus, I set down my teacup and moved a smile through all the ladies, saying, "Thank you so much, this was great. Looking forward to dinner."

"I bet you are," Temperance said in a tone that pretended she didn't want me to hear it, but she did.

Oh, she knew they were putting on a show, and I was lapping it up.

And that begged the question of why she assumed the role of star of that show, if she didn't want me to witness the production.

Chastity said nothing.

Prudence replied, "See you at dinner."

I got up and followed Fitzgibbons out.

As we walked down the central wing, I looked into open doors to see a variety of rooms along the lines of what I'd already seen, with those to the front having grand views of the glory of the parkland, and those to the back having the same of the splendor of the gardens.

We turned into the south wing, and about halfway down, to the right side, the butler knocked on the only closed door we'd encountered along the way.

"Come," a man called from inside.

All right, I had to admit, I was a little tingly.

I'd never met a real-life duke, for one.

I'd read about plenty.

Meeting one?

Nope.

Then there was the mystery. The lore. The history.

All of which, being an ex-librarian, current writer, I was super into.

And here I was, about to meet the keeper of it, a man who, no matter what he did, would not be forgotten in the annals of history just because of who he'd been born to be.

And that was all kinds of cool.

I almost rubbed my hands together like an over-excited idiot when Fitzgibbons opened the door, walked in, I followed, and the butler intoned, "Miss Dupree is here for your meeting, Your Grace."

The man at the desk looked up from whatever he was writing.

And I froze solid.

I heard him say in a deep, lush purr, "Thank you, Fitzy."

Some part of me processed the fact that Fitzgibbons walked out and closed the door.

But mostly, I was all about the man sitting at the desk.

Thick, dark, chestnut brown hair. Handsome tortoise-shell glasses covering rich brown eyes.

But his face.

Damn.

His face.

In any romantic fantasy, that strong jaw, straight nose, prominent brow, those sumptuous lips and hooded eyes would be the face that would emerge when the knight on his mighty charger flipped up the visor of his helmet.

It was the face you'd see after the Scotsman in the kilt swung his broadsword, ending the life of his opponent, and whirled to face his next.

It was the face splashed in blood you'd see looking up from his kill after the Viking berserker brought down his battle-ax.

It was the face of the vicious mobster in the movie you felt wildly freaky about because he made you root for the bad guy mostly because you were dying to fuck him.

It was the face of a warrior, or a villain.

It was the face of Satan, Lucifer, who used to be God's most beautiful angel.

And then he stood.

Tall, broad-shouldered, lean-hipped, thick thighed, the desk hid the rest, but I didn't have it in me to process more.

Not with the strength of the electrical pulse shooting through me after taking in only what I could see.

And it wasn't just an, "Oo, this guy is *hawt,*" pulse.

Oh no.

It was something bigger.

Stronger.

Scarier.

Utterly terrifying.

How did I know?

Because for the first time in my life, after that man took his feet, and the shock tore through me, I fainted.

Dead to the carpet.

CHAPTER 3

THE DUKE

I came to with a view of that damned face.

"She's awake," Battle Talyn murmured in that purr of his, just before he straightened away, and Prudence was in my face.

"Oh my goodness, Vivi!" she cried. "Are you all right?"

I pushed up.

I did this because I was lying on a leather chesterfield. I had no idea how I got there, but my concern was, the lord of the manor carried me.

Beyond Prudence, I could see a glorious, carved stone fireplace.

The only other things I could see were three Talyn women and one Talyn man. Two of the women (Prudence and Chastity) were hovering over me. Temperance and Battle were standing off to the side, both with arms crossed on their chests, studying me.

I pushed back until I hit the arm of the chesterfield and once there, I lifted a hand to rub my neck.

"God, I'm so sorry," I said.

Okay…how embarrassing was this?

The answer was *very*.

It was *very* embarrassing.

Nope.

Excruciating.

It was *excruciatingly* embarrassing.

"I don't know what happened," I finished lamely.

"Jetlag is weird," Prudence decreed.

Could I hang fainting at the sight of the most beautiful man on the planet on jetlag?

Oh yes.

Yes, I could.

And I was absolutely going to do just that.

"I think I've been pushing myself too hard," I told them. "I probably shouldn't have hit the Tate. Or the British Museum. Or the British Library."

"You did all of that in just three days?" Prudence's voice was pitched unnaturally high.

"Well, yes," I admitted, then, due to her tone, cautiously added, "And more."

"Then of course that's too much!" she declared and straightened from me to turn on her siblings and announce dramatically, "On top of driving all the way from London!"

I looked among them.

Okay.

Seriously.

How were these four siblings?

Not one of them looked like the other. Not even a nuance.

Prudence couldn't be more than five three, though I couldn't tell her body type because her clothing masked it. However, Chasitity was willowy, probably only average height, however, even willowy, she had tits and ass. Temperance was my height, five eight, and she was slender as a pole. And Battle couldn't be shorter than six four, and he was built like a brick shithouse.

With the eye color, the hair color, even the bone structure, there was nothing remotely alike about any of them.

Maybe Rebecca had started playing around way before she jetted off to Greece.

Prudence claimed my attention again by grabbing my hand. "I think you should go upstairs, lay down, take a nap. We'll have a tray brought up for you for dinner. We can do the big welcome party tomorrow night."

I shook my head and gently extricated my hand while swinging my legs off the side of the couch, though I didn't go so far as to stand. When I did that again, I wanted to be sure I didn't hit the deck after.

"No, no, no. I'm okay. I mean, sure. I think having a bit of a lie down will be good before dinner. But Battle and I have some things to iron out, and it would be better to get on that straight away." I took my chances with another bout of unconsciousness and met his eyes. "I really am very sorry. But honestly, I'm okay."

He didn't reply to me.

He turned his head and shook it.

I looked over the back of the couch, the direction he'd turned his head, and saw the desk and wing chairs in front of it were on that side of the room, we were on the other side, where there was yet another seating area by a fireplace.

So yeah, the guy probably carried me.

God.

Excruciating.

Fitzgibbons was also there, entering the room with a woman at his side.

He was carrying a first aid kit in one hand, a silver tray with a glass of ice water balanced on the other.

I was impressed.

The woman was carrying a basin with a bright white towel folded over the side of it.

"I'm sorry, but it appears Ms. Dupree is recovering, and now we don't need any of that," Battle told his staff.

"You're sure?" the woman asked, examining me with kind eyes.

"We're sure, Patsy," Prudence said.

"You don't wish for me to call the doctor?" Fitzgibbons asked Battle.

"No. Apparently, Ms. Dupree has not had a mind to her jetlag," Battle answered, still in that delicious purr of his, however this time it was incongruously accusatory.

My attention returned to him.

He was still speaking.

"But leave the glass of water." He shifted to his sisters. "And you three can go. I'll mind Ms. Dupree. Our business shouldn't take that long."

"Are you sure? I can stay," Prudence offered to me.

"I'm fine," I said at the same time Battle ordered, "Go, Prue."

She shot her brother a scrunch-face look that was cute, before she gave me a reassuring smile and pat on the shoulder.

Chastity and Temperance didn't need further permission to exit the scene. They were already leaving.

Patsy was gone, but Fitzgibbons came forward *sans* the first aid kit and put the glass of water on a leather coaster he unearthed from somewhere so he could set it on the coffee table in front of me.

"If you need anything, Miss Dupree, simply have His Grace ring," he encouraged.

"Thank you, Mr. Fitzgibbons."

He smiled kindly, something I thought was really sweet, then he moved away.

I watched Battle fold his very long body in a leather Queen Anne wing chair that flanked the chesterfield.

"Better here," he murmured, crossing his also very long legs. "More informal."

"Again, I'm sorry," I told him, reaching for the water and wondering if I'd paid any attention to hydration the last four days.

I had not.

I took a healthy sip.

"It's unnecessary for you to keep repeating that," he replied.

I stopped drinking and my gaze shot to him at his curt words.

"I do believe our conversation will be simple and straightforward," he went on. "Our solicitors have been belaboring this, but I'm certain you and I can come to an understanding."

I wasn't certain of the same thing.

"I've read your work, at least the historicals," he informed me.

And goodness, that got another tingle that was both fear and excitement, knowing this man had spent time with my babies.

The fear was because I hoped he liked them.

The excitement was just that he'd read them, my words to his eyes.

For me, this was like this magnificent man had spent hours with me.

He continued talking. "You have a flair for the dramatic, which obviously makes these books marketable, but a bent toward historical accuracy."

Well, if that didn't deflate my balloon, primarily the cold way he laid it on me.

"This is rather the point of a book written in the historical fiction genre," I pointed out.

"However, as my family's history is what you'll be writing about next, I don't think my demands are that far-fetched," he stated like I didn't speak.

Oh yes.

This was what our solicitors had been "belaboring."

This is your host. Keep your cool, Vivi, keep your cool.

I took another sip of water then set it down and turned fully toward the duke.

I then took a moment to let my retinas recover from looking at the man full face.

Only then did I share, "As you're not a writer, I can understand how you might feel that way. What I need for you to understand is that what you're requesting is categorically not something any writer can abide."

"And if you were to have a book written about you, would you not request to have final approval of what's published?"

I shrugged. "To be honest, unless it was something libelous, I wouldn't have any choice. However, the only choice I'd have was after publication, suing if it was libelous, but the book would still already have been published."

"As we don't have a choice," he agreed. "Although it would be difficult for you to write with your exacting precision if you don't have access to my family's papers."

Mm-hm.

This was exactly what our solicitors had been "belaboring."

"I do believe it's been communicated to you that this book is not going to be about any living Talyn. In other words, it won't be about you at all."

"Any Talyn, living or dead, is mine to protect," he returned.

"All right, if you're worried about Prudence's idea of a curse—"

He threw both hands out to his sides. "There is no curse. Prue has always had an overactive imagination."

I got the sense Chastity didn't dismiss the whole curse thing.

But this wasn't about the curse.

I sought patience and clarified my position.

"As has been explained to you through your solicitors, my goal is to write a novel, loosely based on the Burleigh Duchy and The Downs, but mostly a fictionalized account of how the generations that experienced staggering advancement in a very short period of time adjusted to that advancement, correlating it to the times we're in now, where we're experiencing the same thing. With the central story being about Harmony and Charlie, albeit mostly fictionalized since, so far, we only have his letters from her, and that doesn't explain much of anything. However, even if I uncovered more, as this was clearly mostly a clandestine relationship, until Harmony asked her father's permission to marry Charlie, I doubt there's very much to find. Unless Harmony's letters from Charlie are discovered, and even then, the bulk of the love affair will have to come from my imagination. This is hardly going to paint the Talyns in an unflattering light. Even your great-great grand-father was acting in the manner of a man of his time, that being for the protection of his daughter."

"Be that as it may—"

I interrupted him this time, and I could tell immediately by the flash in his eyes (the glasses were gone, by the way) and the thinning of his full lips, he not only didn't like it, he wasn't used to it.

"Be that as it *is*, my Lord Duke," I stated. "That *is* the book. That's the outline I sent to my publishers. That's the contract I signed for a manuscript I received an advance to write for them. And the advance was received. I have a deadline about six months from now I'm oblig-ated to meet. And they, too, aren't overly thrilled with your demand to have approval of the copy."

"Then perhaps you should have finalized arrangements with me before you entered into those obligations with your publisher."

Was he for real?

"Are you truly not going to allow me access to your records if you don't have final approval of the book?" I asked.

"As my solicitors have asserted in my stead the last two months of negotiations, Ms. Dupree, allow me to communicate it directly to you. No. I am not going to allow you access to our records unless I have final approval of your manuscript."

Well.

Shit.

I stood, and I did it angrier than I ever thought I'd been in all my life.

One could say I had a temper, but if that one knew me, they'd also say it was rare it reared its unpleasant head because I was usually pretty chill.

Now, I was not.

I was also freaked, because no way could I grant approval, and I had to write this book.

But who knew what his approval could mean.

He could scrap the whole manuscript I spent six months writing.

He could decide he's suddenly a content editor and redline the hell out of it with suggestions of what he'd like to see that had nothing to do with the story that burst forth from me, or nothing to do with bona fide content editing. Or he could see I was telling no lies and have no notes at all.

This could be a minor inconvenience.

Or it could be a nightmare.

What I knew for certain was that I was in a different kind of nightmare.

I'd sold a book I couldn't write. Of course, I could, but it wouldn't be as thoroughly researched as it needed to be.

I was (mostly) living off my advance.

So yeah, oh yeah, I was definitely living a nightmare, because this man was being a stubborn ass.

And it ticked me off.

He stood when I did.

And as I tipped my head back to catch his gaze, I declared, "Well, I guess that's that."

He cocked his head to the side. "I'm sorry?"

"I guess I'm not writing the book."

He righted his head but said nothing.

"I'll have dinner tonight with you all so I can spend more time with Prudence," I went on. "Then I'll get out of your hair tomorrow."

Though I had no idea where I'd go, but it seemed I had no choice but to go.

I was about to walk out of the room when he spoke.

"You threatening to leave, take yourself from Prudence, truncate this visit she's been looking forward to for months, is not going to get me to agree to your terms."

Of all the...

"That's not what I'm doing," I denied hotly. "As my grandmother always said, fish and guests stink after three days, Your Grace. If I had my nose stuck in journals and letters for two weeks, and you all rarely saw me, that's one thing. But now I have to figure my shit out, and I have no reason to be here, so I'll be doing that elsewhere."

"And what will Prudence do?"

"I have a six-month lease on a cottage about an hour away." That lease started in two weeks, but he didn't need to know that. "If I have breaks from writing whatever I'm going to need to talk my publishers into wanting to publish, she and I can take some day jaunts."

His attractive chin jerked into his corded-with-muscle neck, and he said, "Day jaunts?" like I suggested Prudence and I fly to Australia to have lunch on a cruise of Sydney Harbor and then fly back.

"Day jaunts," I reiterated.

"Except to go to the village, Prue hasn't left this estate in six years."

I blinked.

And then I said, "But just at tea, she said we had to go to Glastonbury."

Suddenly, it looked like he was seeing me.

Of course, it wasn't as if he didn't know I was in the same room for the last however long we'd been in the same room.

But now, for some reason, he was *seeing me*.

"She hasn't left The Downs or the village in six years?" I asked softly.

"I take it in your online friendship, she didn't share that with you," he replied.

Perhaps we were getting somewhere, and his mention of "your online friendship" was what made me wonder if he thought I was some kind of reprobate, using a relationship I formed with Prudence to get through the front door so I could steal the family silver.

"No, she didn't share that," I informed him. "Is she…" I looked to the door and again to him. "Is she okay?"

"As years passed, Prue's world narrowed. I don't fully understand it. Tempie doesn't. Nor does Chastity. It's concerned us, she only felt safe in this house and its surroundings. Both my sisters talked to her. It makes Prue uncomfortable. So they stopped talking to her."

"And have you talked to her?" I asked.

"I don't need to talk to her."

Okay.

I was getting mad again.

It wasn't my business, but Prudence was a friend. If that friendship formed online or not, she was still my friend, and if she was dealing with something so huge she'd made herself a kind of hermit, well…

"Why not?" I demanded.

"Because Prue has always been what many consider odd."

Oh dear.

I was getting madder.

"She's always had her head in the clouds," he continued. "She's clumsy. She gets distracted easily. She enjoys reading far too much, drawing even more, she lives in imaginary worlds most of the time, and she has far too many pets. If I allowed it, the place would be crawling with animals. As it is, she has six cats."

Six?

Normally, that was a lot.

In a house with more than a hundred rooms that sat on more than five hundred acres, not so much.

I hoped I got to meet them before I left.

"As such, she was bullied at school," Battle carried on, making my heart squeeze. "Brutally," he added, making that squeeze tighten. "Our father thought it best not to intervene. He believed it would toughen her up. And therefore, it never stopped. As such, it went on for years."

Again, with the getting madder, just this time, not at him.

"But instead, it made the interesting girl, the one who wasn't like all the other girls, she was better, precisely because she wasn't like all the other girls, feel weird, wrong," I deduced, and I kept on deducing. "And to protect herself from a world that doesn't understand her, she's allowed her world to become one that does. This house and the village."

He jutted his chin. "Precisely."

"Has she seen a therapist?"

"And how, exactly, do we tell our sister we think she needs a therapist when we don't want her to feel she's strange, or worse, feel we think she is, when we don't, but she'll take it that way?" he retorted.

He had a point.

Slowly, I looked to the door again, my heart still hurting for Prudence, though, on the flipside, much of her behavior was now explained.

I went back to him when he ordered, "Stay the two weeks."

"Without the book to work on, I'm not sure I'd be comfortable doing that. Although you might not feel my friendship with Prudence is real, it is. However, we still just met, and I don't know any of the rest of you at all."

"Then please explain further why you would take such a drastic step to scuttle this book you so wish to write when I'm simply asking to protect my family's reputation."

"I would think that's obvious."

"Since I've been clear it's not, humor me."

Okay, was it just me?

Or was this guy an arrogant ass?

"Because I can't spend six months on a book you scupper within weeks of deadline," I explained.

"You have an editor, yes?"

"Of course."

"And you make changes he suggests."

"*She* suggests, sure. But not all of them. Though I take them into account."

"Is this not the same thing I'm requesting, however, likely with a much lighter hand?"

"I don't know," I returned. "Can you promise you'll have a light hand?"

His natural purr was a scoff when he replied, "I don't want to write the book for you, Ms. Dupree."

"And I'm afraid you're asking me to give you permission to do a version of that by giving you the power to decide if it'll be published or not. By giving you the power to stamp it approved or denied after I've finished it. I don't know you. Maybe you have a creative outlet. If you don't, then allow me to educate you, just writing it knowing what might happen at the end will impede my creativity. Every writer has a different process. For me, my characters exist, not just the historical ones, the fictional ones too. The story is already there, real, even if the fictional part exists in my imagination. My part is to breathe life into the characters and their story. If I'm not free to breathe, how am I going to tell the story?"

"Perhaps we could come to a compromise?" he suggested.

"And that would be?" I asked warily.

"You share each chapter after it's written. I'll read it, and if something is concerning me, we'll discuss it immediately in order that you don't move forward worrying about what might befall the final manuscript. I would assume, after a few chapters, we would be on the same page and this process would become routine. Obviously, I'd want a final read through, but that should be no issue if you don't change anything or add anything in between."

I'd never done anything like this.

So could I do this?

To buy time to make a decision, I asked, "Would you want some kind of acknowledgement or something?"

"Hell no," he answered so forcefully, I was now pissed that he clearly didn't want anyone to know he'd had any part of one of my babies.

"Well, I wouldn't wish to insult you by giving the reading world an indication you had anything to do with one of my books," I said snottily.

"Again, I'm not writing your book for you, Ms. Dupree. I don't need an acknowledgement."

"You could just say, 'thank you for mentioning that, but it won't be necessary,'" I retorted.

"I see I've offended you," he murmured, and I'd always thought brown eyes were warm and gentle, but this guy managed to make his condescending and haughty.

"This is what I do for a living, Your Grace. I'm proud of doing it. So, you saying," I mimicked his forceful, "'*hell no*' at being offered an acknowledgement, uh, *yeah*, that's offensive. Most people think an acknowledgement is an honor."

"I only meant to say that's not necessary. And my name is Battle."

I ignored the invite to call him by his Christian name and retorted, "Well, as I just said, you could have said that."

He sighed before he requested, "Allow me to understand what's happening here. We were at an impasse, one that was rather calamitous for you. I offered a compromise as a solution to our differences, which would allow you to write the book you've been contracted to write. And now you haven't addressed my suggested compromise because you're angry I don't want an acknowledgement I don't deserve because I won't be contributing to your writing, simply approving if the direction you're going works for the Talyn legacy."

Ulk.

It stunk that he was right in pointing out I was being unreasonable.

He was still kind of a dick.

I shifted to the matter at hand.

"I've never written that way," I told him. "But it would be vastly preferrable to completing the project and having you nix it."

"Then we're agreed," he said with strained patience.

"I guess," I replied.

"Excellent. Shall I have my solicitors draw it up?"

"Can we agree that this verbal agreement holds while that's happening so I can get to work tomorrow?"

He shook his head and crossed his arms on his chest. "Unnecessary. They'll have the agreement ready before dinner. Simply meet me here, you can sign, and I'll escort you to cocktails."

If they could pull that off, one could say his attorneys worked fast.

"I'll have to read it," I warned.

"As it'll probably be a single page, I doubt that will take long."

"If there's something fishy, I'll want my agent to look over it."

He let out a beleaguered breath. "There won't be anything fishy about it, Vivienne."

Oh Lord.

That purr gliding over my name?

It was the single most beautiful thing to ever hit my ears.

Shit.

"Okay, fine. We have an agreement," I conceded.

He uncrossed his arms and offered me his hand to shake, stating, "Brilliant."

Considering I passed out when I first laid eyes on him, I was more than a little scared to touch him.

I did it anyway, putting my hand in his, watching and feeling his long, strong fingers curl around, annnnnnnnnnnd...

Yep.

An electric pulse shot up my arm from our connection, exploding at my shoulder and scattering deliciously across my back, neck and chest.

Fortuitously, I didn't slide into unconsciousness at the contact, but this was partly because he broke our connection, his focus on our hands, his brows inching together in confusion, like he felt it too.

"I think now, I should go lay down for a little while," I whispered like I couldn't talk louder (and I couldn't because...what the hell was going on?).

"I believe that's for the best."

He shifted, and since I didn't, he raised his arm for me to precede him, so I did.

I also tried to salvage this situation by saying, "I appreciate you coming up with a compromise."

Under his breath, he replied, "If I was a diarist, I'd tally this as one of the few instances a female could agree to such a thing, albeit not without some headache."

And thus, I stopped dead. "Pardon me?"

His patronizing brown eyes came to mine. "We have a détente, Vivienne. It's lasted all of two minutes. How about we nurture it for a bit longer?"

"A good way to do that is not to mutter about women not being able to compromise. We can compromise."

His wide, burgundy-cashmere-sweater-covered chest expanded before he released another beleaguered sigh.

All right.

What was I doing?

This was my host.

Sure, he was kind of an asshole, but I was going to be living under his roof, eating his food, reading all about his family history, and he'd come up with a doable compromise so I wouldn't be thrown into a career tailspin that would have my agent and editor hunting me down to strangle me.

"Okay, yes, you're right," I said swiftly. "Détente, Duke."

He scowled at me, and let me tell you, the man could scowl.

It was gorgeous, and petrifying.

"You could fortify that by calling me by my bloody name," he said.

"Of course," I mumbled.

"Are you always this disagreeable?" he asked irately.

I opened my mouth to retort.

Then I closed it.

He watched my mouth doing that, something I hoped he never did again because my nipples liked it way too much.

And then he said, "Good idea."

Uh-oh.

My mouth again opened immediately to retort.

His gaze came to mine, and I didn't miss the dare in his eyes.

This is my host. This is my host. This is my host!

I shut my mouth again.

Luckily, he didn't gloat.

Instead, he indicated the smart unit on his desk and said, "You can intercom me when you're ready for dinner. I'll have the agreement ready for your perusal and signature."

"Perfect."

"Indeed."

"Thank you."

"You're welcome."

"Did you carry me to the couch?"

His head ticked before he replied, "I thought it better than leaving you lying on the floor."

I was never eating another dessert again.

"Well, thank you for that too," I said, and I felt badly, because even I could hear it was begrudgingly.

His beautiful mouth moved, and I watched in no small amount of fascination, because his mouth was beautiful, but also because I thought he might smile.

He didn't.

He prompted, "You were going to rest before dinner?"

"Right," I muttered.

"Until then, Vivienne."

My purred name again.

God!

I just waved.

And got the hell out of there.

CHAPTER 4
THE ANIMALS

Whoever modernized the mattresses, and the sheets, had my undying love and admiration.

The mattress on my bed in my pretty room with a view to a garden was a firm, supportive, cushiony cloud.

The sheets were downright heaven.

But sadly, both made me nap half an hour longer than I'd planned.

I'd wanted to luxuriate in the use of that vanity, but instead, after a quick shower and face cleanse, I had to hurry.

Making matters worse, my slinky, full-length, pine green satin gown had a mock turtleneck formed by a scarf tie at the back side of my neck, which made hairstyles a challenge.

Therefore, I'd had to intercom the staff to get the Wi-Fi info, which made me feel weird...*again.*

Obviously, these people had money. But I was still sleeping on their celestial bed, eating their scrumptious cream scones and using their very fast Wi-Fi.

In truth, it'd taken Prudence some doing to talk me into staying this long. The Downs being The Downs, I *wanted* to stay, but everything drilled into me by my mother and grandparents dictated I shouldn't stay as long as I agreed.

Prudence had worn me down.

I shouldn't have let her, but here I was, with a gracious invitation from a friend, an agreement with Battle and a job to do.

So I just had to shake it off and do it.

Two weeks would fly by (I hoped).

But the Wi-Fi gave me access on my iPad to watch the hair tutorial on YouTube the fifteen times it took me to get it down, though it took me five times of trying with my actual hair to get it right.

I did my makeup in subtle shades of smoke and drama, allowing my ruby-red lips to do the heavy lifting.

Fortunately, the simple gown, which bared not only my shoulders but also, with the low elevation of material at my back, my shoulder blades, skimmed my body like a lover, so I didn't have to go gung-ho on accessories.

This was good, since I did not live a life that would leave me dripping in jewels at age thirty-two.

I put in the simple diamond studs Mom gave me on my thirtieth birthday and strapped on the champagne metallic, high-heeled evening sandals. I then touched my signature scent (one of my few splurges: Carolina Herrera) behind my ears and at my wrists, and I was ready for my first dinner with the Talyns.

There was a smart screen on the vanity.

I touched it to activate it and then I touched the intercom icon.

I was given a dizzying array of choices that I scrolled through until I found the one noted as STUDY.

I tapped it.

As I waited for a response, never having had a formal dinner in a home, I didn't know if you were supposed to take an evening bag. But with this lipstick, reapplication was going to have to happen so I wasn't left with a ruby ring around my lips making me look like a clown, and I didn't have pockets.

Therefore, I was tucking my phone, compact and lippie in an evening bag when Battle's purr came through my smart unit.

"Vivienne?"

God, even remotely, his voice wrapped around my name gave me a physical reaction.

"Are you ready for me?" I asked.

"As I have been for the last hour."

Hmm.

We had not set an exact time to meet, and he knew that.

Don't bite, Vivi!

"I'll be right down," I said, though "right down" was relative since I was on the upper floor in the north wing, he was on the ground floor in the south, and the space in between was a lot.

"Excellent," he drawled.

I decided not to say anything else, grabbed my evening bag, took one last look at myself in the mirror, touching the chignon at my nape crafted of fluffy curls, checking if I had lipstick on my teeth, and then I took off.

I ran into no staff, no Talyns and no cats on my way to the study.

The door was open.

I steadied myself so I wouldn't do anything stupid, say faint or act like a bitch, before I rapped on the door.

"Yes?" Battle called.

I took a breath and walked in to see Battle behind the desk again, this time wearing a dinner jacket, a crisp white shirt and a bow tie.

One could say, he worked it.

Sublimely.

He had his glasses on, and behind them, his eyes were on me.

I immediately became unsteady.

He stood.

And I was unsteadier.

God, this man was something.

"And naturally, she excels at being tardy," he murmured, his gaze gliding the length of me.

I stopped dead between the two wingbacks in front of his desk.

And I forgot about not acting like a bitch.

"I beg your pardon?" I snapped.

His gaze came to mine.

"It's nearly seven," he shared.

"I was under the impression you hit the parlor whenever you were ready."

"But you're expected by seven."

"Well, please accept my deepest apologies, Your Grace," I said snootily. "But it's your fault, considering your mattresses and sheets are the foam and springs and Egyptian cotton versions of heaven, and they made me oversleep during my nap."

After I said this, something lazy entered his eyes as he watched me, and since that caused something not lazy at all to happen between my legs, an inappropriate response, but clearly one he was going for with that look, I nearly threw my evening bag at him.

Because…

Right.

Now what kind of games was this man playing?

To curb that desire, I tucked my bag under my arm and bit out, "Shall we do this?"

He gestured to the chairs. "Allow us, this time, not to impersonate bickering MPs on the floor of Parliament and instead sit and do this like civilized people."

I sat, muttering, "You started it."

Lame, also immature, but I did not care.

I heard his heavy sigh.

But what I saw was movement on the floor by the side of the desk.

I looked that way, jumped in my chair and let out a muted scream.

"What on…?" Battle murmured, having seated himself, he rose to his feet.

But I was staring.

Then I was smiling.

After that, I was crying out, "Oh my God! It's Hagrid's dog!"

The animal crept up to me, so I dropped a hand low and held it out to him.

He got close enough to sniff it.

It didn't take long for him to cast judgement, since after a single sniff, he dipped his snout low and used it to toss my hand up to his head.

Approved.

I laughed, carefully leaned the dog's way and gave his head a rubdown, cooing, "Aren't you a gentle brute."

"That's Bartholomew," Battle explained.

"He looks like his face is melting. He's adorable."

"He's a Neapolitan Mastiff, and be cautioned, he's hell on satin considering his propensity to drool."

I gave Bartholomew a good scratch behind his ear, leaning closer and fussing, "We don't care about drool, do we? We are who we are, and people have to accept us just so. Am I right?"

Bartholomew panted his agreement.

I kept petting as I turned my head to look at Battle, who had again taken his seat. "Where did you hide him earlier?"

"I wasn't hiding him," he retorted.

I looked back at Bartholomew. "Did I witness your gloriousness and that's what made me pass out?"

"No. He was in the gamekeeper's cottage with Christian."

I returned my attention to Battle.

He kept talking. "We went out to speak with him, and as that journey of about three hundred meters was rather taxing for my pup, he fell into a snooze whilst Christian and I conversed, so I left him there."

Again, I went back to Bartholomew. "I totally understand. It's hard being gorgeous, large and packed with muscle. It's good to take frequent rests from lugging your amazingness around."

Bartholomew licked his floppy chops, sending a string of drool curving around his short snout.

I laughed again.

Bartholomew pressed his head harder into my scratches.

"If we could do this so I can finally have a drink," Battle prompted.

I straightened, catching his eyes then looking to the right where I'd spied a drinks cart earlier.

And there it sat right now.

Back to him and I raised my brows.

"With my sisters," he added, lifting a leather portfolio and plopping it in front of me.

So we were going old-school, and this agreement was on paper, not electronic.

Interesting.

I tucked my bag in my lap and reached forward to take it.

Bartholomew realized pet time was over, but he didn't return to Daddy.

Oh no.

He shifted his bulk against my knee, then, no other way to put it, he dissolved down my satin-covered shins with a hearty groan to rest his considerable mass on my feet.

This meant I was smiling when I opened the portfolio.

"Who's Christian?" I asked as I scanned it.

"A botany PhD candidate from Oxford. He's writing his dissertation, studying the physiology or genetics or some such of the plants in our gardens."

This must be the sandy-haired handsome guy who'd been checking out Chastity as much as the roses earlier that day.

"Is he a member of the family or something?"

"No. He's a PhD candidate who reached out to us to ask if he could study our gardens for his dissertation."

With all the mystery surrounding The Downs, this surprised me.

"And you said yes?"

"Apparently," he drawled, eloquently pointing out that was a stupid question.

I gestured to myself with the portfolio. "You seem to say yes a lot."

"I'm not an ogre, Vivienne. Though, I might seem to be if I'm dealing with a stubborn American."

Oh my God.

This guy.

"I'm not stubborn," I retorted. "And being American has nothing to do with anything."

"Allow me to amend. An argumentative American."

Yet again I was opening my mouth to retort, then I bit it back, feeling the heat of annoyance sting my cheeks, and I forced my attention to the agreement.

"When she blushes, the freckles across her nose come out even stronger," he said under his breath, but even if he was pretending to talk to himself, I was oh-so supposed to hear.

I gave up reading the agreement and snapped, "I wasn't *blushing*. That was *annoyance*. And I'll ask you to refrain from commenting on my person."

"Does that mean you'd prefer me not to tell you I think that's a rather fetching frock you're wearing?"

Oh yeah.

Mm-hmm.

He was playing games.

"Yes," I gritted.

"Then I won't share I think that's a rather fetching frock."

Regardless I very much liked that he liked my dress, I glared at him.

He smirked at me.

Oh boy.

The man could smirk.

God.

He tipped his head to the portfolio. "The agreement?"

God!

It took me a second, I had to start over several times, but eventually I got into it.

Straightforward, no hidden agenda, no unnecessary legalese, no need to contact Natalie, my agent, to have a look at it.

Even so, I read it twice just to be ornery.

Finally, I requested, "Do you have a pen?"

He picked up a Mont Blanc from his desk and, in a belated effort at gallantry, rose from his chair so he could reach across the leather blotter so I wouldn't have to before he offered it to me.

I took it, uncapped it, saw it was a fountain pen, which I refused to admit I thought was cool (though, it totally was cool, and I made a mental note to buy myself one on the hopeful day I got my next advance for another book), and I signed both copies.

I closed the portfolio, capped the pen and put both on his desk.

Taking his glasses off and dropping them to the blotter, he stood, stating, "I'll ask Fitzgibbons to have your copy delivered to your room."

I remained seated. "Thank you."

He quirked his brows. "Shall we go?"

"I'll meet you there later."

Now he appeared suspicious. "You're not coming?"

"I have one hundred and fifty pounds of dog on my feet."

His head twitched and he moved around the desk to stare at the dog on my feet.

He opened his mouth, more than likely to call to the pooch, but I said quickly, "Don't."

He looked to me. "Don't what?"

"Disturb him. He's napping. I'm sure it took grave effort for him to walk around your desk. He needs his rest."

His eyes narrowed. "You're joking, right?"

"Yes and no. The no part is that I have a bizarre personality trait where I find myself emotionally unable to disturb a sleeping animal."

"Will you be emotionally distressed if I do it so I can get a fucking drink?"

The answer to that was…probably.

"Just…go gentle," I warned.

"For fuck's sake," he muttered, then, "Bartie."

The dog's head snapped up, and I was pretty sure that was as fast a movement as he had in him, because when Battle let out a low whistle, *I* got exhausted watching the animal push himself laboriously to his feet.

He loped over to his daddy.

I grabbed my bag from my lap and stood.

"After you," Battle invited, sweeping a long arm toward the door.

I started that way, praying I wouldn't turn my ankle in these four-inch heels. I wasn't a stranger to heels, but I was to four inches of them.

Once we left the study to walk down the plush, creamy, gold carpet runner of the hall, Battle fell into step beside me, Bartholomew trudging beside him.

We spoke no words, which I found unsettling.

When we hit the entryway, my heels clicked on the marble, while his soles drummed against it, both echoing through the cavernous space, and still I had no conversational gambit, and he didn't bother to offer one.

The sounds of our shoes disappeared as we made the runner in the hall that led into the north wing.

"This is us," Battle said, beginning to make a left turn into a room three doors down from the foyer.

He did this, so I did this, and then my evening bag was flying because I was flying, because something darted between my feet and tripped me.

Battle's body jerked in surprise before he whirled and caught me.

Batholomew got closer to his daddy, maybe in support, but his movement nearly took Battle off his feet.

His arm around me tightened.

A fluffy white cloud raced between us, further thwarting either of our efforts to remain standing, thus Battle hauled me around, my back was slammed into a wall, Battle's hard body slammed into mine, and the palm of his hand slammed against the plaster at the side of my head.

All of this took my breath away, so it came back in a whoosh as I tipped my head back to peer up at him.

His extraordinary face was close.

Very close.

His eyes were brown, yes.

But radiating from the iris was a gold tone that was mesmerizing.

And my breath left me again.

"I...uh...thank you," I whispered.

"Don't mention it," he whispered in return.

But he didn't move.

Except his eyes, which dropped to my mouth.

"Snowball! You rascal!"

We turned our heads at Prudence's shout to see all three Talyn sisters lined up in the hallway, along with Fitzgibbons, all of them regarding us.

I could have guessed it, but I'll run it down anyway.

Chastity was in a light-blue-shot-with-silver, off-the-shoulder confection reminiscent of the dress Princess Diana wore when she was snapped sleeping in a chair at some event, except it was much more princessier and exponentially girlier.

She accompanied this with diamonds.

Temperance wore a black, strapless tube dress that clung to every inch of her, and on her feet were a pair of killer, red slingback pumps.

She accompanied this with rubies.

And Prudence wore a shapeless, but stunning, flowing marbled black, white, and gray silk kaftan, which was fashioned so it had a dramatic cape in what appeared to be all black at the back. And she had a bizarre black fascinator on her head that looked like a plate with a veil that came down over her eyes.

She accompanied this with ropes and ropes of pearls.

"My, my," Temperance drawled, her lips curving meaningfully.

Pink hit Chastity's cheeks, and her eyes darted over our heads.

Fitzgibbons was having a hard time fighting his grin.

Prudence wasn't looking at us.

She was chastising a fluffy white Persian cat with green eyes who was sitting, faux innocently, on the carpet runner a couple of feet away, her poofy tail sweeping the rug.

"Naughty girl," Prudence admonished the cat.

The cat, as all cats do, remained visibly unrepentant.

It was important to note at this juncture that Battle didn't move.

Thus, I looked up at him again.

"I'm okay," I whispered.

For a second, it didn't seem like he heard me.

And it was important to note at *this* juncture, he was again staring at my mouth, and his long body was both *very* warm and *very* hard.

Then he nodded, and with exquisite slowness, he traced his large hand over the small of my back, my hip, and only then did he step away.

I gulped back a breath, hoping no one would notice me gulping back a breath.

"Shall we get that drink, Vivienne?" he asked.

Not trusting my voice to come out as more than a squeak, I nodded.

He offered his arm, a gesture both chivalrous and hot, and one I accepted because I didn't want any more incidents to happen.

Not at all.

Especially not with Battle Talyn, the Duke of Burleigh in attendance.

We made it into the parlor further unscathed.

And for this, I was grateful.

CHAPTER 5

THE PLAN

"What can I get you to drink, Miss Dupree?" Fitzgibbons asked after Battle led me to a seat, I sank down into it, and Fitzgibbons had retrieved my bag and returned it to me.

"Please call me Vivienne, or Viv, or Vivi," I invited.

He smiled. "What can I get you to drink, Miss Vivienne?"

I guessed that would have to work.

"Amaretto sour, if you have it?"

"We have everything," he murmured and stepped away.

When he did, I took the opportunity to look around the room.

Unlike the blue salon (but a lot like the warm woods, leather furniture and bookcases filled with books of the study), this parlor eschewed any creamy creams or light colors and was done in tones of plum. It was also the smallest room I'd been in, it trended toward the vintage side of the modern/antique aesthetic the rest of the place had going on, and it had a lot of seating.

Primarily, two Regency armchairs (four in all, a coupling at each end) upholstered in a mulberry shade flanking two Duncan Phyfe sofas upholstered in raisin were arranged around an oblong, cherrywood coffee table.

Battle had deposited me in a chair.

Prudence and Chastity took a sofa.

Temperance sat dead center of the other sofa.

Which meant, when Battle returned from working with Fitzgibbons at the drinks cabinet, he gave me my beverage and sat in the chair beside me.

He could have forced himself next to Temperance, it wouldn't have been tough, there was plenty of room, or he could have settled in one of the two chairs opposite me. They weren't that far away.

But nooooooo.

He sat beside me.

Maybe it was because Bartholomew had settled on his belly between our two seats.

But I didn't think so.

"I'll go ask Cook how dinner is progressing," Fitzgibbons said while exiting the room.

"Thank you, Fitzy," Temperance called after him.

Prudence clapped her hands, and everyone looked to her.

But she was looking at me. "Did you two sort everything?"

"It's all good," I assured her.

"Told you Battie would be a pushover when it came down to it," Prudence replied.

I wouldn't call him a pushover, but I didn't share that.

I said, "Your dress is freaking amazing."

When I finished uttering those words, her whole body froze, not to mention, the air in the room went static, though I felt some pretty extreme heat flowing from Battle toward me.

But...

Oh my God.

Did I somehow put my foot in it?

"I didn't mean—" I began.

Prudence spoke over me. "You really think so?"

I was confused.

"Well, of course. Don't you like it?" I tried a smile. "I mean, you're wearing it."

"I love it," she said like it was an admission.

"You should. It's fabulous," I stated.

"It's weird," she replied before adding, "I have weird taste."

What Battle shared earlier about Prudence being bullied came to me, my anger at learning this refreshed, and it drove me to speak.

"I don't know what weird is," I returned. "I'm sure some could say Vivienne Westwood is weird, but there are few with any true knowledge of fashion who would agree. The same with Alexander McQueen, God rest his soul. John Galliano. Jean-Paul Gaultier. Would you call any of them weird?"

"Well, no." Another admission from Prudence.

"And one could say that the costume designers who dress Sarah Jessica Parker put her in some pretty extreme getups, but she pulls them off, because they might be extreme, but they're awesome. Do you like *Sex in the City*?"

"I haven't watched it, but I know what you mean," Prudence said.

I took a sip of my drink then brandished it while concluding, "Therefore, weird is in the eye of the judgy, bitchy, fashion-ignorant beholder, wouldn't you agree?"

A small smile played at her lips. "Yes, I'd agree."

"But also, it takes some courage to like what you like and not worry about what other people think about it. Though, mostly, if they have something to say, it's probably because they're jealous they don't have the guts to be who they are and let that show, not giving a stitch what others might think, which takes some seriously strong ovaries to pull off, something you do effortlessly. Am I wrong?"

"I-I don't think so, no," Prudence stammered.

"I'm not," I affirmed and looked around the room, but avoided Battle when I did so, and not only because of the question I asked. "So we can all agree Prudence's dress is fantastic?"

"I already told her that, but she never listens to me," Temperance said.

"I told you that too," Chastity whisper-spoke directly to Prudence.

"You're my sisters. You're supposed to say nice things to me," Prudence replied.

"Not true," I stated. "A real sister, blood or otherwise, will lay it out for you. What she won't do is say something that would make you feel you have to hide your light under a bushel. What you wear might not be their tastes, but does that mean, since what they're wearing isn't yours, you don't like what they're wearing?"

"They always look lovely," Prudence asserted.

"And I'm sure, so do you," I returned. "At least, that's what I've noticed about you."

"Thanks, Vivi," Prudence said shyly.

Glances were being exchanged, so I chanced one at Battle to see he wasn't participating in this.

He seemed deep in the study of what appeared to be a G&T.

He only looked up when Chastity unusually took the reins of the conversation, and her whisper was slightly louder when she lifted what appeared to be a daiquiri and announced, "I think now we should toast our guest and officially welcome her to our home."

"Hear, hear!" Prudence exclaimed, lifting what appeared to be an old fashioned.

Temperance just tilted her glass to me.

Battle did the same, but then he took his sip with his eyes aimed over the rim right at me, a move that was seriously damned sexy, and he knew it.

Instead of throwing my drink at him, I said to the room, "Thank you. I'm really looking forward to my visit with all of you."

"And we are going to have *so much fun*," Prudence decreed.

Well, she and I probably were.

The rest...we'd see.

Everyone sipped.

"Battie, before you and Vivienne made your dramatic appearance," Temperance changed the subject in a manner I was coming to realize she was wont to utilize, "Prudence was discussing the attics with us."

"Mm?" Battle hummed, a sound that was like a physical touch to me, and seriously…

Why couldn't the man have sat across the coffee table, damn it?

"She thinks, while Vivienne is here, we might want to tackle that project," Temperance went on. "And by 'we,' I wish it to be clear, I do not mean me."

I was about to get fidgety, because if the attics were a mess and I was helping change that status, I wouldn't be able to have my nose in Talyn family papers.

"Not to be presumptuous or anything," Prudence said quickly to me. "Just that, you know a lot about history. Even fabrics, fixtures and furnishings. You describe them so perfectly in your books." She turned her attention to Battle. "I'm sure there are many things of worth up there that we'll never use. But, sitting up there, collecting dust, it's not doing anyone any good." She came back to me. "So I thought you could have a glance at it, not go through it or tidy it or anything. That'll be my job. But just to confirm I'm right."

"And if you're right?" I asked.

"Then you can help me figure out what's next," she answered. "An auctioneer or a curator of a museum or something."

"That is, if you'll let us sell it, Battie," Chastity whisper-added.

"I'd put the lot on the curb for anyone driving by to take what they wanted if it was my choice," Battle said into his glass before taking a drink.

"Oh no, Battie!" Prudence chirped. "Not if we can make money for our charities, or for The Fund, or donate pieces a museum might want."

Battle turned to his sister and said in a loving tone I'd not heard before, and was uncertain whether I wished I still hadn't, or wanted to hear it for a lifetime.

"In other words, sweetheart, whatever you want to do, do it."

Prudence clapped again as she jumped in her seat. "Thanks, Battie."

"Just to reiterate, I will, of course," Temperance began while flourishing a nearly empty martini glass that had three fat olives on a silver pick rolling around in it, "be nowhere near this escapade involving junk, dust mites, and more than likely, mice."

"We can't live in a house with cats and have mice, Tempie," Chastity whisper-contradicted.

Temperance graced her youngest sister with a sly smile. "I'm not taking chances, dear."

Prudence and Chastity's attention went to the door at this point, so we all looked that way to see Fitzgibbons standing in it.

"Cook says dinner is ready when you are," he announced.

"Drink up, I'm famished," Temperance ordered as she sucked back the tail end of her martini and put the glass on the coffee table.

"You can take yours with," Prudence told me.

"Thanks," I replied, rising from my seat.

I made note of where Bartholomew was and scanned for any errant felines before I turned and witnessed, what seemed crazily, the three Talyn sisters rushing to the door.

Of course, Temperance did it while sashaying, but she was still rushing.

Boy, they must be hungry.

Then again, I was the only one who went for seconds on the scones.

This meant two unfortunate things occurred next.

One, Battle offered me his arm (likely not wanting me tripped or to swoon again), and so I wouldn't appear ungracious, I was forced to take it.

And two happened when we walked next door, to a dining room papered in gold damask with cream wainscotting and a large, oval, luscious African mahogany table dressed in a stunning candelabra, the candles flickering, more beautiful but unique floral arrangements, and five place settings of crystal, fine china and silver cutlery cuddled at one end.

This wasn't what was unfortunate.

What was unfortunate was that Chastity was already seated to the left of the head of the table, Temperance next to her. And on the opposite side, Prudence sat at a setting that left only the head of the table and the seat right next to it open.

And this meant I'd be sitting directly to Battle's right.

Marvelous.

Things got worse when Battle demonstrated more gallantry by helping with my seat.

"Thank you," I murmured, setting my drink down and tucking my bag in my lap.

"My pleasure," he purred while taking his own seat.

I hoped the boob tape I was forced to use to pull off this dress held up as that part of my anatomy reacted to his words.

Ugh.

Kill me.

As I put my napkin over my bag in my lap (and made note none of the other ladies had them), in came Fitzgibbons with a bottle of wine wrapped in linen, and Scotty with a soup tureen.

"Did you ever meet your great-grandfather, Charlie?" Chastity spoke directly to me for the first time by whisper-asking this while Fitzgibbons filled our white wine glasses and we served ourselves soup (creamy prawn and crab bisque, it smelled delicious).

"No, he died before I was born," I told her. "Though, he lived a long life. And my mom adored him."

"Obviously, he married," Temperance said. "Did you know your great-grandmother?"

I shook my head and spooned into the soup I'd placed into the bowl over my gold charger. "She was still alive when I was born, and I'm told I met her, but I was too young to remember."

"Harmony never married," Chastity whispered forlornly to her soup.

"And good for her she didn't," Temperance stated firmly. "Serves Saint right to be robbed of more progeny after breaking his own daughter's heart."

"Yes, but perhaps she was lonely," Prudence said, performing a miracle since what she said made me shift focus from my delicious soup to her at my side.

She didn't look upset, just earnest and into the conversation.

"There isn't a female alive who needs a man," Temperance retorted.

At that, I turned to Battle to watch his reaction to this statement, however, what I saw was that it had no effect on him.

Though he, too, liked the soup.

"But maybe she wanted one," Prudence suggested.

"We all want *something* from them, darling," Temperance drawled. "But once that's had, the rest of what they have to offer is superfluous."

At that, Battle stopped sipping his soup and smiled indulgently at his eldest sister.

And yes.

You guessed it.

I not only wished I'd never witnessed that smile on his fabulous lips, I also wished I'd see it again and again and again, all those times aimed at me.

"It's like you agree with her, Battie," Chastity whisper-rebuked his magnificent smile.

"I do agree with her, Chassie," he replied.

"You do?" Prudence asked.

"Men wouldn't have put so much effort into holding women down over the millennium if we actually thought you were the weaker sex," Battle stated. "They did it because they knew women would do a better job if they had the running of the world, and one thing a man's ego can't abide is anyone doing a better job than him."

Oh crap.

Was I going to have to like this guy?

"I adore you," Temperance cooed at her brother.

"Only when I agree with you," he replied.

"Indeed." Temperance smiled an icy-cool, but somehow genuinely loving smile.

No question, I totally liked Temperance.

In order to guide myself out of the zone of Battle (maybe) making me like him, or at least tolerate him, I addressed Prudence, "So tomorrow, tour of The Downs and having a look at the attics, then you'll show me the studio?"

"That sounds perfect," she chirruped.

"Then, I'd like to get into what you've uncovered, get a plan to organize it. Could you give me a day or two with that, and after I feel I have a handle on it, we can head to Glastonbury?"

That weird static feeling came back to the air after I said this.

But Prudence suddenly appeared uncomfortable. "Well, about that—"

After what Battle told me, I wasn't going to let her wheedle out of it.

"Or, we could go the day after tomorrow," I suggested. "Before I get stuck in."

Heading off Prudence's response, Temperance said, "I say you go then. You're in danger of running into a town overflowing with week-end-tripper flower children, white witches and Druids if you wait much past that."

I started laughing. "Druids?"

"It's supposedly a mystical place," Prudence said.

"I know that, my lovely," I replied. "But Druids?"

"They're still a thing," Prudence shared.

"They're essentially hippies who wear white robes," Temperance put in. "Or is it witches who wear white robes? Don't answer. I don't care to know the distinction."

"Maybe Ravenna will want to come with us to Glastonbury," Prudence suggested while I took a sip of soup.

At this proposal, I nearly choked, and for some insane reason my gaze flew to Battle.

He was scowling at me.

How I knew what his scowl was saying, I couldn't tell you.

But I did.

And he punctuated it by nudging my foot with his, a move that caused Bartholomew, who had miraculously followed us in without me noticing and settled between Battle's and my seats, also without me noticing, to groan.

I bugged my eyes out at Battle.

He subtly jerked his head toward Prudence.

I mouthed an exaggerated, *I know, but what do you want me to do about it?*

He did the subtle head jerk again.

"Oh, for goodness' sake," Temperance complained. "I'll say the quiet part out loud."

Battle's brow lowered dangerously as his attention shafted to his sister.

"Tempie," he growled warningly.

Temperance ignored him. "We all think Ravenna is full of shit."

I sat back in my seat, rethinking if I liked Temperance.

"She is not," Prudence said defensively.

Chastity emitted a whisper-peep.

Prudence's voice was rising. "You too?" she asked Chastity.

"And Battie, also Vivienne," Temperance took it upon herself to confirm.

Now my brow was lowered dangerously and aimed at Temperance.

I smoothed my features when I felt Prudence look at me.

I caught the *et tu?* look in her eyes and explained, "I'm one hundred percent all about tarot. You can use the cards as a means of digging deeper into what's happening in your life, things you might not be seeing, things you might be avoiding, feelings you might not fully understand, but should. I guess you can say that about pretty much every"—I put my spoon down to do air quotation marks—"'fortune telling' thing. Like tasseography, astrology, crystallomancy or palmistry."

"What's tasseography?" Chastity whisper-cut in.

"Reading tea leaves," I told her, and turned back to Prudence. "But honey, curses and actual fortunes and some of the stuff you told me Ravenna said to you…" I trailed off and shook my head.

"Though, I will say the woman knows fortunes, since she charges you one every bloody time you see her," Temperance added.

"Enough," Battle said low.

Temperance pressed her lips together.

I grabbed a dejected Prudence's wrist. "But I do want to meet her. I didn't lie about that." I shrugged and gave her a smile. "I might be wrong. Though, how about we take another day to do that and do Glastonbury on our own?"

"With Chassie," Temperance unpressed her lips to declare.

"Of course," I said, then looked to Chastity, and instantly, my scalp started tingling.

She appeared downright panicked.

"Glastonbury isn't my thing," she whisper-asserted.

"Nonsense," Temperance said. "You loved the ruins of the abbey when you were a kid."

"I have—" Chastity whisper-began.

Temperance talked over her. "Sorted. You three girls head to the mystical mecca and peruse crystals and buy flower crowns and be sure to bring back some of those Viennese biscuits dipped in chocolate from Burns the Bread."

Chastity cast rattled eyes at her big brother.

He ignored her while he calmly sipped soup.

I read the room (I hoped) and announced, "Agreed. We have a plan. Girls trip. And I'll drive."

It was then His Grace, Battle Talyn aimed an indulgent smile at me.

I had no idea what was happening or what I was getting into.

But whatever it was, I knew one thing from that smile.

It was worth it.

CHAPTER 6
THE TOUR

I swam out of sleep the next morning to what appeared to be another dreary day in England and the understanding my slumbering self was the entertainment of a green-eyed Persian.

Snowball was sitting beside me, regarding me condescendingly.

"You're a bed hog," I accused.

And she was.

No matter where I turned last night, there she was, sprawled out and purring so that eventually I had the edge of the king-size bed, and she had the rest of it.

As response to my accusation, she licked her paw and cleaned her ear with it.

"Ugh," I groaned, falling to my back then turning my head to see the smart screen told me it was seven fifteen.

Last night, Prudence showed me where breakfast was served (another dining room in the north wing, this one smaller, less formal, with a gleaming round table and a sideboard set up with fancy silver chafing dishes).

She'd also told me I could order a tray to be brought up to my room or come down whenever I wanted. The staff kept the chafing dishes full from seven to nine thirty, but I could order anytime.

I had plenty of time to make breakfast downstairs, but I wasn't going to take it.

I was getting the tour, including discovering what the aristocracy considered junk, and I was finally going to be able to lay my eyes on all the documents Prudence had been able to unearth for me.

And no, this wasn't about maybe catching Battle at breakfast.

It definitely was not.

(Okay, it was, but I didn't want it to be.)

Last night I'd learned he might be arrogant, and a player, with broad hints of dick, but he was also a devoted older brother.

He didn't say much, but outside of curtailing Temperance's character assassination of Ravenna, he not only gave them all the space to be who they were, the way he did it encouraged that same thing.

So...yeah.

I had no idea what he was playing at with me.

But he was a super cool brother, as much as I didn't want to admit it.

On this thought, I turned back to Snowball.

"Should we face the day?" I asked.

As answer, she gracefully leapt over me, as well as the side of the bed, and I watched her fluffy butt with lifted-high floofy tail saunter toward the bathroom.

I smiled, tossed the covers back and muttered, "I'll take that as a yes."

Thus, I swung out of bed and followed Snowball.

Thankfully, I'd learned the lesson a long time ago that I endeavored to teach Prudence last night.

Therefore, when I arrived at the breakfast table, I was wearing a pair of wide-legged, cropped white jeans, a slouchy, soft beige sweater

French tucked, and a pair of peanut suede booties with a stacked block heel and pointed toe that had a slight Western flair in the panel stitching.

Yes, I looked like a well-heeled American (or at least I thought that was the look I was pulling off), because I was one.

Battle, fortunately (unfortunately?), was not at the breakfast table.

No one was.

But Prudence.

And God, I loved this chick.

Today she was wearing a black turtleneck that had the addition of a collar coming out of it that rose up over her ears giving her a petite female Count Dracula look.

That was all I could see since she was seated, but it was enough to absolutely adore it…and her for wearing it.

"Good morning," I greeted while entering.

"Vivi!" she cried. "How did you sleep?"

"Snowball hogged the bed," I told her as I sat next to her and reached for the ornate silver coffee pot.

"Oh no!" she exclaimed. "Do I need to lock her up? I don't usually lock up my babies. They don't like it. But you need to sleep."

This made me pause in pouring, because, when I returned to my room last night, I'd closed my door.

I resumed pouring as I asked, "I closed my door, how did she get in?"

Prudence made a *puh* noise. "It drives Battie…well, *batty*." She laughed. "But they've learned to open the doors. You have to lock them to keep them out. Though, if she wants to get to you, be sure to lock the door to the hallway in your dressing room too."

"I don't mind her joining me," I said, putting the coffee down and reaching for the jug of creamer. Once I poured, I turned to her. "Do I get to meet the others?"

Her eyes lit with excitement. "You like animals?"

"Love them."

"Then…absolutely," she answered and waved a hand at the side-board. "Oh, and just grab a plate and help yourself."

I got up, querying, "Has everyone already come down?"

"Temperance, no. She sleeps until at least nine. Chastity, also no, she took a tray in her bedroom. And Battle, again no, he had his breakfast in the study. He has some computer meetings this morning. He's not usually here during the week, and he works a lot, so we probably won't see him until dinner."

I was peeking under lids, but what she said made me stop and turn to her.

"He's not normally here during the week?"

And no, I didn't ask this because I was interested in all things Battle Talyn.

(But yes, I absolutely did.)

She shook her head. "No. He's at our house in Knightsbridge. His office is in London. He usually leaves early Monday morning and returns Friday evening."

"Every weekend he comes home?"

She nodded.

I grinned at her. "So he's here on a Wednesday to make certain the American stranger you invited to the house doesn't steal the Burleigh jewels."

She returned my grin, but asserted, "Don't be offended, Vivi. It's not like we don't ever have visitors, or guests who stay over. Temperance has a lot of friends. So does Battle. We have house parties. We entertain all the time."

I noted she didn't include her and Chastity in having "lots of friends."

She continued, "It's just that, to him, you were an unknown, and no matter how stridently I vouched for you, as you've learned, he's protective."

I'd sure learned that.

"I would be too if this was my legacy and I had three younger sisters," I replied.

Though they were younger, they weren't *young*.

One thing I knew about Prudence, because she told me, was that she was around my age, thirty-one (I was thirty-two). But in my research, I learned Chasitity was twenty-eight, Temperance was thirty-three, and Battle was thirty-six.

I went back to the chafing dishes, because under one was English sausage, bacon, and black pudding, and I'd vowed to myself I was going to stuff as much of that in my face as I could while I was in the country. And for the four days I'd been there, I'd succeeded in besting this challenge.

I wasn't about to fall down now.

After I filled my plate, I returned to my seat, seeing Prudence had a coffee cup aloft and was staring blankly across the room.

I didn't know whether to leave her to her thoughts or ask after them.

When in doubt with a plate of food in front of you…

I started eating.

It was the right choice.

Prudence jolted and then said, "Sorry. Miles away. Thinking about the attics and hoping we find Aunt Harmony's letters from Charlie there."

"Were you able to find a journal of hers?" I asked before taking a bite of sausage.

Oh yes.

Yum.

"No. Though, we did find Marie's. And Harmony's sister, Unity's."

That made my heart skip a beat, because Marie was Saint's wife and Harmony's mother.

"Really?"

She smiled thinly at me. "Just to warn you, I had a quick scan, and Marie didn't say much of anything, ever. Just a few lines in each entry, mostly about household things, meals they had, etc. And I don't think Harmony shared her love affair with her sister. Then again, Unity was much younger. She couldn't have been more than thirteen at the time. Probably not a planned pregnancy. So also probably not a confidante."

"Well, I'll have a good look to make sure."

"Of course." Her smile grew without bad news to impart. "It must be terribly exciting to embark on a new book."

"Best feeling ever."

"I'm so excited to be a part of it, even a small one."

"I love that we get to share this too," I agreed genuinely. "So I'm going to eat up so we can get started."

Prudence watched me cut off another bite of sausage and said, "I'm just going to get one more sausage."

I didn't blame her.

In fact, I thought that was the perfect plan.

We started below stairs, an area of an estate like this I always found just as fascinating as what sat on top of it.

And at The Downs, it was no different.

There was the vast kitchen (modernized, but it still had the bones of antiquity to it). The buttery, pantries, a comfortable staff lounge, and Prudence unlocked the storage rooms to show me where they kept their crystal, china, silver and booze safe. There was also a laundry area, and a massive linen cupboard we spent some time in because, call me a freak, I found all the tablecloths, runners, sheets, coverlets, quilts and throws fascinating.

Fitzgibbons had an office down there, as did Patsy, the house-keeper, who was also Fitzgibbons's wife.

Those two were the only live-ins, and Prudence shared that Battle had completely renovated what used to be the servants' quarters so they had a rather large apartment (an area, obviously, Prudence didn't show me) that not only had its own entrance off the north side of the house, but also a private terrace and garden.

This space was needed, apparently because, Prudence told me, they had three kids, two of whom lived in the village, all of whom were married, had children and came calling frequently.

The staff included Cook, a woman Prudence's and my age whose name was actually Emily, who I met during the tour.

I also met Amelia and reacquainted with Mary, both maids, and Scotty and Harry, who lugged, served, ran errands and did handyman work, but I got the impression they were also there to provide security.

Don't ask me why I had this impression, maybe it was because they were both tall, fit, alert, and just gave off that vibe.

And last, the lawns and parkland were overseen by a gardener, but Prudence informed me that Chastity did all the gardening, not only in the gardens, but also the greenhouse.

For that big of a house, it didn't seem like that big of a staff.

But the book I was writing was about modernization and how that shifted the world on its axis.

Including having the effect of blurring the lines of the haves and have-nots as many more people had many more opportunities to make a lot more money. But on the other hand, with telephones and vacuums and cars and gas stoves and washing machines and lawn mowers, it made having a vast staff who needed to offer copious manual labor obsolete.

We moved to the ground floor, and Prudence started in the south wing, introducing me to sitting rooms (the most formal of them an exquisite study of greens and cream), a couple of salons, a morning room, the library, Battle's study with its door closed (we skipped that, and not only because I'd already seen it), and at the very end, a fantastic armory.

We went upstairs next, which was mostly bedrooms, though, at the end of my wing, there was a nursery, music and school room.

All the Talyn family's bedrooms were in the south wing, obviously including Battle's, which Prudence waved a vague hand toward the door at the end of the hall, stating that was the duke's chamber, and where it was situated meant he had the whole cap of the end of the wing.

And for that reason and that reason alone (I told myself), I was dying to see it.

I didn't share that desire with Prudence, however.

As we were heading back downstairs, Prudence said, "I want you to be able to get some work done, so we'll save the attics for the weekend. Though I'll head up there after I show you the studio. I'll have a dink around to see if I can find anything of Harmony's, or anything else you might be interested in."

I was chomping at the bit to see what she'd pulled for me, so I was grateful for this offer, and to share that, I hooked my arm in hers as we kept walking.

"That would be awesome."

She smiled at me as we turned towards the stairs.

I took that opportunity to probe.

"Battle tells me you have six cats."

She stiffened, which I thought was strange.

"I do," she confessed. "I don't know where they all are. They're masters at hiding."

"I love cats, so I'm bummed that over the last year I didn't get to oo and ah over cute cat pictures."

Even walking down the stairs, she looked at me. "You don't think having so many cats makes me some kind of crazy cat lady?"

Fuck her father and all the bitches who bullied her.

I forced a laugh hoping it didn't sound forced and shared in all truth, "Girl, if I had this huge house, I'd have eight cats, five dogs and probably a colony of guinea pigs."

That made her laugh, and hers was straight-up genuine.

I stopped her at the table and chandelier.

"Is that why you didn't tell me?" I asked. "Because you thought I'd think you're a cat lady?"

Her humor was gone, and her shrug was uncomfortable.

As such, I wasn't sure she was up for another one of my Let Your Freak Flag Fly lectures.

Then again, I didn't think she was at all freaky.

She was just...

Prudence.

I set us to walking again, saying, "Well, let's get one thing super straight. I like you. And unless you admit to something dire, like you have a side hobby of poisoning, nothing about you is going to make me *not* like you, though it'll probably make me like you more."

She leaned into my arm, but other than that, didn't say anything.

Though, that was all she had to say.

The north side of the house had what I'd describe as the entertaining rooms: the breakfast room, dining room, the parlor we'd been in last night. There were also more parlors, salons, a games room, a billiards room, a smoking room, and what Prudence called "the ladies' lounge."

All of this was not surprising considering we were nearing the end of that wing, which I could see from the open double doors was the ballroom.

My heart started thumping.

It was like Prudence felt it, because she whispered, "I saved this for last."

We held each other close as we came to a stop in the threshold of that stunning room.

A room that brought us together.

The room that brought us to right now.

Three grand crystal chandeliers lined the center of the ceiling. The floors were intricate Versailles parquet. The walls were stark white as were the floral garland moldings. There were massive gilt-framed mirrors on the walls in between the big windows that showcased the gardens and parkland. And along the walls were several Georgian settees upholstered in ivory and early Georgian armless chairs upholstered in gold.

"Where Harmony and Charlie fell in love," Prudence whispered.

"Yes," I whispered back reverently.

"Marie didn't want to do it," Prudence told me something she'd already shared. "Open The Downs to soldiers, nurses, doctors, officers, as a convalescent hospital. She didn't want the common riffraff filling her bedrooms, making offices of her salons and messing up her ballroom. Harmony guilted her into doing it."

"Other great houses went so far as to tear down structures to donate iron and other materials to the war cause," I added. "Also offering space for makeshift hospitals and turning over formal gardens to plant vegetables."

"But not the Duchy of Burleigh," Prudence said. "Until Harmony intervened over a year into the war."

"It was do it or she was going to London to offer her services, meaning she'd have been in London during the Blitz."

"I wonder, since she had such determination, how they managed to tear her and Charlie apart," Prudence mused.

This was a great question.

And hopefully Harmony journaled and didn't destroy her letters from my great-grandfather, so we might find out.

Prudence shot me an impish look. "Shall we?"

I grinned at her. "We shall."

And with that, we stepped onto the parquet.

Instantly, my world turned blue, then green, then purple, the kaleidoscope of colors all a haze as I found myself among couples twirling around the floor in a waltz. I could hear the muted conversation, the orchestra playing, even the wisp of slippers and hems of ballgowns sweeping the wood.

Prudence's arm in mine guided me into the miasma swirling around me as women's feather-bearing heads turned this way and that, men's coattails fluttered, jewels glowed murkily.

I heard a giggle, a low chuckle, a whispered insult.

We kept walking.

And the view changed.

The colors were gone, it was all in a mist of blue that I saw the lines of beds, the privacy screens, the old fashioned IV stands, nurses wandering, doctors reading charts, patients hobbling.

A woman sat by a man in bed, and I listened to him dictating a letter to her as she carefully scribbled.

He did this because he had no hands.

To my darling Jane…

My attention shifted to a set of double French doors at the end of the room as I saw the back of a man with a crutch under one arm, his other arm busy with the woman at his side clutching his other arm at his elbow.

He was smiling down at her as he led her out into a blinding blue sunshine.

"Vivi?" I heard Prudence call as I pulled from her hold to go after them. "Vivi!"

I hit the doors; they were closed.

I tried to open them; they were locked.

The key was in the lock.

I turned it and stepped out onto the terrace.

And it all faded away.

"Vivi!" Prudence cried again as she grabbed my hand.

I looked down at her vaguely, then turned my attention to the ballroom, which was just an empty ballroom.

Okay.

All right.

Okay.

Holy hell.

What the fuck just happened?

"Are you all right?" Prudence asked, pumping her fingers around my hand.

"Did you—?"

I couldn't finish.

Because…*did I?*

Did I just see what I just saw?

Did I just hear what I just heard?

Did that just happen?

"Did I what?" Prudence asked.

I said nothing.

"Vivi, you're worrying me. Are you okay?"

"I…have a very vivid imagination," I told her.

Her smile was shaky. "I would suppose so, considering you're a writer."

"And I could swear I just saw a ball happening in that room, circa the Regency," I rushed out. "And then it morphed into a convalescent hospital during World War II."

Her head drifted so she could look into the room, and she asked, "Really?"

"You didn't…you…?"

Of course she didn't.

How long was my jetlag going to last?

Prudence came back to me. "There's a lot of history here."

I nodded, fervently.

Yes, she was right.

Historical places had *feels*. So did historical things.

I'd twice seen the Declaration of Independence, the Constitution and the Bill of Rights displayed in the Rotunda of the National Archives, and both times, all those around me spoke in hushed tones in the presence of such important documents written and signed by men who changed the entire world.

Hell, just a few days ago, I was fortunate enough to see both original copies of the Magna Carta on display at the British Library, and the same thing happened.

This was my thing.

This was my gig.

This was my muse.

Since I found Great-Granddad Charlie's letters, I'd been obsessed by what happened between him and Lady Harmony Talyn in that room.

So of course my imagination would stir up something spectacular the instant I stepped foot in it.

Right?

Right?

Okay, so nothing that profound, and frankly bizarre, had ever happened to me before.

But I wasn't blood relative to anyone involved in writing the Constitution or the Magna Carta.

So of course this would be more powerful.

"Should we go to the studio now?" Prudence asked hesitantly. "Or do you, maybe, want to lie down again?"

She was worried I'd think she was a crazy cat lady.

Now I was worried she thought I was just crazy.

I shook my head and plastered on a smile. "No. No. Let's go to the studio. I was just…overwhelmed I was finally where it happened. Maybe, I guess, you know, if it had worked out for them, I might not be here. And maybe that all just…got to me."

"Maybe," she agreed.

"It was actually kind of cool," I lied.

Because it was *not.*

It was freaky as fuck!

She giggled. "I wouldn't mind being in the middle of a Regency ball."

"It was pretty rad,' I lied again.

So, maybe it was.

It was still freaky as fuck.

She guided me to the side of the terrace where there were some steps down to the gardens, doing this saying, "I bet it was."

Note to self: avoid the freaking ballroom.

Our feet hit soft turf, and I finally felt the cool air against my face, so I focused on it.

Later, I'd think about passing out the instant I saw Battle and wandering among phantoms waltzing in the ballroom and what those wild things happening might mean.

Now, I had a job to do, and I was finally going to be able to start doing it.

And that was all I was going to think about.

CHAPTER 7

THE DAY TRIP

I swam out of sleep the next morning to what appeared to be an unusual sunny day in England and the understanding my slumbering self was the entertainment of a green-eyed Persian who, last night, brought a friend.

Snowball was lying beside me, concentrating on bathing her ruff with her tongue, and accompanying her was Gingerface, a cat I'd met last night. He was a thick-furred ginger with huge round eyes and an adorable round face, the former now aimed at me curiously.

"You're both bed hogs," I accused.

Snowball ignored me.

Gingerface took my speaking as an invitation to cuddle, which he did, easily and with practice, since last night he made clear his cuddling tendencies.

I buried my fingers in his fur at the same time I fell to my back and turned my head to see the smart screen told me it was six fifty-two.

I then looked up at the canopy above me.

Yesterday, I'd discovered that Lady Marie Talyn's painting studio was a living dream.

A little cottage tucked in a corner of the gardens, abutting a field that held fluffy sheep and was flanked with two forests. It was about a five-minute walk from the main house.

And come time for the wisteria to bloom, considering the amount of it crawling all over that cottage, it was going to be an extra something to see.

It had lots of sparkling-clean windows, whitewashed walls, and just outside the front door that was off to the side, a little patio adorned with a cute cast iron bistro table and chairs and lots of pots filled with flowers.

Inside, there was a desk in the center, a black stove in a corner and a Victorian chaise lounge draped in fringed shawls across from it in the other corner. A stool at an easel with a half-finished watercolor on canvas sat across the room, just in from the door.

There was a breakfront filled with a disorganized collection of paint things, all old and undoubtedly not a bit of it fit for purpose anymore.

There were scattered threadbare rugs on the wood plank floors that had probably been usurped from the main house.

And there was a long shelf in front of the side-by-side, diamond-paned windows opposite the desk, all of it and all the space under it, containing boxes of…everything.

Journals, ledgers, letters, framed photos, unframed photos.

A cornucopia of Talyn history laid out like a mouthwatering smorgasbord in front of me.

Prudence knew I'd hit my Nirvana (probably around the time I shouted, "Oh my God, this is Nirvana!"), so she just gave me the skinny before she took her leave.

First, if I got cold and wanted a fire, since there was no other heating, I should just use the telephone (which only called to the main house) to ask if Scotty or Harry could build one for me.

Second, if I needed anything, like lunch brought out or something to drink, again just use the phone.

Third, the place might not have heat, but it did have electricity, and they'd set up Wi-Fi for me out there (so sweet!).

En fin, last night's protocol held with people turning up in what I thought of as the plum parlor at around six thirty, and since it wasn't going to be a celebration like last night, what I was wearing would be fine for dinner.

She then let me have at it, and I didn't want to be that person, but I was, because I barely noticed her going.

I was dying to just grab anything, sit in the beige, buttoned, arched, tub backed antique rolling Victorian chair behind the leather-topped Victorian desk and dive in.

But that wasn't how it worked.

I had at least a solid day of organization in front of me, and that meant cataloging and dating so when I finally jumped in, I could start at the beginning.

Therefore, that's what I did.

By the time it occurred to me that quite a bit of it had lapsed since Prudence left, the entire space was covered in stacks of papers, books and pictures, my phone said it was six forty-seven, and since I missed lunch, I was starving.

"Shit!" I cried, shoved my phone in my back pocket, turned out the lamps and hightailed it to the big house.

I hit a parlor full of Talyns.

But only Battle (of course) raised his eyebrows at me.

Fitzgibbons smiled at me.

"Drink, Miss Vivienne?"

Since he said they had everything, I challenged him with, "A paloma, please, Mr. Fitzgibbons."

"Right away," he replied without missing a beat and headed to the drinks cabinet.

Everyone was sitting where they had been the night before, so I decided to sit in one of the chairs opposite, not beside, Battle.

He had no response to my changed situation whatsoever.

I didn't want to be, but I was disappointed about this.

"How'd you get on?" Prudence asked me.

"Well, I'm about a third of the way done with cataloging and organizing."

"Cataloging?" Temperance asked.

"Everything set out there for me," I answered. "My book won't have footnotes, but my author's note will, as will my personal notes, and I'll need to keep track of where I read something. To make this more straightforward for me later, I start by cataloging my research documents. It also helps if I have to go back to something. It'll be easier to find it."

Fitzgibbons was there with a tray on which was my paloma. I took it and thanked him.

"No offense, dear, but that all sounds dreadfully boring," Temperance decreed.

I shrugged. "To each their own."

"Indeed," she replied.

I glanced at Battle to see he was having some quiet conversation with Chastity.

And that would be the theme for the night, through drinks and dinner.

Prudence, Temperance and I would chat, Chastity and Battle had their own whisper thing going on, and only occasionally would they join in with ours.

And on those occasions, it was only Chastity that joined. Battle would just listen.

No one acted like this was weird.

But it was kinda weird.

For the most part, even if I was seated right next to him again, it was like I wasn't there.

Outside the brow raise, gone was the high and mighty duke, also gone was the flirty player.

At least Bartholomew hadn't forgotten me.

He'd left his daddy to come lie beside me during drinks and resumed his snooze between Battle and me at dinner.

But I discovered the five-course meal the night before was, in fact, a celebration, because last night's dinner started with a salad, then a main and finally a dessert.

It was just as delicious, but it wasn't as grand.

Or as long.

And after it, Chastity and Battle immediately disappeared (alas, Bartholomew went with them). Temperance joined Prudence and I for another drink in the plum parlor, but she eventually wandered away, leaving Prudence and I to chitter chatter for a spell, this being when Gingerface made his appearance, and he and I got introduced.

Eventually, we both got drowsy enough to call it a night, and Prudence and I walked up the stairs together, parting on the landing for her to go south, and me to go north.

Which brought me to now.

Glastonbury day.

We were leaving after breakfast.

And I was thinking His Grace probably thought I was a bit of fun.

But now he had his signed agreement. I wouldn't write anything he didn't want anyone to read. I was his sister's friend, not his. A guest in his house, though he wasn't there normally, and after he went back to regularly scheduled programming, he would rarely see me.

I'd then be in a cottage an hour away, and except for him approving my chapters, he'd have nothing to do with me.

And I would have nothing to do with him.

Although this left me with a stupidly crushed feeling that made no sense (right, so it did, since he was that gorgeous and that good of a flirt), it was for the best.

I did not need to be flirting or sparring with a friend's older brother, or my host.

Acquaintances, good.

Anything else, bad.

Looking on the bright side, after my walk through the ballroom, nothing peculiar, paranormal or eerie befell me, so there was that.

"Ugh," I said to Snowball and Gingerface.

Gingerface purred.

Snowball stepped delicately onto my chest and stared down at my face.

She then jumped off the bed.

And she was right.

Time to get ready for breakfast.

And Glastonbury.

It was only Prudence and I for breakfast again.

And I knew when our breakfast ended.

That being when Fitzgibbons showed at the door and announced, "Your car has been brought around, Miss Vivienne."

I smiled my thanks to him and immediately looked at Prudence.

She was taking a final sip of coffee and seemed to be okay.

Well then…

Shoo.

The hermit wasn't freaking about being unhermited.

That was good.

I got up and grabbed my tan crossbody.

Today, I was wearing another slouchy sweater, this one a soft gray-blue, with a flippy navy skirt with little gray-blue flowers that hit a couple of inches above my knees. Also, another pair of booties, these tan with a lower heel, so I could walk farther more comfortably, but they were still cute.

I settled the strap of my bag across my chest, sucked back the last dregs of my own coffee and turned to Prudence.

"Ready for our adventure?"

She studied me a moment before she asked, "How do you make everything seem so fun?"

I tipped my head to the side, contemplating this.

I righted it, sharing, "No clue. But you're home. I'm not. This might be a once in a lifetime opportunity for me, and that's always exciting. On the other hand, you've been there before, and you can trundle down the road and experience it anytime you want. That said, all of life is an adventure, and we can choose how we face it. I choose to decide it's going to be fun."

"I might take that advice," she mumbled.

I hoped she would.

We left the breakfast room, walked down the hall, through the foyer and out the front door.

As expected, my Peugeot was there.

Not expected, Battle and Temperance were there too, with Bartholomew…and Chastity.

Whereas Prudence was in a gray number that looked like the sweater version of Princess Leia's outfit on the Death Star (complete with full sleeves and dangling hood at the back), a pair of flowy white pants that had slits up the sides (even if her sweater went to her knees, so it could be a dress), and the big-toe-separated Mary Janes, Chastity was in a long, pale-pink pleated skirt and a punch-pink sweater set, complete with a strand pearls.

She had a cute pair of unblemished white Keds on her feet.

She was also wearing a beige, felt fedora pulled low over her brow with her splendiferous mass of blonde frizz poofing out from under it.

She did not look like she was going on a day jaunt to visit a spiritual mecca adjacent to where one of the biggest musical festivals in the world was held, doing this wearing a super cute outfit that, from what I could tell, was totally her.

She looked like she'd finally come to terms with her fate right before being led to the gallows.

I was uncertain about this, and when I say that, I mean…*very*.

But I wasn't certain who to talk to about it.

Prudence seemed to be hanging in, but I didn't want to give her any excuse to cry off.

Battle had decided I didn't exist.

Chastity was out, for obvious reasons.

So it would have to be Temperance.

That decision was made for all of two seconds, even if I hadn't quite decided how I'd pull off a chat with Temperance when everyone was hanging around, when Prudence and I hit the bottom of the steps and Battle prowled to me.

Yes.

Prowled.

He then took my hand and dragged (yes...*dragged*) me to the back of the Peugeot and then some.

When we stopped, he turned into me.

I'd just tipped back my head to look at him, and, I didn't know, maybe ask him what the hell with the whole dragging me somewhere business, when he asked, "You'll look after them?"

"Um..."

"You'll look after them." This time, it was a demand.

So I guessed I was going to be talking to Battle about this.

I set about doing that.

"Am I missing something here?"

A muscle ticked in his jaw before he lied, "No."

A thought occurred to me.

"Do we need security or something?"

His brows shot down. "Definitely no. Why would you ask that?"

"Because you all are super, crazy, stupid rich?"

"We take pains," he stated. "No one knows who either of them is."

I'd lived that nightmare.

Forsooth, it would have been good to know how gorgeous he was before his looks made me faint right in front of him.

"It kind of gives it away when we drive out of a massive heritage estate, one you all happen to live in," I pointed out.

He took a moment.

And only then did he admit, "Chastity has been staying close to home for a while too."

And there it was.

"How long of a while?" I asked suspiciously.

"Three years."

I felt my eyes get big, and I snapped, kinda loudly, "What the hell is going on?"

He took my hand again and dragged me farther away.

When he was done dragging me, he faced me and bit off, "Keep your voice down."

"What's going on?" I whisper-snapped this time.

"It's not my story to share. Just that Chassie is…dealing with a few things."

Dealing with a few things?

For three years?

My gaze drifted to the Peugeot to see both Temperance and Prudence seemed to be smothering Chastity as they helped her into the back seat of the car.

Yes, even Temperance was doing this.

I went back to Battle.

"Is she okay?" I asked.

"She will be."

"Is there something I should know?"

"Just be gentle with her."

"With you acting all hinky, and me about to set out on a girls' trip one of the girls on the trip isn't all that fired up about, and you all casting me as the ringleader, that doesn't give me much to go on, Your Grace," I pointed out the obvious, and I did it sarcastically.

But I said the wrong thing, I knew, when I was being dragged again.

This time we went a long, *looooooong* way, turning onto a path that took us down the side of the house.

Only when we were out of sight of his sisters did he stop me again.

And when he faced me this time, he did it *right* in my space.

So in my space, I had to tip my head way, *way* back to catch his eyes, and when I did, he was all I could see.

"What did I say about calling me that?" he asked, his purr silken and sinister.

"You're being weird!" I defended hotly.

"I'm simply requesting you have a care with my sister."

"Uh…considering she never raises her voice above a whisper and comports herself…no, wait…you *all* comport yourselves around her like she's made of fine porcelain, I already got that," I returned.

"This is family business."

"Conceded," I agreed. "She's still going to be spending the day *with me*. What I'm sharing with you is, I'm sensing I don't have the tools I need to handle it, primarily because I don't know what tools to pack in my toolbox."

"It's Chastity's business," he continued. "You have Tempie's, Prue's and my gratitude for offering her the opportunity to break her self-imposed exile. You're aware she's fragile. You'll have a mind. That's all I need to know, and it's all you need to know."

"Did something happen to her?"

He said nothing.

Oh God.

Something happened to her.

I stumbled away from him as the immense weight of this knowledge landed on me.

I didn't even know what it was.

I just knew that beautiful girl with her riot of hair and delicate features and whispered words endured something awful.

He caught my jaw in his hand and his face was in mine again.

His hold wasn't harsh, or cruel, just supremely attention-getting.

"Don't," he whispered fiercely.

I realized only then my eyes had filled with tears.

And I knew what he was saying.

I didn't need to lose it, start crying, acting weird and letting Chastity know I knew, even if I didn't.

With us having this convo, she probably had some sense of what was going on.

But I didn't need to return with red eyes, a runny nose, or any visible indication Battle shared his sister's secrets, or that I felt sorry for her.

"Okay," I said shakily.

He waited until I got my shit together before he asked softly, "You'll have a mind?"

I nodded even with my jaw still in his hand. "Yes. I'll totally have a mind."

He let me go, stepped back and said, "Thank you."

I swallowed.

Then I shook out my hands like I could shake off what I didn't know, I just knew it was bad.

Finally, I squared my shoulders.

And I said, "We best get going."

He nodded.

We walked silently, side by side, back to the car.

Bartholomew had made an effort to follow us but either got distracted or too tired halfway, so he joined us at that point and accompanied us the rest of the journey.

Chastity was in the back seat of the car.

Prudence was in the front.

Temperance was staring at me like, if I gave a single hint I didn't have this, she'd tackle me.

I opened the driver's side door and turned to her. "Burns the Bread. We have our instructions. But if those cookies are that good, and we eat them all on the way home, you only have yourself to blame for not coming."

Temperance's eyes rolled, but, even if it was a miniscule movement, I still saw her shoulders slump with relief.

Oh yes.

Chastity endured something awful.

Temperance then pushed beyond me to stick her head into the car and declare, "If no biscuits arrive with you on your return, there will be consequences."

"We'll buy loads so we can't physically eat them all," Prudence offered.

"This is acceptable," Temperance said.

She pulled out of the car, but it was only me who saw, and obviously felt, when she grabbed my hand, gave it a firm squeeze and let it go.

If she was so worried, I didn't understand why she wasn't going with.

But then, when I climbed in, shut the door, and looked out the side window at Battle and Temperance standing there together, I did.

Battle and Temperance, the two strong ones, the two eldest, the two the others could lean on, needed the two who leaned on them to fly the coop.

On their own.

(Or, with me.)

And by damn, that was what they were going to do.

I started the car and opened my window.

"Any biscuit orders from you, Your Grace?" I asked.

At that, the muscle leapt across his whole cheek.

I smiled smugly.

"Battie likes their jam donuts," Prudence said from beside me.

"Donuts it is," I said. Then, "Ready, girls?"

"Ready!" Prudence cried.

Chastity said nothing.

"Tallyho!" I shouted and hit the gas.

Prudence giggled.

Chastity was silent.

And off we went.

CHAPTER 8

THE VISITORS

Prue, Chassie and I fell through the front door of The Downs, weighted with bakery boxes and bags of souvenirs, wearing (oh yes, we went there) flower crowns with streaming ribbons down the back, and we did this giggling.

"Oh my goodness, I think you're the only person alive who could have a serious conversation with a white witch about love spells," Prue was saying.

"For half an *hour*," Chassie whisper-added (yes, she was still whispering, but as we all knew, Rome wasn't built in a day).

"And you bought every single book she wrote," Prue said.

"About white witchcraft," Chassie again whisper-added.

"And there are four of them," Prue finished.

"A girl never knows when she'll need a love spell," I stated blithely. "Or a bitch eradication one, though I think those require eyes of newt, and what bums me out about that was learning from my new friend Anastasia, that's just mustard seed."

Prue and Chassie started giggling again.

A throat was cleared.

We turned to see Fitzgibbons in the hall.

He looked freaked.

Oh shit.

What now?

"My ladies, we have visitors," he announced.

"Who?" Prue asked carefully, totally feeling his vibe.

"Lord Raleigh. Miss Courtney Wright. And Miss Chelsea Renfrew," he intoned.

Prue groaned.

Chassie gasped.

"They're waiting for you in the green sitting room," Fitzgibbons stated.

Prue's "Now?" sounded choked.

"Lady Temperance requested you attend them…*immediately.*"

"Bloody hell," Prue whispered.

"What's going on?" I asked.

"Rally's a friend of Battie's," Chassie whisper-told me. "And Courtney is his fiancée."

"Okay," I said.

That didn't seem so bad.

"And *Chelsea,*" Prue said her name like it tasted bad, "is Battie's ex-girlfriend."

Oh boy.

"She just doesn't like to be his ex-girlfriend," Chassie whisper-appended. "She prefers the 'ex' not to be a part of that and is committed to the act of reversing Battie's decision about it."

"Yikes," I replied.

"Shall I take your things?" Fitzgibbons had come closer.

"No…no, I think, no," Prue mumbled and focused on Fitzgibbons. "Did I miss something? Was this visit planned?"

Fitzgibbons's face, a man who always seemed like a super friendly guy, got tight.

"It is not," he said shortly. "And they're staying the weekend."

Oh boy!

"The entire weekend?" Prue was back to sounding strangled.

That being a *long* weekend, since it was only Thursday.

"They had a good deal of luggage. And Miss Renfrew informed me to inform my wife that she needed to prepare so Cook has enough food in for company," he stated stiffly.

"She sure does like to act like she's duchess when she's around," Chassie whisper-bitched. "She did it even before her and Battie were a thing."

"And Tempie sure hates it when she does," Prue agreed. "We better get in there."

I wasn't sure how three people could show up—unannounced and with luggage—and everyone was just going with it.

What I was sure of was, I didn't want any part of it.

I was about to make my excuses, when Chassie grabbed my arm in a surprisingly firm grip, and yet again I was being dragged by a Talyn somewhere.

I looked helplessly over my shoulder at Fitzgibbons, and he had the good, albeit unhelpful, grace to wince.

"How is she even here when she's an ex?" I whispered urgently to them as I was dragged.

"She gloms on to whoever might get her through the door of wherever Battie is. This time, it's Rally," Prue explained.

"Or Courtney," Chassie whispered. "Tempie likes Courtney."

Sadly, since the sitting room was close to the front hall, that was all I got before we were in.

Temperance was casually lounged in the corner of a sofa. She had a martini in hand. She was wearing all red today, and she looked amazing.

However, even if I didn't know her very well, I knew she wanted to kill somebody.

Battle was standing at the mantle in what he'd been wearing earlier, one of his fabulous sweaters and a pair of jeans.

He looked over his shoulder at us when we entered, and the expression on his face made me wonder if he actually *did* kill somebody.

I did a quick head count of the rest and noted gratefully my next adventure wasn't going to be burying a body, because there was a man with thinning blond hair, but he was quite good looking, sitting on the couch opposite Temperance and next to a brunette who was very pretty.

And sitting next to Temperance on her couch was blonde so gorgeous, she'd make Blake Lively weep with envy.

She was wearing a slouchy cream sweater that was better than mine, because it fell down her shoulder, matching cream, lightweight wool slacks and a pair of soil brown Laurent Vendôme slingback glazed leather pumps.

She looked like a magazine spread advertising fabulous sweaters, or wool slacks, or Saint Laurent pumps.

Oh, and she looked like she matched the room, which could be by design.

What she didn't look like was a blonde freckled-nosed chick who'd recently received the devastating knowledge that Queen Guinevere wasn't *actually* buried at Glastonbury Abbey. It was just a trick the medieval priests there played to get the medieval version of tourists to show up.

"Good Lord," the blonde cried through burgeoning hilarity, "what are you women wearing on your heads?"

I noticed Prue's hand start to move to the flower crown, even as I sensed a calamitous scattering of emotions beating into the room from Battle and Temperance, and both Lord Raleigh's and his fiancée's shoulders curled in like they were trying to disappear themselves.

Obviously, this meant I had to forge into the breach.

I mean, what else could I do?

And I did this by striding forward quickly, before Prue could take off her crown, with mine firmly and proudly in place, and I dumped my baker's box from Burns the Bread on the table between them.

"It's a flower crown," I answered. "We just returned from Glastonbury."

"You're the American," she observed unnecessarily.

"In the flesh." I stuck my hand out to her. "Vivienne Dupree."

"Bestselling author," Temperance drawled.

Chelsea Renfrew stared at my hand, and for a beat, I thought she'd ignore it, but then she leaned forward and put her fingers limply in mine.

I squeezed them…hard.

Then I let her go and flipped open the baker's box.

"Viennese fingers for you," I said to Temperance and turned to Battle. "Chassie has your donuts."

"Here they are, Battie," Chastity whisper-announced and took her box to him.

"Thank you, sweetheart," he murmured.

I pushed in front of Chelsea and plopped down between her and Temperance.

Temperance hummed delightedly.

Chelsea gasped audibly and scuttled deeper into her corner.

I dug into a bag and pulled out the black and red flower crown we got Temperance.

I handed it to her. "You don't have to wear it. But we agreed it's *so you*."

She took it and replied in a question, "Thank you?"

I grinned at her and turned to the other two people I didn't know.

"Hi, I'm Vivi."

The man got up and reached over the coffee table. "Rally. Great to meet you."

I shook his hand.

When he sat back, the woman gave me a pained smile that I sensed was not caused by being pained at me, and pushed out, "Courtney."

"Hi," I replied.

"We also bought books. And crystals," Prue said, upending her bag on the table where a bunch of crystals skittered out.

"I wanted to buy some sage sticks," Chastity whisper-told Battle. "But Vivi told me it's cultural appropriation."

"The shopkeeper wasn't a fan of that," Prue shared with the room at large.

"I'm not sure it's a thing, like Native Americans care if white people use smudge sticks to get rid of bad juju," I explained. "But my motto is, better safe than sorry you not bastardizing something meaningful to some other culture's spiritualism."

Temperance's low chuckle was amused, beautiful and sultry.

Chelsea emitted an annoyed noise.

"I didn't know those were Native American," Courtney put in.

"They are," I confirmed.

Prue, getting in on my game, encouraged, "Show them your books, Vivi."

I pulled all four of my big, how-to-be-a-white-witch books out of another bag, announcing, "First, I'm going to write my novel. Then, I'm going to get this whole love potion thing down and open a shop in Glastonbury."

"I take it you enjoyed your day," Battle purred.

"We had so much fun, Battie," Chassie, hanging on his arm, whisper-assured.

He turned and kissed the side of her head.

Mostly an ass (probably).

But totally a good brother.

I put the books on the table, taking the top one with me, sitting back and flipping through it, saying, "That place is my new favorite place on the planet." I turned to Temperance. "And yes, this decision might have something to do with me eating three of those Viennese fingers."

"I'm stunned and insulted you'd assume I have poor taste in anything," Temperance returned.

"Lesson learned," I replied.

"May I get you ladies drinks?" Fitzgibbons was now there asking.

"Usual for me, Fitzy, thanks," Prue said.

"Can I have a white wine spritzer?" Chassie whisper-requested, then she looked up at Battle, who she was now leaning on, also who had his arm around her (the box of donuts was on the mantle). "It was such a sunny, happy day. Like summer, almost."

He smiled tenderly down at her.

Completely and totally a good brother.

"Miss Vivienne?" Fitzgibbons prompted.

I tried to dream up a good challenge for Fitzgibbons in the drinks arena, but with what was going on, I didn't have it in me.

So I asked, "Gin fizz for me, please."

"Right away," he said and left the room (there was no drinks cabinet there, though, the speed in which he left probably had to do with him making an escape).

"As you see, we have unexpected company," Temperance pointed out unnecessarily.

"I really did think Rally phoned you," Courtney said.

"And I thought Court phoned you." Rally pointedly aimed this at Chelsea.

Chelsea was studying her rounded, cream-polished fingernails.

"It's terribly rude just to pitch up and—" Rally began.

But Chelsea cut him off before he could suggest, maybe, that they leave. "Though, we're all here now. A lovely spring weekend in the West Country, away from the city. Perfect."

No one said anything after that.

Snowball broke that crust of ice by sauntering in and brazenly jumping on the sofa between Chelsea and me.

Chelsea pressed herself even deeper into the corner of the sofa.

I tucked my witch book at my side and put her in my lap.

She settled in, booty to my lap, belly to my belly, paws to my chest, and started purring when I started stroking.

"I'm allergic to cats," Chelsea proclaimed.

"If you were, which you are not, you should have avoided a home that is home to six of them," Battle stated.

"Darling, how could you say I'm not?" Chelsea pouted. "You know how sniffly I get when I come here."

"His point, I believe, is, if that's the case, don't come here," Temperance explained.

Prue, who'd seated herself in one of the two chairs at the end of our arrangement, shot me big eyes.

I bit my lip in return.

"Thank goodness I brought my allergy pills," Chelsea said, showing signs of being oblivious to everything, except what she wanted to be happening. "Though, for now, could I ask you to put it down?" she asked me.

I didn't put her down.

Instead, I got up, and Snowball and I settled in the chair next to Prue.

"I suppose that's better," Chelsea sniffed. She then looked to Battle. "Are we dressing for dinner tonight?" She shifted her attention to Courtney. "It's tradition here the first night anyone comes to call."

"I know," Courtney replied tersely. "I've been here before."

"Repeatedly," Temperance added.

"Oh!" Chelsea cried and turned to me. "Or...maybe not. Do you have a gown?"

"I have three of them," I told her. "Forewarned for packing by my darling friend Prudence."

"Are the other two better than the green one?" Battle asked.

"Depends," I answered. "But they're all awesome." I smiled at Courtney. "Says me."

She smiled back, and she was openly relieved that at least I was making it plain I didn't think she was behind this lunacy.

"What I mean is, will they make me want to fuck you in them like the green one did?" Battle asked.

Chastity whisper-peeped.

Temperance smiled widely before taking a sip of martini.

Prudence didn't quite swallow the nervous giggle she eventually swallowed.

Rally looked to his lap, but his shoulders were shaking.

Courtney turned her head toward her fiancé and further hid her face behind her drink, but I still saw her massive smile.

Chelsea looked like she was about to explode.

I glared at Battle.

Then I stood, handed Snowball to Prue and pointed at the duke.

"You, a word," I demanded.

With that, I stormed out.

I ducked into the blue salon, and mercifully, not making more of a fool of me, within a few seconds, Battle followed.

It was my turn to get up in his face.

This I did.

"What the fuck?" I asked.

He closed the door he'd barely cleared before I confronted him and turned back to me.

"I didn't make a secret of the fact I liked you in that dress," he said, like it was the most natural thing in the world to say what he'd said in the other room in front of his friends…and his *sisters*.

"Listen, I don't know what's going on with that woman, but I want no part in it," I declared.

"Allow me to educate you in English manners. Even if you have no idea someone is going to arrive at your door with luggage, you open your door for them and their luggage."

"I'll file that tidbit away for the never I'm going to need it."

He let out a massive breath and shared, "Somehow, she found out. In other words, she knows you're here."

"Well, obviously, since I just got used in whatever game you're playing."

"It's not my game, it's hers. And I didn't use you. I stated a truth."

My head ticked to the side angrily. "No?"

"Again, Vivienne, *she knows you're here*," he stressed. "Did Prue or Chassie tell you who she is?"

"Your ex."

"She was not at one with my decision to end us."

"No shit?"

His lips twitched.

As hot as that was…

Oh no he didn't.

This was *not* funny.

"Leave me out of it," I ordered.

"Unfortunately, I've no choice. You're in it."

"So now you're going to pretend something is happening with you and me so you can use me as your shield to keep your ex at bay?"

"I'm not pretending anything, Vivienne. I very seriously wanted to fuck you in that dress."

I stared.

But my thighs quivered.

"Or, more accurately, fuck you after that dress hit my bedroom floor," he amended. "Though, the way you looked in that dress, I might not have been able to wait that long."

Ugh!

This man!

"So it's back to games, is it?" I asked.

"I don't play games."

"Could have fooled me," I shot back.

He dipped his face so close, the tip of his nose nearly brushed mine.

"Hear me, Vivi," he whispered, and him using my nickname for the first time, coupled with him being so close I could smell his musky, woodsy cologne, regrettably at that juncture, all of that did a number on me. "I. Am. Not. Playing. *Games.*"

What the hell did that mean?

"Fitzgibbons will be back with your drink by now," he said after he leaned away. "Shall we return?"

To hell with the fact he was my host.

"You're kind of a dick," I shared.

"You aren't the first woman to say that to me."

I fake gasped. "Color me shocked, Your Grace."

And then I was against a wall.

And Battle was against me.

I struggled to breathe, from sheer shock at how he'd backed me to a wall, its swiftness and its ease, and damn him, also from his sexy proximity.

"What do you call me?" he asked silkily.

"Battle," I whispered.

Because…

Seriously?

What would *you* do?

His eyes dropped to my mouth. "Precisely."

Oh God.

What was happening?

"Now, shall we return?" he inquired.

"Leave me out of it," I repeated.

"I'll do my best."

"Try hard to make that your bestest best," I warned.

He stepped back and offered me his arm. "You have my solemn vow."

I stared at him.

Then I took his arm.

(Again, seriously…what would *you* do?)

He escorted me back and deposited me in my chair.

He returned to Chastity at the mantle while everyone pretended to avoid watching us even as they totally watched us.

Except Chelsea, who was glowering openly at me.

Fabulous.

In the crosshairs of a scheming woman who was wearing a sexier sweater than me.

My drink was sitting on the table in front of me.

I grabbed it and sucked half of it back.

"So, we decided while you two had your little chat, it's gowns tonight," Temperance drawled.

Fuck.

My other two gowns were also sexy.

Shit.

I glared at Battle.

He smirked at me.

Snowball jumped from Prue's lap to mine.

Thank God.

Moral support.

I'd take it.

And with no other avenue open to me, I did.

CHAPTER 9

THE CHAT

I sat at my vanity, all ready to head down to drinks, but even so, my mind was casting about for any viable excuse I could give for chickening out of drinks *and* dinner.

And it had to be an excuse they'd buy that wouldn't scream I was chicken.

Sadly, I was not coming up with any ideas that would convince anyone I wasn't a coward.

In the midst of me doing this, or more to the point, failing at it, I heard a knock on the bedroom door.

This was probably Prue, come to ask what was going on with me and her brother. Though, my thoughts, she should ask him.

I didn't have a brother.

However, I understood her play because, even if I did, I'd probably talk to my friend about my brother announcing to the room he wanted to sleep with her and not confront my brother about it.

Especially if he could be scary, like Battle.

Because...yeah.

Talking to your brother about his sex life, I could see, was a serious no-go.

Doing that semi-adjacently?

Not great, but better.

I didn't want to do this, and I blamed Battle for putting me in this position too.

But I had to do it, however, I had no idea how I'd manage it.

Alas, the time was upon me.

"In here!" I shouted to be heard through the dressing room, bathroom and bedroom.

I heard the door open while I swiped on one more coat of my ruby-red lipstick and tried to devise a plan.

But I saw in the mirror, when she arrived, it was not the she I expected her to be.

It was Temperance.

Temperance in a stunning red sheath gown, straight line across her neck, sleeveless, a pair of beautiful gold evening sandals with a huge flower on the toe adorning her slender feet.

She was carrying a sleek black cat with yellow eyes in her arms. A cat, unlike any other cat I'd ever seen, who looked content to be held there for the rest of its life.

"Oh yes," she drawled, her cool gray eyes roaming over me. "Battie is definitely going to like your dress."

Argh.

I had no choice. It was either sexy or sexy.

I picked sexy.

A black gown made of chiffon, the sheer top pleated at a slant across my midriff and chest, making a one-shouldered bodice that hinted at nude underneath. The black skirt had a chiffon overlay with subtly scalloped sides that fluttered when I moved and added to the overt sexuality of the dress, giving it an ultra-feminine feel.

My hair was pulled softly back from a side part to another fluffy chignon at my nape that took forever to pull off.

My diamond studs and champagne sandals completed the ensemble.

The whole getup was another reason why it was regrettable I didn't come up with a believable excuse to skip dinner.

Even I had to admit I looked hot.

"I went down to ask Patsy for a trash bag I could wear, but she just laughed at me," I joked.

Temperance smiled her Cheshire cat smile.

I turned on my vanity stool to address her not in the mirror.

"Who's that?" I tipped my head to the cat.

"Soot," she answered, gliding gracefully down to sit on the round bench and letting Soot go.

The sleek cat, moving as slinky and gracefully as Temperance did, hopped off the bench and started to explore.

"Prue is rubbish at naming the animals," she decreed. "There's Baby Blue, Battie's ragdoll. Floofy, Chassie's white tiger. And Greystoke, Prue's gray. You know Snowball and Gingerface."

"Wait." I was confused. "I thought they were all Prue's cats."

"They are, in a manner. She rescues them and adopts them. But animals have their own way of doing things. They lay their own claims. So Soot sleeps with me. Baby Blue with Battie. Floofy with Chassie. Greystoke with Prue. And, as we were all claimed, Snowball and Gingerface, the newest additions, hadn't yet found their person."

She finished that gazing at me meaningfully.

And I had a feeling I understood her meaning, my heart beating hard with it, I just didn't know what to do with it.

I mean, I'd only been there three days.

And I was leaving in less than two weeks.

"Prue even named Bartholomew," she went on. "This is why that poor creature has such a ridiculous name. He is, of course, Battie's dog. But Prue wanted to name him, and Battie is a soft touch, so he let her name him."

I was stuck on an earlier part of what she said.

"A cat sleeps with Battle?"

She inclined her head. "Baby Blue doesn't hold a great deal of love for Bartie. But she does for Battie. Once Bartie is down for the night, Baby Blue finds my brother's bed. Even when he's not here to be in it."

I tried to visualize Battle sleeping with a ragdoll cat.

It was so easy to visualize, and such a good visual, I stopped trying to visualize it.

Though, I was so enthralled by this endeavor, I jumped when Temperance surged elegantly to her feet and walked to the side of the vanity so she could look out the window.

"Imagine," she said in a soft tone that had me instantly bracing, "being a young child and growing up in a house with no love."

Oh my God.

"And then," she went on, even softer, "this adorable red-haired baby comes home to you. She giggles. And she's loud. And as she grows up, she's excited by everything. She consumes books like chocolate and draws on everything with a surface. She's utterly enchanting. She's all that's good and right, and since you never had that, you and your brother cling to her because she is."

Oh *God*.

"Tempie," I whispered.

She didn't even look down at me.

"And then she goes to school."

I closed my eyes and dropped my head.

I opened them and lifted my head when she spoke again.

"Day by day, all that joy, all that exuberance leaks out of her, little by little. She hides how much she reads. She draws in secret. She wears clothes she doesn't like so she can fit in. But she never brings girls home for play dates or sleepovers. She's never invited to parties."

My eyes started stinging.

"And it just carries on," Temperance continued. "Until she's restricted her happiness and safety to this tiny bubble in the world where the people in it understand her." She pulled in an unsteady breath. "But she's so very alone."

God.

Temperance looked down at me. "And then one day, she's coming to breakfast with her laptop so she won't delay in replying to an email she received from her friend."

God.

"And some time later," she kept at it, "she comes home wearing a crown of flowers, with sun on her cheeks and a spark in her eyes."

"Tempie," I whispered again.

She took in a delicate breath before saying, "In the powder room next to the parlor, there's a drawer in the vanity. I secret my lipstick and a compact in there and nip to the loo if I need a touchup."

And we were done with story time.

I was glad.

Though I was also honored.

"Thank you," I said.

She inclined her head again and started to leave.

But that was when something else hit me.

"Chastity told Battle she didn't want to go to Glastonbury."

Temperance turned back to me. "No. She told me. I told Battle. And Battle, as he always does, handled it."

This was why they were in their own world at dinner last night.

Whatever happened between big brother and baby sister, he had to continue to nurture it, or she wouldn't have gone.

Therefore, this was why he had no mind to pay to me, or, as I hadn't noticed at the time…anybody, but Chastity.

One of several reasons why Temperance was right there with me.

"You're quite the multi-tasker," I noted.

"I try," she replied. "And in that regard, rest assured, Chelsea Renfrew is a sheep in wolf's clothing, though she firmly believes it's the other way around."

Good to know.

I nodded.

"However," Tempie went on, "Battie is a wolf in wolf's clothing. If she steps over the line he's drawn that she will more than likely not see, he will not countenance it. No, Vivienne. Be warned, he'll not delay. And when the time comes, he'll eviscerate her."

"What you're saying is, I have nothing to worry about."

"Nothing at all."

I struggled with what to say next, and decided on, "I'm not a big fan of being drawn into this."

"Courtney is a friend of mine. I told her you were here. I told her you were lovely. I also told her it seemed my brother agreed. Unwisely, it seems she shared this with Chelsea and Chelsea wasted no time in setting up her next play. Then again, Courtney is one of the few in our set Chelsea hasn't used up...yet. Though, I think that happened this afternoon. However, Courtney didn't have any idea she'd been set up. Until she did."

I harked back to an earlier part of what she said.

"Your brother agrees?"

Her brows drew down, she tipped her head to the side, and she drawled a highly sardonic, "Dear."

Hang on.

Was Battle...genuinely into me?

I. Am. Not. Playing. Games.

Oh God.

Maybe he was into me.

God!

Now what did I do with *that*?

Not that I would have, but I still didn't get the chance to ask Temperance.

She patted her leg, and again unlike any feline behavior I'd ever seen, Soot reappeared from wherever Soot was exploring, and he pranced at her side as she walked out.

This was when I saw she had a little train at the end of her gown, and her back was completely bare.

When I heard the door of the bedroom close, I whispered, "Damn, that woman is the shit."

Then I grabbed my compact, my lip liner, my lippie and took one last look at my hair before I took another moment to pull my courage together.

And I got up to follow her.

~

I found the drawer in the vanity was littered with tubes of lipstick and mascara, lip liners, compacts, dress tape, tampons, panty liners and anything else a lady might need for touchups or emergencies.

Once I made my deposit, I hit the plum parlor.

The women were in the seating area, Prue and Chassie on one couch, Tempie and Courtney on another, Chelsea in a chair.

The men were huddled at the drinks cabinet, including Fitzgibbons.

Bartholomew lifted his head when I arrived. He was lying between the other two chairs.

In fact, everyone looked at me when I arrived, Chelsea's expression shifting to one like she'd sucked hard at a lemon, and oh yeah.

My dress was better than hers.

But it was Battle whose gaze raked the length of me, his face got lazy in a way that made the gusset of my panties need to get busy, so of course, I shot him a dirty look.

He smiled.

My gusset got busier.

Okay.

Shit.

Maybe the Duke of Burleigh *was* into me.

"Miss Vivienne, drink?" Fitzgibbons called.

I came prepared.

"White Russian."

That would get him.

No one kept cream in their drinks cabinet.

"Coming right up," Fitzgibbons said with a twinkle in his eye, turning to his task.

"That's rather sweet for a predinner drink, isn't it?" Chelsea asked.

"Vivienne enjoys challenging Fitzy's bartending skills," Battle answered for me, doing so sharing the heretofore unknown knowledge that he was on to me. "What she doesn't know is that Fitzy was a bartender in a club in London for five years."

And there it was.

No bartender worth his salt was ever without a needed ingredient.

"That's where I met my Patsy," Fitzgibbons shared. "She was a waitress. Prettiest girl I'd ever seen. Then and now."

"I love that story," Prue declared on a contented sigh.

I sat in a chair not in Chelsea's grouping and leaned over the arm to give Bartholomew some love.

He rolled to his side and exposed his belly.

I could take direction, so I did.

I only stopped when my drink was in front of my face.

I looked at it, and up, to see Battle was handing it to me.

I took it with a mumbled, "Thank you," as he bent close, closer, closest, so his mouth was at my ear.

Obviously, this meant I turned my head, and he was so close, the skin of my cheek grazed the skin of his, I got a nose full of his attractive cologne, and we were almost lips to lips.

I ignored what all of that did to my gusset (and it was getting busy down there), stared in his brown and gold-star eyes and warned, "Don't."

"Don't tell you you look lovely?"

"Yeah. That."

"All right, I won't tell you you look lovely."

I rolled my eyes.

He dipped back to my ear and whispered, "Good enough to eat."

I jerked my head back and stared murder at him.

Okay, so yes.

Maybe he was into me.

But we were in company!

His gorgeous lips curled up before he straightened away, walked in front of me and angled into the chair beside mine.

My attention went to Prue, scared she'd be upset by this, but I found her smiling dreamily into her old fashioned.

With Prue, that could mean she was in her own little dreamworld, or it could mean she didn't have an issue with Battle openly flirting with me.

Unfortunately, I was probably going to have to have a conversation with her to ascertain where she was with that.

More unfortunately, it was seeming likely I was going to have to have a chat with Battle before I did that.

Even though I wasn't thrilled with the shit Battle was pulling, I couldn't say I didn't love and adore the infuriated expression it put on Chelsea's face.

One could say this weekend she'd finagled was not going her way at all.

"So," I said into the utter silence that was another result of Battle's shenanigans, since everyone (but Chelsea) was doing a version of Prue smiling into her drink. I aimed my next at Courtney and Rally. "It's my understanding you two are getting married?"

"Yes, next month. May is perfect in England," Courtney replied.

I then wielded the conversational gambit everyone used with someone like Courtney in order to manipulate the conversation for a long period of time.

"Is everything set? Where are you going to have it?"

As expected, an excited Courtney launched into a detailed litany of her wedding, the venue, her flowers, the breakfast, the song they'd dance their first dance to, the song she'd dance to with her father, and quite a bit about the villa they were letting in Cannes for their honeymoon.

Okay, so she didn't do this on her own. I egged her on.

But this safe topic took us through drinks and into dinner, where I discovered the full table was set, with a tablecloth this time, more bouquets, candelabra, and little gold swans with calligraphed place cards set in their wings above each setting.

And again, I was impressed by the staff. Being able to pull this off with very little notice was astonishing.

My place was to Battle's right, as had become per usual.

Courtney was to his left.

Tempie had the foot of the table with Rally to her right, Chelsea to her left.

Chastity was between Courtney and Rally.

Prue was between Chelsea and me.

Courtney had just finished talking about some day trips she and Rally might go on in the south of France when she asked, "Chastity, did you design these bouquets?"

Chassie nodded.

I was shocked.

"You did?" I queried.

"Chassie does all the flowers for the house," Tempie stated.

"My God, they're amazing," I replied. "But I should have known. The gardens are stunning. You totally have the touch."

"Thanks, Vivi," Chassie whisper-replied.

"It's too bad you don't do wedding flowers anymore," Courtney said to her fish course.

And this caused Tempie to shoot a look to Battle, whose attention raced to Chastity.

Uh-oh.

"I would absolutely have used you," Courtney finished.

Chassie's face was flaming red.

It was Prue, surprisingly, who forged into the breach.

"Yes, well, the shop was coming to be a bit much," she said. Then immediately, "We should probably discuss tomorrow, since Battie and Vivi both have to work, and I'm going to need Tempie and Chassie in the attics for this project we're doing."

Tempie's brows rose.

But I thought, *you go, girl!* since she just put the unexpected guests in a place where they'd have to find a way to entertain themselves.

"Court and I already discussed that," Rally put in. "Considering you weren't planning on having us. We've decided we're taking Chelsea to the sea."

"You are?" Chelsea asked.

"Yes. Torquay," Courtney said.

"*Torquay?*" Chelsea inquired like one would say, "*A sanitation plant?*"

"Yes. A touch of shopping. A cream tea. The sea air," Rally stated, then to Battle. "We'll be back by cocktails."

"Sounds perfect," Battle purred.

Chelsea glowered at her fish.

I exchanged a beam with Prue.

"Okay, I can't stand it anymore," Courtney announced, everyone looked to her, and I was sure I wasn't the only one who braced.

But I braced more when I saw she was gazing at me.

"I've read all your books," she gushed.

I relaxed.

"I'm a big fan," she said.

"Well, gosh. Thanks," I muttered.

"My favorite is *What Could Have Been*," she declared. "Your reimagining of Elizabeth's relationship with Christopher Hatton was *so romantic.*"

"It's my understanding there were rumors they were at it," Rally put in.

"Oh yes," Courtney practically panted. "I'd never heard of him before your book," she told me. "So I looked into him, and it's clear he was a particular favorite of hers, he built that big house, but wouldn't sleep there until she did, which she never did, sadly, and he never married. Do you think maybe your conjecturing is true?" she asked hopefully.

"Sorry, it's doubtful," I replied on a small smile to take the sting out of dashing her hopes. "Most historians agree, although he was a favorite, earned nicknames from her and quite a bit of land, status and wealth, and he wrote copious love letters to her, so did many men at her court. Although there were rumors, no one really believes they were lovers or even in love. That said, it's pretty clear she had his utter loyalty and devotion, and in her way, she returned that."

"Fools," Tempie said, "thinking, because she's a woman, she'd be swayed by empty avowals of love."

"I don't know," Battle replied. "I'm relatively certain her father reacted rather positively to people stroking his ego and shoving their heads right up his arse."

Everyone laughed, including me.

"I can't think of anything more boring than talking about dead people," Chelsea announced.

The laughter died.

She put a flake of fish between her lips, swallowed and finished, "Or reading about them."

"You don't find Cleopatra fascinating?" Tempie asked.

"Another fool for love, I would say," Chelsea answered.

"Marie Curie? Anne Frank? Amelia Earhart? Maya Angelou? Mary Wollstonecraft? Jane Austen?" Tempie pressed.

Chelsea turned to her. "I'm just saying I prefer to be in the here and now."

"Oh, my apologies," Tempe replied. "I thought you were insulting Vivi's choice of a career and path to writing bestselling novels. My mistake."

Chelsea turned to me. "Obviously, to each their own, Vivienne."

"Obviously," I replied as Harry and Scotty came in to remove the fish course.

"One thing I learned about you during our brief fling, Chels," Battle started.

Oh boy.

I braced again.

Mostly because the "brief fling" comment made Chelsea look both pissed as shit and wounded as hell.

Battle kept going.

"You put grave effort in not wasting your time on anything of value."

I pressed my lips together.

Chastity whisper-tittered.

"I wasted my time on a relationship with you," Chelsea pointed out.

Battle caught her in the crosshairs of his gaze.

"Exactly my point."

Ouch!

And…

Score!

He then turned to me.

Uh-oh.

"I hope old Bess fucked her way through her entire court. I do believe from your book that you don't believe she died a virgin."

"Uh…no. But I think she gave up the goods to Dudley. Though, obviously, no one is sure."

"It actually sickens me they still refer to her as the Virgin Queen like that's some kind of remarkable challenge she bested," he returned. "Like virginity, something we're all born with, is something for a woman to aspire to guard, only if she's not married. Elizabeth is arguably one of the most brilliant politicians in all of history. She demonstrated the depths of her intelligence from a very early age. For better or worse, better only for the Englishman, and yes, I denote the gender of that purposefully, she started the British Empire. The Ingenious Queen, the Cunning Queen, the Crafty Queen, the Wily Queen, all of these are better epithets for her rule and the state she left her beloved country in after her death. Frankly, calling her the Virgin Queen, like that was all she accomplished in her reign, is a bloody insult."

And shit.

Yeah.

I might just have to like this guy.

"Says the man with three crafty, talented, intelligent sisters," Rally quipped.

"And how would you describe me, love?" Courtney queried.

Without missing a beat, Rally answered, "Oh, my Beautiful, Kind, Loving, Supportive, Eternally Interesting Queen, obviously."

"Well said," Prue murmured as Courtney cast adoring eyes to her fiancé.

Fortunately, dinner after that, along with discussion continuing when we returned to the parlor for after dinner drinks, involved a rather spirited and definitely stimulating discussion about Queen Elizabeth, Walsingham, the Cecils, the Spanish Armada, Drake, the historical Raleigh (no relation) and a profound dissection of both Cate Blanchett movies (passable, but entertaining), the Helen Mirren miniseries (excellent) and *The Tudors* TV show (also entertaining, but mostly twaddle).

Chelsea didn't utter a word.

"I cannot believe I'm going to say this, but I'm historied out," Courtney eventually announced.

"Shall I whisk you to bed, my love?" Rally asked.

"If you would." She turned to Tempie. "I know tonight was unexpected for you and your staff, but as ever, it was fabulous."

Tempie rolled a hand at this like she was what we'd been discussing.

A queen.

Courtney turned to me. "And I know this is gauche, but I hope you don't mind. I brought my books, hoping you'd sign them for me?"

I leaned toward her and stage-whispered, "I'll share a secret. Authors like to be asked to sign their books maybe more than readers like them signed."

She smiled in relief.

Wishing us all to sleep well, they took off.

Chastity whispered some words of goodnight and melted from the room after them.

"I think I'm for bed too," I announced while setting aside my cognac glass and standing. "I want to get an early start tomorrow so I might be able to dive into some reading."

Battle stood too, stating, "I'll walk you."

I froze.

Prue shined a smile at us.

Tempie cast a smile into her glass of port.

"I'll walk with you," Chelsea said, rising.

Prue frowned at Chelsea.

Tempie glared at her.

"Shall we?" Chelsea asked.

Pointedly, Battle took my hand, rested it in the crook of his elbow and walked me out.

Chelsea trailed us.

He walked so fast, I wasn't sure I could keep up with him in my heels.

As he intended, Chelsea had the same problem. What she didn't have was him to hold her up.

I managed it, though he was holding me so close, my fluttering chiffon skirt wisped around the legs of his slacks in a manner that was bizarrely, but intensely, titillating.

When we made my room, Battle did no more than glance over his shoulder and say, "Until cocktails tomorrow, Chels."

And then he pulled me right into my room, closing the door behind us directly in her stunned, irritated face.

I opened my mouth.

He put his finger to it.

I said nothing.

He listened.

From a distance, probably/maybe we heard a door close.

He took his finger from my mouth.

"What the—?" I began.

"Thank you for taking the girls to Glastonbury."

Oh.

Well then.

This wasn't a play.

He wanted me alone so he could say that to me.

I pulled my shoulders forward. "Not a big thing. We had a blast."

"It was a big thing, and you three having a blast was the biggest of the lot."

"I really like your sisters," I said quietly.

"I can tell," he replied.

"And Glastonbury," I added.

"I could tell that too."

"Though, I vow right on this spot never to sell a love potion to Chelsea."

For a moment, he just stood there, looking amazing.

Then he burst out laughing.

And let me tell you, that made him exponentially *more* amazing.

Good God.

I'd never seen him laugh.

I'd never even heard him laugh.

I didn't even think I'd heard him chuckle.

It was incredible.

It looked it and it sounded it.

There was a purr to it, naturally, but mostly it was deep, rich, luxurious humor.

I fell in love with it instantly.

When he stopped laughing, his brown eyes were so warm and gentle, I wondered how I ever thought them condescending and haughty.

But he said, "With that, I'll leave you to your sleep."

And now I was instantly bummed.

But I said, "Okay."

He walked to the door, but turned at it and shared, "Along with your highly accessible narrative of the tangled mess that led to Elizabeth signing Mary's death warrant, my favorite parts of that book were your descriptions of Christopher fucking Bess stupid."

My lips parted.

"Very imaginative," he murmured appreciatively. Then, "Goodnight, Vivi."

"'Night," I choked out.

He gave me that lazy look again, and then he was gone.

I stared at the door, wondering if I'd just had an orgasm, or was about to have one.

"He's the single best flirt in history," I said to the door.

This was terribly true.

And terribly annoying.

Because I had a feeling he actually *was* into me.

So now, it was also terribly frustrating.

CHAPTER 10

THE DISCOVERY

I swam out of sleep on Saturday morning to what appeared to be a misty day in England and the understanding my slumbering self was the entertainment of a green-eyed Persian, a round-faced ginger, and a blue-eyed ragdoll.

Snowball was making her status clear by resting curled up on the pillows I wasn't using, those green eyes gazing at me through wisps of her fur.

Gingerface advanced immediately upon me regaining consciousness and cuddled.

Baby Blue just sat there and stared at me.

"Does Battle let you hog the bed like you did last night?" I asked Baby Blue.

She blinked.

I took that as a yes, but I sensed she was lying.

I fell to my back and turned my head to see the smart screen told me it was seven oh seven.

I then looked up at the canopy above me.

When I did this, Baby Blue made her approach, laid on my chest and added her purr to Gingerface's.

I stroked them both.

Thankfully, yesterday had been an uneventful day.

I did not faint, trip, or get tripped.

I did not experience any paranormal activity.

I did not have to engage in trading verbal barbs with anybody.

In fact, both Prue and Chassie came out to the studio with me, and with their help, I was able to finish organizing and cataloging everything before noon. We ate a spot of lunch there, then I looked it up and talked them into going with me to a town not that far away where we could buy crates and separators so I could tidy things away and get cracking.

Prue was all in for this, and shockingly, so was Chassie.

So off we went.

We came back and they helped me tidy.

Then they left and I finally got started reading.

With papers dated 1887.

1887!

Again, I was in my personal Nirvana.

I also began work on the Talyn family tree.

I'd programmed an alarm on my phone (smartening up), so I had plenty of time to get back to the house, go to my room, fluff my hair and refresh my makeup and perfume, and I was down in the plum parlor by six forty.

Dinner went off without a hitch.

There was no tablecloth or candelabra, and we were back to a three-course meal. Chelsea was subdued. Courtney brought seaside souvenirs she lugged into the dining room and passed around (mine was a famous motto ware puzzle jug, it was very cool, and I was touched).

We ended the night in the billiards room with Battle flirting brazenly as he tried (and failed, not his fault, I was hopeless) to teach me snooker with Prue giggling, Chastity almost laughing, Chelsea fuming, and Tempie finally getting up and wiping the floor in a set against Rally.

When the night was over, Battle walked me to my room again, but without Chelsea trailing.

Whether it was for that reason or not that he left me at my door with a chaste kiss on my cheek, I didn't know.

But that was what he did.

My first kiss from Battle Talyn.

On my cheek.

Ugh.

Suffice it to say, yesterday, he was working, I was working, and as such, I had not had the time to corner him to find out what was happening between him and me.

I wasn't sure that day would be the day either, because I intended to work, Battle shared he had some morning meetings, but after that, they were "taking the horses out," and being a gal who didn't grow up with horses in stables, I wasn't sure if that was an all-afternoon activity or not.

I also didn't know they had horses because I hadn't had a complete tour of the grounds. Thus, I had to carve time out to ask Prue if she'd take me, and more time just to do that.

But for the now, I had to eat breakfast then I had crates of history awaiting me.

"Can I get up?" I asked Baby Blue.

She purred and didn't bother opening her eyes.

I gave her time.

Then I gave her more time.

Then she got done with me and jumped off.

So I was free to get up.

I'd jumped ahead because I couldn't wait.

I was reading Marie's journals.

And yes, as Prue said, they were dry as a bone.

If there was ever a more boring woman in history, I did not know.

Discussions with the housekeeper. Lists of invitees to dinner parties. Complaints of rain ending picnics. An endless recitation of the meals she ate.

Ho-hum.

Though it finally got juicier when Harmony started pushing for the duchy to do its part in the war effort.

But this engendered not much more than things like, *Harmony is being troublesome again about that whole war business*, and the like.

I kept reading while sipping the tea Mary brought out for me, and the fire in the stove that Harry started making the studio downright balmy and seriously cozy, especially with the gray outside and the fine mist that had been hanging around all day.

God's honest truth?

I could work in this studio happily on this book and any book I wrote in the future.

That was how much I loved it.

On misty days, gray days, sunny days, I didn't care.

This place was *everything*.

The cottage I'd rented was quaint, but small and cramped. It had an amazing view of the sea (if the pictures could be believed), but right now I had a view to a beautiful garden.

And tea on demand.

It sucked, but I was going to miss the studio when I left.

And The Downs.

I turned a page after reading how offended Marie was that,

that captain has requested we turn over the pink salon for some planning they need to do for some important operation or other. Operation planning! In my pink salon! I don't even know what that means. Bother! It's good he's pleasing to look at, but now I've lost yet another room! Dreadfully tough beef and boiled potatoes and cabbage for dinner. Will there be no end to this rationing?!

I was dying to know what WWII "operations" were planned at The Downs. I'd thought it just a convalescent hospital, but from the number of military staff cordoned there (that Marie bitched about), it stood to reason that it was more.

Though, since Marie didn't care, I doubted I'd ever find out.

But I would forget all about it when I read,

It is as feared. Bishop warned me it was more than harmless flirting. Harmony has actual <u>feelings</u> for that American! She stated this directly to me <u>and her father</u>! I was appalled. The duke is incensed! Oh, what a headstrong girl! We had chicken for dinner, and again, no pudding. Will I never eat a pudding again?

I devoured the next passages, which didn't have much to say about Harmony and "that American" until,

She's gone and done it. Harmony says she intends to marry that young man. An American, of all things. American! Obviously, that means no title, and certainly no money. He told the duke that they take "real good" care of the boys returning home and they should be on their feet "in no time." Balderdash! <u>My</u> daughter will not <u>struggle</u> to <u>ever</u> be <u>on her feet</u>. The nerve. The duke refused his suit, <u>obviously</u>. Harmony refused to come to dinner and sobbed very loudly for all to hear. Humiliating, for all involved. I would sell my soul for a well-seared duck, but alas, it was chicken and potatoes again. I'm not certain whether I hate Hitler or whoever runs the Ministry of Food more.

And then more reading, where things seemed to get worse and worse for Harmony and Charlie, however, in the journal prose of Marie's hand, this was reduced to a few irritable sentences.

Until,

That American boy is finally gone. Good riddance. Harmony is in tatters. She'll soon see. Lamb for dinner tonight, and miracle of miracles, it was actually tasty.

Of course, if Charlie hadn't left without Harmony, I wouldn't be sitting where I was.

I still stared daggers at Marie's throwaway comments about their love affair.

What an empty-headed, pretentious, thoughtless woman, and an unconscionably terrible mom.

Annoyed, I kept going, and although there were hints of Harmony's heartbreak, clearly Marie didn't give much thought to it. At least, not nearly as much as she gave to cataloging the food she put in her mouth.

I was about to give up, especially since I'd gotten to a good six months after the war was over.

But then I read,

It doesn't bear… I cannot even… The deeds that were done <u>in this house</u>. My husband's house. Oh, our beautiful girl! Oh, my beloved Harmony! The only good of it is that it is done. It is well and truly buried. No one will speak of it again. And no one will ever know.

"No one will know?" I whispered to the journal. "Know what?"

I reread the passage, noting it had to have great meaning, because Marie didn't even mention food, something she almost always did.

I then tried to recall Harmony's letters, which I'd read at least four times.

Charlie was begging her to come to America. He offered her the money for the passage. And she planned to go. She was nipping away her allowance. She teased she was doing it to buy her trousseau. From her responses to him, it was obvious he did not tease that he didn't give a crap about her trousseau, he only wanted her.

And then…

"Shit," I mumbled, pushing aside papers to get to the big stack of letters tied in faded yellow ribbon.

I was going through dates to try to match a letter somewhat near Marie's entry when something out the windows caught my eye.

Christian, who I hadn't seen since that first day, wearing a slicker and jeans, mist in his thick blond hair, was walking through the garden in front of the studio.

His eyes were pinned to something.

I turned my head to look out the side window.

Chastity was on her knees in the mist with a bucket of mulch, a trowel, her frizzed hair, frizzier in the weather, pulled back in a huge poof of a ponytail.

I looked back to Christian who had stopped walking, but he hadn't taken his gaze from Chastity.

"Okay," I whispered like he was right there, and I was giving him a peptalk, "I want you to go for it, but I'm terrified you're gonna go for it, so just do it, but you gotta take this *real slow* and be *real gentle.*"

Like he heard me, Christian started walking again.

I held my breath when he stopped next to Chastity.

I kept holding it when she twisted her neck to look up at him.

I continued holding it when I watched her entire body lock.

I knew he was saying something to her.

Inexplicably (maybe), in the middle of him saying it, she popped to her feet and ran—not jogged, not dashed—*ran* toward the house.

And she disappeared.

I let my breath out in a whoosh.

I could only see his profile as he stared after her, but I still could read his shock and concern.

"I sense you went gentle, but...shit, man, that was rough," I muttered.

I watched him drop his head and lift a hand to rub the back of his neck. He stopped doing that, stared for a good long time at the space where Chastity disappeared, and then he walked out of my vision.

"Crap," I mumbled.

I looked to my phone and saw my alarm was going to go off in quarter of an hour to tell me to get back to the house and get sorted for dinner.

I turned off the alarm, grabbed the studio phone and called the house.

"Yes, Miss Vivienne?" Patsy answered.

"Hey, I'm going back in. Do I need to do anything to the fire, or will it just die out?"

"I'll send Scotty out to check it, but it should just die out."

"Thanks, Patsy."

"No worries, dear."

I hung up the phone, nabbed my cell, and dashed through the mist to the house.

But I didn't go to my room.

I took a chance and went to Battle's study.

The door was closed.

I knocked.

"Yes?" he called.

I opened the door and poked my head through. "It's me."

He had his sexy glasses on, and when he saw me, he added a sexier smile on his mouth.

"This is a surprise," he said.

"Am I interrupting you?"

He took his sexy glasses off (alas), dropped them on his desk and invited, "Of course not."

I walked in, closing the door behind me.

"Is everything all right?" he queried.

Now was a good time to get into the whole What's with All the Heavy Flirting, Your Grace? thing.

But first things first.

I sat in one of the wingchairs in front of his desk. "Do you know much about Talyn history?"

"A fair bit."

"Harmony?"

He shook his head. "I'm afraid the only notes made on the females of our line were those who made particularly advantageous matches."

"So you don't know if something happened to her…after the war?"

His brows moved down. "Like what?"

"I don't know. Anything."

"Why do you ask?"

"I've just scratched the surface on my reading, but Marie recorded a very odd entry into her diary. Something about Harmony. Something about the 'deeds that were done in this house.'"

"Jesus," he murmured.

Oh yeah.

That was ominous.

"And I was about to get into Harmony's letters to my grandfather, but from memory, his injury happened at the Battle of the Bulge. So it was close to the end of the war. There was about a year and a half of correspondence between them after he left here, where they were planning on Harmony going to America and them getting married. Her responses seem to infer he was saving for her trip over, along with buying an engagement ring and money to purchase a house. She was helping by putting aside part of her allowance along with attempting to get her father to see reason and approve the match. And then, quite suddenly, she begs off."

"Did she give him a reason?"

"It was a lot of lovelorn, 'go on without me,' and 'my father will never stand for it, he'll disown me, he'll never allow me to have anything to do with my family again.' But it was a real turnabout, and I could tell, my grandfather was blindsided by it."

"'Deeds that were done in this house?'"

I nodded.

"I'm sorry, Vivi, I have no idea what she was referring to."

My eyes drifted from him as I muttered, "Damn."

"You said you're just starting," he reminded me. "Maybe more will turn up."

I nodded again, but asked, "Do Tempie or Chassie maybe know more than you about the history of the Talyns?"

"Maybe Prue. That isn't Tempie's or Chassie's thing."

"Right," I mumbled, dejected.

Because if Prue knew something about Harmoney, she'd already have told me.

"This has shaken you," he observed.

"Since I read the letters, I always thought, after he left here and they were apart, Saint and Marie could put pressure on her. Remind her of her place. Maybe talk shit about what Grandpa Charlie had to offer. Definitely it seemed there were threats. That said, it was clear in her letters she wasn't just dumping him. They were emotional. Heartbroken. She thought she was doing him a favor, being free of her to go on with his life."

"And Charlie was having none of it?"

"There were at least half a dozen letters where she was palpably fending off his pleas for her to reconsider, and considering how long it took for mail to go back and forth, they seemed fast and furious, for the time. So yes, he was having none of it. It was just that nothing he said, whatever it was, made her change her mind." I paused and then reminded him, "And she never married."

"So she didn't meet another man."

"Not that we know. Just because she didn't marry doesn't mean she didn't meet another man. But I'd have to say, she's a damned good liar, even in written word, if all of what she was saying to Charlie was bullshit. But mostly, they were an ocean away from each other. If she was done and moving on, she could just stop writing. It's not like he could do anything, or they'd run into each other at the grocery store or something."

"This has to be both the reason why you do what you do, and the risks you take doing it."

I was confused at his comment, so I asked, "Pardon?"

"You'll dive deeper to find what you can find, even knowing you might never learn what you wish to learn. Much like whether or not Elizabeth and Christopher had a thing."

Ah.

"Yes, that's why I love what I do. But when a mystery remains buried, it sucks huge."

He smiled at me.

Three areas of my body perked up.

Okay, *now* was the time to have the What's with All the Heavy Flirting, Your Grace? conversation.

I did not dive into that conversation.

I remarked, "I know it's not my place to ask, but I wondered why Christian doesn't come to dinner."

He appeared perplexed. "Christian?"

"The PhD candidate."

"I know who he is. Did he say something to you?"

"We haven't met."

"I'll remedy that," he muttered.

"That's kinda not the point."

He focused on me. "What is the point?"

Hmm.

Perhaps this wasn't the best course of action.

Because…

Did I tell the protective big brother that I just watched Christian talk himself into shooting his shot, and then get shot down? Though I wasn't sure Chastity wanted to shoot him down, rather than being terrified of just about everything.

"Vivienne."

Not a purr now, a growl.

Which was better.

Kill me!

"I don't want to say."

"Well, I'd like you to say."

"That doesn't mean I'll say."

"Oh, for fuck's sake," he complained while sitting back in his chair. "Has Christian done something to concern you?"

"Not at all," I replied on a rush.

"So why are we discussing him?"

"Just…curious."

Shit!

Lame!

"I mean, you seem very generous with your hospitality," I included.

Lame again, and I could tell it was by the way his eyes narrowed.

"Are you requesting I ask him to dinner?" he inquired suspiciously.

"Not, erm…yet."

I needed to talk to Prue.

And maybe Tempie.

"Not yet?" he asked.

But first I needed to deal with Battle.

"I shouldn't have said anything."

"Well, you did."

"But I shouldn't have."

"But…you did."

I ticked my head to the side and shrugged.

"We could go around about this for the next hour, and you're still not going to tell me why you mentioned Christian, are you?" he guessed.

Accurately.

"It's like you know me," I quipped.

He pushed up from his chair saying, "Oh yes, I know you. Obstinate and quarrelsome and contrary. Fuck it. Let's go to the parlor and get a drink."

I looked at my phone and informed him, "We have a full ten minutes before we're expected in the parlor."

"Dolores Umbridge did not make me do lines into my arm that say, 'I will not appear in the parlor before six thirty.' We can arrive early."

He had my hand and was pulling me out of my chair.

He was also being funny.

A new thing for the duke.

And I liked it.

Damn.

"I need to freshen up," I told him.

He stopped when he had me on my feet and studied me. "Why?"

"Because I've been out in the studio all day. I need to floof my hair and refresh my makeup."

"Floof your hair?"

"You make it sound stupid," I groused. "Women need to floof before dinner."

"Your hair is arguably your best asset, after your ass and those fucking freckles on your nose. Also, your eyes. And of course your mouth."

I stared up at him, stunned.

"Though, oftentimes, not when you're using it to speak," he continued.

I glared up at him, annoyed.

"In other words, you look beautiful. So fuck the floofing and come have a drink with me."

Who could turn down that kind of offer?

Apparently, not me.

(I will point out, he told me I looked beautiful...mm.)

"Oh, all right."

"Ah, the dulcet acceptance of the fair maiden," he said as he led me to the door with his hand in mine.

"God, you can be super annoying sometimes," I bitched.

He decided, probably wisely, not to respond.

"Where's Bartholomew?" I asked.

"Last time I saw him, he'd made his way up to the attics to keep company with Prue, and then promptly took a nap."

I laughed.

Then I shared, "Baby Blue spent the night with me last night."

"I'd wondered where she'd gone," he murmured.

"She's a bed hog."

"She is that," he agreed.

Okay, *now* was the time to get into the whole What's with All the Heavy Flirting, Your Grace? chat.

I did not.

We made the plum parlor, and I challenged him with making me a Mary Pickford.

He bested it with ease.

Clearly, he'd learned at the hand of a master.

This gave indication he was (almost) perfect in every way.

Drat the man.

CHAPTER 11

THE EVISCERATION

It happened after dinner.

We were in the games room, and I was losing a significant amount of the huge pile of cashews I started with because I sucked so bad at poker.

Chastity, Courtney and Prue were curled up in yet another seating area by a fireplace, the fire lit, having a quiet gab.

So it was Battle, Tempie, Rally, Chelsea and me playing.

"Wait. Tell me again, is a full house better than a straight?" I asked the table.

See?

I was *bad*.

Battle turned twinkling-with-humor eyes to me as Tempie smiled deviously, and Rally started chuckling.

"It distresses me to put a damper on your enthusiasm for the game, but you're terrible at this, darling," Battle purred.

I felt that "darling" in his tone of voice with those twinkling brown eyes in my throat, my chest, my belly, regions south and maybe even down to my soul.

I held his gaze, thrown completely off balance in the best possible way.

I forced myself to speak. "I'll be out this hand anyway. I only have three cashews left."

To this, Battle reached to his massive mound of cashews (a big part of that mass came from my old mass), grabbed a hefty handful and dropped them on mine.

I didn't know if it was the "darling" or how freewheeling Battle was with his cashews.

Or if it was a culmination of the last couple of days, where it was made clear, sometimes subtly, sometimes rudely, but always constantly, she wasn't wanted.

Not to mention, Courtney nor Rally were making any pretense that, once this weekend was done, they were done with Chelsea.

Whatever it was, that's when Chelsea did it.

It started with, "Do you have any family, Vivienne?"

This came so out of the blue, and, let's face it, Battle and I were having a moment, I was liking that moment, so her horning in on it wasn't my favorite thing.

I turned to her. "Yes, why?"

"What do they do?"

"My sister is a mechanical engineer. She works in the healthcare sector."

"Impressive," Rally remarked.

When I spoke no more, Chelsea asked, "Is that all?"

"Well, her husband is a nurse practitioner. And they have two kids, a boy and girl. They don't have jobs, though, since they're two and four."

For whatever her purposes, Chelsea kept at me. "No more?"

What was she driving at?

"No. No more."

"Just a sister?"

"Yes," I said sharply. "Seeing as my mother died not long ago after losing a fight with cancer."

A dead weight fell on the whole room.

"And my father died in a car accident, hit by a drunk driver when I was four," I continued. "Three of my grandparents are still alive, but they're all retired so they don't do anything. However, after Dad died, Mom's parents took us in. We lived with them until we went to college. So part of what they did was help keep us afloat, fed and happy."

"What's going on?" Prue called from the seating area, feeling the vibe.

"Nothing," I called back and dropped my cards. "I think I'm out."

"What was your point?" Rally demanded of Chelsea.

"I just wondered, since she's here for so long, if anyone at home might be missing her," Chelsea explained.

"You could have asked that," Rally pointed out.

I fiddled with my cards.

"I'm sorry about your mum, Vivi," Tempie said quietly.

"It's okay," I lied and looked up from my cards.

Tempie was watching me.

Rally was scowling at his cards.

But Battle was studying Chelsea.

"It's your call, Battle," Chelsea prompted him.

"What was your point?" Battle repeated Rally's question.

"As I said—" she began.

"You lied," he interrupted her.

"I'm just curious," Chelsea retorted with gathering heat. "She's spending time with people I care about, and we know practically nothing about her."

"And you feel it's your job to vet guests in my home?" Battle queried.

"You all *are* ripe to be taken advantage of, Battle," she insulted me not quite to my face, but in very close proximity.

I clenched my teeth.

Tempie tapped the sides of her cards to the table, unmistakably expending effort to keep her mouth shut and allow Battle to field that one.

"Did I hear her right?" I heard Prue demand from the seating area.

"Your father manages hedge funds," Battle stated. "But he studied at Cambridge, as did his father, and his grandfather, and he bought his first flat in Chelsea with his trust fund. You're named after that flat. You do nothing. You live off his money. You do it very well. But you've never accomplished anything in your life."

She looked stricken. "Battle—"

"So let's get back to your point about asking what Vivienne's family does," Battle demanded.

"It was a simple question," she returned.

"Since I haven't done it before, let's not pretend I'll fall for your bullshit."

Now she appeared affronted. "I hardly think—"

Battle sat back, flinging his arm around the back of his chair, but he didn't take his attention from Chelsea.

Oh boy.

My eyes flew to Tempie.

She looked gleeful.

Shit.

"Let's get things perfectly straight," Battle suggested. "You are not better than Vivienne because your father worked hard so you don't have to do anything. In fact, it's the opposite. Even if Vivienne was still working as a research librarian, her pedigree is more impressive than yours. The fact she's published seven books, the last two best-sellers, is an extraordinary accomplishment. You are not going to encourage me to turn my eye to you by pointing out Vivienne works for a living, that her family does, even if they did something where they struggled, or something you thought was beneath you, or me. You are not like me either, Chelsea. I work for a living too."

"Though, you don't have to," she mumbled.

"Do you think this house would run on The Fund alone?" he asked.

Wait.

That was the second time one of the Talyns mentioned "The Fund."

"Christ, you have no fucking idea," Battle went on. "And that's one of your problems."

Chelsea threw her cards on the table and made a big mistake.

Huge.

She asked, "Oh yes, Battle? Please illuminate me, since I honestly *do not* understand why you cast me aside. What are all my problems?"

Battle didn't disappoint.

Boy, didn't he.

"You live in a fantasy world fueled by being spoiled senseless your entire life," he started. "Like using people *you care about* to find a way to pitch up here, embarrassing them, and putting my family in an awkward position, because you've somehow convinced yourself you can win me over. You can't. I've shared that. You're vain. You're entitled. You're a snob. You've been painfully overindulged and criminally pampered. And you're shit in bed."

Oh boy!

I sucked my lips between my teeth and my gaze flew to Prue.

She was pulling a stretched lips *Yikes!* face.

Chastity's eyes were as wide as saucers.

But Courtney looked (almost) as gleeful as Tempie.

"It's entirely unattractive you don't know how hard people have to work to pay a fucking gas bill," Battle went on. "And if I had to suffer through your amateur attempts at sucking me off one more time, I'd have considered putting a gun to my head. The problem with that is, I know you have a lot of practice at the act, you're just so fucking self-involved, you don't realize the man you're blowing is the person who's supposed to feel something."

"I cannot believe you just said that to me," she whispered.

"Three months ago, I told you we weren't going to work," Battle reminded her. "We'd been seeing each other for only three months by the time that happened. There were no promises. We didn't move in together. We hadn't even talked future, because that was never a consideration for me."

He swung an arm across the table and continued talking.

"But here you are. And you just *popped into* my box at the symphony but stayed the entire intermission. And three times, you *just happened* to be at Mangano's during the weekly lunch I take with mates. We do this so we can catch up, but not with exes who I don't want to see. You crashed Alfie and Lulu's house party. Like you did here, they weren't prepared to host you, so their staff was running around sorting a room for you while you drank a martini and complained about the rude sales associate you ran into at Pucci."

"Battle, I just—"

"You called at my house in London and fell into my arms crying about some slight a girlfriend dealt you. Then pretended to fall asleep in my arms. After I left you on the couch, you tried to crawl into my bed. Yes, Chelsea, you need to believe I'm saying these things to you. Because my next step is a chat with your father. And I'll be sharing with him, if your shit doesn't cease, the step after that will be a restraining order, because this is blatant stalking."

She hopped in her seat and snapped, "I'm hardly stalking you, Battle Talyn."

He stared hard at her sitting where she was sitting, a seat she had not strictly been invited to take, but he said nothing.

Chelsea then made huge mistake number two.

She stated, "Oh my God, you can't possibly think you'll do better than me."

"Think, no. Know, yes," Battle replied.

She tossed a hand to me. "With *her*?"

"Chels, maybe—" Rally tried to intervene.

"You've missed the point yet again," Battle growled. "What I have, or don't, with Vivienne or anyone is none of your fucking business. And since I'm making myself clear, you earned this by taking a nice night, where people were enjoying themselves, and forcing Vivi to remember she'd recently lost her mother, some time ago lost her father and only has three grandparents and a sister left in her family, and she's only thirty-two years old. Did you apologize for reminding Vivi of her grief? Fuck no. You stood your ground. Now I'm sharing, that's the hill you're going to die on because we've been done, but I can make it so that we're so done, you'll wish you never heard my name."

With that, he pushed his chair back, stood and looked down at Rally.

"I'm sorry, mate. I need to speak with Fitzy about a taxi and a hotel booking. However, please know, you and Court are very welcome to stay." He turned to Chelsea. "Go and pack. Tonight, you're leaving."

She pushed up too, shouting, "You can't possibly—!"

Battle cut her off. "You can pack and walk out my front door to a taxi, or the police can escort you. Your choice."

"*Fuck you, Battle!*" she shrieked. "You made no promises? What was I supposed to think when you were eating my pussy?"

Oh man, I needed to vamoose and pronto.

We all did.

"That I wondered how I could get you off so splendidly, and you never figured out, when the favor was returned, you were supposed to do the same fucking thing," he retorted.

Eek!

Well, she asked.

"You liked my mouth on you," she asserted.

"One more thing I'll give to you," he drawled. "When a man enjoys your mouth on him, he either wants to come in it, or can't wait to come in you. He doesn't make an excuse to go to the bathroom to finish himself off so he can get some sleep."

Dang.

Chelsea tried tears now, snuffling, "I was a lunatic for ever falling in love with you."

"Go, mate," Rally urged. "Court and I'll get her upstairs."

Battle glanced at Tempie, who gave him a nod, then he stalked out, without looking at anyone else, including me.

Fair play to him.

Because that was *insane*.

Boy, when Tempie told me if Chelsea stepped over his line, he'd eviscerate her, she wasn't joking.

"*I already wish I never knew your name!*" Chelsea shrieked after him.

"Let's go, Chels. We'll get you sorted and somewhere...else," Rally said.

Chelsea turned on me.

"Just so you know," she was still sniffling, "you're the flavor of the month. He collects promising young things. But he won't make you a duchess." She glared Prue and Chastity's way. "Not while he has so much weight hanging on him. He'll *never* make anyone his duchess."

My head was about to explode.

I mean...

How dare she?

Though, one thing good about that, Battle didn't witness it. If he had, I feared he'd strangle the life out of her.

But cool as a cucumber, Tempie sat back in her seat and said, "Bitch, get the fuck out of my sight then get out of *my fucking house*."

Chelsea opened her mouth, but Rally bit, "Not another word. Let's go."

Chelsea shot him a glare before she rolled her shoulders and stormed out.

Rally followed her, his body so stiff with anger, I worried he'd sprain something.

Courtney popped up and started out but turned to us.

"I'm so, *so* sorry. I had no idea all of that was happening. She told me—"

"We know it isn't you, dear," Tempie said in her warm/cool way that only Tempie could manage. "I'm sorry she made you feel like it was. But I do ask you to make sure she gets in the taxi. I don't trust myself to do it. And once she's gone, we'll all much prefer our Sunday."

Courtney nodded and took off.

I turned back to Tempie to see her lifting her hand palm out Prue and Chassie's way.

"But, Tempie," Prue said.

And when Tempie spoke next, the cool was gone entirely.

In fact, her voice was vibrating with anger.

"He can love his sisters, and find a woman to love," she stated. "There are one hundred and two rooms in this house. We vowed, all four of us, this was it. Family. The Downs. Forever. Whoever joins that has to work. And since that woman is Mum, but younger, Battle took what he wanted, didn't like it, and threw the rest back. She never had a chance. It has nothing to do with you. Don't think a second on it."

Prue nor Chassie seemed to let these words soak in.

Especially Chassie.

Of course, Tempie didn't miss it.

"Chastity, did you hear me?" Tempie called.

Chassie's eyes moved meaningfully through me before she whisper-said to her eldest sister. "I want Battie to be happy."

"What makes you think he's not?" Tempie asked.

She flicked a glance at me and mumbled, "That was just...awful. Poor Battie."

"I have a feeling on some level he enjoyed that," Tempie declared. "I know I did. She needed to hear it, and he very much needed to say it. Her lashing out even more in the end is all about her shallowness of character. We just witnessed a thirty-something throwing a toddler's tantrum. More fool her, she has no idea this is precisely why no man alive will keep her. She'll just continue doing this until she has to accept some bottom-of-the-barrel weakling who lets her walk all over him. But I'll lay odds she'll be supporting them, because a man like that won't be making the kind of living she thinks she deserves. She will end up miserable and wondering what went wrong, when Battie, and probably many others, already told her. People like that don't deserve our time. So let's put her out of mind, shall we?"

She stood and walked to the built-in at the wall that held a variety of manly beverages in heavy, fancy, cut crystal decanters, all of the liquid brown.

And she muttered, "I'm having a fucking whiskey."

"Me too!" Prue cried.

"I hate whiskey, but I'm drinking one," Chassie loud-whisper-said.

Tempie peered over her shoulder at me. "Vivienne?"

"I think maybe I should let you Talyns—"

"Oh, for God's sake, the cats sleep with you at night," Tempie drawled. "I can assure you, they don't visit her, nor I suspect, even looked in on Rally and Court, who are good people."

I wasn't certain about this cat thing.

Though Tempie sure did seem committed to whatever it meant.

"Pour one for Vivi too," Prue called.

"Come over here," Chassie loud-whisper-invited. "It's warm and we don't have to shout at each other to be heard."

"I'll just help Tempie first," I told them, got up and went to Tempie.

"You okay?" I asked under my breath.

"Respectfully," she turned to me and peeled her lips back in a terrifying smile, "that woman is a cunt."

I almost burst out laughing.

"Of course. *Respectfully*," I replied.

She rolled her eyes.

Then she poured four neat whiskies.

CHAPTER 12
THE REQUEST

I swam out of sleep Sunday morning, immediately regretting that third whiskey, to note what appeared to be an uncertain day in England—not gray, not sunny—and the understanding my slumbering self was paying company to only two felines that morning, Snowball and Gingerface.

Snowball had graduated to sleeping with me on my pillow, and Gingerface was already cuddling me.

"I'm never drinking whiskey again," I told them.

Gingerface shifted and started making biscuits on my hip.

I gave it some time while I assessed last night's damage, thankfully realizing I was only a mite queasy and headachy.

Then I asked, "Are we ready to face the day?"

Neither moved.

So I got out of bed, scooped up Snowball, took her to the bathroom and laid her on the fluffy bathmat, went back, grabbed Gingerface and added him to my menagerie.

And then I set about facing the day.

I was surprised to arrive in the breakfast room to see only Tempie there.

Of course, dressed all in white, she looked fabulous and not like we all got semi-snockered on whiskey last night. Battle and Rally disappeared, but Courtney returned and joined us, reporting Chelsea was away in her taxi.

We'd celebrated this news with an ill-advised whiskey number two.

How whiskey number three came about was a bit murky.

"Morning," I called.

"Vivi," she replied.

I went directly to the sideboard…and grease.

"How are you feeling?" she asked as I loaded my plate.

"I took some ibuprofen, now I'll eat some greasy food, and then I'll be good as gold," I answered. "How are you?"

"As all good aristocrats do, I've learned quite well to hold my liquor."

That made me smile.

She poured my coffee.

I sat with my plate and added cream to the cup.

"Can I ask you something?" I requested.

"Of course," she replied, sipping coffee, her empty plate (except the crumbs) that looked like she'd only had toast sitting in front of her.

I had a lot to ask.

I wanted to confirm my suspicions about Chastity, but if what I supposed was true, it wasn't Tempie's to give, or mine to have, unless Chassie gave it to me.

I wanted to tell her about Christian, though, upon reflection, I was thinking I needed to let Christian do whatever Christian intended to do.

If he was really interested, he'd make an effort, however that came about, and Chassie was worth that effort.

It was also Chassie's choice how she'd react to it.

I was intrigued about this "Fund" Battle and Prue had mentioned. However, that, again, wasn't my business.

I was also curious about the vow the four of them had made.

However, from what was said, they'd apparently decided as a family they were going to remain a family no matter what, all of them living at The Downs, and if any of them found someone, that someone would have to fit in.

This wasn't surprising, exactly. It wasn't like the house wasn't huge and couldn't fit husbands (and a wife…hmm), children, and tons more pets.

It also wasn't surprising because it was plain they suffered from supremely neglectful parents. Therefore, banding together and creating tight bonds that didn't break was probably a defense mechanism born of a natural desire to seek love and support, and when none was to be found, creating it for themselves.

I couldn't think on that too long, because it was too horrendous to consider, and something I'd never understand because what I had growing up was the exact opposite.

So instead, I thought of how close they were, what an amazing bond they had, and that I thought it was kind of cool they all knew they had a home and a family, no matter what.

And although it seemed clear Tempie was at one with Battle flirting with me, spending time with me and calling me darling, she might be able to tell me if Prue was immune to it, or if she, too, was acting like she was because she was okay with it.

But that I needed to ask Prue.

So I settled on, "Do you know if anything happened to Harmony after the war was over?"

Her sublimely arched brows straightened and inched together. "Happened to Harmony?"

"Yes."

"Like what?"

"No clue. Except Marie recorded an entry in her diary about something dire happening at the house, it was clear whatever it was happened to Harmony, and she said the only good thing about it was that it was 'dead and buried' and 'no one would speak of it again.'"

Tempie took this in for a moment, before she said, "I fear, Vivi, that no one spoke of it again, since I have no knowledge of anything dire happening in this house to Harmony or anybody. Sadly, we don't have the macabre and mysterious reputation of Duncroft."

Duncroft was another famous heritage estate up north.

It was famous for being magnificent (it was bigger even than The Downs), but also because a silent film star plunged to her death over the railing of their grand stairwell back in the 20s.

It was ruled an accident, but rumors persisted to this day that it was murder.

They'd recently been in the news because that film star's great-nephew hatched a scheme to sell more of the books he wrote about the tragedy by sneaking in and doing weird shit in the house to scare the people living and working there.

He'd been caught out by the earl's heir, and prosecuted. My understanding was he was in jail. But the earl's heir was now the earl and married to the American heiress who was there for a house party during this fake haunting.

I'd followed the story, obviously, because it was interesting, included a historical estate steeped in just what Tempie said it was, the macabre and mystery, but also because it was romantic.

Tempie got to the meat of the matter quickly. "Do you think, whatever this is, it's why Harmony ended things with Charlie?"

"I think the dates match from when their love letters switched from being love letters, planning their lives and future together, to her breaking things off," I replied. "It was getting late, so I wasn't able to check." And I'd been interrupted by nosiness about the Christian/Chassie thing, something I didn't share. "I'll be confirming that today."

"I would encourage you not to hope too much you'll find anything," Tempie warned. "Outside of learning to hold our liquor, aristocrats are dab hands at holding our secrets."

"Yeah, I'm aware I might never find out, but I'm going to try."

"Oh God," was said at the door where Courtney was tumbling through. "Why did I drink whiskey? I *hate* whiskey. Lord, I hope there are plenty of sausages."

I exchanged a smile with Tempie, though hers was more of a smirk, as was her wont.

And I cut into my own sausage.

I was out in the studio, having confirmed that yes, the dates matched between the change in tone in letters and Marie's journal entry.

I'd read through quite a bit more of Marie's journals but found not a single word written about anything "dire," and she almost studiously avoided referring to Harmony at all, except to say things like, *Harmony wore the loveliest dress to church today*, and the like.

I'd then turned to Unity's journals, and although Unity, Harmony's younger sister, was far more verbose, she was also quite a bit younger, so her language was dreamy and flowery (whereas Harmony fell in love with Charlie, Unity fell in love with what seemed like every soldier that came through The Downs, both wounded and not).

She was, however, very aware of Harmony and Charlie's love affair, though only as an observer. She fervently hoped they would ride into the sunset for their happily ever after. She was devastated when they did not.

But around the date of Marie's grim entry alluding to something happening to Harmony, Unity was blissfully unaware of it, not only since she didn't mention anything, but also because the blithe, teenaged tone of her entries didn't change.

I'd given up and gone back to where I left off before curiosity got the better of me.

I had a ton of stuff to get through, and now only just over a week to get through it. But also, since Rally and Courtney were leaving after tea, I didn't have a full day to work and needed to be in the blue salon at three because I liked them. They were lovely, it felt good to be around two people who were so in love, and I wanted a bit more time with them and to be there to say goodbye.

So I was hard at it when I sensed movement at the door.

I looked up and my heart jumped into my throat as Battle walked in.

How on earth could he make simple sweaters and jeans look so scrummy?

We'd eventually been joined by Prue and Chassie at breakfast (both of them not as good aristocrats as Tempie, since they were both hilariously hungover), but Courtney told us Rally and Battle were taking a "morning wander with Bartholomew."

This was the first time I'd seen him since last night.

"Hey," I greeted, smiling at him because he was gorgeous, he was there, also, I worried he might feel awkward or embarrassed about last night, and I wanted him to know he shouldn't be.

"Vivi," he replied, walking in.

I looked at my phone and saw I had an hour before tea.

"Something up?" I asked him.

He was perusing the crates, and he didn't answer.

He then turned to my desk, which probably appeared to him as being messy with papers and books, my laptop and notes, but to me, it was organized chaos.

"I see you've made yourself at home," he murmured as he reached out to one of the three framed photos I brought with me, all three standing pride of place facing me from a corner of the desk. This where they always were anywhere I worked.

I had to steel myself as he looked down at it, because him just touching that photo felt like a caress.

Not a sexy one.

A tender one.

It was a picture of Mom and Dad horsing around at a campsite before they were married.

He studied it, and as he did, I felt something tingly move over my skin. Not unpleasant, but wholly intimate.

"Your parents?" he asked the picture.

"Yeah. Mom and Dad. The soon-to-be Amy and Brian Dupree. That was taken before they were married. Actually, it was taken on the camping trip where Dad proposed."

After a moment's more contemplation, he put that down and picked up the picture of me and my sister.

"Me and Solène. My sister," I said. "And yes, Dad's last name was French, and he has French ancestry, obviously. But he wasn't that big into it, according to Mom. She was the one who was fascinated by all things French, so she named us."

"Like you're fascinated with all things English?" he asked.

And yeah, all three of my historical fiction books had been about English history, obviously my next book was, and two of the four romance novels I wrote were set in England.

Though, admitting this seemed like I was admitting something bigger.

Therefore, it was whispered when I said, "Like I'm fascinated with English things."

Fortunately, he made no response to that and instead put that picture down and picked up the one of me cuddling my niece and nephew.

"Matías and Estrella. And their names are because my brother-in-law, Alex, is Mexican American," I explained.

"Mm," he hummed before he put that picture back and moved to the shelf bearing the crates to look out the window. "I'd like to request a favor," he said to the garden.

He was acting strange, and because of that I was on my guard.

"Shoot," I invited.

"I know you have a lot of work to do, but I'd like to ask you to work in tandem with Tempie to get Prue and Chassie to London."

Oh dear.

He turned to me. "You can come on the train. I'll have a driver pick you up at Paddington. Thursday morning. Spend the day in the city. We'll all meet for dinner that night. Spend Friday in the city, and we'll all come back Friday evening."

"Is there a reason you feel you can share that you're asking this?"

"I know you took Prue and Chassie to town to do some shopping," he replied, "I think it would be helpful, considering the seal has been broken, to challenge both of them to move farther afield. But definitely make sure they don't have time to reseal that seal."

This made sense.

But losing two days, when I already lost one (and today, several hours of another) would be hell on my work schedule.

It was like he knew what I was thinking, because he glanced at my desk before moving his gaze to my face.

"I understand it's asking a lot, but I feel I can share that I worry Tempie and I allowed things to go on too long. We should have pushed harder far earlier. But now, we have an advantage, and I don't think we should squander it. I know this isn't your issue—"

"It's my issue, Battle. I care about both of them. And before you say anything else, I'd be down with going to London. I can take some stuff to read on the train, so I can keep my momentum going."

"I'm fucking furious Chelsea forced you to speak about your mother's loss like she did."

I sat still and staring, taken aback by his swift change in topic and the emotion in his voice.

"It's okay," I said softly.

"It is not," he said, all steely. "You must know, I had you vetted before you came. Nothing intrusive, but you were to be a stranger in my home with my family. I needed to know you were who you said you were. As such, I knew about her loss."

"That tracks, and I'm not offended. I'd do the same thing if I were you."

"I behaved badly last night."

Good God.

Was this man...*apologizing?*

"I'm not sure I agree."

His head cocked to the side.

"Battle, she's a bitch," I pointed out. "You were right. Rally and Courtney felt awful. It was hard to witness how awkward they felt. But they were stuck. You were all stuck. Fitzgibbons, Patsy, Emily, everybody had to run around and do shit to adjust to suddenly having three more people in the house. It wasn't cool. All the stuff you laid out she'd been doing wasn't cool. Frankly, I'm surprised you didn't carve into her way before last night. You have a lot more patience than me."

"I have three sisters," he reminded me. "It makes it very difficult to treat a woman poorly, always having it in my mind how I'd want my sisters to be treated."

Okay.

Shit.

Official.

I totally liked this guy.

"Even if she deserves it?" I asked.

"Even if that, Vivi. Chelsea is who her mother and father made her. In a sense, it isn't her fault. She genuinely does not understand a world where she doesn't get everything she wants."

At least that explained why he'd been so patient with her through all he'd described she was pulling last night.

"Well, it's time she was introduced to it," I retorted. "Or she's going to be even more disappointed sometime in the future. I'm just sorry you were pushed into the position to have to teach her that lesson."

"And I'm sorry you had to watch it happen."

"I'm not." I grinned. "It was kind of rad."

With that, everything about him changed, in the sense I was both thrilled and terrified that in about two seconds, he was going to be fucking me on the desk.

We stared at each other, the heat blistering between us, and this lasted so long, I was both thrilled and terrified that it was going to be *me* who jumped *him*.

To my utter dejection, he broke the spell by asking, "Did you learn more about Harmony?"

I had a new obsession with finding out what went down with Harmony.

But I was more obsessed with jumping him, or better, him jumping me.

Alas, all I could do was say, "Just to confirm that Marie's entry corresponds with Harmony breaking things off with Charlie."

"Pity," he murmured.

"Battle—"

I was going to ask what was going on here.

Or request he confirm what seemed obvious was going on was actually obvious it was going on and then discuss what we were going to do about it.

But he said, "I've asked you to cut into your research time, so now, I won't take more of it. I'll see you at tea."

He might have said that.

But me?

I was heartily *over it*.

So when he hit the door, I snapped, "I think, my Lord Duke, you're a massive tease."

He turned, seared me with a look so hot, I one hundred percent creamed my panties, and purred, "Darling, you've no idea."

I blinked.

He walked out of the studio.

CHAPTER 13

THE CALL

I swam out of sleep Wednesday morning, bleary-eyed and still tired, to what appeared to be a day struggling to be sunny in England, with Snowball, Gingerface and Prue's (but really Chassie's) long-haired, white and gray tiger-striped cat, Floofy, hanging with me.

I'd met Floofy last night while I was teaching the girls how to play euchre in the games room.

Tempie was vicious, gloating with every trick she took.

Chassie, my partner, was surprisingly sly.

So much so, she and I won the best of ten we were playing.

It was a blast.

And Floofy was seriously…floofy.

"This book is going to kill me," I told the cats.

I rolled to my back and looked to the smart screen to see it was six fifty-eight.

I then stared at the canopy, stroking cats if they were in reach, and going over the last two days.

Battle left Monday morning, very early.

He didn't say goodbye, as such.

But I did wake up to a text from an unknown number that said,

Didn't want to wake you. I'll see you Thursday. The girls will be on the return train. You'll be riding back with me.

So I guessed Battle had my number, and it was clear he could be bossy in texts too.

Sexy bossy with that whole "riding back with me" bit.

I didn't even think he knew how teasy he was being with some of it. It was just him, like his brown eyes or his hot guy height.

It was crazy awesome.

And it was doing my head in.

I programmed him in, replied, *Righty ho, Your Grace. Be safe out there,* then set about my plan of alternately cramming on Talyn history and figuring out how to get the girls to London.

With Prue, I would find, it was easy.

When the topic was addressed by Tempie over cocktails Monday evening, Prue simply clapped and cried, "Oh yes! I can finally meet François!" She turned to me and shared, "He makes most of my clothes. I've always wanted to meet him, and he works out of his boutique in London."

For her part, Chassie was watching Prue's excitement with eyes that I could tell, behind them, her brain was working hard to come up with an excuse not to go.

Thus, I chimed in, "I always wanted to go to Kew Gardens. It's one place I've never had the time to see when I've been over here. I know it's a bit out of the way of all the good shopping and stuff, but I'd love to visit. Do you think we could fit that in?"

"Of course," Tempie drawled smugly while Chassie made a scrunch face of frustration.

Prue clapped again and said to Chassie, "Oh, you get to go to Kew. You love the botanical gardens!"

And with that, Chassie was apparently foiled for an excuse, though I didn't think the battle was won. There were still two days she could dream up reasons not to go.

"I'll ask Fitzy to book our tickets on the train," Tempie said, and finalized, "Sorted."

At least it was for then.

In order to make up for lost time, I told them I was on a roll, so after dinner, I headed back out to the studio, read and took notes, enhanced my outline and jotted down ideas until almost midnight, when I trudged back to the house, cleaned my face, brushed my teeth and fell into bed.

The same thing happened yesterday after we finished euchre. Though, last night, I got into it, so it was after one in the morning before I came back to the house.

But I was making progress.

Though, it would appear I'd have to dream up even more of Harmony and Charlie's story than I thought I would, because I'd definitely hit the WWII time period, and I wasn't finding anything.

And in the now, I had to make more progress.

Doing it missing Battle, as I had for the last two days.

What could I say?

The guy had gotten to me.

Seriously.

I had to admit, I'd looked forward to seeing him at cocktails and eating dinner at his side, and it sucked he wasn't around.

God help me.

"Are we ready to rumble, babies?" I asked.

None of the felines answered.

Since none of them was lying on me, I rolled out anyway.

But they followed me.

I was in the studio with Snowball and Gingerface.

Yes, I had Prue's permission to bring them with me. I had to seek it out because they'd taken to following me, which made it nigh on impossible to get out the door with them trying to escape with me.

But since I didn't know if they were indoor or outdoor, and I didn't want to introduce the outdoors if they were in, I had to find Prue.

She was in the attic.

I sensed she sensed I needed to work, so she hadn't pressed my visit to this space.

But once me and the cats got there, I was thrown.

"Holy crap," I exclaimed.

Her head popped out from behind a massive, broken chandelier deep within the bowels of a huge mess. "Vivi!"

"Hey," I called, wending my way through bureaus and boxes and armoires and ancient ice skates. "It's like the room of requirement in here."

She giggled. "I know. I'm about to ask Scotty and Harry to help me lug some stuff out into the hall so I have more room to move around." She frowned. "I found more papers for you, but not anything from Harmony."

"I'll take all I can get," I said, gazing at a pair of large, elaborate gilt torchères balanced on top of something covered with a heavy, quilted mover's blanket. "Jesus, honey, I think these are Chippendale."

She picked one up and examined it. "You think?"

"Babe, if they are, those alone might be worth a million pounds."

Her gaze flew to me. "Really?"

"Totally."

She looked back at the candlestick. "How do we know?"

"Chippendale didn't put a maker's mark on his pieces," I told her. "They have to be authenticated by an expert. Unless you have some documentation somewhere."

She glanced through the room. "We probably do, it's just finding it."

I glanced through the room too, saying, "Prue, I had no idea, but I don't think this is a project you can handle on your own. You need to call Christie's, or Sotheby's, or Criterion and ask them to send someone out here. Though, they'll be salivating to get this stuff on the auction block, so maybe contact the National Trust or the British Museum or the Victoria and Albert. I mean,"—I did a full circle—"it appears to be at least three centuries worth of a lot of stuff. They needed a bigger boat in *Jaws* to take on the great white. You're gonna need a fleet of coast guard to handle this white whale."

Prue grinned at me.

I touched the torchère with the reverence a possible Chippendale piece deserved, saying, "But man, I'd kill to dig through this mess."

"First things first, Vivi," Prue advised. "I promise not to do anything with this stuff until you have a look at all of it. But you keep at your book."

Ah, my Prue.

I just knew she'd been guarding my book time.

She continued, "In the meantime, I'll make a few calls. And I'll definitely ask Scotty and Harry to help me move some things out so anyone who wants to look at it can get around better. But I have this crazy feeling there's something in this house *somewhere* that you need. I just can't seem to find it, and since I can't get to half this stuff because the other half is piled on or in the way, I can't get my hands on it."

"Not that you won't, but please, you and Harry and Scotty need to handle all of this with the utmost care. I think this may be a treasure trove, honey."

She beamed. "I thought so too. And since we probably won't keep most of it, we can auction it off and augment The Fund!"

Again with The Fund.

I didn't ask.

I said, "Listen, I came to find you because Gingerface and Snowball want to come out to the studio with me. Can they come?"

"Oh, sure," she replied breezily. "They aren't outdoor cats, but they won't do anything but follow you. Sometimes Floofy gardens with Chassie. She never leaves her side. But she does like to snooze in the sun."

And that was my conversation with Prue and my introduction to the attics before Snowball, Gingerface and I went to the studio and got to work.

She was right.

They pranced through the turf and along the walkways right behind me all the way there.

And now I was studying the butler's ledgers from 1946.

Primarily, two weird entries for two footmen.

Okay, we'll begin with the fact that The Downs still had footmen in 1946, which, for that time, was very rare.

Sure, they had Scotty and Harry now, and even though they served dinner, like a footman would, I still thought they were around more to look after the occupants of the house than to serve food and tend fires.

But that wasn't the weird part.

Bonuses, the line item in the ledgers denoted them. But when I kept going back and forth, there were no other bonuses listed for any staff that I could find.

Ever.

And they each got three hundred pounds, and once I adjusted that number for inflation, it made it over ten thousand pounds in today's currency.

That was a massive bonus.

Especially since the footmen made the whopping amount of forty pounds per year.

And if that wasn't enough, it was dated the day after Marie's entry about something dire happening at The Downs.

"Bribes to be quiet? Or bribes because they were asked to do something they shouldn't have to do, and they also had to be quiet about it?" I whispered to the ledger as my phone vibrated on the desk beside me.

I knew the number, it was my soon-to-be future landlord, so, feeling despondent at this reminder I was shortly going to leave this studio, the house, and the people I cared about in it, I took the call.

"Hello, Mr. Atkins."

"Miss Dupree, how are you?"

"Great, and ready to move in on Monday," I lied.

"Uh, luv, about that."

I stilled at his tone.

"The old tenants moved out, and we moved in to do a tidy up for you, and I'm afraid they were a bit careless about a few things."

Oh no.

"What things?"

"Well, there are several repairs that have to be done. However, sadly, we can't get to them because we discovered black mold."

Holy shit!

"This means the council won't allow us to have another tenant until it's been eradicated," he continued. "Obviously, we wouldn't want you there until that happens either. But not only do we need to see to that happening, we need to make the repairs. In the end, it doesn't look like we'll be able to have you for two, maybe three months."

Oh no.

Two to three months?

"I can imagine this is very inconvenient for you," he kept talking. "I'm so sorry. So very sorry. I asked around to see if anything else is available, hoping to find a stopgap for you, but with the summer holidays coming and tourist season picking up, I wasn't able to find anything. Of course, we'll do what we can, money-wise, to make this hurt a bit less. And obviously, if you find someplace, we'll let you out of your lease with us. But that mold is highly toxic, and even if the Council hadn't deemed it unfit for use until the mold is gone, I wouldn't want you in there."

Okay, this had to suck for him. He was losing rental money on top of whatever it had to cost to clear out black mold and do repairs.

But…

Shit, shit, shit, what was I going to do?

My phone vibrated with another call.

I took it from my ear and looked at it.

Battle.

Calling me.

For the first time.

My stomach pitched.

This reminded me I'd see him tomorrow.

My stomach pitched harder.

I put the phone back to my ear and said, "I have another call coming in I have to take, Mr. Atkins. Um…can I call you back?"

"Of course, luv, just…anything me and my Molly can do. She's still looking and making calls. We're so sorry."

"Yes, thank you. I'll call you back."

"Okay, luv."

I disconnected with him and took Battle's call.

"Hey," I greeted.

"Vivi," he replied.

"You might have a million-pound set of Chippendale candlesticks in your attic, and that's for starters."

He was silent.

"Instead of sitting on the motherlode, the motherlode might just be sitting on you," I shared.

"Interesting."

This guy.

Regardless of my recent disastrous news, I smiled. "An understatement worthy of the Duke of Burleigh."

I heard his chuckle through the line and my breasts swelled.

"Why are you calling?" I asked.

"Chassie phoned, seeking an excuse to get out of coming to London tomorrow."

Crap.

"I was worried she was being too quiet about it once we fenced her in," I admitted.

"I didn't give her the excuse, but just warning you, she might make some plays this evening. I've already warned Tempie."

"Okay, but…I mean, do you think it's right to force her if she really doesn't want to go?"

"She really didn't want to go to Glastonbury, but she had a lovely time. And then, the next day, she was nipping into town like she did it frequently. So, yes. I do think it's right."

"You're the big brother," I mumbled.

"Prue came into the house giggling and baby talking, practically from birth," Battle stated, and my attention sharpened. "She was like a baby sunbeam."

Oh yeah.

This guy.

"So sweet," I whispered.

"Chassie was like a little doll. I've never seen a more beautiful child. Quiet and watchful, fascinated with flowers, always. Though, in the beginning, she tended to try to eat them."

I laughed softly.

"She looked it, but she wasn't fragile," Battle continued. "She knew herself. She knew what she liked. From an early age. Maybe she watched what happened to Prue and took it in more than we expected a child of her age would, and she made certain no one was going to beat her down like they did Prue. Of course, she didn't have the same personality as Prue, but she was self-contained for as long as I knew her, and that's her entire life. She could entertain herself as a child. And when she grew up, she asked for one thing. The money to open her own flower shop. She did this in Bath. It was successful within six months of opening."

"Right," I said, finding the "wasn't fragile" comment a tragedy, and having the mystery of Courtney's comment about wedding flowers explained, albeit only partially.

"We need to reintroduce her to herself, darling," he concluded.

He was right.

"Okay," I agreed.

"How are you getting on with your research?"

"Great. I'm making up for the time I'll be losing by working into the night."

I could actually hear the frown in his voice. "Is this London trip putting you that far off schedule?"

"Probably not, but now that I have to find a new place to live by next week, I'm glad I did it because, at this late date, I think I might be screwed, but I still have to put in the time to look for something."

"Find a new place to live?"

"The cottage I'm renting has black mold. It won't be safe to move in for at least two months," I shared. "And it wasn't that easy to find an appropriate space that would rent to me for only six months. Now I need something fast, and that cottage is cute. I'm bummed I don't get to stay there. But I don't know when it's going to be ready, and I can't ask a prospective landlord to let to me for two to three months or ask Mr. Atkins to wait for me if I'm in a place for three months and his place is ready to let earlier. I think in the end, I'm probably going to be bouncing around Airbnbs for three months, and that sucks."

"Vivienne, you have a home."

My back straightened, and one could say, him uttering those words set an electric bolt through me, much like the one I felt when I first met him.

"You'll stay at The Downs," he decreed.

"I can't ask—"

"You didn't."

"Listen—"

"This isn't a discussion, Vivienne. You're staying at The Downs."

My back got straighter.

"Battle—"

"Now, I must go."

"Battle, no, hang on a second."

"What?"

"I can't stay here."

"Why not?"

"Well, I'm using your Wi-Fi. And eating your food. And your staff handwashes my sweaters for me."

"And?"

And?

"All of that costs money," I stated the obvious.

"Agreed."

"So…" I let that hang.

"Vivienne, as you pointed out so eloquently not long ago, we're super, crazy, stupid rich."

"*You* are. I'm a freeloader."

"Hardly." Now his purr had a sting.

"Look at it from my perspective," I urged.

"What I'm asking you to do, something you seem incapable of doing, is looking at it from mine."

"Okay, I know you all really dig me, and that's sweet. Super sweet. I love it. Because I really dig you all too. And I know you're really happy that Prue is blossoming after she let those schoolgirl bitches take away her shine. But I already felt like I'm taking advantage of you, this will only make it worse."

"You aren't."

"But I feel it."

"However, you *aren't*."

"I still feel that way, Battle," I said heatedly.

"More of your American eloquence, I can confirm we do *dig you*."

That would be funny, hearing him say those words in his posh accent, if I wasn't nurturing a temper tantrum.

It was also very sweet to have confirmed, however, I was nurturing a temper tantrum.

"My sisters enjoy having you there," he continued. "And it would be very hard for me to guide what's happening between us if you're off in a cottage by the sea."

One could say the time was ripe.

So I took a bite.

"Okay, let's get into that. What's happening between us?"

"I very much want to fuck my sister's best friend. I also enjoy her company. So I'm balancing the high wire of seducing my sister's best friend in a way that won't affect her relationship with my sister at the same time I'll eventually get to fuck her, thoroughly and abundantly, whilst enjoying her company in bed and elsewhere."

He was such a fucking *tease*.

"Okay, I'm at one with that plan."

"I know."

And so damned arrogant.

"Maybe we can talk to Prue?" I suggested.

"I doubt Prue has that first issue with it. She wants me happy. She wants you happy. And I'm happy when I'm with you."

Oh God.

He put that right out there.

Right out there!

That didn't make my stomach pitch.

It made it melt.

"However, we must tread cautiously," he finished.

"Battle—"

"So you're staying at The Downs."

Oh my God!

"You can't alternately sweet and sexy talk me into getting your way."

"I was afraid of that," he muttered.

"Okay, we've proved we can compromise. So I'll pay you the rent I would have paid Mr. Atkins."

"Out of the question," he growled immediately.

"Battle—"

"I won't give that comment the respect even to discuss it," he stated.

"And I won't stay at The Downs without paying my way," I fired back.

"Oh, you will, Vivi," he warned silkily.

"You can't make me."

"And you can't leave us, and you already knew that before you learned of black mold," he retorted.

Fuck.

Fuck!

"You don't even want to," he pressed his advantage.

"We'll discuss this in London," I said tightly.

"If you wish."

"And between times, maybe make a passing attempt at thinking about it from my point of view."

"I shall do so, if you make the same promise."

"I'm sorry, Battle, but even if I was rich as fuck, I probably wouldn't let my sister's dear friend hang at my house and eat all my food in perpetuity."

"That isn't my perspective, and you know it."

Okay, okay, okay.

I liked this guy.

He was complicated. He was smart. He was funny. He was gallant. He was handsome as all hell. He was a ludicrously good brother. He respected women. He was protective. He was generous. He was an amazing flirt. He thought I was beautiful. He was interested in what I did. He'd read my books. He was honest. He was frank.

I could fall for this guy.

Hard.

And for forever.

Was he saying he felt the same way about me?

"Now, if you haven't come to your senses by tomorrow, we'll revisit this subject then," he said into my fevered reverie.

Oh shit.

"Come to my senses?" I asked dangerously.

He sighed heavily.

"Fine. Tomorrow," I snapped.

"Until then, darling."

I was never, ever, *ever* going to tell him this.

But I was pretty sure I'd let him get away with anything as long as he called me darling.

"By the way, I might have uncovered bribes in your butler's ledgers for 1946. I think shit went down in that house, and two footmen were dragged into it, or they witnessed it and were paid to be silent. See you tomorrow," I bid.

And then I disconnected.

"So there," I said to my phone.

Snowball, who was snoozing in a combined circle of white and ginger fur in front of the stove (meaning Gingerface was the orange Yang to Snowball's Yin), lifted her head to look at me.

"Men suck," I told her.

She blinked.

"What sucks more is, I want to fall on his dick so bad, I'm probably going to stay here another two months...at least."

Snowball laid her head back down and returned to snoozing.

Bah!

Because I had no choice (and for other reasons I absolutely refused to consider in that moment), I called Mr. Atkins back and requested he share the status of the cleanup, but not to worry, in the interim, I was good.

The bright side of that, Mr. Atkins was blatantly relieved.

After hanging up with him, feeling the cozy warmth of the stove, the crates right there for me to access, the colorful chaos and fertile green beyond the windows, understanding I'd be on a train tomorrow, heading to Battle, I was relieved too.

Argh.

I went back to work.

CHAPTER 14

THE TRIP

I was fuming.

I really didn't want to fume in front of Battle's sisters.

But damn, I was *fuming*.

It was the next morning, and it started with Tempie loading us up into the first-class (oh yes, I said *first class*) carriage of the train, and then we were off.

Although first class was only slightly posher than what the common people had to use, it was a lot quieter (there was only one other person in our carriage). And once we got rolling, they almost immediately came out with the snack cart, which was nicer (when, sometimes, you never got a snack cart offering in the regular class at all).

Within five minutes of embarking on our journey, I asked Tempie how much I owed them for the tickets.

"Oh, you can take that up with Battle," she replied.

Did I decide in that moment to wait until I saw Battle that evening?

No, I did not.

I texted him, *We're away. How much do I owe you for the train tickets?*

To which, immediately, he texted back, *We're not having this discussion.*

Which of course made me text, *Fine, then I'm buying dinner tonight.*

To which, of course, he replied, *Absolutely not.*

To which, of course, I replied, *Brace Mr. 1933. The little woman is buying dinner!*

To which, of course, he replied, *If you even look at your bag during dinner, you'll beg me to end the tease.*

To which…you get the gist, *Are you sexually blackmailing me?*

And I got, *Not if not forced to do so. The decision is yours. I suggest you make the right one, darling.*

Yes!

He pulled The Darling!

Which started me fuming.

"Is everything okay, Vivi?" Chassie whisper-asked.

I stopped glaring out the window at the beautiful English countryside and looked to her.

"Yes, I'm fine," I lied.

"You don't seem fine," Prue noted, regarding me with worry.

She and Chassie were sitting opposite Tempie and me.

"Okay, well, forewarning you, Battle and I are in a fight," I admitted.

Prue's mouth dropped open.

Chassie's eyes got big.

"It's not a huge deal," I assured. "It's just, the cottage I was going to go to has black mold so I can't go. I told Battle. He told me I'm staying at The Downs. *Told me.*"

Not a one of them had any reaction to this.

So I went on, "I tried to compromise by offering him the rent I would—"

I stopped when all three of them hissed breath in between their teeth.

Even Tempie!

I looked among them. "What?"

"You offered Battie rent?" Chassie whisper-whispered, in total shock.

"It's rude to overstay your welcome," I told her.

She seemed flummoxed. "But…you're not."

Man, I was falling in love with all of these people.

"That's sweet, Chassie, but I kinda am," I said gently.

"Do you want to leave?" Prue asked anxiously.

"No," I said fast. "Not at all. It's just…not paying *anything* for room and board?"

None of them had a reaction to that either.

I wasn't sure I could have this discussion again, especially when I was already going to when I saw Battle again.

About the time I had that thought, Tempie noted, "Obviously you know you must stand down from your position."

I turned to look at her. "I do?"

She smoothed the material of her black slacks and stated, "He is that man, Vivi. And I do believe you know what I'm saying."

I had a sinking feeling I did.

She caught my eyes. "It's enough you made the offer. Now leave it."

"I hated the idea of you going anyway," Prue stated, sounding almost petulant. "And if you went, what would Snowball and Gingerface do?"

I also had to admit, I was going to miss those kitties. I didn't have a pet at home. I was waiting for when I bought my house to decide if I was going to go dog or cat, or both (or two of both).

"Well, I'm staying," I muttered. "And not because I have no choice. I was dreading leaving anyway."

Prue clapped happily.

"But now we're quarreling about me buying dinner tonight because he won't let me pay for my train ticket," I shared.

Again with Prue's mouth dropping open.

"If it was any one of us," Tempie started, "I would like to think we would do the same. But I don't know. It wasn't any of us. It was

Battie. Battie who was the oldest. Battie, who saw there was no one there but a member of staff to clean Chassie's scraped knees and palms and calm her tears when she fell off her bike. So he did it. Battie, who knew Dad wouldn't show up, and Mum was already in Greece, so he drove from university to be there when Prue won that drawing competition and got her ribbon."

Okay, I couldn't dwell on Battle cleansing little Chassie's wounds and how that made me feel super melty.

I had other things to deal with.

"You won a drawing competition?" I asked Prue.

She shrugged.

Truth, she'd kept a lot from me.

And with that new tidbit, which shouldn't embarrass her at all, I wondered why.

Tempie kept talking. "You see, it's ingrained in him now, to see to the people he cares about. Especially women, not because we're weaker, or poorer, or anything like that. Because fate gave him three younger sisters. He can't *not* do it, Vivi. I think it would cause him physical pain, if he's in a position to offer something and not do so. I know it would cause emotional pain."

As I started to feel shitty about throwing Battle's generosity in his face, she turned fully to me and kept going.

"So I ask you, don't make him. You offered. You pushed back. He knows your stance and you're not one to take advantage. But that isn't what you're doing it. You're giving him something he needs."

"Oh, all right, I won't buy dinner," I gave in.

Tempie smiled a slow smile.

It was then, Chassie dropped the bomb.

"Well, this is good, because it would be most inconvenient for Battie to keep falling in love with you if you were off to some cottage on the sea."

I froze.

"Chassie," Tempie admonished.

"What? It's not like we all aren't seeing it," she whisper-talked back.

Now I couldn't take the time to deal with Chassie's "keep falling in love with you" remark, because I had to address the matter at hand.

As such, I stared hard at Prue.

She was smiling. "It's so amazing. You might be my actual sister one day!" And she clapped on that.

"He's just flirty. He's just…we're just…it's just a—" I stammered.

"Oh my God," Tempie groaned. "Stop. Watching my brother on the prowl is enough. I can't handle you trying to pretend it isn't what it is. Though, the constant nausea it induces is helping me keep trim."

"Tempie!" Prue snapped.

"I think it's lovely," Chassie whisper-declared. "Finally, Battie's found a good woman. We like her. Bartie likes her. The cats like her. The house likes her." She smiled sweetly at me. "It's perfect."

The house liked me?

I couldn't get into that either.

"We haven't even had a date yet," I pointed out.

"So have," Prue contradicted. "Best dates ever. All at The Downs. If he wasn't my brother, I'd think it was all dreamy. Instead, it's just slightly gross dreamy."

Chassie giggled.

"You're okay with this?" I asked Prue.

"Absolutely," she answered perkily.

"It hasn't even very much started."

Chassie shocked me by rolling her eyes when I said that.

"Okay, it has, but it's new and it might not come to anything," I warned.

"Vivi," Prue smiled brightly, "I'm not twelve. And you're a good person. So is Battie. If it doesn't work, it won't work for whatever reasons you two have. But he won't be cruel to you, and you won't be cruel to him, that I know."

"Chelsea earned what he said to her," Chassie whisper-added.

"I know, honey," I assured her.

"What I mean is, that'll be between you two," Prue continued. "And like he'll always be my brother, you'll always be my friend."

That gave me so much relief, I reached out to her, she took my hand, we squeezed.

"And the nausea returns," Tempie drawled.

Prue and I let go as she and I, with Chassie, laughed.

I also got out my phone and texted Battle.

Tempie gave me a talking to. I won't go for my wallet tonight.

One of the few things I learned from my research into the Talyns was that Battle was a venture capitalist. He was deep into this and had investments in a dizzying number of companies.

So I knew he was probably pretty busy.

He still returned my text, again immediately, *Excellent. Enjoy your day, sweetheart. See you tonight.*

Staring at his text, and my second brand of endearment from him, I realized we'd pretty much been on a weeklong date before he left for London.

And now that would resume.

So I had to bury a bit of my pride and what had been drilled into me during my upbringing.

I looked from my cell to the girls in the first-class carriage, knowing we had a fun day planned, and I'd see Battle again soon.

Okay.

Yeah.

Worth it.

I was in the en suite bathroom of my room at Burleigh House in Kensington.

The outside was a fabulous vision of black wrought iron fencing capped with gold spikes, blond gravel, and pots containing well pruned trees, or poofed or coned shrubs, and bright red geraniums.

Although this house had been owned by the duchy for two

hundred years, Battle had pretty much divested it of anything not from this millennia. It was thoroughly modern, minimalist, bright, sleek, sophisticated and classy.

I loved it.

We had a driver waiting for us at Paddington Station. He loaded us in a big SUV and took us to Kew, which was beautiful. We had lunch there, and although I knew Tempie was done about fifteen minutes in, we crawled over everything, because Chassie was happy.

We loaded back up in the car and were taken to the house.

Prue gave me the tour.

The housekeeper's name was Mrs. Pattinson.

I met her and she seemed very nice, definitely delighted to have us all there.

There was no butler. Prue explained Mrs. Pattinson had cleaning ladies who came in once a week to do a thorough clean of the place, but other than that, she got Battle's food in, cooked for him, dealt with his dry cleaning, made his bed, etc.

There were eight bedrooms, all with en suites.

And they were fabulous, including mine, which was decorated in mauves and taupes, had a massive fainting couch as the end-of-bed bench, and amazing lighting.

There wasn't a dressing table like at The Downs.

But I was oh-so not going to quibble.

It was almost time to meet downstairs for a drink and to wait for Battle's return, whereupon we'd head out to dinner.

I couldn't wait to see him.

Bartholomew was lazing in the doorway to the bathroom.

He'd been excited about our reunion.

Now he was sleeping it off.

And I was putting the finishing touches on another low chignon, this time I had some sultry curls escaping.

For a trip that required eveningwear, I'd of course brought a cocktail dress in a soft jade satin, streamline slim skirt that fell just above my knees, and a blousy, slouchy top that fell off one shoulder.

Bonus, it worked with the diamonds and champagne heels, the only fancy jewelry and footwear I owned.

But my mind was on Chassie, who absolutely seemed happy at the gardens, but grew silent and reflective in the car and disappeared the minute we got to the house.

Even though she did seem a bit panicky before we left The Downs, she'd settled in since and gave the impression she was fine.

Now I was worried we pushed her too far too fast.

I heard a knock on the bedroom door and called out, "Come in!" thinking it was Prue, or Tempie, but hoping it was Chassie, even if she was just coming to get me, but better if she wanted to hang and chat.

I heard the door open and called, "I'll be right out," and headed that way.

I was about to step over Bartie, when he adjusted to come lugubriously to his feet.

Since I had one foot hovering over him, he caught it, catching me off guard, taking me off kilter, and with a truncated cry, I went flying.

This again.

Great.

I landed in a beautiful man's arms.

I looked up at Battle, and my whole world righted.

"Well, darling, if you're going to throw yourself at me," he purred.

I opened my mouth to say I didn't, but then I found my mouth busy, because he was kissing me.

Proper kissing me!

It didn't even take me half a second to process it.

I wound my arms around his neck, tipped my head further back to invite him to do whatever he wanted, melted into him and let him explore my lips with his. He took the opportunity, until the tip of his tongue touched the crease, I opened for him, and he slipped inside.

Oh God.

My belly plummeted, I held tighter around his neck since my legs refused to support me, both because he tasted good and he kissed even better.

I had a hand in his hair and a deep need in my core by the time he lifted his head.

I swam out from under the haze of his kiss, opened my eyes, encountered sheer male beauty and whispered, "Hey."

His mouth and eyes smiled, up close and gorgeous.

"Hey," he whispered back.

He probably never said that word in his life, not like that, but to me, it sounded amazing.

"That was for throwing yourself into my arms," he stated.

"I didn't—"

"This is for agreeing to stay at The Downs," he went on.

And he dropped his mouth to mine and kissed me again.

Right.

The other one?

Superb.

This one?

Hot and wild and *insane*.

After a weeklong tease, we were primed.

God, *so* primed.

He went at me, and I went at him.

Then I was shuffled back, I hit wall, and he went at me harder, so I did the same.

By the time he lifted his head, I was panting, and thankfully (because I didn't want to be the only one seriously affected by our kiss), he was also breathing heavily.

"Christ, I knew that mouth would unravel me," he growled.

Ugh!

He was driving me crazy!

"Stop being sexy," I warned.

He stopped gazing at my mouth to gaze into my eyes. "Is that what you really want?"

"I'm supposed to be having a drink with your sisters right about now."

"They can wait."

"And then dinner with them."

"Maybe they'll go on without us."

"They can't." I took my hand from his hair (soft and lush, *I'm so dead*), smoothed it then smoothed the lapel on his very nice, blue suit. "I don't want you to freak, but I think today was too much for Chassie."

Slowly, his head turned toward the door.

I know it would cause emotional pain.

Damn.

He really was such a good guy.

He looked down at me. "She seemed fine when I arrived."

"Really?"

"She's down in the lounge, having a drink with Prue."

"Oh," I mumbled. "Maybe I'm being overly sensitive."

"Why did you think that?"

"She got quiet on the ride back from the gardens. Then disappeared during Prue's tour. Your house is fab, by the way."

His lips twitched. "Thank you, by the way."

"You're welcome." I used both hands to fiddle with his lapels, watching my fingers move as I muttered, "Maybe she was just being Chassie. Prue and I can talk a blue streak, and Tempie doesn't keep her mouth shut if she has something to say. Maybe she was just being quiet."

He gave me a squeeze, gaining my attention. "We'll have a mind."

I nodded.

Then I tipped my head to the side. "Who told you I decided to stay at The Downs?"

"Prue texted me earlier."

Of course.

Prue.

He pulled back just a smidge and started, "Vivienne, if—"

But I put my fingers to his lips. They even felt good.

"I can be prideful," I admitted.

He wisely kept those lips closed.

I took my hand from them. "It still makes me a bit uncomfortable, but I'll get over it."

"Good," he murmured.

"And I'm sorry I threw your generosity in your face," I carried on. "That wasn't cool."

"Darling."

That was all he said, sweet and tender, and as it was so much of both, that was all he had to say.

I grinned at him. "Do I get a kiss for giving in about dinner?"

"Only if you wish me to close that door and not see my sisters until I deposit you back at The Downs tomorrow evening," he paused, "Or Saturday morning."

"Tease," I accused jovially.

He shrugged.

I rolled my eyes.

He touched his lips to mine as I did it, so I stopped halfway through.

When he lifted away, he asked, "Are you ready to go down?"

"Just need to put on my lippie and get my bag."

With two big hands smoothing along the satin of my dress across my back and down my hips, leaving fire in their wake, he stepped away from me.

Total tease.

I successfully avoided the dog on the way back to the bathroom.

Battle lounged in the doorway watching me slick on lipstick.

"And you call me a tease," he said while I did it.

I took the tube away, looking at him in the mirror. "What?"

"Darling, your ass in that dress?"

I twisted, like I could see my ass.

"Unless you're so inclined," he began, "which thankfully, I just discovered you're not, I don't believe you'll react to it the same way I do even if you could contort yourself to see it."

This hot man thought I was hot.

God, I loved that.

I grinned at him and went back to my lipstick.

It was highly erotic, doing that with him watching me. Even dropping the tube in my bag and walking to him as I finished.

But it was only sweet when he took my hand and led me to the door, Bartholomew lugging himself along with us, as we went to join his sisters.

Hot and sweet.

That was Battle.

Or at least that was what he was to me.

It was after dinner.

Battle and I were just inside my bedroom, standing, wound together and going at each other like teenagers (again).

I was hot and bothered, I felt him hard and ready, pressed to my belly, and I *could not wait* to unveil that present.

His hair had to be a mess considering my fingers had run through it repeatedly.

He had a hand full of my ass, and *dayum*, it felt good there.

I was on the verge of dragging him to my bed when he cupped my jaw and pulled away.

I swam up from the fog of Battle's kisses, opening my eyes just as he kissed the tip of my nose in a manner that was cute, but I wasn't a big fan of it due to what I worried it meant.

"The minute I saw those freckles, I knew I was done," he whispered.

Okay, I wasn't going to get a penetrative orgasm from him first.

I was going to get a verbal one.

"Battle—"

"I go to the office early. We have a gym," he said.

No!

"But I've planned to leave early so we can be on our way," he concluded.

Hang on.

Was he going to leave me in this state?

"Battle—"

He touched his lips to mine, and there, he said, "Sleep well, sweetheart."

Then he glided his hand from my ass so it became an arm around my waist, he gave me an affectionate squeeze, let me go and walked to my door.

I was right, his hair was a sexy mess.

God!

"Are you insane?" I whispered, half frustrated, half irate.

He turned and smiled a roguish smile at me.

God!

He was killing me.

"Not in the slightest," he replied, knowing just what he was doing to me. "Have fun tomorrow."

And then…

The lout!

He was gone.

CHAPTER 15

THE RIDE

Late the next afternoon, the girls having left earlier to make their train, I left it until Battle had navigated London traffic (he needed his concentration) in his red Audi Q8, and we were on the M4, before I launched in.

"Right, François is a scream," I told him.

"Sorry?" he asked.

"Prue's favorite designer," I explained. "She called him to tell him we were showing. He had champagne and caviar waiting for us, which is gross, by the way. The caviar, I mean."

"Mm," he hummed with amusement.

"It was like the Princess of Wales showed up to try on his wild creations. Prue was so stunned. She had no idea he loved her from afar for so long."

"Loved her from afar?"

That held no amusement.

Zip.

Nada.

None.

"He's very gay, Battle, so don't get all brotherly."

Battle said nothing, though I noted he relaxed.

Such a good brother.

But maybe, in some instances, an overbearing one.

Though, maybe that was the way all good brothers were.

"I think she dropped four thousand pounds in there," I informed him. "Four hundred on this crazy black knit beanie with all these curled bits coming down. It looks like an octopus. It suits her to perfection."

He chuckled before saying, "Perhaps why he greeted you with champagne."

"Maybe part of it," I allowed. "But he still adores her. I guess they've been corresponding a little bit after she became a regular of his online store. It was really cool to see her appreciated like that. I wish you could have seen it."

"Me as well," he murmured. Then, "How was Chassie?"

"Okay. Better at the gardens yesterday. But okay."

"I noted what you said over dinner last night. She seemed preoccupied."

She did.

"Agreed."

"But not traumatized."

"Agreed to that too."

"We'll have to see," he muttered, the concern evident.

"She went. She did enjoy the gardens. I know she loves being with all of you. It'll be okay."

"Hmm."

"And it's not my place to say, but I suggest we back off and let her think on things."

He reached a hand my way, I gave it to him, and he curled his fingers around it and rested it on his thigh.

Nice.

"She's had three years to think, darling," he pointed out.

I forced out a breath.

"But no more pushing her," he conceded. "At least for the weekend."

"Well, going back on what I just said, I have a wee bit of an idea in the sense that Prue has an appointment with Ravenna next week, she asked me to go with, and I thought, if Prue's okay with it, we'd ask Chassie to go with us too."

He gave my hand a squeeze. "Perfect."

Then he put my hand in my lap, let it go and returned his to the wheel.

Although I loved holding hands with him, I appreciated him letting me go. We were just out of London, it was Friday traffic, but I'd noticed M4 traffic always seemed heavy. I was glad he intended to concentrate and keep both hands on the wheel.

"At the risk of making you dislike Chelsea more…" he began.

Oh boy.

"What?" I snapped. "Has she done something else?"

"No. It's just that Fitzy and Patsy usually have Fridays and Saturdays off, also Sunday mornings. Emily, Sundays and Mondays. And because Chelsea, Rally and Court showed last weekend, they didn't get their days off."

Ugh!

"Did Chelsea know that?" I asked.

"Unlikely. She still wouldn't care."

God, that woman.

"So, obviously, Tempie gave them Thursday off to start to make up for it," he went on. "And they won't be back to work until Tuesday, in order to fully make up for it."

"Oh, okay."

"That means Tempie will probably head into the village to grab us a curry or hit the chippie for tonight, and it'll be very casual until Tuesday. They'll have left us some croissants or something for breakfast, but we'll be eating out or getting takeaways for lunch and dinner."

I turned to stare at him.

"There are some lovely restaurants around The Downs," he said. "I thought tomorrow, you and I could go to a pub that has excellent steak dinners."

"Battle, I can cook."

"Sorry?"

I was trying hard not to bust out laughing.

"Honey, I know how to cook," I repeated.

But the instant I called him honey, the atmosphere in the vehicle became, well…*honeyed*. Thick and oozing sweet.

I powered through that loveliness and went on, "I'll take that steak dinner, but if Emily's down with me using her kitchen, I can scramble some eggs and make toast and even pancakes or something. Definitely I could throw together some sandwiches or big salads for lunch. And I've got a full repertoire of dinner selections."

He was suddenly frowning.

So I asked, "What?"

"Is this your attempt to pay me back?"

Jeez.

This guy.

"No, Battle, this is what normal people without cooks and butlers and housekeepers do. They make their own food. Anyway, not only do I love to cook, it'd be a dream to cook in Emily's kitchen. It's a chef's kitchen, for one. But for another, I'm a history junkie. Cooking in a space that has fed countless dukes and duchesses, earls and countesses, barons and baronesses, etcetera, would be so fun."

"You're certain?"

"Yes, Battle, I'm certain."

"Not tonight, I'm looking forward to a curry, or fish and chips, or tomorrow, but you can have Sunday and Monday, if it's your wish."

"Awesome," I replied, then asked, "So, Tempie manages the staff at The Downs?"

"Tempie manages The Downs."

Interesting response.

"Is there a distinction?"

"No and yes. The no part being she does indeed manage the staff, insofar as they need managing, which they don't. Fitzy and Patsy take care of everything, but they do report to Tempie. Tempie handles payroll. And manages the house books, alongside Fitzy. She also manages all the enterprises of The Downs."

"The enterprises?"

He glanced at me. "We let some of our fields to adjacent farmers. She deals with that. However, The Downs for centuries has had a herd of Lincoln Longwool sheep. We raise them, sell the wool. Or the shepherds who Tempie hires raise them. We also own six attached buildings on the High Street in the village. We let the ground floors for shops and the upper floors as flats. Tempie manages those as well. The duchy further owns four cottages at the northernmost end of our property. They used to be tenant cottages. She manages those lets as well. The Downs is an income-producing property, and Tempie has responsibility for all of it. She's essentially our steward."

"She's the steward?"

"Yes."

"So she gets email sent to the steward?"

"I have a member of staff who vets any email coming into The Downs for such purposes, so she doesn't have to wade through the chaff. But yes, if it's actionable, she gets it."

"So it was Tempie who forwarded my email to Prue," I mumbled.

"I'm sorry?"

"That's how I met Prue. I got my hands on the steward's email and mine was forwarded to Prue."

"Tempie probably knew she enjoyed your books."

Undoubtedly.

This meant Tempie had a job, and it was a big one. Chassie used to have a flourishing flower shop, though now she managed the gardens, which were a project. She was out there every day, rain or shine. But Prue seemed to be a lady of leisure.

I'd never asked, because I'd never dealt with people remotely like the Talyns.

Though, I would admit that I assumed all three of them just lived off The Downs and frittered away their days doing whatever.

"Are Scotty and Harry security?" I inquired.

"Of a sort," Battle said. "I'm in London most of the time, and I do believe Fitzy can handle most anything. However, that big house, and all it contains, primarily its most precious things, my sisters and Fitzy and Patsy, when I'm away, I need to feel they're all safe."

Okay.

Yeah.

So overbearing and overprotective was a good thing.

He kept going.

"Scotty and Harry live in the steward's cottage, a property we'd probably let if they didn't. And no, we don't need them around to serve. But yes, I do need men around simply to have men around, but also to make sure the pipes aren't leaking, and if they are, to fix them. They're both jacks-of-all-trades, but providing presence is one of those trades. Part of their regular duties is to patrol the property daily. It isn't a fortress. We can get poachers. We can also get people who want to take pictures. And there's always the threat of someone wanting to do something nefarious, even though I'll stress that threat is very minimal. The people in the village know they're right on hand, if needed. And anyone who might be watching would not miss two fit young men who can take care of themselves, and my family."

Mm-hmm.

I could fall for this guy.

Hard.

And for forever.

"There's always one on call," Battle continued. "Tempie manages their days off."

"Do they provide your speaker security at the front gate?"

"No. The gate is watched twenty-four/seven by an outside contractor who Tempie or Fitzy informs if we're expecting guests, workmen, whoever may come to call. They deal accordingly with anyone who shows at the gate. Including notifying Scotty or Harry if someone needs to be handled. Or, if some dire circumstance occurs, corresponding directly with the police."

"Right. Can they check the veracity of an ID? Like a passport or driver's license."

"Yes. They're one of the top of the line of firms who do this kind of thing, and as such, quite costly."

I bet.

"Is this for interest, or are you asking about this for another purpose?" he queried.

"For interest," I said. "What other purpose would I have?"

"That you don't feel safe at The Downs."

His comment surprised me. "Why wouldn't I feel safe?"

"There is the matter of you mentioning Christian."

Argh.

"Forget I said anything," I ordered.

"Has he shown interest in you?"

"I've only seen him twice, and I don't think he's ever seen me."

"You *are* hard to miss, darling, as is your very lovely arse, phenomenally long legs and magnificent head of hair."

All he said was delightful.

But...

Hang on.

Had he been stewing on me mentioning Christian because he was...

Jealous?

"I am quite certain, even if Christian's seen me walking to the studio, he has zero interest in me."

"And you can be quite certain of that because...?"

I walked right into that one.

"Just...a girl knows."

"Mm."

That was a very dubious hum.

He had reason to be dubious.

And I had reason to keep him thus.

"If I ask nicely, will you let it go?" I requested.

"Is that you asking nicely?"

"Yes."

"Then, yes."

I was relieved.

"For now," he finished.

I stopped being relieved.

But, for now, I'd take what I could get.

We drove in silence for a few minutes before he said, "You dropped quite the bomb about the butler's ledgers before you hung up on me Wednesday."

"I didn't hang up on you. We were done talking."

"Did you say goodbye?"

I did not.

Mostly because I'd hung up on him.

I decided not to answer.

He let it go and asked, "You think two footmen were bribed?"

"They were given three hundred pounds in bonuses. Their annual salaries were forty pounds a year. Adjusted for inflation, those bonuses were ten thousand pounds. I did not peruse it in detail to the point I could memorize it, but I did it carefully, and I saw no other bonuses for any staff in that ledger. It covers years of expenditures. Not a single bonus. Except those. And they were recorded the day after Marie's entry about something happening at The Downs."

"That does seem suspicious."

"My guess is, they saw what happened and were paid to keep their mouths shut."

"What's your course to see if you can find something out?"

"Go to the local newspaper and ask to see their stacks. Maybe something was reported around that time."

"Are you going to go to the newspaper to ask to see their stacks?"

"I want to, but it might have to wait. You see, I have this overprotective duke who I've foolishly given approval over my chapters. I'm uncertain he wants me speculating or uncovering nefarious dealings that happened at his country seat, recording them in a book, and publishing it for all the world to see."

He chuckled.

And then he urged, "Follow your trail, Vivi. It was eighty years ago. Anyone involved is probably dead. We'll see what you uncover and deal with it if you find something."

Nope.

I was wrong earlier.

I couldn't fall for this guy, hard, and for forever.

I *was* falling for this guy. Hard. And in a way that felt like it could be forever.

And I was that girl.

That girl who thought stuff like this should be out there so both parties knew what they were dealing with.

So I put it out there.

"I really like you, Battle Talyn, Duke of Burleigh."

Instantly, he held his hand to me again.

I put mine in it.

He then took it, turning it, and he kissed the inside of my wrist.

A lick of heat raced down my arm, smoothed over by the feather-weight sense of deep affection.

That was the best response he could give me, but he one-upped it.

"And I very much like you too, Ms. Vivienne Dupree, bestselling novelist."

He pressed my hand to his chest and then again placed it in my lap.

I let that moment dwell between us with all the warmth and exquisiteness it could give for a few miles.

Then I requested, "Can I ask you something else?"

"You can ask me anything, darling."

Totally really liked him.

"You've mentioned Prue drawing. Tempie has too. But Prue has never mentioned it."

He was visibly surprised. "She hasn't?"

"She also didn't tell me she had cats. When I asked her about it, she shared she thought I'd think having six cats would make me think she was a crazy cat lady. After what you said about what she endured at school, I understood. Someone thinking she was weird and not wanting that. But drawing isn't weird, so I don't know what to do with the fact she never told me she does it, and it seems, she's very good at it."

"She isn't very good at it. She's exceptional."

"So I don't get why she would keep that from me. It seems obvious it's her thing."

Battle said nothing, until he muttered, "Bloody hell."

"What?"

"She draws, yes. She also writes."

Oh my God.

Another thing Prue never told me.

"She writes?"

"Both. She produces graphic novels."

Holy crap.

"Seriously?"

"Although they're not my usual genre, I've read them, and they're all superb. It could be bias, but I don't think so."

"Are they sci-fi? Fantasy? Goth?"

"Fantasy romance. Fae and dragons and things like that. The imagery is beautiful, and the stories have depth."

"Has she looked for an agent? A publisher?"

He glanced at me, and he didn't have to say anything because I read it from his glance.

"She hasn't," I stated what I read in his expression. "She's hiding her light under a bushel again. And she didn't tell me because she thinks...I don't know. Maybe that I might think she's using me for my publishing connections, or she doesn't think her work is good enough, or whatever those fucking bitches at her school, and your fucking father who didn't protect her from them, make her think."

Battle was again silent.

And I realized I'd allowed my mouth to run away from me.

So I rushed into damage control.

"That wasn't my place. To say 'your fucking father.' I never met him, and I shouldn't say things like that about your dad. But I can't hide that it really upsets me, the effect his decision had on Prue. Tempie told me more about it. How she didn't have sleepovers or get invited to parties. It must have been really, really bad, but he didn't intervene. And it had to be so bad, she's thirty-one years old and just met the designer she adores whose boutique is a two-hour train ride from her home."

"My fucking father was a fucking piece of shit. I don't mind you pointing out that truth. But this won't work, Vivi, if you don't feel you can speak your mind. I thought you already knew that, and it was one of the multitude of things that attracted me to you. Many dance around me to curry favor. From the beginning, you didn't. It was refreshing and incredibly alluring."

Well.

Gee.

Was I blushing?

"It's clear we won't see eye to eye about everything," he said. "It's also clear we have the capacity to discuss it if we don't. And I have questioned my sanity about this since I met you, but the truth is, I enjoy rowing with you. You demonstrate a quick wit, a strong will and courage every time you do it. So please don't bury that habit now."

Okay.

It was safe to say it might only take a car ride across England to fall for this man.

Boy, I was in trouble.

"Are we agreed?" he asked.

"We're agreed, honey."

"Brilliant."

"And we might share the same mental ailment, because I think it's hella fun to bicker with you two."

"We don't bicker."

"Battle, we totally bicker."

"We have words."

"Okay, Your Grace, however you want to look at it," I teased.

He shot me a quelling look.

I grinned at him.

Then I pointed out, "Like we just semi-kinda bickered about bickering."

He heaved a sigh.

I let it go and said, "I hope it's curry. I haven't had a truly good curry since I was in England the last time."

At that, within moments, the dash was ringing.

Tempie picked up. "Everything all right?"

"Vivi wants curry for dinner tonight," Battle declared.

"Battle!" I snapped, turning to slap his rock-hard biceps.

"Anything particular?" Tempie asked through the dash.

Battle raised his brows to me.

"Get what you want," I said. "If you want to go to the chippie, that's cool too."

"I was getting curry anyway," Tempie replied.

Battle raised his brows to me again.

So he'd pay attention to the road, I gave my order.

It was long.

Battle was chuckling at the end of it.

"Well, it would appear we'll have plenty of leftovers to nosh on over the weekend," Tempie drawled when I was done. "I consider my mind is a steel trap, even so, perhaps you can text all of that to me so I don't forget anything."

"I will, Tempie," I said.

"Excellent. Is that all?" she asked.

"Yes, love. We'll see you soon," Battle said.

"Ta-ra," Tempie replied and disconnected.

"That was unnecessary," I spoke the minute I knew she was gone.

"She was getting curry anyway," he pointed out.

I huffed in my seat and crossed my arms.

"And now she's irritated because she's getting what she wants," he murmured, but he sounded amused.

"Oh, do shut up, Your Grace."

"As you wish, darling."

Totally amused.

Ugh!

I decided to shut up myself.

Of course, this only lasted about five miles before I took another five miles (approximately) to text Tempie my curry order.

And then I just had to share about the see-through purple monstrosity François told me I just *had* to try on, and I did, but I didn't buy it, and not because it cost two thousand pounds. But because it was a monstrosity.

And what did Battle ask after I told him this?

"It was see-through?"

Because...

Of course he did.

And I'd walked right into that too.

CHAPTER 16

THE WALK

That night, I lay in bed, staring at the dark canopy, the room bathed in moonlight, two cats curled against my body.

A body that was still vibrating after the makeout session Battle treated me to at my door when he'd walked me to my room at the end of the night.

Like in my room at his house in London, it had been hot and heavy, and like our first kiss, he'd eventually pressed me to the wall so it would hold me up and leave his hands free to roam *most* pleasantly.

My hands roamed too.

As did both of our mouths.

One could just say, he would one hundred percent have had lipstick on his collar, if I'd been wearing any.

But then, he'd tipped my head, kissed the top of it then ran a thumb over my lower lip before he said, "I'll see you at breakfast, sweetheart."

And he'd sauntered away.

Sauntered!

Away!

Now, I could see him making the call not to go there with me the first time when his sisters were in bedrooms close to mine in the house in London.

Yes, it, too, was a huge house.

But it wasn't nearly as big as The Downs.

So that begged the question, since all their bedrooms were clustered around the corner to the south wing, and his was at the very end of it, not to mention mine was in an entirely different wing, and as far as I could tell, the walls were very sturdy and practically sound-proofed, why he wasn't going there now.

We were agreed we were exploring this.

We'd been exploring this even before we agreed we were doing it.

And on our trip from London, I'd eventually gotten around to telling him about the conversation in the train and that we had his sisters' blessings.

So…what was going on?

Flirting was fun.

Teasing was fun too.

But this was torture.

"Fuck it," I said to Snowball and Gingerface.

They didn't move.

They did when I threw the covers back and got up.

I went to the bathroom.

They came with me.

I turned on the lights, winced against the brightness and walked to the mirror.

I wasn't a sexy nightie type of gal.

Sure, I had a few, but I hadn't brought any of them.

Therefore, I was wearing a pair of plaid sleep shorts and a shelf-bra cami.

My hair was back in a ponytail, my face clean and shiny with moisturizer.

I did not look like a sex kitten.

I looked like a co-ed.

"Ulk," I groaned, pulled the ponytail out of my hair and fluffed it.

Better, but not great.

"Whatever," I bit off and looked down at Snowball and Gingerface, who were both sitting beside me, gazing up at me curiously.

As they would.

This was not our protocol.

"Let's do this," I said with more bravado than bravery.

If Battle didn't want this, if he wanted to take it slower, if he needed to be in control of it, I knew he'd find some way to say that to me where I wouldn't be totally humiliated I took this walk.

But if he needed some kind of explicit consent from me, something I would have thought he knew he had after I got my hands on his tight ass that night, then he couldn't mistake me knocking on his door in my jammies.

I turned out the lights, and me and the cats stepped into the darkened hall illuminated by low floor lighting that was probably always on when it was dark so anyone could get to and from their rooms without breaking their necks.

The cats bounded after me on the longest walk I'd ever taken in my life.

We could just say, along the way, I changed my mind three times, and once, even stopped.

But I made it to Battle's door to see it partially open, and a light was coming from the opening.

He did what I did.

Left the door ajar, in his version, for Baby Blue to join him without having to faff about with a doorknob with paws and without opposable thumbs.

And that was what happened, even before I gathered the courage to lift my hand and knock.

Snowball and Gingerface slithered into his room.

"Shit," I whispered.

The door flew open.

My eyes flew up.

Battle was in a pair of drawstring pajama pants, navy with little pinstripes.

And that was it.

His broad chest was adorned with the most perfect smattering of dark chest hair I'd ever seen *in my life*.

My mouth got dry, and I was pretty sure I was going to faint again.

Fortunately, Battle's arm hooked around my waist, and he hauled me into his room so forcefully, I would have cried out, but my mouth automatically swallowed it.

He slammed the door behind me...

Slammed it!

And turned me, still in his arms, walking me backwards across his room, his gaze locked to mine.

"Done being teased, darling?" he purred.

Did he...

Did he...!

...force me to take that walk?

Doing it so he could win our game?

One I didn't know (okay, I did) we were playing?

"You're a jerk, my Lord Duke," I tried to snap, but considering I was pretty breathless, it came out breathy.

He smiled a slow, wicked smile that reminded me of my first impression of him.

The villain.

The marauder.

The rogue.

My panties flooded.

He bent his head and kissed me.

During the kiss, he turned, fell, I fell with him, and he landed on his back in the bed with me on top of him.

Oo.

Lovely.

I wasn't on top for long.

He rolled us so he was on top.

He was warm and heavy.

Way lovelier.

We kissed. We touched. We tangled.

This didn't last long before he got his hands in my cami, shoved it up and, *whoosh!* it was gone.

His lips hit my neck, trailed down, and they closed around my nipple.

Nice.

I slid my fingers in his hair.

I was so enamored with what his tongue was doing to my nipple, I missed his hand sliding down my belly, into my sleep shorts, but I sure didn't miss it as it pressed into my panties, down, around, and he sucked hard at my nipple as he filled me with a long finger.

"Oh my God, *Battle*," I gasped.

He surged up to take my mouth as he finger-fucked me, and *damn*, all of that felt good.

And then he was gone.

Entirely.

And then my sleep shorts and panties were gone.

Entirely.

After that, he pulled me to right in his bed, slipped down my body, kissed my stomach, spread my legs, and he went in.

"*Oh my God, Battle*," I moaned, sliding my fingers in his hair as he ate me, and damn, damn, *damn*, the man knew what he was doing.

I undulated under his ministrations, mindlessly begging for more.

Battle gave it to me.

"Baby," I eventually whispered my warning after he took a hard draw on my clit that was a miracle didn't wring an orgasm out of me, then dipped his tongue deep into my pussy.

He pushed up to his knees between my legs, then dropped to a hand in the bed to reach to the nightstand.

I reached to his drawstring.

I tugged it loose, pulled his pants down, and his thick, delicious cock sprang forth.

"For fuck's sake, how are you perfect *everywhere?*" I complained.

"Lie back, Vivi," he ordered after he straightened.

I looked up at him. "Are you high?"

He grew visibly confused.

I shifted to all fours, and with zero fanfare, sucked that beautiful big dick deep.

"Bloody hell," he groaned, his fingers gathering my hair at my nape.

I blew him and I blew him, and then I put more effort into blowing his goddamned mind by blowing him some more.

Eventually, he grasped me under my arms and yanked me up to my knees.

His jaw was hard with the effort of not coming, his pupils were blown, that was the sexiest thing I'd ever seen, and he made it sexier when he growled, "I'm finishing in you."

"All righty," I agreed.

He kissed me, and I knew something else was going on, I heard the foil tear, but I was concentrating on his tongue dueling with mine.

I knew he'd taken care of business when he wrapped an arm around my waist and hauled me up.

I curled my arms around his shoulders and my legs around his hips.

He gazed into my eyes as his other hand moved between us.

And then he dragged me down and filled me.

Oh God.

Beautiful.

Gorgeous.

Life.

My head fell back and then my body fell back because Battle was again on top of me, and he was fucking me.

His eyes holding mine, his hand cupping my jaw in a gesture that was not tender, but claiming (and I *adored* it), his thumb tight on my lips.

He pressed.

I opened.

He slid his thumb in.

I sucked it hard.

He growled and fucked me harder.

He got my drift when I nipped the pad of his thumb, he pulled it out, I gasped, *"Honey,"* bucked under him, curled my arms and legs tighter around him, arched my neck back and came.

Blinding...

Earth shaking...

Mindless...

Amazing...

Oblivion.

With a thumb in the flesh under my chin, he pushed my head even further back, bit hard at my neck, I convulsed under him as another orgasm built instantly and washed through so strong, I had to fist a hand in his hair to hold on lest it sweep me away.

And then he filled me, groaning deep and gorgeous, as I held his big body while it shuddered through his orgasm.

He rolled us even before it was fully done, so I was straddling him and lying on him as he finished and came down.

I knew he was out of the thrall when his hands began to meander, though one meandered quickly to my ass and laid claim pretty vehemently, considering the pads of his fingers were pressing into my cleft.

Oh yeah.

The duke really liked my ass.

"Rule." His thick-from-his-orgasm, luscious voice filled the room. "The first time I have you after I return from London, you don't suck my cock."

I lifted my head to look down at him.

He seemed peeved.

But I was worried.

"You didn't like it?"

He cupped the side of my head. "Vivienne, I nearly blew in your mouth. Twice."

I grinned.

"I see you're proud of yourself," he groused. "But the first time I came in you, it wasn't your mouth I wanted to come into."

"I almost came when you were going down on me," I shared.

"That would be acceptable."

"So why wouldn't it be acceptable the other way around?"

"Because I said so."

My eyes got squinty, then, since I'd lost his dick, I rolled off to my back and bitched to the ceiling. "Oh my God, I just fucked an arrogant, bossy duke."

His amazing face filled my vision. "No, darling, an arrogant, bossy duke just fucked you."

He gave me a quick peck, then shifted, chucking the pajama bottoms neither of us fully divested him of, before he crawled over me to get out of bed.

I watched his criminally fantastic ass (though, I did give his beefy thighs a gander) as he moved into a dark room.

It lit, he disappeared, and I saw a lot of black tile.

The bathroom.

I shifted in bed until I was under the covers and then saw a gray, floppy-eared head pop up over the side.

"Hullo, handsome," I greeted Bartholomew.

He looked at me, gave me a half-sleepy, half-happy pant, then he slid down out of view.

I felt the distinct movement a bed makes when a cat lands on it and looked over my shoulder.

Baby Blue was there.

While I watched, Snowball joined her.

Gingerface came up the rear.

Snowball and Gingerface were checking out the lay of the land.

Baby Blue just plopped down to stake her territory.

I sensed movement and looked the other way to see an equally delicious full-frontal view of Duke Six-Pack-Fabulous-Cock-Even-Semi-Hard strolling my way.

"We have company," I told him.

He made it to me, lifted the covers, slid in beside me, then grabbed hold of me, pulling me on top.

"They'll have to come back," he said.

"Why? Baby Blue is already comfy."

"We're going to be very busy, Vivi."

Oh, lovely.

I thought that.

I went for coy.

"We are?"

"Quiet and kiss me," he ordered.

"So bossy."

"All right, I'll kiss you."

After rolling on top of me (scattering cats), he did.

And then we got busy.

Indeed, we were so occupied, we didn't see the muted blue, green and purple lights dancing through the windows that faced the ballroom.

And once we passed out, we definitely didn't see the light change only to blue.

Before it faded away.

CHAPTER 17
THE BREAKFAST

A soft knock on the door roused me from a deep sleep.

For a second, I didn't know what was happening.

Then my bed moved, since my bed was a tall, built, sex god aristocrat. I was gently set on my belly on soft sheets as Battle slid out from under me.

Blinking and pushing up on an elbow, I watched him pull on his pajama bottoms then go to the door.

He opened it a smidge and immediately looked down.

He then opened it fully, bent, grabbed something and came up with a wide silver tray. He kicked the door closed with his foot as he walked what looked to be breakfast toward the bed.

"Um…" I didn't quite start as I gathered the sheets and duvet to me.

We weren't loud, as such.

But it seemed the girls knew of last night's activities.

Unless they routinely brought breakfast to his door when the staff were away.

Battle set the tray on the bed, stating, "I would be touched if that didn't look appalling."

I turned my attention to the tray.

Burnt toast. What appeared to be solid oatmeal. Badly hacked into grapefruit halves in bowls. A pot of jam. Two coffee cups in saucers, a little jug of creamer, and a cafetière of what appeared to be the strongest pot of coffee ever made.

The only thing on it that wasn't terrifying was an adorable, tiny, stemmed glass with pretty buds sticking out of it.

But there were two cups.

Yeah.

They knew I was in here.

"Your sisters really can't cook," I said to the tray. I looked up at him. "That's the visual representation of 'it's the thought that counts.'"

He smiled at me, then he swooped in to give me a soft kiss.

After he did that, he walked into the bathroom and shut the door.

I kept the sheets around me as I poured coffee.

I gave it plenty of room for cream, but even so, once I'd mixed it, I could tell by the color it needed more.

When he came out, he had a gray dressing gown with him.

He handed it to me, murmuring chivalrously, "Just in case you prefer modesty."

He was just *so great*.

I shrugged it on, climbed out of bed while he climbed in, and I tied the belt, trapping the voluminous material around me as he called while I walked to his bathroom, "I got out an extra toothbrush head, if you like."

So great.

I did my business including brushing my teeth.

And I did this in a very modern, all-black bathroom (it even had a black soaking tub). The only break in the black was some gold fixtures and pendant lights and a few green plants here and there (even the towels and mats were black).

Being nosy, instead of going back to the bedroom, I poked my head into the next room over and saw more black. This had white and gray accents, but it was a closet, about three times the size of mine, and the built-in dressing table at one of the two windows in the space was even better. Though, it was empty.

Put there, waiting for the duchess to move in.

Hmm.

His closet had an island in the middle, where I could see open-sided drawers filled with rolled ties and displayed cufflinks and the like. The island was flanked with benches with tufted ivory velvet tops that you could sit on to put on your shoes.

It wasn't full, but there was a duke in this house who liked his clothes, that was certain.

I headed back to the bedroom, and although I wanted to study the shirtless man lounging in bed with a cup of coffee, I finally took in his room.

Juxtaposition was his thing, because this room was mostly white.

There was a thin black stripe around where his duvet would fall over the edge of the bed when it was made. But the big seating area on the other side of the room (yes, by a fireplace) had two white couches facing each other, flanked with two white chairs, also facing each other. All of this was on a white rug edged in two thin black stripes.

There were no old paintings or portraits on the walls.

But there was a clear crystal Lalique sculpture of the nude dancer, and a black one of a hunting panther.

However, the minimalism was extreme here except…

I stopped dead as I spied the portrait over the fireplace.

It was of a man's torso. He was wearing a light-blue button-down covering his wide chest. He had his hand in the pocket of his jeans.

However, instead of a head, over the open neck of his shirt and the strong column of his throat was a stunning, drifting trail of flowers, cut rubies and prancing cats that filled the black background of the top half of the painting.

Tears instantly hit my eyes.

"Come here, Vivi," he called.

I looked to him.

He was watery.

"Is that you?" I asked.

"Yes. Prue painted it."

Oh my God.

"Darling, come here."

I wandered there.

He pulled me into bed beside him.

"It *is* you," I snuffled, nuzzling into him. "It's so very you."

"I was moved by it, yes."

I looked at his face (or tried, I was still crying). "It's so beautiful."

He tucked my face in his neck and wrapped his arms around me.

"I need to see her work," I mumbled into his skin.

"Prepare to be deeply impressed."

"You make me wish I had a brother.'

"Well, I put a fair amount of effort into our activities last night, so I'm uncertain about that being your response this morning."

I laughed and slapped his chest lightly, pulling back and gazing at him. "You know what I mean. Not *you* as my brother, specifically. Though, a brother just like you."

"I hope that's what you mean."

I touched his face before I glided my fingers over his hair and got my shit together.

Then I dashed my fingers over my cheeks and asked, "Do you think they heard us?"

"Doubtful. What I think is, it's nearly ten, and someone went looking for you. When they found your bedroom and the studio empty, they came to the obvious conclusion."

That tracked.

"Did you see anyone in the hall?"

"No."

I reached for my coffee cup. "Where are the animals?"

"They went out through my dressing room. They need breakfast too."

They did.

"Will someone see to that if the staff isn't around?"

"Even Tempie makes it her mission to provide sustenance to our pets on the rare occasions she's the first one up and they need feeding."

I found this entirely easy to believe.

"It's nearly ten?" After asking this, I took a sip of coffee and came instantly alert in a way I would be until tomorrow at that hour with the power-packed punch of caffeine I just swallowed.

"You were insatiable last night. You kept me up very late," he explained instead of answering my question.

"*I* was insatiable?"

"You have a very greedy mouth," he paused, "and pussy."

"Ugh," I grunted.

He angled in to kiss my neck.

"I'm not complaining," he said when he pulled away.

"Well, I am. The condoms have to go, Your Grace."

He raised his brows.

"I have an IUD. And I'm clean."

It was my turn to raise my brows, and I did it over my mega strong cup of coffee.

"I don't go in unprotected, sweetheart."

I could see why.

He had a lot to take for someone who was up for taking it that way, and I would suspect there were many women who were.

"Your call," I said to the coffee.

"I mean no offense, Vivi," he said gently.

I focused on him. "Honey, I get it. You're loaded. It should be your choice, just as it should the woman's." I smiled at him. "You're deft with application." My smile died. "I just want it to be as good for you as it is for me."

"That's very sweet, darling." He came in for a lip brush. "I'll bear it in mind."

"All I ask."

"But I'm concerned you have any fears it wasn't good for me."

"I said *as* good."

His eyes twinkled. "Ah. Rest assured, I do believe it was *as* good. I promise."

"Mm," I hummed.

"Now, the question is, are we going to attempt to eat this?" He gestured to the tray.

I reached to grab a spoon and stuck it in the oatmeal.

It remained on end.

I turned to him. "I think…no."

"I don't even believe Bartie would clean that mess for us, and he eats everything. I'll go down and see if there are some croissants."

"How about I go down and scramble some eggs and make some non-burnt toast?" I offered.

"How long will that take?" he asked curiously.

He was cute.

"Maybe fifteen minutes. With walking there and back time, maybe twenty-five."

He smiled at me and moved from the bed, saying, "No. It's croissants."

I wasn't going to object.

Though, as I watched the muscles of his back bunch and flex while he walked to the door, I called, "Hurry."

He shot me a smug look before he opened the door.

"That means fast, Battle."

He shook his head and disappeared.

I sank into his big, comfy bed and smiled to myself.

Then I took another sip of super strong coffee, set it aside and reached for a grapefruit half.

We'd just done it again, and miracle of miracles, Mr. Control the Proceedings let me be on top.

Battle was a cuddler after, which made me rejoice, because I was too.

And that was what we were doing.

Cuddling.

Though, it was sexy cuddling, because we were naked, and most of his "cuddles" involved drawing random patterns on my ass.

"I'll return," he whispered, slid me off him, got out of bed and went to the bathroom.

I pulled the duvet up the front of my body and wrapped my limbs round it, waiting for his return.

He didn't take long, and when he came back, he tugged the bedclothes from my grip and positioned us as we were before he left me.

"I see your point about the prophylactics," he muttered after he had me where he wanted me.

Aw.

He didn't want to leave me.

"Still your call," I said.

"We'll see."

His fingers went back to drawing.

I rested my cheek on his shoulder and let them.

Eventually, he wrapped his arms around me and just held me.

Was there ever a better Saturday?

No.

Not ever.

"Do you miss her?" he asked softly.

I lifted my head to look at him. "Miss who?"

"Your mum."

For the second time that day, dang it, tears filled my eyes.

He shoved my face in his throat and said, "Stupid question. I shouldn't have asked."

"She was stay at home. Dad worked. She was going to go back to work when I was in kindergarten. That happened earlier, necessarily. They were young. Just starting out. New family. Crushing mortgage.

He had a life insurance policy, but it pretty much only covered his funeral. I learned this all later, from Gram. Mom had no choice but to sell the house and move in with them. It was only going to be until she got on her feet, but we became a family, so we stayed. I don't think she liked it. But she did like there was always someone there for her girls. Someone to get them from school or take them to a friend's house. Someone to help with the grocery shopping. She worked reception at a dentist's practice. She was there for twenty-three years. She didn't make a ton. We had more because we had them."

"She never remarried?"

I got choked up, swallowed it down, and said huskily, "I guess Dad was a hard act to follow."

He gave me a squeeze.

I pulled out of his throat to look at him. "She was great. The one good thing was, after Solène and I left, Mom could get a little house of her own. She loved that house. Did it up exactly the way she wanted. I just wish she had more time in it."

"I do too, for her, for you."

I gave him a shaky smile and continued, "Gram and Gramps were great too. We were really happy. We didn't know we didn't have much. Both my grandparents were teachers, so they weren't rolling in it either. But we had each other, and the way they raised us, with a lot of love, laughter, support, togetherness, that was all we needed."

"That's beautiful."

"It was. And I'm glad you have a version of that too, with your sisters. I think that's why I'm so comfortable here. There's a lot of love in this house. It's a big house, but it still feels like a home."

It was only after I said that, woefully, when I realized the long length of his body under me had stiffened.

"Shit, did I say the wrong thing?" I asked.

"You think this house is full of love?" he asked in return.

"You don't?" I queried hesitantly.

"I've never thought on it."

"Well," I said carefully, "it is." Even more carefully, I stroked his jaw and whispered, "And it's obvious you're the one who built that."

"She was raped."

Now my body stiffened.

Straight to stone.

"Some monster who was a guest at a wedding she did the flowers for," he went on.

Oh no.

I mean, that was what I was guessing happened.

But I hated to have it confirmed.

"He asked her out. She had a boyfriend. She declined. He refused to be put off and wasn't, in the end. He cornered her in the back of her shop after closing, beat the fuck out of her because she fought, and probably because she didn't say yes when he wanted her to, and he raped her."

I framed his head in my hands and had no words to say except an aching, "*Battle.*"

"She was terrified of him. Closed the shop. Broke up with her boyfriend. Came home. Refused to press charges. She didn't want it in the press. She didn't want anyone to know. She didn't want to have to testify."

I pressed lightly on his head and remained quiet as he recited the litany of what any woman faced when this happened to her: having to make the decision whether or not to endure another violating trauma after experiencing the worst violating trauma a woman could experience.

"Buried herself in the garden. Tempie and Prue begged her to go to therapy. She refused. They stopped because just broaching it brought the subject up and they didn't want to cause her more pain. I..." he swallowed with difficulty, "couldn't go there with her."

"Of course," I said tremulously, because this man, knowing what happened to his sister, had to have come undone.

It didn't happen to him.

But anytime something heinous befell someone you loved, in a way, it happened to you too.

"I fucked up, Vivi. I warned Tempie and Prue off. I told them to let her heal how she needed to heal. But the days turned to months, and now it's been years, and I see all I did wasn't giving her a safe haven to find a way to heal her wounds and accept her scars. It was allowing her to close the door on her own prison."

"You take too much responsibility."

"Tempie was right. We should have pressed therapy. We should have pushed her."

"And maybe push her away?" I shook my head. "No. You did the right thing. It's up to her to chart this course, honey."

"Three years, Vivienne?"

I flinched.

"Right," he muttered.

"That isn't on you. It's not on her either. It's on that man. God. What an asshole. Did *anything* happen to him?"

His face shut down.

Oh boy.

"You did something," I whispered.

"He raped my sister," he said through his teeth. "And I'm stupid rich. Yes, I did something."

I grinned.

Huge.

"What did you do?"

He stared at me like I was crazy.

"You can tell me," I urged. "You didn't make me sign an NDA, but I swear on all the orgasms you've yet to give me, I will take it to my grave."

"We established yesterday we're fond of each other."

Fond?

That was tame for what I was feeling, but it worked for now.

"Yes," I confirmed.

"I'd prefer you remained fond of me."

"All right, allow me to share, as a woman, there is not one thing you can tell me you did to a man who violated a woman that way, especially Chastity, but really anybody, that would make me even an iota less fond of you."

"I had him beaten," he said like a dare, "and raped."

My eyes got big.

Then I busted out laughing.

I pushed up, and through my hilarity, said, "Oh please, tell me you're serious."

"I was emotional at the time, Vivienne. It wasn't my finest hour."

"Oh, you are so wrong, my overprotective duke, it *soooooooo* was. Seriously? The whole hog?"

"It was very costly," he muttered.

"Did he press charges?"

"No, considering they told him it would keep happening if he uttered a fucking word."

"They?"

"I sent three."

This just got better and better.

"Did they all...?" I let that trail off.

"I didn't ask for specifics. Just confirmation it was done."

"Oh my God, this is *magnificent*."

He rolled on top of me and warned, "Chassie and Prue don't know."

I pretended to lock my lips with a key, then said, "Let me guess, it was Tempie's idea."

"No. But she sanctioned it."

"I bet she did," I mumbled. Man, I dug that woman. "This is priceless. I love it."

"It doesn't erase what was done to my sister."

That made me pull my shit together and soothe him with my hands.

Oh yeah, that muscled back was *amazing*.

"No, honey," I agreed. "But even if she was his first crime, she might not have been his last. But I bet that made it so it was."

"Well, since they told him it would happen to him again if he did it to someone else, and they'd be paying attention, I would reckon so."

"Have you been watching?"

"He hasn't even been out on a date."

I tried not to smile.

I failed.

He watched me and noted, "You're rather bloodthirsty."

"I'm actually all about rehabilitation and establishing hearty social programs to alleviate conditions that would lead to disenfranchisement, such as after-school activities, paying for school lunches, increasing minimum wage, redistribution of wealth through taxes—"

I didn't finish because he groaned.

"Oh shit," I said. "You're a Tory."

"Fiscal conservative," he amended.

"A Tory!" I accused.

"Center leaning."

"Oh my God, I spent the night fucking a conservative."

"And you enjoyed it greatly," he purred.

"Thank goodness you don't have a second amendment here."

"The duchy owns twelve shotguns."

I forced my hands in between us in prayer position and begged, "Please tell me you don't hunt. Please, please, pretty please."

"I don't hunt. But I do trap shoot, and we host sporting clays."

"Trap shoot?" And since I didn't know the other either, I added, "Sporting clays?"

"Clay pigeons. Trap shooting is from a stationary position, but the angle the clays are launched is varied. Sporting clays is when you're in a simulated hunting scenario. In other words, I shoot. I just don't shoot anything that's breathing."

I grinned, grabbed his head and pulled it to me to kiss him.

He took over what was supposed to be a quick kiss, and it got interesting.

Some time later, when he put me on my knees with my face in his downy pillows, and he was taking me from behind, it got seriously interesting.

Okay, he was a great fuck and a magnificent man.

I could forgive him for being a Tory.

Or…a fiscal conservative (I decided to think of it like that).

Then again, I was coming to terms with the fact I would probably forgive Battle for pretty much anything.

And that didn't scare me one whit.

CHAPTER 18

THE CANDIDATE

"Battle," I moaned.

Then I came.

For his part, Battle kept fucking me against the wall of his shower.

Around the second time we did it after we returned to the house from going out for steak dinners at the posh pub where he took me on our first out-of-The-Downs, his-sisters-not-around date last night, he'd stopped reaching for the condoms.

I got it, they were a pain.

But I was honored, since it said he trusted me.

And of course, since then, I'd showed him that gratitude…repeatedly (though, right after the first time he did it (or didn't do it, as this case was), I'd touched his face and whispered, "Honey," and from his expression, I knew he understood me, or rather, I understood the immensity of what he'd just given me).

So this time, when he climaxed, I felt the warmth of his cum jetting inside me.

Mm…

So much better.

Just him.

And me.

Nothing in between.

He rocked into me through the aftermath and then held me, because that was his way.

And I loved his way.

Finally, he pulled me off his dick and kept his hands on me until he knew I was steady on my feet (that was his way as well, and obviously, I loved it too).

And we finished our shower.

I tripped on a ragdoll cat when I was stepping out.

But fortunately, Battle was there to catch me.

"They live," Tempie drawled as we walked hand in hand to the breakfast room.

I felt my face get hot.

One could say I never in my life expected to be on the greatest sex-a-thon of all time with the hottest guy in existence, only to end it wandering into a room filled with his sisters.

But there we were.

And as for Prue, for some reason, she was there wearing her octopus beanie.

"Not another word," Battle warned, guiding me to a seat.

Tempie just smiled her cat's smile.

"You two missed the delights of the chippie last night," Prue told us.

"I don't think they missed anything," Tempie was still drawling.

"Stay," Battle said into my ear after he seated me. "I'll get your plate."

Watching him go to the sideboard, and doing this with confusion because he'd told me himself it would be empty, I heard Chassie chime in, "I thought I saw you guys leave last night."

"We had dinner at a pub," I told her.

"The Nag's Head?" Prue asked.

I nodded as I poured coffee.

"They do great steaks," Prue said.

"I learned that last night."

"Good Lord, Battle. Is that a love bite?" Tempie asked, her gaze narrowed on my neck.

I stopped pouring cream into my coffee to lift a hand to cover my love bite.

He scowled over his shoulder at his sister. "What did I say?"

She smiled again.

He turned his attention to the chafing dish. "What's this?"

"I scrambled eggs!" Prue chirped.

This I had to see.

I got up and stood by Battle to peer at the messy, wet, underdone slop in the chafing dish that had cooked bits of eggs floating nauseatingly in it.

Mercifully, Battle put the lid on it and looked down at me. "Darling—"

"Speak not another word," I cut him off and turned to the room. "No offense, Prue, but I'm not sure that's healthy to eat."

"I didn't want them to be overdone," she replied.

She achieved that.

"This is why we're all sitting here, starving, waiting to see if you two would unearth yourselves from Battle's room to ascertain if we should try to find somewhere open to serve us breakfast," Tempie said. "Or if we should send Battle to the grocery store for American muffins or something, seeing as someone ate all the croissants." She narrowed her eyes again, this time on Battle.

"It wasn't us," Battle replied.

"I got peckish yesterday afternoon," Chassie mumbled.

Good God, this lot wouldn't last a day on *Naked and Afraid*.

"Right, consensus," I announced. "You get one thing. Pancakes and bacon? Eggs and bacon? Or French toast and bacon?"

"American pancakes?" Prue asked.

"Obviously," I answered.

"That's my vote," she trilled.

"That sounds amazing," Chassie said.

My eyes homed in on her.

Something was…

Different.

"Is it much effort for you to toast me a muffin?" Tempie requested.

"No," I said distractedly, attention still on Chassie. Then I informed them, "It's going to take about thirty minutes."

"I can wait," Prue said.

"Can I help?" Chassie asked.

"You can flip bacon."

I noted Battle took his seat, reached for the coffee pot and didn't say a word.

Men.

I grabbed my cup and Chassie and I headed for the kitchens.

Once there, it took a second to get the lay of the land.

Then I set about making the batter so it could rest for a bit. After that, I toasted an English muffin for Tempie and sent Chassie up with that and a tray of accoutrement for the pancakes. While she was gone, I got the oven warming and the bacon frying. When she got back, I gave her a set of tongs and instructions and set up the griddle to heat.

It was then I realized this was the first time I'd spent any with Chassie alone, and knowing what I now knew, I was at a loss for anything to say.

Though, glancing at her, she seemed content with silence.

I rarely was, so I asked, "Did you have fun in London?"

"That restaurant Battie took us to for dinner was really good," she said. "And I haven't seen Mrs. Pattinson for a while. It was nice to see her."

She said this.

She didn't whisper-say it.

That was what tweaked me about her earlier.

She still had a quiet voice, but her words no longer practically disappeared the minute they left her lips.

"Well, I had a blast,' I replied. "François was hysterical."

As she nudged bacon, she gave me a shy smile. "He was pretty funny."

"I loved how he was with Prue," I remarked.

"He's got a crazy-big crush on her," she replied with a teeny smile on her mouth.

He didn't, since I highly suspected he was gay.

I wasn't falling into a stereotyping. He wasn't effeminate or anything like that.

It was just that he was so comfortable around women, especially four attractive, interesting women (says me), which would immediately make a straight man go on the prowl with at least one of us.

Though, one could say he did go on the prowl with Prudence.

Hmm.

I poured batter.

She watched.

"I used to cook a little when I was in Bath," she offered.

I fought hard not to show a response to this throwaway comment that was far from throwaway.

Okay, was it good she was talking about her other life?

I didn't know.

And it was so hush-hush, I didn't think to ask.

Then again, I'd spent time with her, and she'd never mentioned it before.

"Just ready-meals and such. Take and bake. Things like that," she went on. "So not real cooking, like this."

"My grandmother used to say that every woman should have a month's worth of meals in her inventory that she can cook without a recipe." I leaned toward her and said *sotto voce*, "But she was from a different generation."

"Do you have a month's worth of meals in your inventory?" she asked.

"Yes. My lasagna, which I'm thinking of making you all tonight. And spaghetti with meat sauce. Tuna casserole. Tacos."

"Oh, I love tacos," she said.

"Do you want those tonight?" I asked.

She shook her head. "No, because one of Battie's favorite things is lasagna."

"Then lasagna it is," I decided, seeing the bubbles forming on the pancakes so I flipped them. "You can turn the bacon over," I told her.

She started turning.

"You like him loads, don't you?" she asked the bacon with more than a small amount of hope in her voice.

"He's infuriating."

She looked to me.

"And maybe the most interesting, kind, thoughtful, generous man I've ever met," I finished.

She smiled.

And this time, it wasn't teeny.

God, I'd never seen that come from her like that. So easy.

And free.

Could her quiet reflection and Battle and Tempie's not-so-gentle-anymore nudging be working?

We cooked in silence—or stared at the food cooking and did it in silence, because there was nothing more to do.

After I set the pancakes on a plate and put them in a warming oven, she waited for the inopportune time when I was pouring more batter to share, "Tempie has a boyfriend. Oh no!"

The "oh no!" part of that was me pouring a stream of batter across the hot griddle.

"What did you say?" I asked her.

She was staring at the griddle. "That streak is cooking, Vivi."

I scraped it off, re-oiled, and poured four more pancakes.

Then I looked to her. "Tempie has a boyfriend?"

"She doesn't want anyone to know. But I hear her talking to him on the phone. I've talked to Prue about it, and she's heard it too."

"Do you know who he is?"

She shook her head. "No. I think he's from London. Or at least, the conversation I overheard yesterday, he seemed mad she was in London and he didn't see her."

Oh boy.

"She has a flat there," she told me. "She isn't there as much as Battie because…"

Because she was at The Downs with Prue and Chassie.

"Battle told me how much responsibility she has here," I remarked.

Her head snapped to the side to look at me.

Shit.

She thought I was talking about her and Prue.

"You know, the sheep and the cottages and the lettings in town and all that," I explained. "It sounds like things are pretty busy for her."

"Oh yes. That." Now she was nodding her head. "I think she's busy. But she's so organized, I also think, in a way, it runs itself."

I bet Tempie ran it like a well-oiled machine.

"I'm hoping, now that Battie's found you, she'll come out of the closet, you know, proverbially," she said.

I grinned at her. "I get you."

"She's funny about her men," she muttered, then asked, "Is this done?"

"Yes, honey, grab a plate and put a paper towel on it. Then put the bacon on the towel."

Her brows were knit. "Paper towel?"

"What do you call it?" I snapped my fingers repeatedly. "Shit. Oh! Kitchen roll!"

"Right," she said and headed to the kitchen roll.

Once she was transferring the bacon and I'd flipped the pancakes, I asked, "She's funny about men?"

"Both Battie and her are about people they're seeing. They tend not to introduce us to the ones who aren't *candidates*."

Yikes.

Candidates?

"Though," she carried on, "Battie isn't as strict about it. However, he will share before we meet someone," she took off his deep purr, "'she's not the one.'"

That made me laugh out loud.

"He hasn't taken us aside to tell us you're not the one," she went on.

I quit laughing as a happy shiver drifted over me.

"I don't think either of us would have gone there if we weren't…if this wasn't…" I faltered.

"I get it," she said and lifted the plate of bacon. "Should I put this in the oven too?"

"Yes, and grab a mitt. I want to add these pancakes to the others. Then one more round and we're done."

We did that, and while the pancakes were cooking, she turned fully to me.

"She likes you, loads and loads, so I think maybe you can tell her, you know, that Prue and I…we're…" She rolled her head on her neck. "She doesn't need to baby us anymore. She can have a life."

Oh yes.

Either she'd done some reflecting, or she just knew what her sister was up to.

"She's known me two weeks, honey," I said gently. "Don't you think it'd be better coming from you?"

"I've already said it to her. She doesn't believe me."

If Temperance was who I thought she was, she had not missed that Chastity was no longer whisper-talking, so she might be more inclined to hear her and believe her now.

"Maybe try again?" I suggested. "And if it doesn't work, I'll…" God, was I going to offer this? I guess I was. "Talk to her."

"That'd be wicked," she whispered happily.

I could only hope that Tempie noticed the change in Chassie herself.

Fortunately, not much slipped by Tempie.

"Wanna try your hand at flipping a pancake?" I offered.

"Please?"

I handed her the spatula. "You have to wait until the batter bubbles, then you can flip."

When the time came, her first go was a disaster. But I tidied it up. The second and third were much better, and the fourth was superb.

"See! You perfected it in four!" I crowed.

A pretty pink blush colored her cheeks.

"Right, grab a mitt and take the bacon up," I ordered. "I'll finish these and be right behind you."

"Will do."

She was on her way with the bacon when I called, "And you tell them, if there aren't two rashers waiting for me, I'm not cooking again!"

"Will do that too!" she called back, loud, no wispy whisper attached.

Healing.

Or at least, I fucking hoped so.

"This is for the birds," I bitched.

"Use your legs. Let go of the pommel," Battle instructed.

"*You* let go of the pommel. I'll hit the dirt if I do."

Battle reached out and grabbed the reins of the beautiful gray roan mare who had the unfortunate luck to have me hauled up on her back half an hour ago.

She was a good girl all through Battle giving me a twenty-minute riding lesson before we headed out.

But she got stuck with a dud in me.

With some "whoas," tightening my reins and his, he stopped us.

"And why don't you have those sticky-uppy pommels like American saddles do?" I demanded.

"Have you ever seen an American saddle?"

"In Western movies."

"So, when you said you'd never ridden, you really weren't joking."

"Look, Your Grace, not all of us were born with an English riding saddle in the barn."

He studied me, visibly fighting laughter, and if I thought I could do it without falling off this damned horse, I would have smacked him a good one.

"Can't we go back, and I'll ride you?" I offered hopefully.

With that, he burst out laughing.

"I wasn't being funny," I said through it.

And I wasn't!

He then took my life in his hands by nabbing me at the back of my neck, pulling me to him and laying a wet one on me.

I was a little dazed when he was done, but miracle of miracles, I kept my seat.

"I like riding," he said softly, his hand still warm on the back of my neck.

"Okay," I replied.

"And I like you," he went on.

The kiss daze was receding, but at that, it came back.

"Okay," I repeated.

"And it would mean a lot to me if you learned how to ride so we can do it together."

Argh!

"However, if you really hate it—" he began.

"No, no, no. I'll get the hang of it."

Maybe in ten years.

"We'll go slow. Find your seat. Trust Noelle. She doesn't want you to fall off either. And you'll start to get comfortable."

I nodded, even if my nod was a total lie.

"Ready?"

I nodded again (and again lie-nodding).

He let go of me and the reins, clicked his teeth and dug in his heels, and I did the same.

We started walking slowly.

How embarrassing.

Well, out of this at least I got a mini-tour of the south side of The Downs, which included mostly parkland, but obviously, the stables along with Chassie's greenhouse (of course, it was bigger than I expected it would be) and the garage, which was a surprising clip away from the house (Battle had told me to hang on the steps while he went to get the car last night, he was gone a long time, now I knew why).

And on our journey, he pointed out the gamekeeper's cottage tucked in the edge of the trees in the south forest (no Christian, though), as well as the steward's cottage, which was opposite the gamekeeper's, close to the tall stone fence at the front of the property.

Now we were riding in the field that I always saw sheep in.

And today was the same in regard to the sheep keeping us company.

"Things go well, cooking with Chassie?" he asked.

I was oh-so not going to point out she was different and how. If he didn't notice, and it wasn't what I thought it was, I didn't want to give him hope.

So I said, "I taught her how to flip a pancake."

"Those were delicious, darling."

Honestly?

It made me feel good to make them all breakfast, and not because I liked to cook.

Because I felt like I was doing something for them after all they'd done for me.

Though, I would never tell Battle that.

Hell no.

I'd hold that to me until I died.

"Glad you liked them."

We walked, or our horses did.

Then I asked, "Hey, do you know if Tempie is seeing someone?"

He turned his head to me. "Why do you ask?"

"Because Chassie said she's seeing someone."

"Chassie knows?"

I guess that rumor was true.

"She is? Tempie, I mean."

He nodded and turned forward. "She is."

"So, he's not a *candidate*?"

At that, he whipped his head toward me.

"Oh yes, Battle, she used the word," I shared.

Again, he turned forward, muttering, "I'm seeing the disadvantages of you being close to my sisters."

"Really? You and Tempie use the word *candidate*?"

"Tighten the reins, don't pull, and squeeze her with your full leg, not your thighs," he instructed.

I did that, and Noelle stopped.

Well, hell.

It worked!

His blood bay, Oberon, stopped too.

"You should know something," he announced.

Oh boy.

"What?" I asked.

"I will never live anywhere but The Downs or Burleigh House."

"You *are* the duke, so I can't say that's a surprise."

"And neither will my sisters."

"But, Chassie says Tempie has a flat in London."

"Tempie has a flat in London because I walked in on her blowing a man in the lounge at Burleigh House."

I grimaced.

"Yes, sweetheart," he agreed. "Click your teeth, slack the reins, and loosen your legs."

I'd already done the leg bit, so I did the others, and Noelle and I started walking again.

Oberon and Battle did it beside me.

"She and I decided to give each other space until we settled," he shared.

"You could have just made a rule that any kind of fornication happened in a bedroom or put a sock on the door to the lounge or something."

"That would disallow both her and I to get creative."

Since I'd been the recipient of some of his creativity, I got that.

"Why does settling matter?" I inquired.

"It was simply a pact we made so we could get beyond how mortifying it was for both of us when I walked in on her. However, from that experience, I believe we both learned our lesson."

I should say.

Tempie was the shit.

But, yuck.

"It was a kneejerk reaction on her part," he explained. "Tempie has her pride, and a certain reputation she cultivates. If she needed that distance, I wasn't going to stop her."

He'd do anything for his sisters, so that was no surprise either.

"But she would also need an excuse to let the flat go and come back," he continued, "And our pact gave her that."

"Ah."

"Did you hear what I said earlier?"

I turned to him. "I heard it all, but which part are you referring to?"

"I'll always live with my sisters, and they'll always live with me."

Their vow.

"It isn't like you live in a two thousand square foot, three-bedroom, two-bath house, Battle," I pointed out. "Either residence."

"That doesn't bother you?"

"Honey, I walked to the breakfast table all three of your sisters were sitting at after a sex-fest and with a visible love bite. If I can survive that, and do it making pancakes, I think I could handle…"

Oh shit.

"You can handle…what? Living with my sisters?" he prompted.

I did the whole tighten-reins/lightly-squeeze-legs bit, and Noelle stopped.

So did Battle and Oberon.

"Are you saying I'm a *candidate*?" I asked breathlessly.

"It troubles me you keep emphasizing that word, but I'm seeing you understand the importance of it, so I can confirm you absolutely are. Now, does that trouble you?"

Okay, he'd had to heft me up in that saddle, something he did with ease, but I wasn't sure he'd be up to doing it again if I got off Noelle and did a dozen cartwheels in the sheep field.

So I focused on something else.

"You know…*already*, that I'm a *candidate*?"

"I would hardly walk you to the breakfast table with a love bite I gave you with all my sisters in attendance if you weren't."

"Chassie says you warn them about the ones who aren't the ones."

His mouth tightened but he loosened it enough to say, "Very much seeing the disadvantages of you being so close to my sisters."

"Battle," I called.

His gaze sharpened on me. "I would also hardly keep my sister's best friend in my bed for thirty-six hours if I didn't feel deep feelings for you, doing it understanding those feelings will only grow deeper."

Why was I on a fucking horse?

And…

Would he beg off if he saw me do a dozen cartwheels in a sheep field?

"Oh my God," I snapped. "Can we get off the horses so I can ride you in a field?"

A slow, very naughty grin formed on his lips. "Sheep shit in this field, darling."

"Gross."

"Indeed." He clicked his tongue and kept going.

So I did too.

"So, these *candidates* will have to know it's The Downs, Burleigh House, and the Talyn family forever, and be all the way down with that, correct?" I asked, just to be sure.

"Are you ever going to stop emphasizing the word 'candidate?'"

"Does it bug you?"

"Yes."

"Then, no."

He grunted in annoyance.

It was fucking adorable.

"To answer your question, yes," he said. "And they lose if they have an issue with it."

"As in, they get kicked to the curb."

"Absolutely."

"I bet Chelsea wasn't at one with sharing The Downs and Burleigh House," I muttered.

"The girls were told she wasn't the one before I even brought her here when I was seeing her."

"I'll bet."

"Then again, I'd known her for years, so she'd been here before."

"Right."

"But yes, if it had ever gotten to that point, though it never would have, she would have been ousted because she's an avaricious, privileged bitch who would want everything to herself, including me evicting my sisters."

"She sure would," I agreed.

"Hamish, however, is madly in love with Tempie. She doesn't give anything away, but they've been together for over a year, and I know my sister. She wouldn't invest that time if her heart wasn't in it. And he's an outdoorsman. He'd love The Downs."

"Hamish?"

"Yes."

"Please tell me he's Scottish."

"I don't know if I've met a more Scottish Scotsman."

I hoped I got to meet him.

And when I did, I hoped I understood him when he talked. A pronounced Scottish burr was practically indecipherable to me.

Though indecipherable, it was invariably hot.

"She's going to lose him if she doesn't quit fucking him about,"

Battle stated. "He's not a man who'd put up with that for long, even from a woman he loves. Maybe especially."

Shit.

"Maybe, have a word with her?" I suggested.

He looked to me and raised his brows.

"Are you saying you want me to?" I bleated in panic.

That made two Talyns putting the lean on me to interfere in Tempie's life.

I dug her, she was awesome, but the only reason she didn't scare the pants off me was because she liked me too.

"Fuck no," he replied to my deepest depths of gratitude. "No one tells Tempie what to do."

"You order her around all the time."

"She ignores me most of that time."

This was true.

"She's sticking close to home, and him out in the cold, for Chassie," I deduced.

"She is."

Shit again.

"Chassie heard her talking to him yesterday, and apparently, he's pissed she went to London without seeing him."

"You and I have had one day and two nights in my bed, and two weeks of teasing, and if you came to London for even an hour without seeing me, I'd be pissed at you."

Wow.

He *really* liked me.

I smiled smugly to myself.

"I see you're coming to understand where I'm at," he noted.

I looked at him to see him watching me.

"The Duke and The Novelist is a shit title, but I bet some publisher would publish it," I replied.

He shook his head but did it with his lips curled up.

"How's this?" I started. "I'll talk to Prue, and I know she'll be okay with it, then I'll talk to Chassie about taking her with us to visit

Ravenna. If that goes well, I'll find some way to remind Tempie that I'll be around for a while, I can keep my finger on the pulse, and if she wanted, I don't know…I have to find a better word for it, but for now I'll say…*a break,* she can take it."

"Darling, you're brilliant. That might work."

I tried not to preen. "I have my uses."

"You're also no longer clutching the pommel."

I glanced down.

"Holy hell!" I cried. "Look at me!"

"Care to try a canter?"

I wasn't sure.

"Do you think I'm ready? I mean, I've only been on this girl for half an hour."

"You know how to stop, so do that if you're feeling uneasy."

I could do that.

"Let's go for it," I decided.

"Loose reins, give her your heels, guide her behind me. She'll follow."

I nodded.

"Ready?"

Another nod.

He studied me a moment to be sure I was all good (he was so sweet).

Then he took off.

I did as told, and Noelle and I took off after him.

I couldn't say I wasn't uneasy. The first few minutes were a little hair-raising.

I could say I didn't give up, and I kinda got the hang of it.

In the end, though, even if it was a little scary, it was still awesome.

CHAPTER 19

THE ABSENCE

Early Monday morning, I woke to a hot guy nuzzling my neck.

I turned in his arms, murmuring a drowsy, "Baby."

He tipped up my chin and didn't bother with preliminaries.

He took my mouth in a deep kiss.

I melted into him, but even so, Battle slid a hand between my legs, cupping me there. Using his hold, he yanked me forcefully so I was plastered to his body and had no choice but to hook a leg over his hip.

I was rewarded for this first by the rush of wet it caused between my legs, and second, with deeper kisses and his fingers wreaking delicious torture on my clit and in my pussy.

Once he had me whimpering into his mouth and pumping against his fingers, they glided away, only for something bigger, thicker, harder and much, much better to take their place when he slipped his cock inside me.

He also stopped kissing me.

But with his hand fisted in my hair at my nape, his eyes held mine all the while our lips brushed, our labored breaths mingled, my hands clutched his back, my nails digging in, and he thrust inside me.

The look in his eyes was carnal, sinful, downright diabolic, possessive, assertive and demanding.

Yeah.

All that.

It was fucking amazing.

And the hold he had on my hair pretty much meant I couldn't move anything but my hands, which felt illicit and crazy exciting.

So yeah, that was fucking amazing too.

Therefore, when he slid his free hand between us and toyed playfully with my clit, I came apart.

"*Battle*, baby," I breathed, rocking my hips to try to get more of him.

"As I said," he growled, "greedy."

He pinched my clit.

I exploded.

His mouth took mine so he could consume my orgasm that way as well.

Talk about greedy.

When it was done, he rolled us so I was on my back. He came up on his knees but rested back on his ankles, dragging my ass up his rough thighs to keep our connection. He wrapped my legs around his hips and grasped mine, slamming me into him as he slammed into me.

I was still panting, my breasts bouncing, as he watched me with that lethally hot look on his face, then he dropped his gaze to my body, our connection, and he watched himself take me.

Seriously.

If I thought the look on his face was carnal before, I was wrong.

That look was carnal.

It was so hot, the pressure built up inside me again, and I almost lost it, but then he shifted his hips, adjusted his angle and banged against *the spot*. So with a deep moan and long whimper, my second orgasm surged through me.

I heard his grunting, felt his pounding come stronger, faster, and I pushed myself out of swimming through the depths of pleasure so I could watch when his handsome head snapped back, the muscles and veins in his neck straining, as he drove into me repeatedly through his climax.

He gentled his thrusts, his fingers moving tenderly over my thighs, his gaze never leaving me.

I lay before him, on display, feeling beautiful, feeling powerful, feeling loved, under the open warmth and affection that he had written all over his handsome face.

I wasn't sure which expression I liked better.

Thankfully, I got both.

What I did know in that moment was, unless something wild and unforeseen happened, I was going to be the next Duchess of Burleigh.

I wasn't the candidate.

As ludicrous as it seemed, from the moment I walked into this house, it claimed me.

And from the moment I laid eyes on this man, he did.

Naturally, this made me deliriously happy.

He fell forward onto his hands at my sides, did the downward part of the pushup and brushed his lips against mine.

"Best lasagna I've ever tasted, darling," he said there.

Oh yeah.

I'd made it for him.

And oh yeah.

He'd liked it.

Also yeah.

So did all the girls.

And the last yeah, and maybe the best part, after we ate it, Battle came downstairs and helped me clean the kitchen.

Straight up, as crazy as it sounded, of the many things that made him insanely attractive, watching him dry a plate was one of them.

"I have to shower and go," he murmured.

I frowned and wrapped my arms around him.

"Keep me with you today," he said.

I didn't get that.

"Pardon?"

He tensed his hips between mine, forcing my lips to part, because that felt so good.

"Don't wash me away."

One could say this was a turnabout from our condom discussion.

"Can you go back to sleep with me slipping out?" he asked.

Right.

Was I weird?

Why was this convo turning me on again?

"Yes," I answered.

"Good," he whispered, touched his mouth to mine and bid, "Go back to sleep. I'll kiss you again before I leave."

"Do you want me to hustle down and make you some breakfast?" I offered.

"I don't want you to move."

I smiled at him and smoothed a hand over his hair.

He kissed me, no brush on the lips this time, before he slid away, arranging the covers over me.

I watched him walk to the bathroom.

I wouldn't have thought it possible, hearing the water of the shower going and knowing he was in there, wet and soapy and naked, that I could fall into a drowse.

But that was what I did.

I woke up when I felt the covers pulled up to my shoulder and then tucked in.

I turned my eyes to the sides to catch him dipping in.

He kissed my temple.

"Back to sleep," he said when he pulled away. "We'll connect during the week. And I'll see if Janelle can rearrange my schedule so I can be back Thursday night."

Janelle, I'd learned yesterday, was his PA.

"Absence makes the heart grow fonder, right?" I said unconvincingly.

"If it were up to me, I'd pack all those crates in the Audi and take you with me. But you've made the studio your space. I'm not creative, but I know a creative needs their space. Am I wrong?"

"No, but—"

He sat beside me on the bed. "And I work all day, darling, late. No point you being stuck at Burleigh House alone only for me to come home, us to eat then fuck and me to leave you alone again in the morning."

I could argue this, but I wasn't going to.

Because I had work to do at The Downs, and not only book work.

"In order that we can continue to get to know one another," he went on, "and I can do my part in alleviating Tempie feeling the need to be here to look after Chassie, I'm going to ask Janelle to arrange my schedule so I can work from here half a week. After this week, I'll try to sort it so I'm home Wednesday evening."

I smiled brightly.

He kissed it from my lips.

When he lifted his head, he ordered, "Now, go back to sleep."

"You be careful on that motorway," I ordered in return.

"Always," he murmured.

Another lip brush, a sweet, sexy smile.

Then he was walking away.

Late that afternoon, I was in the studio, marking photos I wanted to ask Battle if I could use to reproduce in the book, when my phone, lying on the desk, vibrated.

Since Snowball was napping on it, she let out a displeased mew, rolled and glared at it.

I left the photos arranged across the chaise, went to the desk, saw the call was Battle, so I took it right away.

"Hey, honey," I said, rounding the desk and sitting in the chair.

"How's your day been?" he asked.

"Do you want the good news, or the bad news?"

"Shit," he muttered.

"Okay, let me rephrase. None of it is really bad news, as such."

"Let's start with that, then."

"This morning, I called the local paper and asked if they were publishing in 1946. They were. I then asked if they would be all right with me perusing their stacks. When I told them who I was and what I was working on, they said they'd pull all the digital files for the dates I was looking for. So I went into town after lunch and had a good gander at everything two weeks before the date Marie recorded in her journal, and two months after."

"Let me guess. Nothing," he deduced.

"There was a national preoccupation with some viscount from Northumberland going missing. But considering Northumberland isn't super close to Devon, and he was last seen in his club in Newcastle the day before Marie's entry, no. Nada."

"I'm sorry, darling."

"You want the good news?"

"Absolutely."

"I asked Prue to come with to help look, and she did. I also asked Chassie, and without that first hesitation, she agreed to go too."

I could hear the happy in his voice when he said, "Excellent."

"Not even a little hesitation, honey," I reiterated.

"I think you're having a positive effect on her."

I was stunned.

"Me?"

"You *have* been key in urging her out of her shell."

"I appreciate you wanting to hand me so much credit, but I just gave her the opportunities, as have Prue and Tempie, because another stroke of good news is that we're all going to meet Ravenna on Wednesday. Even Tempie."

"And even more excellent."

"But none of us should forget it's Chassie who's doing the heavy lifting. None of us are forcing her into cars or trains. She's taking those steps herself. These are her victories."

For a second, he said nothing.

And then he said, "You know how very fond of you I am."

Fond wouldn't be the word I'd use.

But the way he used it, I was totally down with it.

"I know."

"I hope so, because I am very fond of you, Vivienne."

My heart skipped a beat.

"And I'm very fond of you too, honey," I replied just as something at the windows caught my attention.

Christian was walking through the garden again.

"I've spoken with Janelle," Battle said in my ear while Christian passed. "Alas, she's not very fond of me right now, but I'll be home Thursday evening this week and working there from Wednesday on, for the most part, for at least the next six weeks."

"That's awesome, baby," I said distractedly as I slowly got out of my chair and surreptitiously moved to the windows to see if I could get an angle toward the house and gardens to see if Chastity was on Christian's trajectory.

It wasn't a good angle. I was very much secluded by plants and shrubs and trees. I could see a hint of the caps of the north and south wings, but not much more.

And no Chastity.

"Did I lose you?" Battle said in my ear.

I turned away from the windows to give him my attention, but as I did, I saw something on the other side.

I focused on it.

Chastity was standing, wearing a pretty yellow sundress, and since the day was warm, no cardie. She had garden gloves on her hands, clippers in her fingers, her hair was a chaotic glory…

And she was gazing after Christian with…

Holy shit!

Longing.

"Vivi?"

I stared at her.

"Vivienne," Battle growled in my ear. "Are you there?"

I twirled from the window and moved back to my desk chair, saying, "Sorry, yes. I'm here. I got distracted by some photos."

Lie!

"Photos?"

"Would you be averse, if my publishers wish to print them, to me publishing some photos in the book?"

"No. Though I'll add a caveat it depends which ones. Then again, I can't imagine there would be anything in them I'd have concerns about sharing publicly."

"I'm flagging them. I can show you when you get home."

"That works."

"It's a plan."

"Am I still in you?"

His words gave me a full body shudder.

"Yes," I whispered.

"Brilliant, darling," he purred. "Now I must go. I'll text a goodnight."

"I will too."

"Speak soon."

"I hope so."

"Goodbye, sweetheart."

"Bye, Battle."

We disconnected.

I tapped my phone on my smiling lips.

Then I got up and went back to the windows.

Chastity had moved further into the garden in the direction Christian went. However, now I could only see her frizzy hair.

It was like she was following him.

"Seems the tables have turned," I said to the cats (Gingerface had claimed a precarious perch on the top of a crate). "Or maybe Christian's playing a clever game. Hmm."

Since I had a book to write, I had no choice but to let that go and get down to it.

~

That evening after dinner, Prue and I were in the smoking room, which had been turned into the television room.

It wasn't until then that I noted The Downs had an underabundance of TVs. I didn't have one in my room. Battle didn't have one in his either. The only rooms I'd seen them in was this one, the games room (where the TV was ginormous, like lowkey home theater ginormous), and the study.

It was the first time I'd watched TV since I came to England.

There was something freeing about that. Something even triumphant, living a life so full you didn't turn to mindless things like the telly to fill it.

But it was still nice to laze on a comfy couch with a friend, sharing a bowl of after-dinner popcorn that Fitzy brought us and watching old episodes of *Rosemary and Thyme.*

I'd never seen it.

It had broad hints of goofy, but it was also very charming, and Laura was a scream.

We were at the end of one episode, waiting for the next one to come up, when I broached it.

"I saw the portrait of Battle you painted in his bedroom."

I did it casually, not even looking at her, but I felt the tenseness in the air after I said it.

"Girl, that portrait is unbelievable," I enthused "I, like, instantly started weeping when I saw it. Battle had to comfort me. It's so beautiful, and it captures him so perfectly. It's the epitome of why abstract art is so powerful. If you understand the meaning, it will blow you away."

"You started weeping?"

I turned to her. "Totally. Battle told me he was moved by it, and it hangs in his room, he sees it all the time. But I could tell, he wasn't moved by it. He's *moved* by it. Still. And sister,"—I smiled at her—"that room is as minimalist as it comes, and the man displays it there. Pride of place. The focal point of the whole room. I would say not only does it move him, he treasures it. I had no idea you painted. But you've immense talent."

I was hoping this didn't come off as a why-didn't-you-tell-me whine.

I was also hoping it would open the door to her sharing more.

"I love it that you reacted so strongly to it, Vivi," she said timidly.

"I hope you have more," I said leadingly.

"I...fiddle."

"Well, if you ever want to show me, I want to see it."

She curled her shoulders in.

Shit.

"Your stuff, your decision," I mumbled.

The next episode had started playing, and to end this discussion, Prue asked, "Do you want me to rewind? It's a mystery. We shouldn't miss anything."

"Yeah, honey, let's rewind."

I was disappointed she wasn't ready to go there with me.

But I didn't lie.

Her stuff, her decision.

That said, if her novels were even remotely as imaginative, original and thoughtful as that portrait, they should be seen, and she should get the accolades for them.

Baby steps.

I was falling in love with a duke.

Chastity was emerging.

Tempie needed to be encouraged to get on with her life.

And Prue needed to embrace her talent.

All in good time, I told myself.

All in good time.

The next morning, Scotty said to me, "Repetition is key. It becomes second nature. Like driving a car. And the more you work with the same animal, the more your minds meld. I know that sounds barmy, but it's true. She'll sense what you need from the barest movement of your hands on the reins or your legs on her barrel."

I nodded.

"So stop and start," he instructed. "In a circle. If you feel it, kick her up to a trot or even a canter. If you go canter, lean into it. Reduce your center of gravity to give you balance. Stop and start again."

I nodded a second time and was about to do that, when my phone at my ass rang.

"Hang on," I said.

This time, he nodded.

I pulled it out and saw it was Battle.

"Hey there," I greeted after I took the call.

"Hullo, sweetheart. How's your morning?"

"I'm going to go in and saddle Troilus," Scotty called. "After you do more circles, we'll head to the field."

"Okay," I said to him.

"Is that Scotty?" Battle said in my ear.

Well, crap.

"Yes."

"Troilus?" he asked.

"You all seem to have a thing for Shakespeare," I mumbled.

"Vivienne, what are you doing?"

I'd wanted it to be a surprise.

Though I didn't want to let him go to voicemail.

However, I probably should have given Scotty the heads up about that.

"Scotty is giving me another riding lesson," I admitted.

Total silence.

Complete.

I attempted to read it and said quickly, "Don't be mad. You're a good teacher. It's just that I wanted to get more practice so I wasn't such a dud, and we didn't have to walk the horses so much when you got back home. I hope you don't mind I asked him, and he's teaching me, and I'm riding without you."

"Stop speaking," he commanded.

I stopped speaking.

"I do not mind."

Oh boy.

He was enunciating every word very clearly, and his voice was so far from a purr, it wasn't funny.

It was gravel.

"All is good there?" he asked.

"Yes," I answered quietly.

"Good. I'll leave you to your lesson, and Vivi?"

"Yes, honey?"

"My father loved my mother. My mother used my father. As I was a young boy, even as I felt it, I had no idea I lived shrouded in his devastating heartbreak that she loved the title he gave her and the life he gave her more than anything, and she felt nothing for him at all. It was only when I was older that it came to me. It helped me to understand a little why he was so distant, formal, unapproachable, and eventually bitter. It didn't excuse it. But it helped me understand it."

Listening to him say this, my heart was breaking.

And not for Atlas Talyn.

For his son.

He kept at me. "Your books could soar, and it is highly unlikely you'll ever be as wealthy as me. But don't you ever, *ever*, darling, mistake what you offer to me. Am I understood?"

Oh man.

I was about to start crying.

So my, "You're understood," was croaky.

"Quickly, I've adjusted my RSVP to Rally and Court's wedding to give your name as my plus one. Court texted to say she's delighted you're coming. Is that all right?"

"Perfect," I pushed out.

"All right, sweetheart." Now he was purring. "I'll text my goodnight."

As he did last night, the perfect boyfriend, never allowing me to think I wasn't on his mind.

"I will too."

"Have a good day, Vivi."

"You too, baby."

We hung up.

I managed (barely) not to burst into happy tears.

And by damn, it was true.

Somehow absence *did* make the heart grow fonder.

On this thought, Noelle and I started and stopped, started and stopped, I kicked her up to a trot, then to a canter, leaning into her, and we stopped again.

Eventually, Scotty came out on Troilus.

And we headed to the field.

CHAPTER 20

THE CLAIRVOYANT

I was a little bummed that Ravenna's fortune-telling lair wasn't a cottage covered in vines, surrounded by flowers, and so cute it would attract unsuspecting children so she could cook them and eat them.

It also wasn't a creepy, rundown manor house with dead rose bushes outside and cobwebs everywhere.

It was a flat above a Boots in the town centre.

It was Wednesday afternoon, after we'd gone to a cute bistro in the village for a lovely lunch.

No, my book wasn't progressing very rapidly.

Yes, I was ready to start writing.

However, I could get so stuck into a book when I was writing, I forgot the time, sometimes forgot to eat (or shower), and usually railed at anything that would take me away from it.

So I thought it best to go over notes, augment the outline to help me write more efficiently when I got down to it, and hit the book on Monday when Battle went back to London.

Tempie parked her sparkling black Defender (totally the vehicle of the landed aristocrat with style) in the town centre car park, and as we were walking to a door beside the pharmacy, Prue ordered her older sister, "Be nice when you get there."

"I'm always nice," Tempie replied.

Chastity made a dissenting peep, and it wasn't a whisper-peep.

"All right, so I don't suffer fools," Tempie conceded. "It's a good trait."

"Do as your name suggests with that trait with Ravenna. She's sensitive to emotion and undercurrents and—" Prue didn't quite finish.

Because Chastity, coasting effervescently ahead of us, broke in to tease, "Ley lines?"

Prue gave Chassie a startled hopeful look, then moved it to Tempie, who was giving her youngest sister a contemplative hopeful look. She caught Prue's gaze then they both looked to me.

I shrugged.

I also smiled.

They were getting it.

Yippee!

Prue put in a code at the door, it buzzed, and we went in and up the stairs.

She knocked on the door.

Bummer part two, Ravenna didn't look like Angelica Huston or that chick that played Rowena in *Supernatural,* or Melisandre in *Game of Thrones.*

She was about an inch taller than Prue, had bigger breasts than Chassie, bleach-blonde hair, a heavy hand with makeup, and I suspected she was around my age.

"Come in, come in," she said distractedly. "I'll start the tea."

We walked into bummer *numero* three.

There was no velvet, tassels, fringed scarves thrown over lamps, circular tables with long tablecloths and crystal balls in the center, or pentagrams carved into the floor.

Instead, it was an open-plan kitchen and lounge with slouchy, comfortable-looking furniture and a hint of a mess (nothing gross, only discarded shoes on the floor, cast aside cardies over the arms of chairs, and copious tea mugs scattered about).

"I'm not certain the woman understands how to set a scene," Tempie leaned into me to say under her breath.

I gave her big, shut-up-and-stop-trying-to-make-me-laugh eyes.

I heard the undeniable sound of the button on an electric kettle being pressed as Prue said, "Ravenna, I'm really excited to introduce you to my sisters, Temperance and Chastity, and my dear friend, Vivienne."

Ravenna turned, looked at Tempie, Chassie, and when she looked at me, her head jerked, her body lurched, and she was falling.

"Goodness! Ravenna!" Prue cried, rushing forward to latch on to her to keep her on her feet.

"Please," Tempie whispered skeptically beside me.

Ravenna kept her eyes glued to me as she steadied herself with Prue's help.

"Do you need some water?" Prue asked. "Here, let's get you down and I'll see to the tea."

She walked her to the sofa and Ravenna sat in it, consistently, and freakily, staring at me.

"I'll be on tea," Chastity chirped.

I hoped her tea was better than the coffee whoever brewed for Battle and me.

"I'm fine," Ravenna decreed, finally tearing her attention from me. "It's just, the veil has been unpredictable now for weeks. I don't understand it. I've never felt anything like it. And sometimes, it makes me dizzy."

Prue seated herself beside her clairvoyant. "Do you have any idea what it might be?"

"No, but it's a very strong disturbance."

"We're having Cook's homemade gnocchi for dinner tonight," Tempie leaned into me again to say in an undertone. "I don't have time to go searching for Obi-Wan Kenobi."

I elbowed her.

Ravenna eyed her.

Then she reached to the coffee table, picked up a set of cards and offered them to Tempie.

"You first," she said.

Tempie raised one hand, palm out, and turned her head to the side: the universal aristocrat's gesture of "no thanks."

"Anyone who walks through that door gets read," Ravenna stated inflexibly. "If you're not going to be read, I'll have to ask you to leave."

Hmm.

Seemed Ravenna had some backbone.

With some interest, I watched the staring contest play out.

But I knew how it would end.

And it ended that way, with Tempie lighting the barest glance on Prue before she reached out and took the cards.

"You can shuffle them," Ravenna educated. "You can move them around. You can simply just hold them. And when you feel you're ready, give them back to me."

I pressed my lips together to hide my smile when Tempie instantly handed the cards back.

"Ladies, take seats," Ravenna invited.

There was a couch with two armchairs opposite, a coffee table in between.

Tempie and I took the chairs.

"Chassie, you can bring one of the kitchen chairs over when you're done," Prue called.

"Okay," Chassie replied from the kitchen.

She did this as I heard the switch go off on the electric kettle.

"Is there anything you want me to look for?" Ravenna asked Tempie.

"Aren't you supposed to ask that before you give me the cards?" Tempie asked Ravenna.

Ravenna dipped her ear to her shoulder. "Would you like to tell me how to read them as well?"

Tempie fluttered a desultory hand at the coffee table. "Carry on. Let's do a general reading."

Immediately, Ravenna flipped three cards on the table.

They were neither major nor minor arcana. Prue told me ages ago that Ravenna didn't read with a regular deck but used other cards.

Even though I knew there were many decks, this was one of the reasons I thought she might be a fraud. Easier to hide behind those since, at least the major arcana, such as Death (change), The Chariot (triumph), The World (completion), was easy to read.

"Intrigue," Ravenna said, gazing at the three cards. "Inaction." A long pause and then, "In love."

The room went wired on the last two words.

And although we were all feeling that, mostly it was coming from Tempie.

"This,"—Ravenna tapped what I was guessing was the Intrigue card—"is beyond your control, and although in your realm, it's not in your inner sanctum. You will witness it, but it only peripherally involves you, and you have no control over it."

She put a finger on that and scooched that card aside.

She then picked up the card that I suspected was Inaction. "*This* is a problem."

She picked up the other card.

In Love.

"Because *this* is at stake."

She dropped both cards and tossed two more down.

Without lifting her head from studying them, she said, "You must go forth purposefully, and with consideration, not for yourself, but for the one you've won, but you may lose if you don't act promptly."

She tipped her head back and skewered Tempie with her eyes.

"Your actions have been selfless, but now that you're hiding behind them, they've become nothing but selfish."

Oh boy.

Prue gave me huge eyes.

I wrinkled my nose at her.

A tea mug showed up in front of my face. I took it.

Chastity passed the rest of them around, then set a kitchen chair between Tempie and me and sat down.

Prue and Chassie studiously avoided looking at Tempie through all this.

But I chanced a glance, and I saw her face was the study of banal, but she wasn't fooling me.

She was holding her shoulders very tight, and there was a feeling of almost desperate fear emanating from her.

I wasn't thinking Ravenna was a charlatan anymore.

Yeesh.

The woman could read.

"Would you like me to pull more?" Ravenna offered.

"No, that'll be fine," Tempie said like she was about to ask for the bill.

Ravenna gave her a long look, then her expression shifted to genuine affection when she turned to Prue.

"Ready?" she asked.

Prue nodded eagerly.

Ravenna gathered the cards while we all sipped tea (for your information, Chassie could make a lovely spot of tea, then again, she was English, they were born with natural talent at that). She gave the cards to Prue.

Prue shuffled them, her face screwed up, and she did both a long time.

Then she returned the cards to Ravenna.

Ravenna immediately threw down five.

She looked at them.

She looked at them more.

She squinted her eyes at them.

She then turned to Prue with some alarm and shared, "Your cards are everywhere. What's happening?"

"I asked them to tell me where Charlie's letters to Harmony were," she said.

"Letters?" Ravenna asked.

"For the project I'm working on," I chimed in. "A novel loosely based on a star-crossed love affair between Prue, Tempie and Chassie's great-aunt and my great-grandfather. We have Harmony's letters, but we're not sure she kept his because Prue can't find them."

Ravenna's gaze floated back to the cards. "Well, they're somewhere at The Downs."

The room went wired again.

"She didn't destroy them?" Prue asked.

Ravenna shook her head.

"Any idea where they are?" Chassie asked.

Ravenna studied the cards again.

Then another shaking of her head.

"Well, that stinks," Chassie griped.

This caused Prue and Tempie, then Prue, me and Tempie, to exchange another glance because, boy...when Chassie decided to break out of her shell, she wasn't messing around.

Ravenna took a fortifying sip of tea before she queried of Prue, "Is there anything more you want to ask the cards, hun?"

Prue almost accomplished hiding her quick peeks at Chassie and me before she shook her head. "I think I'm good with that."

This meant she would ask the cards about me and Battle, and Chassie changing at another appointment.

I understood her play.

"Let's do me," Chassie said excitedly.

"All right," Ravenna agreed, did the card gathering and offered them to Chassie.

"Just shuffle and give them to you when I feel it?" Chassie inquired.

"Just that, luvvie," Ravenna said.

Chassie started shuffling. "When do I know when I feel it?"

"You'll know."

Chassie kept shuffling.

"Oo, there!" she cried and handed the cards to Ravenna.

Ravenna gave her a kind smile and took them.

She threw down only one, looked at it then looked at Chassie.

"Yes," she said.

"Yes?" Chassie breathed, her eyes bright, a blush stealing across her cheeks.

What on…?

The rest of us exchanged even more glances.

"Yes, luv," Ravenna said gently, smiling in the same vein.

"Thank you," Chassie said meaningfully.

"It is my absolute pleasure," Ravenna replied.

And with neither of them giving the rest of us that first hint as to what they were on about, Ravenna picked up the card she dropped and offered the whole lot to me.

I took them enthusiastically.

I loved tarot. I read my own. I went to readers.

But this was the best reading by far I'd ever been involved in.

I didn't ask a question. I just wanted the cards to feel how I'd fallen in love with these women, their home, their pets, and yes, okay, also their brother. It was new love, burgeoning love, but I knew what I was feeling was very, very, very, very, *very*…

Fond.

Once I felt I'd imbued all that goodness in the cards, I handed them to her.

She didn't immediately throw any down.

She examined me for an awkwardly long time.

And then she threw them down.

One, two three…

Four, five, six…

Seven, eight…

What the hell was she doing?

Nine, ten, eleven, twelve…

And thirteen.

She set the rest of the pile aside, scrutinized the scattering on the table, shifted them this way and that.

And then she looked at me. "Choose the ring wisely."

I blinked and asked, "Sorry?"

"When the time comes, choose the ring wisely," she repeated.

"What ring?" I asked.

"*The* ring," she answered.

"My precious," Chassie joked using a lisp.

God, I cannot tell you how amazing it was to see Chassie blossoming.

I shot her a smile, and so as not to make a thing of it, I returned to Ravenna. "I'm not sure I know what you're talking about."

She sat back in the sofa with her tea. "Many don't. Until they do."

I flicked a hand at the table. "Thirteen cards, and that's all it says?"

I knew she was lying, though I didn't know how I knew she was lying, when she replied, "Yes."

I gazed down at the cards, mumbling, "Maybe I should reshuffle."

"You're welcome to," Ravenna said. "But you'll have to ask a specific question, or the cards will tell me the same thing."

I did my best to commit the cards on the table to memory, collected them, reshuffled and did that copiously, keeping my mind on nothing but what I had before (not hard), then handed them to her.

A chill raced right through me when she immediately threw down what appeared to be the exact same thirteen cards.

"Holy hell," I breathed, staring at the table.

I could tell Prue, Chassie and Tempie were feeling the same way as they stared with me.

"My cards were blessed by a high priestess at Avebury," Ravenna bragged. "They're very powerful."

"I'll say," Chassie whispered.

"Would you like to ask them a question this time?" Ravenna offered.

"Kinda," I told her. "I want to see if my sister's doing okay. Our mom died a little over a year ago, and it really hit us hard."

"Of course," Ravenna said softly.

I did the reshuffle, handed them to her, she took them, threw down three, and stated immediately, "She has a good husband. And she feels…" She tossed out another card. "Blessed that she has what she has when your mother didn't have it. There is heaviness there, but mostly, she knows your mother was happy for her, and she feels grateful her life doesn't have the challenges, but it does have the bounty that your mother's life did."

That was Solène.

And me.

We'd always been taught to try to find a bright side.

And this made me feel better.

"Though, she'd like you to call her," Ravenna finished.

I decided to do that this evening.

"Can you…talk to dead people?" I asked.

Yup.

In those words I asked that.

Ravenna's expression got kind(er), but she shook her head.

"And anyone who tells you they can is full of it," she advised. "The dead can speak, but they do their own talking."

Eek!

We finished our tea chatting, and Ravenna elevated herself even further with Tempie when we all tried to pay, and she said, "One session, it doesn't matter how many readings. I charge by the hour. So, same price."

This meant Prue forked over fifty pounds, we thanked Ravenna, and Chastity said, "Can I come back?"

"Of course, love. I have openings."

She shouldn't.

The bitch should have them lined up around Boots, for shit's sake.

"I'll get your number from Prue," Chassie peeped.

And I'd get it from one of them.

As we were walking out, and I was the last, Ravenna grabbed my arm.

I turned to her.

"Whatever you choose will be right, but it might not reveal the answers you seek," she said.

"I still don't know what you're talking about."

"You will," she replied, smiled at me, let me go and shut the door on me.

Everyone was silent on the way back to the Defender.

We all got in.

We all buckled up.

And then for some reason, we all sat there while Tempie did the same thing with her hands on the wheel, not switching on the ignition, just staring out the windshield.

Chassie, who was sitting next to her in the front (as she had on the way there), called, "Tempie?"

"I'm seeing someone, all right?" she demanded irately, like we'd been giving her shit for months about it. "And he's a candidate, I think."

"Can we meet him?" Chassie asked quietly.

"No," Tempie answered.

"Why not?" Prue asked carefully.

"I don't know," Tempie said in a voice that made my heart squeeze.

"Leave it," I advised quickly.

Chassie twisted in her seat to look back at me. "But—"

"Leave it, doll," I said gently. Then to Tempie, "But you, sister, have three people in this car who will listen to you and support you. So don't squander those resources. Hear me?"

She pulled out if it, started the car, and drawled, "My brother has fucked some bossy into you."

"Euw!" Chassie cried.

I rolled my eyes.

"Ulk! I love them together, and I can't love them together if I have to think about those things!" Prue complained loudly.

Tempie just smiled smugly at me in the rearview mirror.

Obviously, this made me roll my eyes again.

Tempie set us on our way.

"Wait, there's a possibility my sister might be a duchess?" Solène said in my ear.

I was grinning loopily when I replied, "Maybe. He's very *fond* of me. And I'm likewise *fond* of him."

"Am I missing something with your emphasis on *fond*?"

"If you're missing that I'm falling in love with him, and he's not hiding he's doing the same with me, but he says he's *fond* of me when he's a sex god, thinks Elizabeth the First was the greatest politician in history, and I agree, screw all those Roman senators, though Lincoln obviously had chops. Further, he's an amazing brother and has been since he was a kid through some pretty extreme odds. And he thinks I'm smart, talented, and has a serious fascination with my ass. Therefore, *fond* doesn't cover it by a long shot for either of us. But it is very sexy and also very English. They do tend to master the understatement."

"There was a bit of TMI in all of that, but...wow, Vivi. I don't know what else to say but wow."

"Wait until I send you a picture of him."

"So he's hot."

"Yes. Scorching. And I thought that when I first saw him. But he makes me laugh, Lenny. He thinks I'm funny. I don't know..."

It was late.

I was in my bed in the main house, papers and my laptop and my cats (Prue's, but yeah, mine, and Baby Blue had taken to hanging with me with Battle gone) strewn across the coverlet, but since I was at a loss for words, I fell back onto my pillows.

And admitted, "I could probably talk about him for the next three hours and not explain how amazing he is."

"You've only been there a few weeks, honey."

"When did you know with Alex?"

Heavy pause then, "Point taken."

I grinned to myself because she called me the day after their first date and announced she was going to marry him.

My sister was an engineer. She was STEM. She got her jollies from quadratic equations (or whatever).

She was not a romantic like me.

But she knew with Alex immediately.

And she was right.

Just like I knew it was with Battle.

"Would Mom like him?" she asked.

Instantly, I said, "Yes. She'd spend five minutes with him with his sisters, and she'd know what I was going to get for a lifetime and be very happy for me."

"This is really cool, Viv. Alex and I were talking about taking the kids out there in June or July. It's expensive, and they're too young to remember much of such a momentous vacation, but they miss you, and Alex and I do too. Maybe we need to talk about that more seriously, when it comes time to meet him?"

It was already time, as far as I was estimating.

Though, I should probably give it more and talk to Battle about it.

Even so, I said, "Yeah, maybe talk seriously with Al. But I don't think I'll have to try too hard to get Battle to fly home to visit me when my visa runs out. You can meet him then."

"Let me share this news with Alex. I'm really happy for you, Viv. You sound..." She let that lie for a spell and finished, "Like before Mom died."

Yeah.

Ugh.

"Life will never be the same without Mom," I replied. "And sometimes, I think about the fact she'll never meet Battle, or Prue, Tempie, Chassie, see this gorgeous house, meet the kitties and Bartholomew. And that hurts. But, yeah. I feel lighter here. I feel comfortable here.

This house is beautiful, but it wouldn't be half as pretty if there wasn't so much love here. Even the staff seem like family. So, I guess...yeah."

"I love that," she whispered.

"I do too," I agreed.

"I'll talk to Alex. So, how's the book going?"

We chatted book, Alex, Matty, Rayray, her work, Alex's work and grandparents. And when we hung up, I was glad I called, I was glad she knew, I was glad she sounded good.

And I was glad I could call Battle before I went to sleep.

He answered on the second ring.

"Hullo, love," he greeted.

"So, Prue's clairvoyant is the real freaking deal," I shared.

"You're joking," he replied.

"Battle, I cannot tell you how eerie-cool it was. She outed Hamish!"

His "She didn't," sounded hot-guy shocked.

"She did. And told her off for hiding behind Chassie in not making a commitment."

Battle started chuckling.

"She confirmed that Charlie's letters still exist too," I continued. "Though, she couldn't tell us where they were."

There was hesitation before he noted, "That seems convenient."

"Honey, I believe every word out of that woman's mouth. Chassie's reading was one word, 'yes,' and none of us know what that's about, but Chassie really did, and it made her happy."

"It made her happy?"

Mm-hmm.

He had a treat waiting for him.

"You'll be glad you came home early, baby," I said softly, thinking it was time to give him hope. "She's really coming into her own."

"Fuck," he bit with grave feeling. "That's great."

"It so is."

He gave that a moment before he asked, "Did you do a reading?"

"Yes, but mine was weird. She just said to choose the ring wisely. I didn't get it, she couldn't tell me more, so I challenged her."

"Of course you did," he murmured with admiration.

I was *so fond* of him.

"I reshuffled the cards, and this is where it got eerie-cool, she pulled the exact same thirteen."

"She could know sleight of hand, Vivi," he cautioned.

"If she does, she's the master. When I said I reshuffled, I really did. She just took them and threw down. It was crazy."

"Choose the ring?" he asked dubiously.

"I don't know. Chassie joked it was my precious."

"Chassie joked?"

Right.

Time to confirm that hope and hope I was right in confirming it.

"Honey, shaking her shit, I don't want to get your hopes up, but it seems to be working."

He let that sit a beat too, before asking, "And Tempie?"

"Once we got in the car, she admitted she's seeing someone, and he might be a candidate. Obviously, Chassie and Prue wanted to be all over it, but I warned the girls to back off. They weren't happy about it, but they did. She isn't missing Chassie no longer needs her hovering. Prue either. If she screws that pooch, it'll be all on her. And Ravenna warned her about it."

"I'm still uncertain about this Ravenna character, but perhaps I should find words to say to Tempie."

"I think that would be good."

"It's also good I'm home tomorrow night then."

"Oh so good," I said, adding weight to it.

"I missed you too, darling."

So fond.

"Are you almost ready for bed?" he asked.

"I'm going to do a bit more on my book outline, then hit it."

"Right. It's late. I'll leave you to it. I hope to be home tomorrow around six, latest seven. I'll see you then."

"Will it turn you off if I'm wearing a gauzy dress, draped over the front balustrade, wasting away waiting for you when you drive up to the house?"

He burst out laughing.

"I'll aim a fan at me so my dress can drift off in a ghostly fashion to up the drama," I offered.

He kept laughing.

I loved giving him that.

Then he asked, "Do you own a gauzy dress?"

"Maybe the girls and I can nip back to Glastonbury to look for one."

"Your usual clothes will work as wardrobe to your pining."

"I suppose," I fake groused.

"You do need to go shopping though, love. Rally and Court's wedding, according to their invitation, is 'spring formal.' I don't know what that means, but since I'm in the wedding party, my wardrobe is set. Perhaps ask Tempie if your last gown is appropriate, because I fear the two I've seen may not be."

Considering the fact I was saving two, maybe three months' rent, I could spring for another fancy dress.

And maybe a few sexy nighties.

And a few other things.

I'd packed three huge suitcases, and since I sometimes never even got out of my pajamas when writing, I thought I'd be covered.

I had no idea I'd be courted by a duke.

"I'll ask her."

"Good, darling. Now I'll let you go."

"See you tomorrow night."

"You absolutely will. Sleep well."

"You too, Battle."

We hung up.

I didn't grab my laptop at once to dig into my outline.

I held my phone to my chest and cast my gaze to three cats, all of whom had claimed their own papers to lie on.

"He's so dreamy," I told them.
Only Baby Blue lifted her head.
She looked at me and blinked.
She did not lie.
And she knew what she was talking about.
He was.
So dreamy.

CHAPTER 21

THE RETURN

I was sitting cross-legged outside the threshold to the ballroom, staring into it.

I was terrified of going in after what happened the first, and frankly, only time I ever wanted to walk in that room, so I stayed out.

I should be upstairs, freshening up, because my man was going to be home any minute, but even if not, it was almost time for cocktails, one of my favorite parts of the day at The Downs.

I'd showered after my riding lesson with Scotty that morning, and because Battle was going to be home, I took special care with my makeup and hair, so it wasn't like I was gross.

But still.

My man was coming home.

However, for some reason, the ballroom called me.

No, I knew the reason.

Scotty and Harry had helped Prue drag a bunch of stuff out of the attics to line the upper hall so she could get around better in the space, and even if she'd unearthed an ancient filing cabinet that could prove useful in authenticating some of the pieces up there, still no letters.

I had the book totally outlined. I'd been through all papers, journals, letters, ledgers, notes, and nothing more on Harmony and Charlie, or Marie's cryptic journal entry.

I was raring to dive in.

But it stunk that it seemed that mystery was to go unsolved, and I was going to have to make it up, augmenting what I had only from Harmony.

I felt movement at my side, startled, and looked up to see Chastity folding down beside me.

"Hey," I greeted.

"What are you doing?" she asked.

"Trying to get the dead to speak to me."

She started and looked at me. "What?"

I tipped my head to the ballroom. "Harmony and Charlie fell in love in there. I'm going to start my book on Monday, but I only have half the story."

"Yuck," she replied.

"Yup," I agreed.

She turned to the room. "Are they talking?"

"No."

"Ulk," she replied.

"Yup," I agreed.

We sat there, both looking into the room.

"Can I tell you something?" she asked the room.

Oh shit.

I wasn't a huge fan of her tone.

Even so.

"Anything, honey," I answered.

"Something really bad happened to me a while ago."

Yeah.

Shit.

"I guessed that," I said gently.

She looked at me. "I got raped at my flower shop."

I closed my eyes, opened them, there were tears I would not shed, but they were there, and I whispered, "Chassie, baby."

"After, I did something really stupid."

Three years of healing.

"Nothing is stupid."

"After it happened, I went to Battie."

My body wound up so tight, I thought it would snap.

"I was…in bad shape," she continued. "Bleeding and stuff."

Battle didn't tell me that.

"I refused to go to hospital," she carried on. "He and Mrs. Pattinson cleaned me up. I closed my shop. Battie had to pay back a ton of money because I pulled out of contracts for events I agreed to do. I stayed in London for a long time with Battie. Then Tempie came to get me and brought me home. And I've been here since. I haven't left…until Glastonbury."

I nodded, fighting very hard to tamp down my response to Battle opening the door to his bloody, violated, beautiful, dainty, frizzy-haired sister who he adored (rightfully so) beyond reason.

God, it was testimony to how much he loved her that he didn't leave her to Mrs. Pattinson in order to go out and commit murder.

But what he eventually did was even further explained.

I also had to hold my tongue, because, if she drove from Bath to London in that state, she could have further harmed herself. It was a miracle she made it.

However, this wasn't the time for admonishments (far from it).

And it totally tracked that the only thought she had at that time was to get to Battle.

She leaned into me and put her head on my shoulder.

I wrapped an arm around her.

"Now, I've messed up, Vivi," she whispered.

"How did you mess up, honey?" I whispered back.

"I scared them so much. I worried them so much. They aren't living their lives."

"This is what I know," I announced grandly.

She just tipped her head back but kept it on my shoulder as we looked at each other.

"If that happened to my sister, I'd be on her like a rash, until I knew she didn't need me. And I wouldn't give that first fuck if she needed me for twenty years."

"Really?" she asked softly.

"Absolutely," I answered resolutely. "But what you're missing is, they can look after you and live their lives too. You can't be responsible for the decisions they make."

"But...Tempie—"

"No, Chassie. You heard Ravenna. It's on her now."

She lifted her head, but I kept my arm around her.

"I know she was worried about me going to London," she said. "Seeing Mrs. Pattinson again. All of that. And she didn't see him when she was there. She goes there, not much. Not enough, if he cares about her. And obviously he does. Their row on the phone didn't sound good."

"Her decision to make."

"But—"

I shook her. "You have enough to worry about seeing to you, don't take on Tempie."

Her face grew stubborn, and damn, I was loving Chassie getting back to Chassie.

"So they can take on me, and I can't take them on?"

"They didn't take you on, my lovely. They stuck close to support you. I think it's important you know the difference."

She scrunched her nose, still stubborn, and I'd take it.

Though, I wasn't done.

"But just to say, that would be my advice to anyone. Worry about yourself. What you can do. What you can control. Trying to take on responsibility for another person's happiness is like trying to change the past or manipulate the future. It's fool's work and doomed to fail every time."

She bit her lip and gazed into the ballroom.

I wasn't sure what I said sank in, but I didn't get the opportunity to pursue it.

We heard Prue shouting, "Battie's home!"

We both twisted to see her at the end of the hall.

She then disappeared.

And I didn't know what came over me (I did, I was very *fond* of him).

I immediately jumped to my feet, raced down the hall, turned the corner, raced down that hall (damn, this house was huge), hit the foyer, and there he was, wearing a dark-gray shirt, the sleeves rolled up, the tie was gone, the shirt open, this over charcoal-gray suit trousers—tall, broad, beautiful.

Mine.

I threw myself at him, heard him grunt when he caught me, but his arms locked around me as I slid my hand into his hair to pull his mouth down to mine.

I didn't have to expend much effort. He took my mouth, and we made out hot and heavy in the foyer.

When we finally broke, he purred, "Much better than you draped longingly over the balustrade."

"I thought so," I replied breathlessly.

He kissed my nose (a thing for him, since my freckles were a thing for him).

Then he let me go so he could kiss the waiting cheeks of Prue and Chassie while I greeted Bartholomew, who came home with him.

Prue clapped. "You made it in time for cocktails."

"And a drink is precisely what I need, sweetheart. Traffic on the M4 was a nightmare," he replied, rounding my shoulders with an arm and turning us to the plum parlor.

When we made it, Chassie asked, "Should I ring Fitzy?"

"I can manage," Battle said, because not a single Talyn could toast a slice of bread, but I figured they all could make a variety of cocktails. He let me go and headed to the drinks cabinet, asking, "Orders?"

I tried to think of one to stymie him.

But he called me on it, saying, "I have a phone, Vivi. Whatever you cook up, I can look it up."

"Martini," I ordered on a huff.

He smiled at me.

I got over my huff.

"My usual," Prue chirped.

"Me too," Chassie surprisingly said (she was a non-frozen daiquiri girl, for the most part).

Battle got to work, and we took our seats, me in what had become my chair, next to Bartholomew, who put his slobbery snout on my leg, making me happy I was wearing jeans.

I stroked his head.

Battle had made the drinks, passed them around and folded into the chair beside mine when Tempie floated in looking her usual fabulous in a pair of wide-leg white pants and a red and white sleeveless blouse with a complicated bow at her neck.

She was accompanied by Fitzy.

"Good," she said upon spying Battle. "I missed the reunion. But do tell. Was it mildly pornographic, or wildly pornographic?"

On his way to the drinks cabinet, Fitzy's eyes went to the ceiling, but he was smiling.

Battle grunted disapprovingly.

"Blurgh! Tempie!" Chassie cried.

At that, I saw Battle's body jerk in his chair, and I looked at him to see his eyes narrowed on his sister.

Yeah.

There it was.

"Stop doing that," Prue ordered Tempie. "It probably makes Battie and Vivi really uncomfortable. I know it does me."

"That *is* the point, dear," Tempie replied blithely as she floated her long, lean body down to sit in the sofa opposite Prue and Chassie.

"There's martini in the shaker, Fitzy," Battle called. "That was also Vivienne's selection for this evening."

"Excuse me, I do not do watered down vodka," Tempie replied.

"It's been in the shaker maybe five minutes," Battle told her.

"That'll be acceptable, Fitzy," Tempie said to the butler.

As he poured, he called, "Miss Vivi, if you don't mind, Patsy was hoping you'd pop down and let her know what you want brought in for the weekend. She's sending Harry to the market tomorrow. We're off early to visit the youngest for a couple days." He grinned madly. "We have a new grandson."

Yes, I'd asked Tempie if it was okay.

And yes, I'd told Patsy she didn't have to cook dinner for the throng when Emily was away.

So yes, she took me up on it.

No shade on being served delicious cocktails and meals at home. Especially no shade on not having to do dishes.

But getting to cook a couple of nights a week for people I loved *so* did not suck for me.

"Oo, do you have baby photos?" I asked Fitzy.

He offered the martini on his tray to Tempie, she took it, then he dug his phone out of his inside jacket pocket, engaged it, slid his finger on the screen and offered it to me.

"You can scroll for probably fifteen pictures. They're all of our new little bundle," Fitzy said.

"Good goodness, Granddad, he's the perfect child," I said while scrolling. Then I looked up at him, "Outside my nephew and niece, Matty and Rayray, of course."

Fitzy smiled at me. "Of course."

"And I'll dash down now to give Patsy a grocery list." I turned to the group. "What do we say for Sunday? Tacos?"

Prue clapped. "I *adore* tacos."

I looked at Battle. "Honey?"

"I don't think there's a human on the planet who would turn down tacos," he replied.

Oh so very *fond* of this guy.

"Erm, that human would be me," Tempie said.

Battle scowled at her.

"How about a taco salad?" I suggested.

"Don't make special food for Tempie. She eats what we all eat," Battle decreed.

"It's all the same ingredients, honey," I told him. "It'll take me thirty seconds."

"Mm," was his only reply.

"The concept of a…*taco salad*"—Tempie saying those last two words like she would say *wearing flats* nearly had me cracking up—"intrigues me."

"Taco salad for you it is," I decided. "And maybe my rosemary roast garlic chicken on Monday?" I suggested to the girls, then to Battle, "Or I could do that on Sunday. Proper Sunday roast, with Yorkshire puds, sprouts and gravy."

Prue clapped again. "Oh, let's do a Sunday roast."

"As long as you make your tacos for me at a later date," Battle put in.

"Perfect," I said, sipped my martini, set it aside and got up, telling Fitzy as I returned his phone, "I'll pop down now so it isn't left too late."

"Thank you, Miss Vivi. The missus is in her office."

I grinned at him, and on my way down to Patsy's office, I made a mental grocery list, adding to it the puds I also was going to make.

I met Patsy in her office, wrote it all down and headed back up.

As I walked back into the plum parlor, Chassie was saying, "Capri has beaches."

"Switzerland, though, is so gorgeous. I've always wanted to go," Prue replied.

I didn't know what they were talking about.

I did know that when I sat down, Battle grabbed my hand in a punishing grip, which made me start to pay extra close attention.

"Capri is gorgeous too," Chassie said.

"My skin and the sun don't mix," Prue returned.

"Maybe we should go to Ravenna and ask her where we should holiday," Chassie suggested.

My heart stuttered.

Holiday?

Those two were discussing where to *vacation*?

Now it was me who was holding Battle's hand in a punishing grip.

"Oh! Let's!" Prue agreed. "The cards will tell us where to go."

Crap.

Was I going to burst into tears?

Stupidly, I looked to Battle to see him studying the G&T he had resting on his knee, but a muscle was working up his cheek as he fought to keep his own emotion in check.

That far from helped me in controlling my tears.

In the end, I just kept hold of his hand, even when I retrieved my drink.

I took a healthy sip.

Chassie's attention drifted to us holding hands, and she smiled brightly.

Battle's fingers pumped mine.

Mine pumped back.

"You two are so cute," Chassie said.

"Thank you, sweetheart," Battle replied, his voice slightly thick, but he was hanging in there.

I shifted my attention to Tempie to see she was swirling her olives in her martini.

And she was smiling.

Broadly.

The man practically ran me off my heels when we were trying to escape Chelsea.

But post-dinner, after we'd been apart for four days, and I wasn't teetering in heels, did he drag me to my room?

No.

We strolled there like we had all the time in the world.

We were headed to my room because, during pudding, I'd leaned his way and whispered, "Your room or mine?"

To which he'd found my ear and whispered back, "Considering I intend to fuck you in every room in this house, we might as well start now. Yours."

After that, I made a mental note to initiate no more, even minimally sexy talk in front of his sisters, because my body reacted so strongly to his words.

Fortunately, when we made my door, Battle stopped messing around.

He did this in order to start *messing around.*

As such, he used his hand in mine to whirl me whereupon I slammed against his chest, he wrapped his arms around me and kissed me deeply as he backed into my room, taking me with him.

I was all in to win (in other words, all over him), when he sat on my bed, also taking me with him, only immediately to stand, break the kiss and turn his head to look down at my bed.

In more than a bit of a haze, I looked too.

There was a book there.

The cover was beautifully imagined swirls and flourishes in which were hidden dragons and ridiculously handsome men with wings on their backs, all of this in greens, blues, purples and shades of gray.

And in the middle of all of this, in silver foil, there was the title INTO THE GILT FRAME.

Under it, it said, WRITTEN AND ILLUSTRATED BY PRUDENCE TALYN.

I gasped and my hands flew to my mouth.

From behind them, I asked, "She's been published?"

"No," Battle replied. "Chassie took one of her books and had it printed and bound as a Christmas present a couple of years ago." He reached and nabbed a sheet of thick, soft gray stationery with an artsy, blocky monogram of PJT (Prudence's middle name was Joanna) at the top that was lying beside the book. "There's a note. Addressed to you."

Excited, I took it from him.

And read it aloud.

"Vivi. You liked Battie's portrait so I thought maybe you might want to see this. It's an early thing, not very good. If you don't like it, that's okay. But I thought you might want to see it. Love, Prue."

With big, happy eyes, I looked up Battle.

He smiled indulgently and stated, "I suppose we can have sex in the morning."

Gah!

He was so great.

But…

Was he crazy?

"Are you crazy?" I asked.

He didn't answer.

I took the note and the book and put them on my nightstand.

After which, I promptly returned to Battle.

And jumped him.

The room was dark.

Battle was asleep, head on my pillow, the one I was leaning up against. His arm was resting snug around my hips.

I had a little reading light shaped like a sloth that I was using to read Prue's extraordinary book.

Battle was right.

The story had depth, also emotion, heat, humor.

And the illustrations were crazy-amazing.

However, I'd had two orgasms, so as much as I wanted to keep reading, I was losing it.

I didn't want to miss anything.

I'd have to return to the book tomorrow.

I switched off the light and set it and the book aside.

I slouched down and turned into Battle's embrace.

"It's good, isn't it?" he murmured sleepily.

"No, it's exceptional."

His arm got tighter around me.

I curled mine around him.

"'Night, love," he said.

"'Night, baby," I replied.

And we went to sleep.

CHAPTER 22

THE SPIES

"Up here, Vivienne," Battle ordered hoarsely. "Now."

His cock still deep in my mouth, I looked up his defined abs, over his perfectly-sprinkled-with-dark-hair pecs, his strong throat to his flushed face and dilated eyes and kept sucking him off.

I got in two more strokes with my mouth before his hands were under my arms, and he was hauling me up his body while he sat up.

Then he was grinding me down on his cock while he groaned and I gasped.

He fisted a hand in my hair, yanking it back sexy-rough, so my spine arched.

His arm tight around my hips held me full of him, unable to move, as he kept me positioned for him and tortured my nipples with his lips and tongue.

Such a damned tease.

"God, honey," I begged.

He tipped my head forward, kissed me and used both hands clenching my ass to control my rhythm as I rode him.

Eventually, I had his head in my hands, one of his skated over my hip so he could roll my clit with a strong finger, we were gaze to gaze, lips to lips, Battle purring, me whimpering.

Then I came.

He slid down in bed, pulled me off his dick, planted me on his face, and he ate me through my orgasm, built and unleashed another one, and when I heard him groan up my pussy, I knew he'd taken care of himself with his hand.

A quick squeeze of my thigh giving me the message, and I expended energy I did not have to swing off him, collapse on my back, settling at his side.

"You eat me out while you jack off, you position me the other way so I can watch," I bitched wheezily (what could I say? That was hot. I was still recovering).

"Darling, you'll be where I put you," he replied.

I turned my head to look at him, uncertain I wanted to countermand his order because I always liked where he put me, like I did just now.

I still would have liked to watch.

I didn't get the chance to make up my mind.

He leaned into me, touched his lips to mine and rolled out of bed to head to the bathroom.

After he cleaned up and came back, he didn't come back to me.

He put on his boxer briefs, then his trousers, and shrugged on his shirt but didn't button it.

Only then did he come to me.

Another lean in, another lip touch, and when he pulled back, he said, "Stay there. I'll return."

With that, he walked out.

I didn't stay there.

We fucked upon waking.

Or we fucked upon Battle waking me.

This meant I got out of bed and took care of business, including brushing my teeth.

I went back to bed and considered hitting the smart screen to order a pot of coffee.

By the time he got back, Snowball and Gingerface were hanging with me.

Bartholomew wasn't, but that was probably because he was having breakfast.

When Battle returned, Baby Blue was prancing behind him.

But I was staring at him.

He was still in the same clothes.

And he had a thin, long, darkest dark-blue velvet jewelry box with him.

As I stared at that box, Battle stretched his long body out beside me in bed, still wearing his trousers, open shirt, bare feet...yum.

And he handed me the box.

"Battle," I whispered, now only having eyes for him.

He reached out and flipped the box open.

I forced my gaze to what was inside.

Nestled in a bed of robin's-egg-blue satin was a diamond tennis bracelet, set in white gold.

The diamonds weren't ostentatiously huge, it was a classy piece, albeit it could never be described as lowkey, because even if the diamonds weren't large, it was a tennis bracelet, so there were a lot of them.

But...fucking hell.

"Baby," I said.

"I've noticed you don't have enough jewelry," he stated.

Annnnnd...

Yes.

A tear slid down my cheek.

"Your diamond earrings are set in white gold too," he remarked.

Of course he noticed.

Of course.

He slipped a thumb over the trail of my tear. "Don't cry, Vivienne."

"My mom bought me those earrings."

His face gentled, and he cupped my jaw. "Sweetheart."

"Now I can have her at my ears and you at my wrist."

He took that wrist and kissed the skin on the inside, then he moved his hand to the back of my neck and pulled me to his mouth.

We kissed, wet and sweet, before he ended it, and I asked, "Will you put it on?"

He didn't reply, except to take the box from me, pull the bracelet from its bed of satin, casually toss the box on my nightstand, and when I offered my wrist, he bested the fiddly clasp with a few flicks of his thumb and there it was.

Flashing brilliant, rich and meaningful.

Battle on my wrist.

"I take it you like it," he murmured.

I shifted my gaze from the bracelet to him. "It's beautiful."

"I suppose we're making progress that you didn't throw it in my face," he quipped.

I swatted him.

Then I kissed him.

He rolled on top of me.

And he kissed me.

Tennis Bracelet Day, as it would henceforth be known for all eternity, was Friday morning.

It was now Saturday afternoon.

Battle and I had worked yesterday.

This morning, we had sex (again, my room), got showered, dressed and went down to have breakfast with the girls.

After that, we went riding, and Tempie came with us.

Battle was impressed with how much more comfortable I was on Noelle, but I left my ride to continuing to get used to a canter while they took off at a run.

Watching them race through the field, I doubled down on my

intent to learn how to ride better so I could someday do that with them.

Truth, Tempie was totally the shit (she was wearing black riding breeches and boots, with a crisp white blouse (another mental note: buy riding breeches—not only were they the shit, it seemed like they gave your legs more freedom, even than jeans, which could be restricting), and her horse, Calpurnia, was an unusual, lustrous silver black).

But Lord…

In faded jeans and an olive-green button down, Battle bent forward, racing his sister on the back of his blood bay?

Be still my freaking heart.

After our ride, we cleaned up and Battle took me into the village for a pub lunch and a half pint of cider.

The day was nice, and they were getting warmer, so we sat outside at a picnic table with hanging baskets and pots of England's famous lush, bright flowers all around.

He knew people and nodded when he caught their eyes, or they stopped by the table for a moment to say hello, whereupon he always introduced me, and never failed to wedge in the words "bestselling author," something I freaking *loved*, because he seemed almost as proud of that as me.

It was cool to see him out and about and being just Battle. He was too danged tall, built and gorgeous not to give off a certain presence, but it wasn't a duke-ish one. And it was clear all of these people who he'd lived among all his life were as comfortable with him as he was with them.

In other words, they didn't act like Henry Cavill stumbled into their pub for a bacon and brie sandwich, chips and a pint of Guiness.

When we returned, I took him to the studio to show him the photos I wanted to use (he approved). We then sat on the chaise so I could show him my outline on my laptop (he approved of that too).

After that, he asked if he could see Marie's journal.

I dug it out for him.

He then lounged all sexy-hot duke on the chaise, one hand behind his head, the other holding up the diary, legs stretched out, ankles crossed, Gingerface hunkered down on his chest (Snowball, by the by, was on my desk (her favorite spot in the studio if the fire wasn't going), Baby Blue hadn't ventured out with us, but Bartholomew had somehow wedged himself under the desk and was resting his head on my feet).

Battle read while I went to the desk and did some online shopping.

Tempie had confirmed "spring formal" for Rally and Courtney's wedding meant some springtime-esque formalwear…

"But, dearest, Battle is a man, so he missed part of it," she stated. "The ceremony will be smart dress and hat. Everyone is changing for the evening reception to formalwear."

So I needed two outfits.

And a hat.

Although shopping for a wedding hat was a fun online trip (I'd never purchased a hat that wasn't a baseball cap), I got sidetracked in this endeavor (though, before that happened, I'd found two sexy nighties, which I bought).

What sidetracked me was doing a bit of side research on something that had been intriguing me since I learned of it.

I was in the middle of that when Battle ended our companionable silence.

"Christ," he said. "This woman is tedious." He rested the book on his thigh with his thumb in the page and looked at me. "Did you get through this whole thing?"

I nodded.

"Bloody hell. How?"

I smiled at him. "It's my job."

"I actually feel foul this woman's blood runs through my veins. She was vapid to extremes, and a revoltingly slipshod mother."

I grimaced, because I got him as well as agreed with him.

His eyes dropped to the laptop and came back to my face. "What are you doing?"

"Researching the disappearance of Lord Arthur Hughes-Davies, the viscount from Northumberland who went missing in 1946."

His brows inched together. "Why are you doing that?"

I shrugged. "Because it's a mystery." Then I got into it. "Get this, the dude was not a good dude. He got three deferrals, all medical, all suspected to have happened because he paid people off so he didn't have to serve during the war."

"If he had that kind of pull, he could have done the same thing and found himself a safe officer's commission where he didn't leave English soil and not taken that kind of hit to his reputation," Battle noted.

"He could. Another reason people thought he was an asshole. If you didn't do your bit for the war effort back then, whatever that bit might be, you were *persona non grata*. And as far as I could tell, he didn't do anything. It was like the war didn't happen for him, and he worked hard to make it that way. But there were also rumors he cheated at cards, left his companions with bar and dinner tabs, maybe had fascist tendencies and was inappropriate with the ladies."

"So did anyone give a shit he was gone?"

"The dowager countess, his mother, kicked up quite a fuss."

"And no one ever found him?" he asked.

I shook my head. "Not hide nor hair. Nothing. He vanished. One day there, one day gone and never heard from again."

His tone had changed, taken an edge, when he queried, "How was he inappropriate with the ladies?"

"The articles and entries paint him as a bit of a cad, he was single, however reading between the lines of such things being reported in 1946, it could be a lot worse than that."

"Then I hope someone got sick of his fuckwittery and put an end to him."

"Now who's bloodthirsty?" I teased as something caught the corner of my eye.

I looked out the windows.

Then I blinked and stared out the windows.

Prue, in a dove-gray tunic-length top that looked like two squares stitched together with openings for armholes, and matching gray leggings with equally matching gray flats on her feet with pointed toes that curled up, making her look like she was wearing tiny boats on her tiny feet, was lurking behind a shrub.

She was also wearing her octopus beanie.

How Atlas Talyn didn't recognize his third child had strong artistic tendencies was beyond me.

What a moron.

But I couldn't think on that.

Because she was furtively glancing around the shrub at something.

"What?" Battle called.

I didn't know what, so I couldn't answer him.

Carefully extricating my feet from under Bartholomew's jowls, I stood, and my movement must have shared I was in the studio, because Prue looked my way.

She then started waving, not in a hello way, in a get-out-of-the-way way. Since I had no idea what way I was supposed to get out the way of, I didn't move. And after a spell of her gesticulating wildly, she raced across the grass.

I got up and went to the door.

I opened it just as she came crashing in.

And that would be *crashing*.

And the crashing would be into *me*.

"Get down!" she said urgently and in a hushed voice.

But she didn't give me the chance to get down.

She yanked me down to my knees.

I hit the floor hard, and that was probably one of the reasons Battle did an ab curl to sit up and growled, "The fuck?"

Bartholomew bumped his head on the desk when he lifted it to see what was going on.

The straight edges of Prue's hair fanned out when she snapped her head to Battle then pointed at him. "Don't move!"

"What's going on?" he demanded.

But, as per usual with Battle giving everything he could to someone he loved, big brother didn't move.

Prue dragged me to the side window.

I glanced in confusion at Battle.

I returned to her when I felt movement and saw her popping up so only her beanie and eyes were over the bottom edge of the window frame, then down, and up again, and down, then up.

I inched up to look over the edge of the window and gasped.

Christian was out there, crouched by a bush, stabbing some kind of long stick into the soil beside it.

Chassie was out there too, wearing a lavish sundress that was pink and had deeper pink flowers on it, was mega flowy and had lots of ruffles. She'd paired this with a wide-brimmed, straw hat with a corresponding pink ribbon tied in a big bow at the back.

Her hair was floofy under the hat, and Floofy was lounging bedside her as she did some pruning.

At this point, Christian moved with his sticks, acting like she wasn't there, five feet away from him.

He crouched by another bush and dug the stick in.

Chassie shifted so he was in her eyeline.

Or she was in his.

I moved from the window and landed on my ass, whispering, "Oh my God."

Prue landed on her ass beside me. "I know!"

"I don't, so what the fuck is going on?" Battle demanded.

"Shh!" Prue waved at him.

I eyed Battle.

Oh shit.

"She's on the prowl!" Prue said animatedly to me.

She so was.

"Who's on the prowl?" Battle asked.

"*Shh!*" Prue repeated.

I could tell Battle was getting pissed.

I could also tell he was done with this because he was making moves to get up.

I knew no way could Battle witness Chassie trying to mend the damage she caused by pretending Christian didn't exist, only for Christian to make his move to prove he did, and her racing away from him, so he was leaving her alone, without Battle…doing something.

I didn't know what.

I just knew he couldn't do whatever it was because that was the message Chassie had been sending.

She wasn't sending it now.

However, she wasn't being overt in the new message she was sending.

Ugh.

Shit.

"Don't move," Prue ordered. "They can't suspect we're in here."

Battle stopped moving, but clipped, "Who?"

Prue ignored him and told me, "She used to garden in old jeans and sweaters and beat-up wellies. She only started wearing dresses since Christian's been around."

Oh shit!

That made Battle move.

So I crawled on all fours quickly across the room, knowing I looked like an imbecile, but this was too important for him to engage.

I got to him, looked up at him to see him staring down at me like he thought I needed medication and a straitjacket.

I grabbed his hand and tried to pull him down.

He didn't budge.

"Just sit, Battle, please," I begged.

He glowered at me.

"Please?" I repeated.

Slowly he sat.

"That's what the 'yes' meant at Ravenna's," Prue called quietly.

Mm-hmm.

That was what the yes was about.

Either did he like her, or should she make a play, but something like that was what she asked the cards.

And the cards said yes.

"Allow me to guess," Battle began sarcastically, "whatever you wouldn't tell me about Christian is happening out there right now with my baby sister."

I bit my lip.

"Is he bothering her?" Battle asked.

"I would say…no," I answered. "If there's any bothering happening, Chassie's bothering him. But she's actually not."

"You're telling me…" He couldn't bring himself to say it.

He was so cute.

I turned to Prue. "Really? About the sundresses?"

"I don't think she knew what she was doing." Prue smiled a radiant smile. "I think she knows what she's doing now."

"For fuck's sake," Battle growled, making another move.

But I pushed between his legs and grabbed onto his shoulders to hold him down.

"You know she's healing," I said quickly. "I know you've noticed it."

This didn't appear to make him any happier.

"Honey, you told me she's had boyfriends before," I pointed out.

Still not happy.

"Do you not like Christian?"

"He's a solid bloke. Very intelligent. Serious," he said like someone was waterboarding him.

"Tall. Blond. Fit. Good looking," I added.

He scowled.

"Baby," I put a hand on his chest under his throat, "this is very, very good. Chassie wanting to feel pretty. Chassie wanting a man to notice she's pretty. Chassie wanting a man to notice her at all."

His lips thinned, he still didn't say anything, but I knew I was getting to him.

"I love this for her. And you should too," I advised.

And it might be time to invite Christian to dinner.

"Under her brother's nose?" he asked.

My eyes got huge.

"Your Grace, you announced you wanted to fuck me right in front of her," I reminded him, and kept doing it, "In fact, in front of *everybody*."

He got quiet again.

"And I came to breakfast with a love bite," I went on. "And let us not forget, there were flowers on our breakfast tray, and those were all Chassie. What's good for the gander..." I let that trail.

"I mean, seriously, Battie," Prue chimed in, "we're all going to be in this house, filling it with babies eventually. And we all know too well you know how that comes about."

I looked to her, happy she used the word "we're" and hoping she'd eventually go on the prowl.

I wondered what her guy would be like.

Doing this, I watched her pop her head up to look out the window again before she took to her boat-shoed feet.

"They're out of sight. I can still see them, but they're closer to the house than the studio now," she announced.

"Stop stalking them," Battle ordered.

"But, Battie—" she tried.

"Let it play out however it plays out," Battle continued being bossy, though I knew that particular tidbit cost him.

Prue heaved a sigh.

I got off the floor, sat beside Battle and changed the subject.

"Hey, thanks for letting me read your book," I said to Prue.

Prue stopped looking annoyed at her older brother and got fidgety.

"It's fantastic," I went on.

She stopped being fidgety and stared at me.

"You think?" she asked.

"No. I know," I told her. "The story is great. I'm totally into it. It pulled me in immediately. But the illustrations are *life*, Prue. So gorgeous. Have you approached a publisher?"

"I—"

"You should get an agent. They'll be better able to negotiate a deal for you."

Battle's pissed vibe was now gone, and as I spoke, he stroked my back.

"Do you really think I should…try to find…uh, somebody?" she asked hesitantly.

"I think you'll have a bidding war. Your work is better than *Lore Olympus*, and I fucking love those volumes."

"Better than *Lore Olympus*?" she breathed.

Oh yeah.

I knew she loved those books too.

I probably should have gotten a hint she was into graphic stories with how much she loved that one.

"It's a different genre, so not easy to compare, but yes. Your work is really that great. I can get my agent to get in touch with you. I don't know if she does graphic novels, but she'd know who to refer you to."

"I didn't give my book to you so you'd—"

"I know, Prue," I cut her off. "I also know I never approach my agent unless I believe in what I'm going to pitch her. I believe in your work. If you want to share it, I think publishers would fall all over themselves for the opportunity." I smiled at her. "And I kinda love you, therefore I wouldn't blow sunshine, get your hopes up. If I didn't have total confidence in what I was saying, I wouldn't say it."

"Oh, Vivi!" she cried, raced across the space, and threw herself at me.

I stood so we could hug more easily.

I'd had a lot of great hugs in my life.

But this one ranked close to the top.

She bopped back and looked up at me. "Do you want to see more?"

"Absolutely."

She became confused. "Should I leave it in your room, or Battie's?"

"Either works," Battle said.

She looked from him to me. "Do you really think someone will want to publish it?"

What I thought was, it would be so popular, she'd get a movie or streaming deal.

I didn't share that.

"I really think someone will want to publish it, and a lot of some-ones will want to read it."

"Okay. I'll show you my other stuff. Would you help me with submissions?"

"I'm all yours."

She hugged me again.

Then she hurried to the door.

"No stalking," Battle warned.

She threw an exasperated look over her shoulder and left.

The minute the door closed, Battle dragged me into his lap.

I rounded his shoulders with my arms. "I think that went well."

He just stared at me, hard, with lots of lovely things working in his starburst brown eyes, all of them making words unnecessary.

I framed his face in my hands and put mine closer to his. "And Chassie is going to be okay. It's time you all let Chassie be Chassie."

He grunted.

I grinned.

Then I kissed him.

In the middle of that, I found myself on my back with a handsome duke on top of me.

"Do you get many visitors out here?" he asked.

"Occasionally."

"Do you have a sock to put on the door?"

Another grin from me. "Alas, no."

"Are we done out here?"

"Absolutely, yes."

He got up, pulled me up, and he, I, the cats and dog walked to the main house.

We saw no Prue, Chassie or Christian on our way.

We went right to his room.

And I was glad.

It felt like coming home.

After round one, and before a hoped-for round two, I lay pressed to Battle's side in his bed.

He was on his back.

While he traced random patterns on my hip (and, of course, my ass), I was tracing the same through his perfect chest hair on his equally perfect chest.

My eyes caught on the tennis bracelet I hadn't taken off since he'd put it on.

This man noticed the tiny prongs of white gold on the earrings my mother gave me.

This man was becoming everything to me.

So I wanted everything from him.

"At the risk of ruining the atmosphere…" I trailed off.

He clasped my ass and gave it a squeeze. "I'm naked with you in bed after having you," he announced unnecessarily. "Nothing could ruin the atmosphere."

Oh yeah.

This was a man who would notice those tiny prongs.

This man was everything.

I pushed up at the same time I partially covered him so I could look into his eyes.

No surprise, his hand stayed on my ass while I did this.

"I'm taking us into the getting-to-know-you-better department," I shared.

He smiled wolfishly. "I thought we'd already accomplished some of that."

I smiled back, but replied, "Non-sexually, honey."

His smile turned to just being his lips curved up before he invited,

"Hit me."

"Your mum and dad."

That was all I said, and I expected he'd at the very least frown, but he just sighed.

However, since I started it…

"The girls told me he was very traditional," I said. "And Tempie said he was an ass. She also said he had other women."

His brows knit, and with them, the mood finally shifted to what I'd expected it to be.

"Do you worry it might be like father, like son?" he asked.

"Hell no."

That response came automatically because one thing I knew, Battle Talyn would never cheat.

You could never predict life. Unless you had the talents of Ravenna, you also could never tell the future.

And shit could always go south.

But deep in my heart, even if, for some crazy reason, things went that way for us, it would never be about that.

For him or for me.

The mood shifted again at my answer, his arm slid up so he could wrap it around my waist to hold me close, and he purred, "I'm gratified by your swift response, darling."

I smiled at him.

He studied my smile then lifted his gaze to mine.

"He had other women, yes, as the whole world sadly knows," he confirmed. "Understandably, we never spoke of it, so my conclusion as to why he did it might be incorrect. However, I think he was trying to make her jealous. Mum, that is. Or, perhaps, make her feel something. Anything."

Something.

Anything.

"Was she that distant?" I inquired gently.

"I was fourteen when she left. After she did, I would try to recall any kind of mother-son or family moment I'd shared with her, or I'd witnessed her share with my sisters. I couldn't recall any."

I could not process that.

I could only process how destroyed I was for him that he experienced it.

And one could safely say, I had trouble doing it.

"Oh, baby," I whispered, those two words being all I could get out.

"And yes, Dad was very traditional. I didn't understand it. Our grandparents weren't. I don't know if he was attempting to make us live some storybook life to remind her he was duke, she was duchess, she'd birthed a marquess and three ladies, and to snap into the program of what he'd offered her when he'd offered for her hand. I don't know if he was just strange. He had a variety of old-fashioned ideas, hence Prue toughing it out with her bullies."

Hmm.

"I know I felt something when he was gone, and not just annoyance that I had to deal with the press frenzy of how he went," he continued.

"Just...something?" I prodded.

He rolled into me and kept rolling until he was on me, resting some weight in a forearm under my shoulder blade so he could stroke my jaw with his thumb.

"For your book?" he asked.

I didn't understand the change in topic, so I repeated in my own query, "For my book?"

"We'll call it a kind of research," he stated, then explained, "My telling you that isn't a thing in aristocratic families. That distance. The unemotionality. That boys are hoped for to continue the line and not much else, and girls are used to form or strengthen alliances, and nothing else. Perhaps that used to be the way, but it isn't anymore."

I nodded.

Battle kept talking.

"Rally's an example. He has a big family, they're very close and loving. I have many friends in the peerage, and all of them are the same. Perhaps not always as close, or some siblings don't get along, some parents divorce. But familial love is there."

"And it wasn't there from your parents?"

He shook his head, but said, "Mum, no. Dad, I think he was so invested in getting her not only to love him, but to see him as the man who loved her and not the title she wanted, that for the most part, he forgot us." His tone changed to one where it sounded like he was talking to himself. "Though, I could be making that up to give him excuses."

"I hate that for you. For all of you," I stated vehemently.

He came back to me and ran his knuckles along my jaw. "I'm not tremendously thrilled by it either."

"And this is a sucky part," I declared. "Not *the* sucky part. You four not having even decent, much less loving, supportive parents is *the* sucky part. But *a* sucky part is that it might be the reason why you're all the awesome that's you."

His lips quirked. "All the awesome that's me?"

I wasn't finding it amusing.

"All you are to your sisters. Thoughtful. Observant. Clicked in. Not many dudes are as clicked in as you, Battle."

He smoothed his free hand down my side. "I'm delighted you think I'm clicked in, darling. But shall we return to the 'might be' in your comment?"

"Pardon?"

"You said it 'might be' the reason why I'm as completely and utterly awesome as I am."

I squinted at him. "I don't recall using the words 'completely and utterly.'"

"It was subtext."

That made me roll my eyes.

"I know you're being serious, sweetheart," he said, and now his tone was serious too. "And I cannot express how much your compliments mean to me."

"Well then, I'll share that the reason I used the words 'might be' is that I think you're so much who you are, you'd be this man anyway. I just think it sucks you were forced to be. Does that make sense?"

"Absolutely."

"Does it suck for you?"

"Being placed in the position, well before I was fourteen, to look after my sisters in all ways, including emotionally?"

I nodded.

"Not in the slightest," he answered.

Ugh.

Every day it was becoming clearer and clearer.

He was perfect in every way.

"Oh, all right," I grumbled. "So the words 'completely and utterly' were subtext."

He burst out laughing.

When it was down to chuckles, he brushed his lips against mine before he said, "It's my life. If I could change things, I would change Prue being bullied. I'd obviously stop Chassie from being assaulted. I would wish for all three of them to have a mum who was around to give them the things I couldn't, which would mean Tempie wasn't forced to become that person for Prue and Chassie after she was forced to find her own way. But other than that, I have no complaints."

I was about to kiss him to share how his statement made me feel (which was ever-increasing levels of *fond*) when that movement of a bed made only by a cat jumping on it happened.

I looked to the side and gasped.

There was a chubby, thick-short-haired gray cat there with tawny eyes.

"Oh my God," I whispered excitedly. "Is that Greystoke?"

"One in the same," Battle replied, reaching a long arm to the cat and further extending a long finger.

Greystoke sniffed it then butted his head against it.

Battle started scratching behind his ears.

"I haven't met him yet," I said. "He's so chonky."

"He's around Prue the most, and she has copious cat treats stashed throughout The Downs, so he's usually the beneficiary of those."

"Hence why he sticks close to Prue," I deduced.

"Hence, that," he replied, his voice shaking with humor.

Greystoke took a chance and came closer to cuddle with us, doing this at my hip.

Which meant I got to start stroking.

Oo, his thick fur was so soft!

"Fuck," Battle grunted.

"What?" I asked.

"Grey is here, and that means we can't move until he's gone. Am I right?"

I bit my lip.

He read that as what it was.

An affirmative to his question.

As such, he griped, "To use your terminology, *a* sucky part of all that's completely and utterly wonderful about you, is that you refuse to disturb a content animal."

"They never stay long."

"Mm."

"And I just met him," I added.

He said nothing.

He also didn't move, because I was stroking Greystoke, and I didn't want him to.

White gold.

Clicked in.

My guy.

"You know, I had the weirdest feeling before I turned into the drive at The Downs," I informed him. "It was kind of like before you go into a haunted house. You're scared, but you're excited. I don't know what that shit was about." Haunted ballroom notwithstanding, but I wasn't going to tell him that. "I just know my vibe-o-meter was malfunctioning, because turning into your drive was the best thing I've ever done in my whole life."

"Vibe-o-meter?"

"You get what I'm saying."

"I do, and a very not sucky part of what makes you so attractive is that you're an unabashed loon."

I grinned proudly. "I am that."

He looked at my grin for half a beat before he kissed me.

At this point, Greystoke had no choice but to vamoose, because thus commenced round two.

At least I got to meet the wee fur baby and get a little cuddle in.

But I would only think about that after Battle redemonstrated one of the very *not* sucky parts about him.

His unending creativity in finding ways to give me orgasms.

And to make me feel beautiful, precious and adored while he did it.

CHAPTER 23

THE CLEANSING

It happened when I was headed from Battle's room, a place he'd left fifteen minutes ago because he had a text that sent him to his laptop in his study.

I was going down for cocktails.

I had a pep in my step (for obvious reasons—spending a late afternoon in bed with Battle talking deep shit and making love was the perfect afternoon activity, says me) and was nearing the bend of the hall of the south wing, when it happened.

Soot dashed from out of nowhere, tripping me.

I was about to right myself before Floofy was there, sending me careening in the other direction, tag teaming with Greystoke, who came from the other side to keep me going in that direction.

After that came Baby Blue, Snowball *and* Gingerface, and since I couldn't keep my feet under me, there was nothing for it.

I tipped over, my hands hitting a door that wasn't quite closed.

It flew open and I fell into the room on my hands and knees.

The cats scattered.

I shifted to a hip and waved out my wrists because both hurt like fuck from landing on them.

For a second, I was out of it, discombobulated from the fall.

Then I looked around the room I was in, one I hadn't been in before, but I knew it was Chassie's.

A study in pinks, not like mine—softer, paler, more feminine, but not girlie.

There were lots of flowers in vases, and her straw hat was on the bed.

She wasn't there, thank goodness.

But I was freaking.

It was not an unknown occurrence to trip over a cat.

In fact, if you had cats, you knew it was commonplace. We'd had cats all through growing up. I'd been tripped countless times.

So yeah.

I knew it was commonplace.

As such, the night I tripped over Snowball and into Battle's arms didn't seem weird to me at the time.

Tripping over Baby Blue getting out of the shower wasn't weird either. Cats had fascinations with bathrooms. And Baby Blue had an attachment to Battle. Not to mention, every female of any species (also says me) would have an attachment to Battle when he was naked.

Even if we shifted to canines, it stood to reason Bartholomew would get up to greet his daddy when he got home, so him tripping me at Burleigh House didn't seem odd to me either.

But...

What just happened with all six cats tripping me at once?

No.

And because what just happened wasn't your normal occurrence, maybe the Snowball and Bartholomew thing...

Perhaps those were something else.

"It's like they wanted me in this room," I mused to myself, and since the sting was out of my wrists, I pushed to my feet.

It felt weird being in Chassie's room without her knowing I was there, I certainly wasn't going to search it.

And maybe I was being funny.

So, some cats tripped me.

But six of them tripping me at once, like they were leading me to Chassie's door?

I walked out, closing it like it was before, not fully, and still feeling way the hell creeped out.

I considered chatting with Prue about it.

But that was a problem because I was down with Battle thinking I was an unabashed loon, but I didn't want anyone to think I was an actual lunatic.

I'd told her about what happened when I walked through the ballroom, and she hadn't experienced it, but I knew that sounded cray-cray to her.

And of course, there was passing out the second I laid eyes on Battle.

But Prue did go to Ravenna and write fantasy books. Maybe she would think what just happened was, indeed, freaky, but meaningful, like I did.

And maybe, with her, we could ask Chassie if there was anything Harmony-and-Charlie-related in her room.

She might not understand it, so perhaps we could all have a look.

I thought this because I thought the phantom couple I saw walking out of the ballroom, the ones who I ran after, were Harmony and Charlie. I didn't see their faces, just their backs. I had photos of my great-granddad, and I'd seen some of Harmony. It could have been them.

I mean, I wasn't completely at one with cats being motivated by supernatural forces to guide you where you were supposed to be.

I was no UFO, conspiracy theory, reincarnation, etc. believer.

But I still thought there were things that were unexplained.

I didn't believe Lee Harvey Oswald acted alone, for one.

And I saw what I saw in that ballroom.

That was not jetlag.

Nor was my reaction to seeing Battle. The bolt that hit me, the charge I got when he first touched me.

And I saw Ravenna throw my cards…twice.

Not to mention, she said Charlie's letters were in the house.

Okay, so it was more than minorly loopy that I thought maybe the cats were pointing me in the direction of Chassie's room to tell me Charlie's letters were in there.

But everyone on board The Mary Celeste disappeared without a trace, and to this day, no one knew why. And hundreds of people danced for days, some of them dropping from exhaustion and even dying in Strasbourg during the Dancing Plague, and to this day, no one understood how that happened.

So I wasn't closing my mind to anything.

This taking my thoughts, along with avoiding any cats at my feet, I was rounding the south landing of the stairs only to see Battle climbing the first grand sweep.

"Hey, take care of business?" I asked as he stopped to wait for me to get to him.

"A quick email I needed to read and respond to, and not on a phone keyboard."

Yeah, those phone keyboards were no fun to type on.

"I hear you," I said as I made it to him.

He turned and curled an arm around my shoulders, mine went around his waist, and we walked down the rest of the stairs.

We hit the plum parlor that had Tempie and Prue, both with drinks.

Battle deposited me in a chair and then locked eyes with me.

I understood his look.

"Amaretto sour," I ordered.

He jutted his chin and went to the drinks cabinet.

Tempie opened her mouth to speak.

But Prue got there before her. "If you're going to say something about Battie and Vivi and afternoon sex, I'm throwing a pillow at you."

"I don't need to, dear, you just did," Tempie replied.

Prue shot her a pointy face.

It glanced off Tempie.

"Where's Chassie?" Battle asked from the cabinet.

"On her way, I expect," Tempie said.

"You can relax, Battie," Prue told him. "I saw her come in from the gardens earlier." She turned to me. "She didn't look happy."

Hmm.

I wasn't sure hard to get was Christian's best play.

"Didn't look happy?" Tempie queried, the thread of worry in her voice going undisguised.

"Chassie has a thing for Christian," Prue announced.

Tempie, for the first time since I met her, seemed thrown.

She blinked and asked, "She does?"

Prue took a sip of her old fashioned before she answered, "No one wears three-hundred-pound dresses to garden, Tempie."

Tempie appeared stunned.

Miracles never cease.

"We're not to get involved," Battie commanded while walking our drinks toward me. After he gave me mine and folded in beside me, he looked at Prue. "Any of us. I'll repeat, your stalking is done."

"Fine by me," she replied and looked at me. "The curator from the V and A is coming on Tuesday anyway. I'm going to be busy."

"I cannot wait to hear what they have to say," I enthused.

"Me either," Prue agreed.

I took a sip of my drink and said to Battle. "This is yummy, honey. Thank you."

"My pleasure, darling," he murmured into his G&T.

"I forgot to inquire," Tempie said. "Did you call your sister?"

I nodded. "Wednesday night."

"All good on the home front?" Prue asked.

"Yes." I smiled big. "And Lenny and Al are thinking of bringing the kids over to visit in June or July."

"That would be so lovely for you!" Prue clapped. "And we'll get to meet them." She sat back in the sofa. "It's been forever since we've had kids in the house." Her brows shot down. "Wait, except for when I was a kid, I don't know if we've ever had kids in the house."

"I'd love for them to see the house," I remarked.

"See?" Tempie asked.

"Yes. See. If you're all groovy with me giving them a tour," I answered.

Battle entered the conversation. "I believe that would be necessary for them to navigate it and find the parlor for drinks, Vivienne."

"Oh, they won't stay here," I said breezily.

And got one set of surprised (Prue), one set of amused (Tempie) and one set of annoyed (Battle) eyes aimed at me.

"What?" I asked.

"We're not having this discussion again," Battle said.

And I got it.

"Battle, I don't think they'll be comfortable with staying here."

"Then you best be very convincing, darling," he purred.

"You and I are very new," I pointed out. "That's a lot to ask for all involved."

"You and I are very solid," he returned. "It would be insulting if they stayed elsewhere. You know we have more than enough space."

Since I wasn't going to bicker about this in front of his sisters, I said, "Okay, I can float the idea by them. But if they're not into it, you have to be okay with them getting a BnB or something."

"That would be the you-convincing-them part," Battle retorted smoothly.

Changing my mind about bickering, I was about to open my mouth to say something when the vibe in the room tilted on its axis.

Battle felt it and we both looked between Tempie and Prue.

Prue was staring at the door with her mouth agape.

Tempie was following her sister's gaze to the door, and when it got there, I didn't think she could get paler than her naturally paler than pale, but she did when her gaze hit whatever was at the door.

Then her face got red, and she took her well-shod feet.

I looked over my shoulder at the door to see Chassie in her pretty pink sundress.

And with her was a brute of a man, probably six two, built like a pro wrestler, with a mess of very dark-red hair and an equal mess of a big russet beard. He had sky-blue eyes that practically shone out of his face. And I was glad I was sitting, or I would have swooned again.

Battle stood.

I chanced it and stood too.

I sensed Prue standing with us.

I saw Chassie's fingers fiddling with the skirt on her dress and she was also carrying a massive bouquet of flowers in her other arm.

"Hamish, mate," Battle broke the silence, and he did it tentatively. "This is a surprise."

Hamish?

The Hamish?

This handsome bear of a man was Tempie's boyfriend?

Oh, God.

I loved this.

"I asked a friend in London who we both know," Chassie said to Tempie on a rush. "She got me Hamish's phone number, and I called to see if he would be up to surprise you at The Downs." An excruciatingly awkward pause and then a lame, "Surprise!"

"That was not your call to make Chastity Louisa Talyn," Tempie snapped.

Hamish's face closed down.

Then it got ticked.

No!

I shot Battle a *Do something!* look.

Before he could do something, Hamish spoke.

"If I'm not wanted," he said (or I think he said—yeah, the burr was strong).

"Hamish—" Battle started.

"It's me who should invite you to my home first," Tempie snapped.

"Aye, love, and I'm hearing your message loud and clear," Hamish fired back (I think).

Tempie tried to look cool, but I could sense her panic.

"I'll just go," Hamish declared. He looked down at Chassie. "Appreciate the effort, lass. Enjoy your flowers."

Battle shot me a look I sadly couldn't read then walked around the chairs, saying to Hamish, "Let's go talk in my study while the women chat."

"Thanks, Battle, but a man knows when he's not wanted and that's been communicated clearly. I just didn't want to hear it," Hamish replied.

My attention shot to Tempie.

"Tempie—" I started.

"You're not leaving," Chassie said over me, this aimed at Hamish.

His face got soft (but I could tell he was still pissed...and hurt). "You're sweet, lassie, but—"

"*You're not leaving!*" she shrieked in his face.

All the air left the room, taking with it our ability to breathe.

Chassie stepped further into the room and kept screeching.

"*I got raped!*" She threw the beautiful bouquet to the floor and pounded her chest. "*Me!*"

I vaguely noted the extremes of Hamish's flinch right before his gaze raced to Tempie.

"What, Temperance?" Chassie demanded. "*What?*" she screamed. "You're going to put your life on hold *forever* just to be sure I'm okay?"

"Dearest," Tempie whispered.

Chassie shot forward at the waist and shouted, "I won't have it!"

"Lovely, let's go somewhere and talk," Prue urged Chastity.

"No!" Chassie yelled. "Chelsea was right. I'm a weight. A weight both of you"—she jabbed fingers at Tempie and Battle—"have been carrying *for too long.*"

"What the fuck?" Battle growled low.

I gave him a *Later!* look.

"Not anymore!" Chassie was still yelling. "Vivi comes to this house, and she's sweet, and she's funny, and she doesn't take Battie's shit, or your shit, Tempie," she aimed that at her sister. "Then, one day, she's flirting and playing cards, and she says, 'Oh yes, my mom died a year ago.' And you could tell by the ache in her voice it *kills her* that her mum is gone, but she *keeps going*. I saw it. I felt it. I understood what I'd done. So now you, all three of you"—she jabbed her finger again, this time including Prue—"are off duty."

"You've been—" Tempie tried.

"I know what I've been, Tempie," Chassie snapped. "I'm not that anymore. I figured it out. He took *everything* from me. *Everything*. My boyfriend. My shop. My life in Bath. My strength. My courage. He took everything, except the three *of you*. And *I let him*."

Tempie started an approach, beseeching, "Please don't look at it that way, darling."

"How should I look at it, Tempie? It happened. I let it. And now I'm going to stop letting it. Chelsea was right. But I've been watching Vivi and that's how I'm going to be. Life punches you in the teeth. You bleed, wipe away the mess and keep going. I'm not going to let him scare me anymore. I'm not going to let him take any more from me. And I sure as *fuck* am not going to let him take any more *from you*."

"You go, Chassie," I whispered encouragingly.

She shot me a timid look then pulled it together and tossed her chaotic curls.

She locked eyes with Tempie. "So Hamish is here because you want him here. You're just scared I'm going to worry that Battie found Vivi, and you have Hamish, and Prue will become a big-time author, and I'll be alone. Well, I know I'm never alone. I know I'll never *be* alone. Prue can take me with her on her book tours, and Prue's good company. That will make me happy. But however it happens, I'm going to get on with my life. I haven't figured out what I'm going to do, but that's for me. It is not for you. All I know I *am* going to do is get out of the way of *your* life."

No one said anything.

And then Tempie did.

"You were our wee china doll."

Oh God.

Her voice was an open wound.

"Everybody out," Battle ordered, his gaze glued to Hamish.

I wasn't about to move, at least not toward the door.

But I saw Hamish, his handsome face a mask of anguish for Chassie, also for his woman, heading toward Tempie.

And I didn't have a choice.

Battle took hold of my elbow, he grabbed Chassie on the way, and Prue scurried after us.

Battle closed the door on Tempie's first sob.

My heart shattered.

He turned from the door and Chassie fell into his arms.

Her sobs were quiet.

He stroked her hair.

We stood just outside the door for a bit, hearing the muted humming burr of whatever Hamish was saying, the feminine weeping coming from Tempie, but eventually, Prue herded us to the smoking room.

When we got there, Battle took Chassie to the sofa, and they sat in it with his arms still holding her close.

"I'll just tell Cook dinner might be delayed," Prue whispered, and she took off.

I was so agitated, worried about Chassie, about Tempie, I couldn't sit.

So I went to the windows, stared at Chassie's beautiful garden and listened to a woman I loved weeping.

"I-I knew she'd be m-mad," Chassie eventually wept into Battle's chest. "B-b-but Ravenna told her she was going to l-lose him. And sh-she's still here. Sh-she d-didn't go to London. Even with you here. I h-had t-t-to do *something*."

"You did right, love," Battle purred. "Just right. It's going to be fine."

I turned my head their way.

Battle's gaze was on me.

The expression on his face was harsh and hopeful, an odd combination, but pure beauty.

Prue returned.

"Cook's good," she announced, going directly to Chassie and taking control. "Let's get you up. See to your face."

Chassie rose, sniffled and wiped her cheeks. "Did you go by the parlor? Is she still crying?"

"I just heard Hamish when I walked by," Prue told her, leading her toward the door. I saw her big smile. "That was a totally crazy idea. I wished I had it."

Chassie looked at her, startled.

Then she giggled a little bit as they disappeared in the hall.

I turned to Battle. "Are you okay?"

He lifted one long finger then stood from the couch.

He stared at the door his sisters walked through for a beat, two, three…five, and then he went to it and closed it.

After that, he came to me.

"Did you hear whatever Chelsea said?"

Oh boy.

"Yes," I admitted.

"What did that bitch say?"

"Battle—"

He got in my face and clipped, "Vivienne, *what did she say?*"

"She just hinted, rather strongly, that you'd never find a duchess because you had to look after Chassie and Prue."

"To their face?"

"To my face, but they were there and didn't miss it. Tempie told her to get out of her sight right after she said it. Rally was pissed as shit. Courtney was a mess. If she didn't walk out of the room, I think Rally would have tossed her out."

Battle's jaw clenched.

"Tempie had words with them after," I rushed on. "I thought she'd handled it."

"She didn't."

No.

But Chelsea did.

"Honey, I hesitate to give Chelsea any credit, but I feel at this juncture I should point out that, even if what she said was cruel, and wrong, it did get Chassie to thinking."

"*You* got Chassie to thinking. She found out that same night your mum died not long ago. And here you are, calling 'tallyho' erroneously and peeling out of the front drive."

"Erroneously?"

"It's a call to the hounds on a hunt, or if you see a fox. Not what you shout before taking a day trip."

"Oh."

"Bloody hell, Vivi," he bit out. "Stick with me here. My sister just had a goddamn meltdown."

"No, Battle, your sister just asserted her power."

His body jolted.

"That"—I pointed in the direction of the plum parlor—"took some serious ovaries. Calling Hamish? Going head-to-head with Tempie, of all people? Hell, I like to think I'm no pushover, but she scares the bejesus out of me."

His head cocked to the side. "She does?"

I flipped out my hands. "Not really, but yes. She's the coolest bitch on the planet, and I've seen her make mincemeat of Chelsea. I never want that aimed at me."

"She adores you."

I sighed. "I know, honey. Just…forget it. It's a woman thing. Like tampons and periods and never talking to a friend again if they let you chat up a hot guy with lipstick on your teeth."

He assumed a baffled look that was outrageously adorable.

I put my hands on his chest and leaned into him. "What I'm saying is, what just happened is good. Very good. Cleansing. For Chassie, and since she decided to pack a punch at her impromptu coming-out party, hopefully for Tempie."

Slowly, his gaze moved to the door.

I put a hand to his cheek to bring him back to me.

"To put a fine point on what we talked about earlier, one of the myriad reasons I'm falling in love with you," I began, "is how much you love them. I grew up surrounded by love, but I've never seen anything so beautiful."

His hands came to my hips, his face got soft and gentle and warm and oh-so-very beautiful, and he whispered, "Darling."

I loved his reaction to my admission, but I couldn't let up on him.

This was too important.

"But right now, your challenge is going to be letting them sort themselves out," I informed him. "However this is going to go down from here has to be about Tempie and Chassie and Prue. Chassie's ready to figure it out, and she has to have the space to let that happen. Tempie is going to have to stop hiding from what she feels for Hamish and take that risk or lose him. And Prue is going to be a huge star one day, and you all are going to have to learn to deal with her outshining you. None of that is going to be in your control, baby. You're just going to have to let them roll the dice and see."

For a second, I thought he'd retort.

After that second, his arms curved around me, so mine did the same to him, and I put my cheek on his chest.

"I know it's going to be hard," I said gently.

"It'll probably kill me," he admitted.

Totally wished I had a big brother.

I tipped my head back. "In the end, they're going to be happy. They're going to be all they should be. And you'll have given them the foundation to be that and the freedom to be all of it. That's good, isn't it?"

"Yes, Vivi." He went in for a lip touch. "All good."

He moved to let go of me, muttering something about drinks.

But I didn't let him go until I could see from his face he was dealing.

Only then did I let him go.

Battle went to make us more drinks.

After a spell, the girls came back with the news that the door to the plum parlor was open, no one in it, so they crept up to Tempie's bedroom, and definitely someone was in there.

"I've told Cook we're ready when she is, and to leave something warming in case they want a tray," Prue declared.

Chassie still had red eyes, but she was veritably *preening*.

Oh yeah.

She done good.

We went into the dining room when Scotty came to share dinner was ready.

And when Battle and I went up to bed in his room, there was a tray on the floor outside the door of Tempie's room with spent plates, and a cork, but no bottle of wine or glasses.

As we kept walking, I shot Battle's stony-face-shit-my-sister-is-in-that-room-fucking-her-hot-Scottish-guy expression a smug smile and asked, "See?"

He tucked me tight to his side and kissed my head as he kept us walking.

And he took me to his room, so he could fuck his hot American girl.

I was almost asleep, worn out by my hot English guy and draped over his chest, when he said, "So...falling in love with me?"

I stiffened.

He rolled on top of me.

"I'm thinking Sophronia," he stated.

I forced my lips to say, "What?"

"That's for a girl. Noble, Archer or Journey if it's a boy. Maybe Endeavor."

Oh God.

He was talking children!

I melted under him.

"You want kids?" I whispered.

"Yes."

"How many?" I asked.

"However many you wish to carry for me."

Oh God!

I stared up at the shadowed planes and angles of his face in the moonlight.

He was no less gorgeous in shadow.

And I *loved this*.

However.

"Sophronia?"

"It means sensible. We can call her Phronsie."

Uh.

No.

"Yes on Noble and Archer," I decreed, because those were shit-hot boy names. "Endeavor is a maybe. It's rad, but not sure how to make it a nickname. No on Journey, or I'll never get 'Don't Stop Believin'' out of my head."

He chuckled.

It sounded and felt nice.

Then he took us to our sides but kept me gathered close.

"Grace?" I suggested.

"Pretty, but unimaginative. Sorry, sweetheart. You know the rules."

I did, and I'd always thought the Talyn penchant for naming their offspring unusual names was just…unusual.

But now I was seeing it was all kinds of fun.

"How about Verity?" I suggested.

"A contender, but I think I have a great-great-great aunt with that name."

"Gilda?"

"Hmm," he hummed.

Another contender.

"Genesis is interesting," he said. "We can call her Genny."

I wasn't sure about Genesis, but it *was* different. And Genny was sweet.

"Constance is also good," I said.

"Yes, it is."

"But it's also kinda normal. So what about Lyric?"

That got me another "hmm," so that meant it was another contender.

Battle followed up his hmm with, "Fury could be for a boy or a girl. Though, I like it better for a girl."

Fury was a kick-ass name. Especially for a girl.

"That's an option," I agreed. "Electra?"

"Maybe."

He wasn't keen on that one. And it kinda didn't fit the theme.

"I want to add Shepherd and Hero to boys' names," I declared.

"Acceptable," he grunted.

I smiled.

And we whispered in the moonlight, so caught up in the importance of what we were discussing, what was happening, what was growing...

We again missed the dancing lights coming from the ballroom.

CHAPTER 24

THE AFTERMATH

The next morning, Battle and I walked into the breakfast room hand in hand to see Prue at the table, which was covered with sketchpads.

"Oh my God!" I nearly shouted, letting Battle go and rushing in. "Is this your work?"

I reached for a sketchpad as Prue answered, "Some of it. These are the roughs of the stories and illustrations. I like to hand draw my ideas before I get down to it. Most of it is digital."

With a sketchpad in my hands and Battle's hands on me, he guided me into a chair and went to the sideboard.

"With all of this out on the table, can I assume I can look at it?" I asked enthusiastically.

Prue smiled happily at me. "Yes."

I eagerly started flipping.

Okay, I immediately saw what she meant about "early" work when referring to what she'd previously given me.

What she gave me was stellar.

This was off the charts. I'd frame any of these for my wall.

"Holy shit, honey, this is…*wow*."

"Even I'm kinda proud of that one," she mumbled.

Proud?

The English and their understatements.

Yeesh.

I kept flipping even after Battle put a plate full of food in front of me, one in front of him and seated himself beside me.

He then reached to the coffeepot to pour us both a cup.

Eventually, the bacon called to me, not to mention caffeine, and I set the sketchpad carefully away from anything that might mar it.

"You say you have that on digital?" I asked.

Prue gestured to the pads with her fork. "All of it."

"Perfect," I replied while spreading lime marmalade on my toast. "I can look through them and we can strategize which ones to send my agent."

While I was saying this, Chassie roamed in sporting a pair of cute pajama bottoms with little pink and peach polka dots on them, a peach babydoll tee and a frizzy head of hair that was exponentially frizzier after sleeping on it.

I'd never seen someone come to the breakfast table at The Downs like it was what it was, the breakfast table of a family.

I loved it.

Especially coming from Chassie.

"Coffee, sweetheart?" Battle asked as Chassie roamed right up to the sideboard.

"Please," she answered, lifting a lid and peering inside. "You need to teach Patsy how to make your pancakes, Vivi."

"Whenever you want them, I can make them for you," I replied.

"Or you could teach me how to make them," she said while spooning scrambled eggs on her plate.

"I'd love that," I returned.

Prue clapped. "And me. Teach me. I also want to learn how to make toast and oatmeal."

"We'll have some cooking lessons next Sunday when Emily is gone," I decided.

"You'll have them whenever you feel like you're up for a break from your book," Battle butted in. "You're being lovely as usual, darling," he purred to me. "But don't let anything take away from your process."

I'd warned him about my process since I was starting the book tomorrow, and I didn't want him to be caught off guard by the obsessive nature of my work.

"What process?" Chassie asked, folding a leg under her as she took her seat by Battle and put her plate on the table.

"I get obsessive when I write," I explained. "I usually write at home, so it's going to be interesting, having a space just for writing that's away from everything. But it's good Battle brought it up, because you guys should know, I'll probably hole up in the studio for long periods of time."

"We don't want to mess with your process, Vivi, so whatever you need," Prue said.

"And don't forget, just buzz to the house if you need anything," Chassie added.

"Thanks, guys," I replied. Then, "Listen, speaking of the book," I turned to Prue, "when you were searching for Charlie's letters, did you look in all the bedrooms?"

Prue was confused. "Bedrooms?"

"Like yours and Tempie's...and Chassie's?"

This was the way I decided to play it rather than share about what happened the evening before with the cats.

I was falling for their brother; I didn't need to give them reasons to move me out of The Downs and into an asylum.

"I would notice some letters hanging around," Chassie remarked and took a bite of toast.

"I would too, as would Tempie," Prue said. "Especially since I've been looking for them for months."

"A journal? Something tucked in books? Anything?" I asked.

They both stared kindly, but ruefully at me while shaking their heads.

It was Battle who spoke.

"All the family bedrooms have been redecorated in the last few years, love. And except me, we've all been in the same rooms since we were children. They would have noticed something like that after several decades, and definitely when things were moved out so the redecorating could happen."

I frowned and forked into some eggs.

"The letters will turn up when you most need them, Vivi," Prue said. "Ravenna never lies. They're here. We just have to happen on them when the time is right."

I hoped so.

It was then, wearing smart red capris, a white sleeveless top and white Versace pumps with the flat bow on the toe, Tempie strolled in.

Her expression was bland when she did, but it shifted instantly to cross when she looked at Battle.

So I looked at Battle.

He was gazing at her with a smug expression so extreme, it turned me on as much as it confused me.

"Don't start," she warned, melting into a chair and reaching for the coffeepot.

"I said nothing," Battle purred, and even his purr was smug.

"Let me see," Prue began. "We all heard Battie's door slam at... what? Eleven o'clock on a Friday night? And we didn't see Battie and Vivi until Sunday morning. So that makes it..." She started counting on her fingers.

"Yes, dear," Tempie drawled. "But I just left a Scotsman immobile on his stomach in my bed."

"I still win," Battle said into his coffee cup.

Good Lord.

Were they competing about who was the bigger sex god?

"Thirty-four hours!" Prue crowed after she stopped counting.

Battle smirked.

"You're at only fourteen hours, Tempie," Chassie rubbed it in. "Battie beat you by a whole twenty hours."

"They took a break to go to the pub," Tempie pointed out.

"Maybe so," I chimed in. "But it was a miracle that happened considering Battle induced a lot of immobility in me. This meant he was forced to do quite a bit of the work, also forced to take me to fuel so I could move."

Prue's giggle peeled through the room.

But Battle turned his head and gave me a look so magnificent, I knew I'd never forget it.

Not all my life.

And it didn't make my nipples tingle.

It made my heart skip a beat.

It said both I was officially one of them…

And he was falling in love with me too.

I already knew that last part.

But the first part felt nearly as amazing.

"A warning," Tempie broke into our moment and fluttered a disparaging hand Battle's and my way, "that will never happen with Hamish and me."

"What won't happen?" Chassie asked.

"Being gooey-eyed at the breakfast table." Tempie paused. "Or anywhere, for that matter."

"We'll see," Battle murmured.

"Are you and Hamish all right?" Chassie asked, her words threaded with worry.

"Although I'll never forgive you, dearest," Tempie stated, and Battle got stiff beside me, "I'll also never be able to find the words to thank you."

Battle relaxed.

Chassie grinned.

Tempie sipped coffee.

I shoved bacon in my mouth.

Fifteen minutes later Hamish sauntered in.

And with a light kiss on Tempie's upturned lips, she belatedly introduced him to everyone.

And he joined the family.

I leaned my weight against the handle of my mallet, stating, "All right, this is a shade too far."

Prue, standing next to me, asked, "What?"

I looked down at her. "We're playing croquet."

"And?" she inquired, openly perplexed.

"Do you play croquet often?" I asked in return.

"Yes, in the summer. Why?"

"My darling!" Tempie cried before I could say word one about the Bridgertons, and we both turned that way to see her planting a lavish kiss on Hamish's beard.

Battle was frowning.

"Oops. I think Hamish just got in a good shot," Prue mumbled.

"My turn!" Chassie yelled and bellied up to her ball.

I watched as everyone watched, a good deal of my attention on Hamish, who—new to all this drama and being introduced to it rather dramatically—had a keen and concerned eye on Chassie even as he slid an arm around Tempie's shoulders.

Yeah.

He was a good guy.

Chassie's hit connected with my ball and sent it flying.

She twirled to me. "Oh no, Vivi! I'm sorry!"

"Honey, that's the game," I said as I trudged to my ball.

I had to get it back on the appropriate trajectory.

My hit failed and it went too far the other way.

"Revolting luck, darling," Battle cooed, coming to me, curling his arm around my shoulders and tucking me into his side.

"Luck has nothing to do with it. I suck at this," I replied.

"You'll get the hang of it."

Maybe I would.

But even if I never did, when the croquet set came out, I'd be there.

Because the sun shone, the flowers bloomed, spring was in the air, croquet was fun (no matter how bad I was at it), and I was happy.

I leaned my weight into Battle and whispered, "I wish Mom could be here."

His arm tightened and he kissed the side of my head.

He didn't need to say anything.

That was perfect.

In the end, Hamish won, and I thought Battle would pitch a low-key aristocratic fit (one could say my guy was competitive).

But he just said to Hamish, "Shall we set up the thrower and shoot?"

Hamish's strong white teeth emerged from his bushy red beard. "Works for me."

But me?

I knew Battle's game.

Hamish was an outdoorsman.

And here we were, doing a bunch of shit outdoors.

He was doing his bit to help his sister win Hamish to The Downs.

So falling for my fucking guy.

And with his suggestion, people scattered.

Then we reunited in the south parkland (for your information, Tempie had a pair of shiny red, short shaft wellies that she was so cool wearing them, she made them look hot).

The thrower shot clay pigeons in the air that Battle, Tempie, Hamish, and even Chassie shot out of it (if they hit it, and just to say, Battle definitely excelled above all the others in this, though Hamish wasn't far behind and Tempie rocked it) while Prue and I sat on a thick blanket wearing ear protectors (Battle insisted—we all had them, then again, shotguns were *loud*) and looked through her sketchbooks.

Admittedly, it wasn't super close to spending time with Battle in his bed.

Still.

Lawn croquet and trap shooting in the sun with all of these lovely people was second runner-up for how I liked to spend time at The Downs.

The chicken was under foil and resting.

The potatoes were done and in their pot of hot water waiting to be whipped.

I'd just put the Yorkshire puds in the oven.

And the pavlova smeared in thick cream, lemon curd and covered with berries was in the fridge.

This meant I could dash up for a drink before I had to come back down and finish everything.

When I made it to the plum parlor, I saw everyone was there but Prue.

The minute I stepped in, Battle pushed up from his chair.

"Drink, darling?" he asked.

"Please. Can you make me a Cosmo?"

"Of course," he murmured as I made it to him.

I got a lip brush, a gentle shove into my chair, and he headed to the drinks cabinet.

"You sure you don't need help in the kitchen, Vivi?" Chassie asked.

"It'd help if you'd go back down with me in twenty minutes," I answered. "I can tell you how to mash potatoes while I whip up the gravy. Then you can help me carry everything up."

"Oo, that'd be great," Chassie replied.

I looked from her to Tempie and Hamish, tucked close together on the sofa opposite Chassie.

"Where's Prue?" I asked.

"Somewhere," Tempie said unnecessarily.

I gave her the side eye.

She smiled.

"Maybe I should text her," Chassie suggested. "She's usually always one of the first ones down."

"She probably doesn't want to be pressed into kitchen drudgery," Tempie remarked.

Hamish chuckled.

"I'm going back to London with Hamish in the morning, dears," Tempie said to Chassie and me. "Is that all right?"

"That's perfect," Chassie whispered.

I just smiled and transferred my smile to Battle who was heading my way with a Cosmopolitan in a martini glass.

He didn't make it because he stopped dead, his eyes to the door.

I looked over my shoulder.

And I nearly burst out laughing.

Prue was walking in.

With Christian.

His eyes went right to Chassie.

Chassie emitted a panicked peep.

Prue spoke.

"I asked Christian to join us for our Sunday roast!" she announced superfluously. She looked to me. "I hope there'll be enough, Vivi."

"Oh, there'll be plenty," I replied.

She clapped. "Brilliant!"

Battle stopped scowling at her, put on his host's face and said to Christian, "Good to have you, mate. Would you like something to drink?"

Before Christian could answer, Prue took his hand, dragged him to Chassie's sofa, and all but shoved him in it.

Chassie's face flamed.

I nearly snorted.

Tempie whispered something in Hamish's ear.

Battle looked to the ceiling.

"Cider would be good, if you've got it," Christian ordered, his voice deep and pleasant.

When it filled the room, Chassie's face flamed harder.

"They have everything!" I peeped.

Battle gave me my Cosmo and a *cool it!* look then headed back to the cabinet.

"Hey, I'm Vivi," I introduced myself.

He got out of the sofa just enough to offer his hand, I took it and found he had a nice, firm grip. "Pleased to meet you."

"Hamish," Hamish said after Christian and I broke.

They did the shake thing and then both sat back down.

After that, no one said anything.

Fortunately, by the time Battle handed Prue her old fashioned and Christian a pint glass of cold cider, Tempie came up with a conversational gambit.

"How are your studies going?" she asked Christian.

"The Downs have one of the most flourishing organic gardens I've ever seen," Christian stated after taking a sip.

At his remark, I worried Chassie's flesh would melt right off her skull *Raiders of the Lost Ark* style.

"I'm comparing your results to six other gardens in the area. They all use chemical compounds," Christian went on. "You use nothing but organic compost. And the results are startling."

"All our Chastity's idea, you know," Tempie drawled, gesturing to Chastity with her martini glass.

Christian turned his head to look directly at Chassie.

Chastity popped to her feet and asked me, "Is it time to mash potatoes, Vivi?"

"I—"

She slammed her daiquiri glass down, had to veritably leap over Christian's long legs (and Battle's) to latch on to me and tug me from my seat.

"It's time!" she all but shouted, and as I desperately attempted not to spill any Cosmo, she dragged me from the room while I looked over my shoulder at the inhabitants of said room.

Christian looked crestfallen.

The room disappeared from view.

I left it until we were on the servants' stairs before I pulled her to a stop.

"Get right back up there and send Prue down," I ordered.

"But, Vivi—"

I cupped her face in my free hand and put mine in it. "Honey, I get you. This is scary. But you like him, am I right?"

"He's really handsome," she whispered. "And he likes plants, like me."

"So why did you escape the room?"

"I don't—"

"Listen, you know this is all about vibes and cues. And I don't want to freak you even more, but you're giving that man riotously mixed vibes and totally indecipherable cues."

She blinked. "I am?"

I took my hand from her face and leaned back. "I know we *want* men to get what us wearing pretty sundresses to garden means. But let me educate you, men are clueless."

"He tried to talk to me a little while ago," she admitted something I already knew. "I made a fool of myself. I think it turned him off."

"I'm certain you didn't because he didn't know a single person was in that room, but you."

Hope lit her face.

I seized on it and kept at her.

"It's going to be hard. I know it is. But you have to give him something to go on. And I can tell you, racing from a room he's been in all of five minutes is not the cue you want to be giving him. Go back. Send Prue to help me. Or Battle. Sit with him, and…I don't know. Ask him what those sticks are that he shoves in the ground."

"But I know what they are. They're soil probes."

"Okay, then ask him what readings he's getting on his soil probes…or something."

"I could…maybe ask him what the title of his dissertation is," she suggested.

"Go with that," I encouraged.

She looked uncertainly up the stairs.

"Go, honey," I prompted. "He's into you. Trust me. And if he made the first move, and you froze him out, since now you're giving him an in, I suspect, once you break the ice, he'll take over."

At least, I hoped so.

"I…okay," she said.

"Okay."

She didn't move.

I gave her a gentle push, verbally and physically. "Go, baby."

She gave me a wild-eyed look.

But then she went.

I watched her go.

Once she disappeared, I mumbled, "Fuck, I hope he's not a dick."

And I headed to the kitchen, chicken, mash, sprouts, pud…

Dinner for my people.

I was sitting cross-legged on Battle's bed wearing nothing but the button-down he'd worn that day.

He was coming out of the bathroom in heathered gray pajama pants with a black drawstring.

He had a face like thunder.

I guessed the orgasm I gave him ten minutes ago wore off.

"Honey—" I began.

"Does Prue have some secret crush who'll be coming to dinner next Friday?" he demanded.

I took a second to control my hilarity before I responded.

"Not that I know of."

He stretched out beside me on the bed, head to the pillows, and lifted his hands to rub his face.

"It was good tonight," I told him.

He grunted behind his hands.

I lightly slapped his abs. "It was good."

He took his hands from his face and looked at me.

"I thought Tempie and Hamish were going to whisk the china and cutlery from the table so they could fuck on it, and Chassie and Christian got to the point, it was like no one else was in the room."

One could say, Tempie and Hamish's heated glances and more heated whispering in each other's ears did not take body language experts to interpret.

And once Chassie and Christian got started on compost, plant anatomy, seedlings, algae (yes, algae!) and bioethics, I thought Prue, who was sitting close to them at the table, was going to nod off to sleep.

"We aren't the only ones who get to have fun," I remarked.

His eyes dipped to the gape in his shirt I was wearing, they heated, then what was probably happening, or already happened (like with Battle and me) and was inevitably going to happen again in Tempie's room came to him, I knew, because he rubbed his hands on his face again.

I stretched out against his side.

And I did my own whispering in a hot guy's ear.

"Everyone in this house, right now, is happy."

He dropped his hands and turned his head to me again.

Then his whole body.

When I was in his arms, I asked, "Why'd you put on pajamas?"

"Because you're obsessed with my chest, so I thought I'd help you out with some framing. If I give you too much, you get distracted."

I rolled my eyes (even if he spoke truth, the distracting part was his pretty cock, also his muscled thighs).

He chuckled (he knew he spoke truth).

"Move to my rooms?" he asked.

My eyes rolled right back to his face.

"What?"

"I like the idea of knowing you're sleeping in my bed when I'm away."

I liked that he liked that.

However.

"Battle—"

He gave me a squeeze. "If it's too much too soon, don't do it. I'm telling you what I want. If you're not ready..." He shrugged.

"But, the girls," I said.

"And what's the difference between you being here right now, and them knowing you are, and you being here when I'm not here?"

"You know there's a difference."

"I do? Really?"

Man, he was so into me.

And he didn't give a shit who knew it.

Including me.

Another reason I was falling for him.

"I'll think about it," I gave in.

He brushed my lips with his. "Thank you, love."

"Am I going to get another orgasm? Or are we going to sleep?"

"Do you want another orgasm?"

"You might as well ask if I want another scoop of ice cream in a hot fudge sundae."

He grinned.

We rolled again.

And Battle Talyn, Duke of Burleigh, as was his way, set about giving his all so a woman he cared about would have everything she wanted.

And he did it splendidly.

CHAPTER 25

THE WEDDING

I came out of the bathroom and into Battle's and my bedroom at Primrose Lodge, the country seat of Rally's viscounty up in Somerset.

I did it touching my hat and saying, "Okay, I rock this thing."

Then I stopped dead.

Holy shit.

Battle was wearing gray trousers, a cream waistcoat, a white shirt, and a black morning coat with a peach tie.

Fucking hell.

"I knew this was a mistake," he groused.

My attention shifted from the vision of him being a full-on, super-hot duke in that getup to his face to see him scowling at my outfit.

Since I was finding my online shopping trawls tedious due to me being in the middle of writing my book, Tempie had taken me in hand.

So, to Rally and Courtney's wedding ceremony, I was wearing a lilac suit with a complicated lapel that showed off a lot of my chest, the straight skirt molded to my ass and hips, and a matching hat that sat at an angle and went up high on one side to showcase some intricate net swirls.

Bummed at his reaction, I looked down at myself. "Is this not okay?"

"I knew I should have let you go to the ceremony with the girls," he stated.

"Why?" I asked.

"Because, seeing you looking like a sex-kitten duchess, I no longer want to go at all."

If I could glow, I would have burned a hole in the side of the lodge.

"Well, you're not so bad yourself, my Lord Duke."

He reached a hand to me. "Let's get going," he said tersely, then he told me something I already knew, "They're taking some of the groomsmen pictures before the wedding."

I was very aware going with him to watch him and a bunch of other dudes have their pictures taken would probably bore me silly.

But last night, in a little Talyn Family huddle at a small (if you called fifty people small) pre-wedding dinner party, Tempie had dropped the bomb that Courtney had dropped on her.

This being that she'd made the unhinged decision not to revoke Chelsea's invitation after her behavior at The Downs.

"So Battle can rub Vivi in her face! She'll just *die*. Isn't it smashing?!" Tempie had taken on Courtney's excitement in a droll way when she related this to us.

Normally, I'm all for vengeance.

But after what Chelsea said about Prue and Chassie, with them right there listening, Battle was concerned he might not be able to handle being anywhere near her without causing a scene, something he didn't want to do at one of his best mates' weddings.

He also didn't want her to say anything else to them or to me.

And this was why I was sticking close.

I went to him and took his hand.

"You are the very model of the modern duke," I said. "You'll keep your cool, I know you will. And as Tempie said, with Chelsea's personality, she's eventually going to whittle down her choices to some loser who she can walk all over who will make her extremely unhappy. We've already won, baby. She can't do anything to us."

"That doesn't mean, if she does, it won't piss me right off."

Well then.

What did you say to that?

Because he was right.

But for Rally and Courtney, I knew he'd keep his cool.

Thus, I decided on saying nothing, just sticking to my plan of keeping an eye out.

He tucked my hand around his elbow, and we headed out.

Primrose Lodge was outstanding from the outside, though smaller than The Downs.

But inside, they'd kept décor that had probably been there since two turns of a century.

It wasn't worn down, but it was worn (mildly) and dated (completely).

Still pretty, in its way.

But it wasn't bright and warm and open, like The Downs.

While all sorts of scurrying was going on throughout the house, Battle escorted me out of it and onto the lawn, slowing his gait as I navigated it in my nude heels.

He then sat me in one of the white chairs arranged before an arch festooned splendiferously in peach, cream and yellow flowers, set up in front of the detached orangery.

He bent and touched his lips to mine, then moved to the other men wearing morning suits who were loitering at the arch.

Okay.

So…

It was a month after the Hamish/Christian weekend at The Downs.

And a lot had happened.

Let's get into it.

∼

First, I started my book, and yes, it was obsessing me.

Though, two things were cool about writing in the studio.

One, I found it was kind of fun to "go to work" rather than stumbling to my desk in my house with a cup of coffee and a bedhead.

At The Downs, I got up.

I took a shower.

I got dressed.

Then the cats and I headed out to the studio, now covered in blooming wisteria, which if the wind blew, sent confetti petals all over the place. And the wind blew often.

It was like being in my own magical little world.

I would arrive in the studio to what Patsy sorted for me to be treated to: a big carafe of coffee, a jug of cream in a bed of ice and something lovely but easy to eat, like an almond croissant and some fruit or a bacon butty (and some fruit).

The second thing that was cool about writing my book in that studio (okay, so this wasn't strictly about the studio, but it was about what I was doing there) was running my chapters by Battle, I found to my surprise, was awesome.

Due to that response, obviously, he hadn't nixed anything (yet).

But his compliments and enthusiasm meant the world.

Better?

When he was home, he didn't get all demanding of my time, or pouty that he didn't have it.

No, in fact, if I called to the house for a sandwich or something, often, it was Battle who brought it out to me.

Not to interrupt me. I only got my delivery and a quick kiss.

He did it to support me.

In other words, we could say, for a variety of reasons, the "falling" bit of falling in love was no longer part of the equation (and that was the best of all of this).

Other than that, everyone left me alone to do my thing, and that was crazy kind.

However, that didn't mean things didn't happen.

They did.

The unsurprising stuff:

We still hadn't run across Charlie's letters.

I was beginning to think this might be a rare miss in Ravenna's psychic powers.

The only thing I knew was, it was what it was, and as usual, I just had to sally forth.

So I did.

The kinda boring stuff:

I took Noelle up to a run and I didn't fall off.

Progress.

I also, at Battle's suggestion (all right, it was a demand, but I decided to think of it as a suggestion), phoned Mr. Atkins and told him I'd found other accommodation, and I wouldn't be taking the cottage.

As he said he would be, Mr. Atkins was cool with it.

And so I wouldn't miss out on time by the sea, Battle promised to take me there for a weekend, if I found a time in my writing where I could go.

So that was something to look forward to.

The oh-so-not boring stuff:

Those candlesticks were Chippendale.

Yep.

They were.

And that only scratched the surface.

The curator from the V and A lost her mind, and since her visit, Prue had more than a half a dozen experts out to look at things, authenticate them and value them. She'd found tons of stuff in that old filing cabinet to help (but alas, nothing that would help my book, all the stuff in the cabinet predated 1880).

There were two more Chippendale pieces, gorgeous giltwood and painted satinwood pier tables that the four siblings agreed would be perfect on either side of the opening to the great hall. Thus, they'd been taken away to be cleaned.

Further, there was a Hepplewhite piece, three by Alexander Roux, five by Lannuier and one by Eileen Gray (Prue, no surprise, was keeping the Gray).

There was also a Sisley painting (which had been taken away as well to be cleaned so it could be displayed somewhere in The Downs).

And then some.

A lot more *some*.

This engendered a spirited conversation at the dinner table one weekend, the only times now when both Battle and Tempie were home (as such, Hamish was also always there, and a not so important aside: he was hilarious, totally down-to-earth, super friendly, and so much Tempie's opposite, it made them perfect).

And that was when I learned what The Fund was.

Not at the table.

I asked Battle when we went back to his bedroom.

"There's an untouchable endowment that pays for property taxes, maintenance, upgrades and staffing of The Downs and Burleigh House," he shared. "I manage this carefully, though I can only make moderate- to low-risk investments to keep it growing, as the terms of the endowment dictate. Outside those reasons, it cannot be touched, and by that I mean, withdrawals made. We can deposit whatever we wish, but once it's in, it can't come out."

"That makes sense."

Although it did, it only partially explained a fascinating question I had that I hadn't asked (because…truth: even if Battle and I were what we were becoming, still, at this juncture in our relationship, it would be rude).

That question being how they managed to keep that property and their lives the way they did.

Battle had already explained some of the estate's income, and even if he didn't get into detail, I knew no way would that cover all of their lifestyles.

And sure, I knew Battle was very wealthy, but there's wealth and then there was The Downs and Burleigh House, horses, cars, security, staff, recent redecoration, the way all of them dressed, etc.

And *Battle* was wealthy. Tempie managed income they'd probably had for centuries, and Prue and Chassie didn't have jobs.

Therefore, it did not explain Prue's four-hundred-pound beanie, Chassie's three-hundred-pound dresses or Tempie's Versace shoes.

Battle must have seen my confusion, because he continued, "There's a surplus from The Fund at the moment, which I reinvest. The income Tempie makes, which is considerable, is split between the three of them. Not equitably, since Tempie does all the work, but Prue nor Chassie has any other expenditures, so it's rare they'll ask for more. And when they do, it's for something like Chassie's flower shop, which I funded personally."

"Right, so what's the big deal about augmenting The Fund?"

"Growth from moderate- to low-risk investments sometimes won't cover the cost of inflation. We can only use the interest we make on those, so it's consistently necessary to augment The Fund to keep on top of paying to manage both houses."

"And if you don't keep doing that, what? You'll lose property?"

"Fortunately, I make enough that wouldn't be a problem. But it's my job, all of our jobs, to secure the future of the duchy."

"So selling those two hideous Louis XV gilt candelabras with porcelain chickens in the middle of them will assist in keeping the duchy running smoothly," I deduced.

He smiled. "Precisely."

I smiled in return.

At this point in our discussion, he cocked his head to the side and reiterated, "I make enough that wouldn't be a problem."

"Okay," I said so he knew I'd heard him this time, even if I'd heard him the last one.

"Darling, I'm an independently wealthy man."

I didn't know why he was saying that out loud since I already knew.

He came to me, gathered my hair at my nape in both hands, resting his forearms on my shoulders, and he dipped to me.

"That money, my money, will be placed in trusts for my children, their educations and their futures, as well as set aside for a very comfortable retirement for myself and my wife. Not to mention, in the interim, used on important things, like tennis bracelets," he said quietly.

Ah.

I grinned up at him.

He used my hair to tip my head further back, and he kissed me.

And we quit talking about The Fund, as fascinating as it was, and started doing better, far more fascinating (and fun) things.

In the end, with all that stuff in the attics, they decided on non-equal thirds.

Except for a few pieces they intended to keep, some of it was being donated to museums, and the rest of it was going to be auctioned, with three quarters of the proceeds going into The Fund, and one quarter to charities the duchy patronized.

That said, Battle told me, the low end of what they expected to get from the auction would, "Make things much easier for Fury and Noble, darling."

Oh yeah.

We'd picked our top favorites.

Mm-hmm.

Things were progressing very nicely (see? I could do an understatement too).

Just saying, I didn't think Battle was falling anymore either.

But when it was all said and done, all of what was in the attics was going to go so Prue could reconfigure part of them into her own studio. And Battle was going to reconfigure the other parts into apartments so Scotty and Harry (or whoever was in their positions) could be closer to the house for security purposes. They could then rent the steward's cottage to increase the estate's income, and his sisters' allowances.

Which I thought was a rad idea.

Onward from all of that, I'd taken an afternoon off to clear the cobwebs, and we'd all gone back to Ravenna for another reading (*sans* Tempie, and not only because she was in London).

Ravenna still didn't know where Charlie's letters were.

But she decided it.

In August, Prue and Chassie were going to visit Switzerland.

And spending that time with the clairvoyant decided it for me.

Ravenna was the shit.

Last semi-boring but still not boring (because it was fun) thing that happened: I'd taught Prue and Chassie how to toast bread and make oatmeal (considering there was instant, it was just showing them how to measure milk, and they both already knew how to use a microwave).

We also made pancakes together.

Chassie did all the flipping.

She didn't mess it up once.

The big stuff:

As mentioned, Hamish had become one with the crew.

Tempie spent more time in London, but they both always came back to The Downs for the weekends.

I missed her.

But I loved how happy she was with Hamish, with Chassie and Prue moving on with their lives, just happy.

And speaking of Chassie…

She and Christian were dating.

Christian, we would come to learn, was not only smart about gymnosperms (don't ask me, but Christian could chat with Chassie about them for an hour), he'd clued in that Chassie was at the very least shy, so he was taking it slow.

That said, he came to the roast I made every Sunday.

Further, I'd sent a picture of Battle and me to Solène, and she immediately called after she received it.

And when I picked up, she shouted, "Holy fuck!"

I was not surprised at this reaction.

They were coming out next month.

And yes, they were staying at The Downs.

I didn't have to try too hard to be convincing. I just sent her photos of the place (mostly Chassie's gardens), and she'd texted, *We're in.*

Her response was so swift, I wasn't sure she'd run it by Alex.

What I suspected was that he was a man in the manner of Battle, so my sister wouldn't find him hard to convince either.

Another total non-surprise, my agent lost her shit when she saw Prue's work.

She signed her within days, and they were planning to go out to bid soon for *Into the Gilt Frame* (they were going to start at the beginning).

Natalie had already given a few editors some advanced looks, and she told Prue what I knew from the beginning.

She needed to strap in, because it was about to get very interesting.

Prue was nervous, excited and anxious.

But she'd soon have objective input into how talented she was.

So she'd soon come to understand that was the bottom-line truth.

And the last bit of news, the weekend after he'd asked me, I moved into Battle's rooms.

This did not have to do with the better vanity.

It also didn't have to do with the pink star sapphire topped and tailed with a triangle of three diamonds in a pendant and matching earrings he brought home from London with him that week (and yes, because Tempie had a big mouth, I now had an amethyst tennis bracelet, an emerald-cut amethyst ring, the stone sitting in a band accented with pavé diamonds, and an amethyst and diamond choker, because they matched my wedding outfits—this was a lot from Battle, but I could tell he seriously got off on spoiling me, so I kept my mouth shut, something I found hard at first, but I was getting used to it).

The move to his rooms further wasn't because I wasn't a fan of schlepping things I'd need to the south wing, or Battle doing it when we were in my room, or either of us leaving because we needed our clothes or deodorant.

I moved because he wanted me to move.

And because it felt right.

Before I did it, though, I called and talked to Lenny about it, primarily how fast this was going.

And she said, "One thing I know, Viv, you are no dummy. You're also not a sucker. And last, that man wouldn't move this fast if he wasn't right there with you. He has to have trust issues a million miles wide with all the gold diggers who want to dig into him. And he's all in with you. Not sure why you'd fight it or question it. It's not like he's chained you in his dungeons. If shit goes south, you can leave. But since it isn't, why not do what you always do? Roll with it and make it work, if you want it to work. Or cut your losses if you don't."

My sister was wise.

Therefore, me and the cats were in with Battle and his babies.

And everything was good.

Watching Battle pose for pictures with the other groomsmen was totally not boring.

Why I thought it would be meant someone should evaluate me.

Eventually, after coming to me to kiss my nose, he went with the others to hang with Rally pre-big-moment, and I went to the patio where pre-big-moment champagne was being served to arriving guests.

I joined Prue, Tempie, Hamish and yes, Chassie had squeezed Christian in at the last minute as her plus one.

"Ah, there she is," Tempie said loudly as I got close. "Our budding duchess."

Prue giggled.

Christian sent me a bewildered smile.

Chassie hid hers behind her hand.

Hamish hid his looking at his shoes.

And yeah.

Chelsea was in earshot.

And from the sour look on her face, Tempie's shot landed in her ears.

"Be good," I snipped at her quietly when I got to them.

"For heaven's sake, why?" she asked, sounding genuinely perplexed as to why I'd snip that warning at her.

She also didn't wait for an answer.

She turned to Hamish and requested, "Will you fetch Vivi some champagne, darling?"

He angled in to kiss her jaw then took off to find a roaming server.

"Battle's on edge," I said. "He's pissed at the potshot Chelsea took at Prue and Chassie—"

"Wait up, what did she say to you?" Christian interrupted me to ask Chassie tetchily.

Oh yeah.

I liked him.

"It wasn't a big deal," she replied.

He looked right at Tempie (the boy was a fast learner). "Was it a big deal?"

She took a sip from her champagne flute, swung her hand out to the side, and drawled, "What can I say? The woman is a cunt."

Christian was going to say something, but thought better of it and muttered to Chassie, "We'll talk about it later."

Chassie shot Prue big eyes from over the rim of her own champagne flute.

"As I was saying," I started up again, "he's on edge and we, none of us, should do anything to push him over the edge."

"You know I'll be good," Prue said.

"Of course, I wouldn't do anything," Chassie said.

Hamish returned with my champagne, I thanked him, then aimed a hard stare at Tempie.

She put her hand to her throat, "Are you asking me not to be *me?*"

"Just…tone it down so Battle doesn't make another speech ripping her to shreds in front of Rally and Courtney's four hundred guests," I suggested.

"I'll do my best," Tempie replied.

I didn't believe her.

"Love," Hamish warned in his scrummy burr.

She gazed up at him. "I said I'd do my best."

"Do that and do better," he replied.

She turned her head and did such a brilliant rolled side-eye, I wished I had video of it.

Since I missed my chance, I sipped champagne instead.

"I'm so glad they have a beautiful day," Chassie enthused.

With that, we settled into chitchat, and I was looking forward to when we got to sit down. My heels were already killing me.

When the music changed, and the staff started to guide people to the seating area, Prue and I looped arms together, and I did my best to avoid her fascinator/hat, which was wire covered in gray material wound around and around in a spiral that had a cluster of forget-me-nots in the middle.

"Is that hat François?" I asked.

She beamed up at me and cried, "He made it especially for me! Can you believe?"

I'd been to his shop.

I'd seen how he'd fawned all over her.

I totally believed.

"You rock it, sister."

"It's not too much?"

It was big, but people could see through the spirals, and she was short.

"It's perfect," I decreed as we got to our row and slid in.

We sat.

We waited.

Other people sat.

The parents were escorted in.

The groomsmen came out.

Once Battle got to where he'd be standing (he wasn't the best man, he was one over), he looked for me.

When he caught my eyes, I threw him a kiss.

He smiled his sexy smile.

The bridesmaids came down the aisle.

The flower girl strewed her petals.

The music changed.

We stood.

Courtney walked down the aisle with her dad.

She looked stunning.

And very, very happy.

It was closing in on the end of the evening, and Battle and I were on the dance floor.

He'd changed into a tux, and he looked dashing.

I was wearing a flowy, long dress with big purple flowers on it. It had a feminine, frilly ruff around the neck that formed the halter, leaving my shoulders and entire back bare.

And as I swayed in Battle's arms, he took advantage of that exposed skin by skating his fingers up and down my spine.

It was affecting, but mostly it was affectionate.

With me in my heels, we fit perfectly.

He was a good lead.

And I was so intent on being in his arms, I wasn't even sure what song was playing.

We were very close, with Battle holding my hand to his chest, my other arm was around his shoulders, and he'd pressed his jaw to the side of my head.

Thus, I just had to adjust it slightly to whisper in his ear, "Do you wanna know something?"

"Is it about you?" he returned my whisper.

"Yes."

"Then, yes. I want to know everything about you."

I closed my eyes and drew in a soft breath like I was drawing in his words to hold inside me forever.

Then I shared, "I'm maybe-probably sure that I passed out the minute I saw you because you were so hot."

His head came up so he could look down at me. "Sorry?"

"Oh. What do you all call it? Not hot. Fit," I amended.

"I know what you mean, darling. But I'm trying to process the delightful fact you're telling me you fainted at first sight of me because you wanted to jump me."

I couldn't even be annoyed at his interpretation, because it was the correct one.

Though, I gave him an alternate scenario that was definitely fantastical, and only maybe true.

"Also, there might be paranormal activity at The Downs that had me in its thrall."

He put his jaw to my temple and said, "I prefer the other option."

I grinned. "I bet you do."

The music ended, a fast song came on, people who loved to dance and people who were drunk off their asses flooded the dance floor, as per protocol at a wedding reception, and Battle guided me to a chair at a table.

He didn't sit me in it.

He sat in it and pulled me into his lap.

Definitely.

He was the best chair *ever*.

He wrapped his arms around me and called my name.

I looked from the dancers to him.

"The second I saw your freckles, I knew I was done for," he shared.

My heart thudded, and I wrapped my hand along his jaw, whispering, "Baby."

"I have to stay until the bitter end, darling, but you can go up anytime. Just don't go to sleep."

I touched my mouth to his and replied, "If you're staying, I'm staying with you."

His fingers at my hip gave me a loving squeeze.

I turned my attention back to the dance floor, but on my way, my gaze caught on Chelsea, who was staring such hate at us, it felt like acid burning my skin.

Battle must have sensed my reaction, because his arms tightened around me protectively and he asked, "What?"

When I looked down at him, I saw him staring at Chelsea.

He turned to me. "Ignore her. She's behaved, but she's still a bitter cow. Don't let her shit ruin a good day."

"All right," I agreed.

But, Lord.

Her look of such hostile animosity, I had to admit, it shook me.

However, Battle was right.

It'd been a good day.

Rally and Courtney were happy.

We'd all had a great time.

And I was in love with a man who was in love with me.

Nothing could mess with that.

Not a thing.

~

Sex that night at the Lodge with Battle was unlike anything we'd done before.

And we'd pretty much explored the smorgasbord.

But fortunately, there were always new things to introduce to the menu.

Though, I knew what we had that night would always be the best dish served.

Because Battle allowed me to lavish every inch of him with everything I could: lips, fingertips, tongue, eyes.

I did suck his cock, but I didn't suck him off.

It wasn't a tease.

It was making love.

And eventually, when I ran the tip of my tongue along the underside of his cock, up his belly, between his pecs, up his throat and took his mouth, he rolled us so he was on top, and he slipped inside.

The touch continued on both our parts as he slowly glided in and out of me, our hands moving on each other's skin, caressing, giving. I even used my heels to touch him, running them up and down the backs of his thighs as he moved inside me.

And we did all of this while kissing.

As much as I might want it to, it couldn't last forever. Battle's movements grew faster, his drives more powerful, our breaths became heavier.

In order that we could breathe, he slid his lips to my neck to nuzzle me there, and I threaded my fingers into his thick, soft hair.

It was the right time, the perfect time, and I wasn't going to squander it.

I turned my head and whispered, "I'm in love with you, Battle Talyn."

In response, his face came out of my neck and his mouth took mine in a branding kiss as he shifted his hips and his thrusts slammed into me.

I fisted my hand in his hair, grasped his tight clenching ass in my other, and used my heels in his thighs as leverage to lift my hips to meet his drives.

The whimper that warned of my impending climax vibrated against his tongue, he growled in return, then my moan of orgasm mingled with his groan of the same, and we came simultaneously.

Oh yes.

It was the perfect time.

He glided inside me for a while as he gentled our kiss, before he planted himself and traced his mouth to my ear.

And there, he said, "I'm in love with you too, Vivienne Dupree."

The best part about that?

I didn't question it.

Because I already knew it.

Undeniably.

CHAPTER 26

THE CLIPPINGS

I was out in the studio, studying a picture of Harmony alongside a picture of Charlie.

It was Tuesday, a week and two days after we got back from the wedding.

Battle and Tempie were in London.

They were returning together tomorrow evening, because the folks from the auction house were coming to get the stuff from the attics, and since it was such a huge job, Tempie wanted to help Prue oversee that, and Prue wanted Tempie's help.

Battle was coming home because he still worked from The Downs half a week, no longer to be there to look after Chassie, but to be close to me.

And yes, him making that effort, changing his work schedule like that, made me feel all squidgy.

I'd arrived at a place in my book where it was now time to turn my attention to the ill-fated love affair of a duke's daughter and an injured American soldier.

And for the first time, I was seeing something eerie.

The pictures were in black and white, but even so, Harmony was blonde.

Like me.

She was also not petite or dainty.

Like I wasn't.

And Great-Granddad Charlie was dark-haired, dark-eyed, tall, fit and handsome.

Like Battle.

Those were the only similarities.

I didn't look like Harmony, and Great-Granddad Charlie didn't look like Battle.

But Harmony didn't resemble any of the other Talyns (and from perusing many pictures, this seemed a trait in that family).

More to the point, I looked not a thing like Great-Granddad Charlie. Neither did Mom or Solène.

I dropped the photos to the desk, telling Snowball, "Now I'm just looking for weird shit to get to me."

Snowball had no response.

But I knew I was being stupid.

Nothing the least bit strange had happened since the cats tripped me into falling into Chassie's room, and so much time had passed, I was now feeling like a huge dork that I thought there was anything weird about it.

I gazed out the windows at the rainy, dreary day (Prue told me May and September were usually very fine, but June, July and August were hit and miss, a lot of miss, and the weather was proving her right).

I was doing this gazing while trying to decide if I should go back to my laptop or call the house for an afternoon snack and a Fanta orange, when my phone vibrated.

It was Battle.

I took the call. "Hey."

"Hey," he replied.

My I'm-speaking-to-the-love-of-my-life antennae zinged at the tone in his voice.

Before I could ask after it, he asked his own question.

"Are you writing?"

"No. I was about to call to the house for a snack."

"So I'm not interrupting?"

Oh yeah.

That tone was still in his voice. I'd just never heard him sound like that before—flat, dull—so it was tweaking me.

"Yes, I can descend into a book," I reiterated. "Yes, it would annoy me if I was consistently interrupted while writing it. But no, even if I was writing, I'd want to hear from you just because I always want to hear from you. So…what's up?"

"Mum rang."

My head shook so violently at this news, I might have given myself whiplash.

But I couldn't concentrate on having possibly given myself a neck injury.

"Your mother called you?"

"I haven't heard from her in twenty-two years. But, yes. I just got off the phone with her."

"Oh my God, Battle. What the fuck? What did she say?"

"Apparently, she had some friends at Rally and Court's wedding. One of them called to chat and shared that her children were there, and even though Tempie was very with Hamish, and Chassie was with Christian, the only thing Mum cared about was that her friend told her we seemed very close. Therefore, she phoned in order to understand, should I marry, if she can continue to use her title."

I sat, stunned silent.

No, I sat, pissed-off silent.

Called to chat and shared that her children were there?

What kind of person was a friend who casually dropped, "Hey, saw your kids you haven't bothered yourself with in decades. Don't worry about the youngest three, but the eldest is seriously hooked up. So you might want to check the status of your title."

Scratch that.

What kind of person could be a friend to a woman who would desert her children so she could frolic in Greece and make everyone call her duchess?

"Vivi, have I lost you?" he called.

"You're telling me,"—my voice was vibrating with fury—"that woman phoned you after decades of desertion, solely to learn if she can continue to be a duchess after you get married?"

"Yes."

"You have to be joking!" I shouted.

Snowball glared at me, but I was too incensed to check how Gingerface and Baby Blue, snuggled together on the chaise, responded to me suddenly shouting.

"Sweetheart—"

"Fuck her," I spat. "What a fucking bitch."

"Yes, darling, and as lovely as your response is on my behalf, if you'd calm down, I can share I'm calling to ask if you think I should tell the girls she phoned."

"Fuck no," I bit.

"Vivi—"

"Did she ask after them?"

"No."

"Then, again, fuck no."

"I've thought about it, and if she called one of them, I'd want to know," he shared.

"Did she give any inkling her call was a clumsy attempt to reach out and maybe begin communicating with you again?"

"Not an inkling."

"What did you tell her about the duchess thing?"

"Strictly speaking, since they never divorced, she'll always hold that title. Though it has a dowager in front of it, she doesn't have to use that bit."

"And you told her that?"

"No, I told her Tempie is very much in love, and I was too, Chassie was dating a fine man, and Prue was on the cusp of signing a lucrative publishing contract. I further told her I hoped she was healthy, wished her well, and hung up on her."

"Good," I said shortly.

"Vivienne."

Okay, he needed me, and he didn't need me to be an angry shrew.

I blew out an irate breath and said, "Yes. Okay. You're right. You should tell them. But do it somewhere safe and good, like during Sunday lunch."

"You think I should wait that long?"

"I think Hamish and Christian should be there to temper Tempie's tantrum, and soothe Chassie's hurt feelings, and we can see to Prue."

"I knew you'd have a wise response," he murmured.

That almost made me smile.

Almost.

"Are you okay?" I asked.

I heard his deep sigh, before, "My concern is, I just don't care."

I looked to the picture of my mom and dad.

I didn't even remember my dad, but seeing them, young and happy and on the verge of a beautiful life, one that would tragically be cut short for both, I felt the shaft of pain drive through my heart, like it always did.

This was also always followed by a squeeze of tenderness, because at least they had that time, and I hated it was so short, but I loved they'd found each other, experienced it, and Mom was left with a part of him: Solène and me.

I couldn't imagine not giving a shit your mom phoned, be it just to ask you over for dinner, or after decades of absence.

"I hate that for you, even if I think it's healthy," I replied.

"Healthy not to give a damn I spoke to my mother after two decades?"

"Yes."

"I'm not angry. I'm not hurt. I'm not anything, except worrying about how my sisters will react, Vivi."

"When someone gives you nothing, it stands to reason you won't miss it when it's gone."

"She's my mother, love."

"She's a womb that nurtured you," I retorted. "I know that's harsh, but it's true, and no matter how much it deeply sucks, somewhere along the line, you've come to terms with it, and that, Battle, is healthy. Perhaps your sisters have done the same. But we'll be there to look after them if they haven't."

"We'll be there," he said softly.

"Yes," I confirmed.

"I very much love you, darling."

Okay.

Now I felt better.

"I very much love you too," I replied.

And I hoped he felt better.

"We'll do it over Sunday lunch," he decided.

"Terrific," I lied.

I heard a smile in his voice when he said, "It'll be fine."

At least I could agree to that.

"It will."

"Right, you ring for your snack. I'll text before bed and see you tomorrow."

"All right, honey. I'm glad you called and worked that out with me."

"I am too. Get back to work."

So bossy.

"Will do. Love you."

"And you."

He rang off.

I put my phone down and wondered if I could sneak to Greece to deliver an all-mighty bitch slap and get back before Battle returned home tomorrow evening.

Since I couldn't, I swiveled in my chair to nab the house phone and called for a snack.

~

I'd gotten into it.

Thus, it was late.

Just after midnight.

And I was bleary-eyed and drooping.

I needed to drag myself (and the cats) to the house, brush my teeth, wash my face and fall into bed so I could keep this clip up tomorrow.

Decision made, I was calling to the cats, heading out, about to flip the light switch, when my eyes fell on the box of stuff by the door, which Harry brought out earlier in the day.

It was the forgotten box of stuff Prue told me about ages ago that she found in the attics. The stuff she thought might be useful since it was from the time period I was writing about.

I spied a cloth-covered diary with tattered edges in the box, and my natural curiosity had me reaching to pull it out.

There was a gold 1946 stamped in the corner.

Goosebumps suddenly covered my skin as I moved to flip through it.

But as I did, newspaper clippings dropped to the floor.

I bent and retrieved the folded pieces, straightened, unfolded one, and those goosebumps became full body tingles.

The headline said, VISCOUNT STILL MISSING, POLICE SCRATCHING HEADS, and there was a picture of Lord Arthur Hughes-Davies with his pomaded hair and Clark Gable pencil mustache above his supercilious smile.

Completely awake now, I wandered blindly back to my desk and sat down.

There were seven clippings in all, the totality of them about the missing viscount.

"Holy shit, shit, shit," I whispered, dropping the clippings to the desk and frantically flipping to the date in that diary that corresponded to the one where Marie recorded the dire news.

There was nothing in the journal for that date except a heavily written, large X.

My heart thumping, I went to the front of the book.

Inside the cover, in cursive so perfect the writer could teach it, it said, THE DIARY OF AILEEN FLANNERY.

I knew from the butler's ledgers Aileen was lady's maid to Unity...

And Harmony.

I dashed back to the dire date and read the passage before it.

Dear Diary,

Another house party starts tomorrow. Everyone belowstairs jokes that the duchess is making up for the lost time of the war. It seems like we have dinner parties every night and house parties every weekend.

I don't find it funny. Dresses to iron, shoes to brush, stockings to wash, it's all a bother.

And my Lady Harmony is in no mood.

Especially since that odious (as Lady Harmony refers to him, but her opinion is just) Arthur Hughes-Davies telephoned to say he was coming.

He wasn't even invited!

Lady Harmony detests him. Even Lady Unity doesn't like him, and she's boy crazy.

I fear the duchess has her sights set on him to marry Lady Harmony. Which, frankly, is a slap in the face, disallowing my lady that lovely American man, and expecting her to bear the ring of that bellend (but in the end, Lady Harmony will get the last laugh).

The duchess will be sorely disappointed, considering Lord Bishop dislikes him almost as intensely as my lady does, and the duke can barely countenance him.

Why they had a room prepared for that man is the mystery, when only the duchess seems to care for him.

But a lot of what these people do is a mystery to me.

She didn't sign the entry, or any of them.

Among many things that passage shared with me was an explanation of why The Downs had footmen far longer than other great houses did. If the duchess did that amount of entertaining, they'd need them.

I skipped past the ominous X to the next entry, which was dated several days later.

And this one wasn't any less ominous.

Dear Diary,

Tenterhoooks, tenterhooks, tenterhooks.

I am sworn to secrecy.

And for my lady, who has lost everything, I will never breathe a word.

That was it for that entry, and the next wouldn't be for over two weeks.

I read it, and it was studiously, even painfully, about the frustration of mending a tear in one of Lady Unity's dresses in a way that wouldn't show, and a flirtation escalating between the milkman and the cook.

I put the diary down and picked up a clipping that had another picture of the viscount. In this one, he was wearing a tuxedo with a white double-breasted dinner jacket that had serious shoulder pads. He was holding a coupé glass of champagne.

Mr. Smooth.

But it was all wrapping.

He wasn't at all handsome and he had a receding hairline.

"By damn, whatever happened to you, it happened here. You crashed a party, told no one you were coming, and because of whatever happened to you, no one shared word one that you were at The Downs."

What was it that Tempie said?

Outside of learning to hold our liquor, aristocrats are dab hands at holding our secrets.

"Fucking hell," I whispered right as the lights went out in the studio.

Abruptly being plunged into the dark, I let out a little scream of surprise, then I felt like an idiot.

It had been raining all day. Not a surprise the electricity might go out.

On that thought, another one hit me.

"But no lightning," I said out loud.

That was when the cats started hissing into the dark.

The hair on the back of my neck stood up.

And it was then I saw the blue, green and purple shades revolving through the space, coloring Snowball's fur.

My gaze shot to the house, and I saw those lights shining brighter from there.

No.

Not from the house.

From the ballroom.

But even though that was happening, the lights Fitzy kept on to guide my way back were illuminated.

The electricity hadn't gone out at the house.

Just at the studio.

Creeped out, coasting through anxious straight to alarmed, I reached to the house phone.

It was late. No one would pick up.

I still did it because I had to check.

I put it to my ear.

And what I feared was correct.

The line was dead.

At that point a shadow raced across the front windows.

I sped right through alarmed straight to scared shitless.

"Okay, shit. Okay, shit," I whispered.

The door to the studio wasn't locked.

I grabbed my phone, engaged the screen, looked at it and saw I had a red bar.

Not a surprise. I'd left it in the studio the night before. It hadn't been charged for over a day.

But I had juice.

Though I didn't know who to call.

Did I phone 999 and say, "Hey, listen, the ghosts are kicking up a fuss at The Downs. Can you come out and rescue me from the studio?"

I wasn't sure they'd be all that motivated to race out here on a call like that.

I didn't want to call Prue or Chassie. They'd be sleeping.

I didn't want to wake Fitzy and Patsy either.

Especially if this was probably nothing but my fatigued but always overactive imagination.

Sadly, I didn't have Harry's or Scotty's numbers in my phone.

"Just go to the house," I started my peptalk, my attention fixed on those lights glowing and shifting color. "You're tired. You just made a huge discovery. The cats aren't fond of your mood. You need to chill out and sleep."

I got up, went to the door, and when I opened it, all three cats darted out.

"Fuck," I snapped and moved out after them.

Just get in the house, get in the house, get in the house.

I charged quickly toward The Downs, following after the three scampering shapes of the kitties.

"*Sss,*" I heard from behind me.

Not the wind.

It was a person.

Out after midnight with me, hissing at me while I was alone in the dark.

Oh fuck.

I took off running.

When the house came into view, particularly the ballroom, I lost the rest of the little shit I had hold of because I could see the ghostly apparitions drinking punch, gossiping and dancing.

I never went in that way.

Fitzy kept the doors to the terrace off the ladies' lounge open for me.

I rounded the north wing, skidding on the wet flagstone. The rain, still coming down, was now only a drizzle, but it'd been falling all day so everything was drenched.

I nearly took a header into some shrubbery but kept my feet for once, raced up the steps to the terrace at the ladies' lounge and moved to throw open the door.

It didn't open.

"*Sss,*" the sound came again.

Closer.

Fuck!

I rattled the door.

Locked.

And nowhere near anyone who could hear me pounding on it.

I was not going back from where I came, either the studio or the ballroom.

And it was hell to the no on the ballroom, and not only because that was the direction the noise was coming from. The people in it were still dancing and the lights coming from it were now almost blinding.

I took off running again, down the steps, across the courtyard to the door opposite, which went off one of the salons to the terrace.

I tried it.

Locked.

"*Sss, sss, SSSSSSSS.*"

It was following me.

I was not going to look.

I raced down the terrace to the armory, trying all three sets of double French doors at that end.

Locked.

All of them.

Damn Fitzy and him taking his butler responsibilities so seriously!

I raced down the steps, onto the walkway, around the edge of the southern wing and skidded across the wet turf.

This time, I went down, hard, both hands and knees slipping over the wet lawn as well as the fine gravel of the path there, the pebbles cutting into the skin of my palms and knees.

I heard a low chuckle.

It was a man.

I was alone in the middle of the night with some strange stalking man!

Fuck!

I pushed up and kept running, the fine drizzle winning, soaking through my shirt, my jeans, into my hair.

I rounded the front (this huge fucking house!), sprinted across and bounded up the steps two at a time.

I heard running feet coming my way.

I yanked frantically at the bell pull and pounded on the door.

My heart felt like it exploded, and in my moment of panic, fortunately, my mind recalled what Prue had told me.

Fitzy and Patsy had their own entry into the house.

I bounded down the steps this time, three at a clip, getting a stitch in my side as I raced blindly along the front of the house, around the side, straight toward the shrubs that had been planted to give Fitzy and Patsy some privacy for their outdoor space.

I found the entry, practically jumped down all of the steps, ran across their patio, hit their door and pounded on it.

I did all of this terrified out of my skull.

Because I did it hearing the heavy footsteps following right behind me.

A hand landed on my shoulder.

I screamed and whirled, ready for anything.

And there was Christian.

Oh fuck.

Was Christian a creepy stalker?

"What's going on?" he demanded.

"Were you following me?" I asked.

The door behind me opened.

Christian's hazel eyes flicked there but returned immediately to me. "Were you with someone?"

"No."

"Who was chasing after you?"

"You saw them?" I breathed.

His jaw got hard, he shoved me, I landed in someone's arms, and he growled, "Call 999," and then took off into the night.

"You're trembling something fierce," Fitzy said, pulling me inside. "What's happening?"

"Terry, she's bleeding!" Patsy cried.

Fitzy sat me in a chair and grabbed my hands.

While he was rotating them to look at my palms, I said, "Someone is out there."

His gaze snapped to my eyes then he turned to his wife. "Call 999, luv. Now."

She raced away.

"Lock the door," I begged. "Please lock the door."

"It's locked. It's on a latch, Miss Vivi."

I nodded and couldn't stop doing it.

"Breathe, luv, just breathe," he urged. "I'll be back."

And then he disappeared.

I stared down at my hands.

They were a mess.

God, I went down harder than I thought.

Patsy hustled in with a first aid kit. "I've put the kettle on. Nice spot of tea will do you good." She knelt in front of me, set the kit on the floor and took hold of my wrists. "These are going to need a bit of cleaning. Just a tick and I'll have some nice warm water and soap."

She got up, reached for a throw, tossed it around my shoulders and took off again.

I looked out their windows.

Just dark night. No colored lights.

The cold of my wet clothes and hair hit me and my teeth started chattering.

Patsy came back, and was in the middle of bathing my hands when Prue and Chassie rushed in.

"Oh my goodness!" Prue cried. "What happened to you?"

"I—"

"Kettle's boiled," Patsy interrupted me. "You girls, make us all tea. Be sure to make one for Christian too, for when he gets back."

"Christian?" Chassie asked.

"Please just make the tea, dear," Patsy said.

They both ran to the kitchen.

"Just a lot of cuts, luv," she said to me. "Nothing too deep. Might be hard to type for a few days, but it won't be long until you're good as new."

"My knee really hurts."

She looked to my knee.

I looked to my knee.

On my right one, my jeans were torn and blood was oozing.

Shit.

Totally went down hard.

"I'll get to that next," she said.

"The cats are outside," I told her.

"We'll have a look for them in a tick."

"Okay," I whispered.

She grasped hold of my wrists firmly, and I focused on her.

"You're safe, Vivi, all right?"

I took in a super deep breath.

And I nodded.

She reached for the Germolene to put on my hands.

~

I was pacing the green salon.

Not true.

I was limping through the green salon (my knee hurt like a mother) and doing it back and forth.

Prue, Chassie, Fitzy, Patsy and Scotty were with me.

We were here because it was at the front of the house, and we wanted to see when Christian and Harry got back.

Fitzy had called the steward's cottage and sent the men out to help Christian.

As Patsy tended to me, the police came.

They then left, with Christian and Scotty, because they caught whoever it was who'd been fucking with me, so they all went to the station.

We were now waiting for them to come home and give us the lowdown.

I'd toweled my hair, but it was a frizzed disaster and still damp (hair didn't dry very fast in England, just sayin'), and I'd changed into a knit lounge set to keep warm.

I'd had four cups of tea.

But it wasn't those that made me revved.

Phantoms in the ballroom.

Someone chasing me through the night.

And I knew, down to my soul, those phantoms were dancing to warn me to get to the house.

Do not ask how I knew that, but I knew.

They were a beacon to guide me to safety.

I just hadn't noticed them until too late.

What I did notice was that they went away when I was in the house and safe.

That was why I was revved.

Outside the good news that the men had caught whoever-the-fuck was dicking with me, when Fitzy went out to see if he could find the cats, he didn't have to go far. They were wet and cranky (cranky because they were wet) and loitering by the door off the ladies' lounge.

So they were in there with us, along with Soot, Greystoke and Floofy.

Chassie, at the window waiting for Christian, abruptly turned to the room.

"They're back." Her attention came to me. "Battie is with them."

Battle?

It'd been hours, but…

He was in London.

How was he here?

"I called him, luv," Fitzy told me.

That explained that.

But…shit.

Battle was going to be flipped out, and I wasn't sure that was a good thing.

About a minute later, I would find I was right when he stalked into the room appearing homicidal.

He did a head count but landed and stayed on me.

"Are you all right?" he asked tersely as Chassie ran to Christian, who came in behind him, followed by Harry.

"Were you at the police station?" I asked in return.

"Are. You. *All right*?" he gritted between clenched teeth.

I went to him and put my bandaged hands on him. "I'm all right, baby. Now tell us what's happening."

He didn't tell us what was happening.

He took my wrists in a gentle grip and looked down at my bandaged hands.

That muscle in his cheek danced, then it did it again.

Oh boy.

"Battle, honey, I'm *fine*," I stated. "Really. But I'd like to know what's happening."

His gaze lifted to mine and he said one word.

"Chelsea."

I gasped.

Prue gasped.

"What on earth?" Chassie whispered from where she was tucked with Christian's arm circling her shoulders against his side.

"She hired someone to mess with Vivi," Christian shared.

I pulled my hands from Battle's hold and snapped, "Oh my God! Seriously?"

"He's been watching you for a few days," Christian said. "Getting your habits down. He crept up to the house, locked the door you usually use. He cut the electricity and phone line to the studio, doing that just to spook you, but also to get you out of the studio. And when you took off, he stalked you. As he was ordered to do."

"This will be explained," Battle said dangerously Harry and Scotty's way.

Both had hangdog faces.

Both nodded.

I'd have a word with Battle later about Scotty and Harry. They weren't responsible for this, and they couldn't be expected to have a mind meld with every inch of The Downs so they knew when there was an intruder.

But that wasn't for now.

I should have known from the way she was staring hatred at us at the wedding reception that Chelsea would pull something.

But this?

The woman was deranged.

"How did you see Vivi?" Chassie asked Christian.

"I was up late, working on my paper," he told her. "Good luck, I was looking out the window when I saw a shadow trying to get into the armory. I couldn't tell who it was, until I went out. Then I saw it was someone chasing Vivi in the rain."

At this moment, I realized my mistake at allowing Chassie to request the story before I calmed my man down, because hearing Christian say that, Battle prowled to the teapot, picked it up, and hurled it violently into the fireplace, shattering it with splashes of the remains of the tea wetting the stone.

It was probably Limoges or something.

Yikes.

"That bloody, *fucking cunt!*" he exploded.

I moved to him to put a soothing hand on his back. "It's okay. I'm okay, honey."

He turned furious eyes to me. "It is not okay, Vivienne. It's fucked up."

It was that.

"But I'm fine and the bad guy was caught," I reminded him.

"As will be the true villain in this scheme, darling," he said sinisterly. "We're pressing charges against Chelsea. I don't give a fuck we'll be splashed all over the tabloids, *she* will be. She'll be humiliated. Ridiculed. And hopefully, after she faces the likely minimal consequences she'll receive for her part in this plot, she'll need to retire to some island like my mother to escape the scandal."

But…

He couldn't do that.

He worked so hard to protect their privacy.

Nevertheless, I didn't think now was the time to remind him of that.

"How about we all get some sleep and discuss it tomorrow?" I suggested.

"We can do that, but I won't change my mind," he replied. "They've already phoned the Met. They're picking her up in London for questioning tonight."

Well, that was happening, and I wasn't about to stop it.

Chelsea needed a good, hard scare.

"Okay, then everyone is all right. Everyone is safe. We can't do anything about that, not that we'd want to, so let's all get some rest," I suggested.

"A good idea," Fitzy decreed as Patsy started gathering the unbroken china onto a tray. "Sleep helps all ailments."

"It's so lucky you're so diligent in your studies," Chassie whispered to Christian in a *my hero* tone.

"Let's go to bed," I whispered to Battle in an *I'm fine and I love you're so pissed on my behalf, but you can chill* tone.

My tone didn't work. He scowled at me.

I hooked my arm in his and looked to Patsy and Fitzy. "Thank you guys for taking care of me." I turned to Christian. "So much."

Chassie beamed.

Christian nodded.

Fitzy and Patsy tutted and herded everyone out.

I guided Battle to our room.

Once inside, he turned the light on by the bed.

I sat on it as he stalked to the bathroom.

I stayed where I was as I saw the light go on there and then in the closet.

Not long later, the lights were extinguished, and he came out in blue and white thin-striped pajama bottoms.

I knew it wasn't the time, but just to note, I would never get tired of my hot guy unintentionally modeling his never-ending supply of pajama bottoms.

"I hesitate to say this," I began carefully, "but, love of my life, you need to chill."

He jerked to a halt two feet in front of me.

And his head slanted sharply to the side.

"Love of your life?" he asked.

"Well...yeah," I answered.

"Love of your life." It was a statement this time.

"Um, I love you," I said. "I love you very much. I love you more each day. I'll probably love you more every day for, like, eternity. I hope we have a boy and a girl we can name Noble and Fury. So, since I believe that's the definition of the love of someone's life, you're mine."

He moved then, lifting me off the bed, pulling me into his arms and kissing me hard.

I had arms with bandaged hands wrapped around his neck when he was done.

"You chill?" I asked.

"I'm pissed as fuck," he answered, then his lips twitched. "But the thought of that bitch being taken to the station in the middle of the night, needing to phone for a solicitor, which means needing to phone her father, and then being questioned because she was caught, helps a bit."

I smiled. "Helps me too."

He got serious. "And you're all right."

"I am," I confirmed.

"And you're probably exhausted."

I was still coasting on four cups of exceptional earl grey tea.

I didn't say that.

I said, "I could use some sleep."

Of course, Battle didn't mess about in making that happen.

It was dark, the cats had joined us, and I was in Battle's arms when I said, "Thanks for driving from London in the middle of the night for me."

His response.

A hefty arm squeeze and "Darling."

That was it.

Then again, that was all he needed to say.

CHAPTER 27

THE RING

I swam out of sleep to see the day was bright and the cats had had breakfast, because they were all in bed with me, snoozing.

I could also see my hot duke striding toward the bed with hair wet from a shower, in jeans and a button-down.

I pushed up to an elbow. "Hey."

He said nothing until he sat on the side of the bed and curled a hand around the side of my neck.

Then he said, "Hey."

I looked to the smart screen and saw it was twelve after ten.

"Holy crap, it's late," I said, pushing up further, then wincing as I tweaked my knee.

"Still," Battle ordered and took my wrist.

He carefully peeled back the bandage a tad and peered at my wounds.

"That doesn't seem too bad," he murmured, pressing the bandage back down.

"The hands aren't. Just gouges and some scrapes. But I did a number on my knee."

He looked that way even if he couldn't see anything through the duvet.

"It's fine," I assured. "Just a deep cut. Not so deep it needs stitches, though. Patsy pushed it together with some plasters and bandaged it. It just aches a little, and since it's on the bend, it gets irritated easily. I tweaked it pushing up."

Battle, being Battle, didn't take my word for it and shoved the covers down (seriously pissing off Gingerface, I really needed to work on his habit of blithely disturbing the animals) so he could peer under the bandage at my knee.

"Fuck, that looks bad," he murmured.

"It's okay. I'm okay. But I need a toothbrush and then I need caffeine."

He pulled the covers back over me. "I'll have some coffee sent up."

"No, I need more to make sure Prue and Chassie are okay."

"Prue is in the breakfast room. Because of the late night, Cook adjusted the schedule and set out a brunch."

I started to get out of bed. "All right. Let me do my biz and we can head down."

"Darling." I stopped moving and looked at him. "They are dear to us, but we still pay them, and we pay them well, to serve."

He was just so sweet.

"I need to move," I replied. "I feel achy and still revved. I don't think I can lie in bed, baby."

At that, it was Battle who pulled me from under the duvet.

"I'll meet you down there," he said.

I gave him a peck on the lips, nabbed the lounge pants I took off to go to sleep last night, hit the bathroom, did my thing, including taking off the bandages on my hands (they really weren't that bad, and I didn't want to have to deal with them whilst using cutlery). I put my pants back on and walked (okay, kind of limped) out.

The cats were still snoozing on the bed.

Last night, they'd tried to warn me too, my lovely furry babies.

I'd ask Patsy if we had any tuna.

On that thought, I headed down to the breakfast room.

I'd hoped Chassie would also be there by the time I made it there, but it was only Battle and Prue.

The minute I walked in, Battle started pouring me coffee.

He also started issuing commands.

"Sit. I'll get your plate."

I did as told, reached for my coffee cup and smiled at Prue. "How are you doing?"

"I think I slept for about an hour," she told me something I could guess, considering her tired eyes and the messy edge to her fringe, which was always razor sharp.

Man, Chelsea was *such* a bitch.

"How are you?" she asked.

"Knee aches. Otherwise," I showed her my scraped palms. She winced. "They look worse than they are."

My filled plate clattered in front of me.

"Where are your bandages?" Battle demanded.

I looked up at him. "Honey, again, *I'm fine*. They need air. After brunch, I'll clean them in the shower again, put on more Germolene and ask you to wrap them. But only so the antibiotic ointment can get to work without me rubbing it off. They don't need the drama of being wrapped all the time."

His lips thinned, he sat down, but he said nothing.

I looked down at my plate to see beans, mushrooms, sausage, hashbrowns, toast and a fried egg.

Perfect.

I grabbed my cutlery.

Battle got up and went to the window.

He peered out and came back, sitting again and saying, "Tempie and Hamish are here."

I was hoping one day I'd know the house sounds so well, I'd be like the rest of the Talyns.

But I didn't dwell on that thought because I had more important things on my mind.

"What? Why?" I asked after swallowing a forkful of mushroom-topped hashbrowns soaked in beans. "They aren't due back until tonight. At least Tempie isn't. Hamish wasn't coming until the weekend."

Battle studied me like I had a screw loose.

It was Prue who spoke.

"Vivi, you were attacked last night."

"I wasn't attacked," I said to her. "I was chased in the rain."

Prue looked to Battle.

I looked to Battle.

The homicidal expression had returned.

Mental note: do not refer to my midnight trauma with Battle in earshot.

I'd managed to stuff another bite in my gob before there was a commotion at the door, and then Bartholomew was loping in, ears and jowls flying, drool sailing, skidding to his rump between Battle and me.

"Hullo, my handsome boy," I cooed as I pet his head.

"Don't pet the dog with your injured hands," Mr. Overprotective ordered.

"Battle," I snapped. "For the last time, I'm fine!"

"I see Midnight Mayhem hasn't broken your spirit," Tempie drawled as she sashayed in with Hamish. "Brava, dearest."

"You didn't have to drive all the way to The Downs. As you just heard, I'm fine," I told them.

"Man and dog can't be separated for long," she replied, sitting and reaching to the coffeepot (Hamish went straight to the sideboard). "Regardless, I had *the most delicious* phone call early this morning and I had to share about it in person."

My gaze darted to Battle, worried myself, but more worried he would be that Rebecca might have also phoned her daughter.

"She's right," Hamish said from the sideboard. "Tempie's side of it was so hilarious, I wished I could hear the whole thing."

"Hilarious?" Battle asked.

Tempie took a sip of her coffee and put the cup back in its saucer. "Newton Renfrew."

Battle stretched his neck ever-so-slowly to the side, and I didn't think that was a good thing.

"Is that Chelsea's father?" I asked hesitantly.

"One in the same," she answered as Hamish put a scone in front of her and sat behind his own very full plate.

"Why the fuck is he calling you?" Battle demanded.

"Well, he didn't share. But one would suppose he did it because he knew, if he attempted to speak to you, you'd tell him, he and his daughter could go fuck themselves."

"I'd maybe have more words," Battle said scarily. "But the message is spot on."

"I had several words myself," she stated while slathering butter on a bite of her scone, then going for the pot of jam. "And as you could probably guess, Mr. Renfrew is quite keen to keep his daughter's name out of the papers and her face out of a courtroom."

"I don't give a fuck what he wants," Battle replied.

"Yes, however, since he'll be giving a million pounds to Vivi as an apology for his daughter's erratic behavior, as well as another million pounds to the Talyn family, which we will in turn donate to the RSPCA,"—she looked to me—"I picked that charity, dearest, since you're an animal person." She returned to Battle. "Along with a written apology from Chelsea to Vivi, his assurances that she will be spending the next year...at least...in their flat in Sydney, and his solemn vow none of us will ever hear from her again, I thought you'd reconsider."

I was so stuck on the first part, I forgot about shoving more of the full English on my plate into my mouth.

"He's giving me a million pounds?"

She turned pensive. "Should I have demanded two?"

"You did!" I cried, beginning to freak. "The donation."

"Of course. I mean three," she amended.

I collapsed back in my chair.

Tempie delicately bit into her scone, chewed, swallowed and remarked, "I did not promise discretion. He knows we won't go to the papers. He also knows I will tell every fucking person who has the ability of hearing, and I will learn goddamned sign language to share it with anyone who doesn't, what a daft nutter his fucking daughter is."

At this speech, Hamish had lost interest in his food and was gazing at his woman with open adoration.

"You, of course, can decline his offer. I only brokered it," she concluded.

"He can—" Battle started heatedly.

"We're taking it," I said.

He snapped his head toward me.

"Somehow, honey," I began, "no matter how totally gorgeous all of you are, how rich, how interesting and how titled, you've managed the miracle of pretty much keeping yourselves out of the limelight. But if you let that light in, you know it will never let up. Don't let her do that to you. Even if it means she won't be publicly scorned, I'll bet Tempie has some pull in your circles, and she'll be shunned. That'll hurt worse. I guarantee it."

"And she'll be in Australia, Battie," Prue chimed in. "Far away from you and Vivi."

"I'll add that Newton did not hide he's done with her shenanigans," Tempie said. "I do believe he used the term 'very short leash.'"

She grinned malevolently.

I *so* understood Hamish.

I simply adored this woman.

Prue clapped. "And Vivi and the animals each get a million pounds!"

"What am I going to do with a million pounds?" I asked.

Again, Battle looked at me like I'd gone 'round the bend.

Tempie had an answer for me. "Obviously, that means shopping trip to Paris, and perhaps Milan. Equally obviously, I'm going with."

Hmm.

I'd never had anything designer that wasn't pre-loved.

No, strike that.

Both my wedding outfits had been found by Tempie, and as such, they'd both been designer.

Fortunately, there wasn't a quota on that.

"I've never been to Milan," I said. "After I finish my book, we can go there, and Paris, and then I'll go home for however long I have to go home before I can get another visa to come back and stay for a spell." I missed the shift of the vibe of the room and started talking to myself. "I need to make a note to look into the rules about that."

"Go home?" Battle asked.

I turned to him.

And…

Whoops!

"Honey—"

"Go home?" he repeated.

"My visa is only good for"—I did a mental calculation—"less than four more months. I have to leave. I'll figure out when I can come back and maybe you can come out and visit while I'm in The States."

Bartholomew's head shot up because, immediately when I was done talking, Battle pushed back his chair, got up and strode out.

I stared at the door.

Then I looked between Prue, Tempie and Hamish, mumbling, "Okay, I probably should have finessed that better."

Prue and Hamish kept their silence.

Tempie said, "Dear."

Eep!

I started to get up. "I'll go talk to him."

"Think you should give him a bit, lass," Hamish advised.

I sat back down and bit my lip.

His bright blue eyes shifted to Tempie, making his point eloquently, and then he said, "Just a bit. Aye?"

I nodded but said, "It isn't like I told him I was going to go home forever. I said I'd come back."

"Do you want to go home?" Prue asked quietly.

"No. Yes," I answered. "No, not without Battle. But yes, for a visit. I want him to meet my grandparents. And just see where I lived before I came here. But I don't have a choice. I don't have leave to remain here."

"The law can be rather inconvenient at times," Tempie remarked in her cool tone that was meant to be soothing.

It usually worked.

Now it didn't.

I pushed my food around on my plate, gave up, and went after my coffee.

When I was putting the cup back in the saucer, Battle returned.

And he was carrying two thin…

Drawers?

He balanced one on the other, shoved my plate aside, his, then he upended both drawers on the table.

Tinkering flashes of precious jewels scattered all over the surface in a manner both Prue and I had to act fast so none fell to the floor.

"Looks like someone has been to the vault," Tempie murmured.

"Pick one," Battle ordered after he set the now-empty drawers on the sideboard.

Tempie chuckled deeply.

I stared in shock at the plethora of rings all over the table.

I took too long doing this, because Battle sat beside me, grabbed a random ring, then grabbed my left wrist.

Carefully, he put it on my ring finger.

Oh my God.

It didn't go over my knuckle (which was good, it was a huge ruby in a not-very-attractive setting).

"Not that one," he murmured.

Tossing it aside like it was plastic, not gold and a big-ass ruby, he grabbed another one at random.

This was a round sapphire surrounded by diamonds.

He slipped it on my finger.

It was too loose.

"Not that one either," he said, sliding it off and nabbing yet another.

"Battle," I whispered.

The massive emerald-cut emerald fit snug over my knuckle, but it went and then fit perfectly at the base.

He caught my eyes. "That one?"

My heart was beating like a mad thing.

"Are you asking me to marry you?" I whispered.

"Yes, and no," he said curtly. "Yes, we shall be getting married. Yes, I will eventually ask for your hand in a far more romantic manner. Yes, when we apply for a fiancée visa from the Home Office, we will share we're engaged. No, between you and me, my sisters, Hamish and Bartie, this is a place keeper until you and I are ready for the real thing. And that means, until I can phone my jeweler and set her to finding the ring you'll wear to your grave, which in turn means we'll be official sometime next week."

I stared at him even though he was wavy through the tears in my eyes.

"So, darling, will that one do?" he asked a lot more gently.

"I—"

"Vivi!" Prue cried urgently.

I turned to her.

"The ring," she said.

"What?"

"Ravenna!" she nearly yelled. "The ring! Choose the ring wisely."

Holy crap.

The ring.

I looked down at the scattering of expensive jewelry (seriously, they could cull this lot too, and even Noble and Fury's children would have a still-healthy Fund).

"What's this?" Battle asked.

"I do hate when I'm wrong about something, and with that woman, it seems I'm wrong," Tempie said.

But I saw it on the table.

Like when Indiana Jones picked the proper Holy Grail, there it was amidst all the decadence, wealth and splendor.

A little white-gold engagement ring, art deco style, stacked, with a small round diamond embedded in a radiating stamp of art deco square, two tiny diamonds set on each side.

I reached to the ring and felt it for the first time since the first day I was there.

A bolt charging through me.

Oh God.

I handed it to Battle. "This one."

He didn't look fond of my choice, but he took off the emerald and slid that ring on my finger.

It fit perfectly.

I nearly burst into tears.

I didn't, though not due to any iron will over my emotions.

But because, right at the moment Battle settled that ring at the base of my finger, we all heard Chassie scream.

CHAPTER 28

THE LETTERS

Battle and Hamish were out of their chairs like a shot.

The rest of us got up, even Bartholomew, and raced after them, even Bartholomew, and he did this barking.

Surprisingly, with Bartholmew's bulk and Prue's short legs, they took the lead, because I was mildly hobbling and Tempie was on high heels.

She eventually stopped, took them off, chucked them and sprinted up the stairs a lot faster than I'd ever guess she could move.

This meant I was the last one to get to Chassie's room.

By the time I made it there, skidding to a halt beside Tempie, Christian, in nothing but boxers, was laying Chassie, in nothing but a cute, girlie but sexy nightie, on the bed.

Bartholomew was pacing beside it.

"We need ice," Christian stated, thankfully moving to his jeans. "She turned her ankle."

But one must say, it was interesting to know botanists worked out.

Chassie was scrambling to pull the covers over her, and her face was so red, it was gleaming.

Christian hefted his jeans up and prompted, "Ice?"

Prue squeaked then dashed from the room.

I turned to Battle, Tempie and Hamish.

Hamish was studying the ceiling.

Tempie was grinning broadly at her sister in the bed.

Battle looked homicidal again.

Though, I noted, even though Chassie seemed okay (outside the ankle) none of them appeared prepared to leave.

I shambled to my man, just in case I had to be close for a lockdown, asking Chassie, "What happened?"

Her eyes got big, and she pulled the covers up over her nose.

"She got out of bed and the floorboard went," Christian answered, crouching down. "I was in bed, she was too far away, I couldn't grab her."

I looked down at the floor.

The rug was disturbed, pushed through a hole.

"Took a step, she went right through," Christian finished.

"I must have walked on that spot on the floor a million times," Chassie said from behind the covers. "It's so crazy it went this morning. I didn't even feel it was loose."

First things first.

I looked up at Battle. "Why don't you, um…"

He carefully guided me aside, and I thought he wanted me out of the way because he was going to bum rush Christian.

But he squatted down and slapped the rug back.

He then walked to Christian calmly, they both stared down at the displaced floorboard, then Battle squatted again, shoved it fully aside, reached into the floor and came out with a thick stack of letters bound in a faded green ribbon to what looked like four volumes of journals.

"Charlie's letters, I presume?" he asked me when he straightened.

"Oh my God!" I cried just as Chassie cried, "Goodness!" and Tempie drawled, "Well, hell."

I got grabby-hands and took the letters from Battle.

I looked at the address.

Lady Harmony Talyn
The Downs
Haverbourne, Devon

The return address was Great-Granddad Charlie.

I looked to Chassie. "These are them."

She took the covers from her mouth. "You were right about them being in a bedroom," she breathed.

"Go. Read, darling. Christian can look after Chassie," Battle encouraged.

He *so* got me.

I was dying to dig in.

However.

I turned to Chassie. "You're okay?"

"The scream was surprise. It's not that bad. But Christian won't let me move until it's iced and he can have a look at it," Chassie answered.

"Good man," Hamish said while pushing Tempie out the door.

Battle took hold of me, but his attention was on Christian, "You have her?"

Christian nodded. "I've got her."

I checked out Chassie through this. Her color was back to normal, but her eyes were bright and happy.

Seemed Christian wasn't the only one who received a reward last night for being a hero.

Battle guided me down the hall, into our room, to one of the couches into which he pressed me. He went to the closet, came out with a snuggly, fluffy wool black throw and tossed it over me.

He then said, "I'll go get you some more coffee. Did you get enough breakfast?"

No.

But I was not about to delay diving into these letters in order to eat.

"Yes," I said.

He bent and touched his lips to mine.

When he pulled away, he said, "Weight off that knee as much as you can. Yes?"

I nodded.

He left the room.

And at long last, I pulled the ribbon off the letters.

Five hours later…

After a lot of reading.

After a spot of lunch brought up by Battle.

And after a quick, clandestine (I didn't want Battle to catch me) totter out to the studio to retrieve Aileen's diary and the clippings, I was back in Battle's room with my now-fully-charged phone (I took care of that too, after going to get Aileen's things).

I called him.

He picked up with, "Do you need something?"

"Can you come up here?"

"Of course. Be right there."

He hung up, and he told no lies before he did. No matter how long a walk it was, he strolled into the room within minutes.

"Fucking hell," he said after he took one look at me and then moved quickly across the room to wedge his hip next to mine on the couch. "What's in those letters?"

"Harmony killed Arthur Hughes-Davies."

Battle reared back.

"With all the kerfuffle last night…" I began.

He gave me a warning look at describing it as a kerfuffle.

I ignored him and carried on, "I forgot all about finding some newspaper clippings in a diary Prue uncovered in the attic. Harry brought them out to the studio yesterday. Right before the whole…" I tried to find a word that wouldn't tick him off. I settled on, "*Thing* went down, I looked into the box and found a journal. It was Aileen Flannery's. The clippings were in that journal. And Aileen was Harmony and Unity's maid. Her entries around the date in question were also cryptic, but one thing wasn't. She recorded that Hughes-Davies invited himself to a house party at The Downs the weekend he went missing."

"Bloody hell," he whispered.

I kept with the story.

"Aileen was under the impression that Marie was courting him to marry Harmony. However, Hughes-Davies wasn't interested in Harmony. He liked them younger."

His brows shot up. "Unity?"

I nodded.

"How old was she then?"

"Fifteen."

"Jesus Christ," he bit.

"Yes," I agreed.

"How old was he?"

"Thirty-four."

A smidge of his homicidal look came back, but since the homicide (as such) had already occurred, I reached to one of the journals.

Harmony's journals.

Harmony's journals that would, at the time, see her possibly hanged if anyone got to them, and she wasn't able to prove what happened.

Self-defense.

So she hid them under the floorboards.

I waved it side to side before I set it down again.

"Harmony was onto his game. It was one of the reasons she was putting off Charlie. Hughes-Davies was sniffing around a lot, and that around would be around Unity, and Harmony was terrified he'd try something."

"Fuck, Vivi."

"I know," I agreed, and kept going. "She fretted about telling

Charlie, because she knew, if she did, he'd be on the next boat or plane to, as she noted, 'take care of this nasty man.' Apparently, Charlie liked Unity quite a bit. As she did him, according to Unity's journals. Sadly, Harmony decided not to involve him. Or any of her family, mostly due to the fact Marie was fond of Hughes-Davies, so Harmony thought her father was too. Though, she knew Bishop thought he was a blackguard."

Battle's mouth tightened.

"During that fateful house party," I continued, "she got a bad feeling, and she switched rooms with Unity. Her feeling was correct. Hughes-Davies snuck in with malintent. Fortunately, Harmony was ready for him. Unfortunately, Hughes-Davies decided he'd take whatever he could get. He assaulted Harmony. It was bad, but not as bad as it could be. Still, it was bad. She did manage to get her hands on the letter opener she had waiting. She also managed to plunge it into his neck."

His surprised eyes coasted to the letters and journals then back to me when I kept speaking.

"Saint, Bishop, and his younger brother Flint recruited two footmen to assist them in disposing of the body. Marie, her maid Beatrice and Aileen cleaned up the mess. Unity never learned of it. And Harmony doesn't know where, but Arthur Hughes-Davies's remains are buried somewhere on this property."

"Christ," he whispered.

He could say that again.

"Harmony was undone by the events," I carried on. "She understood Hughes-Davies was a rapist, pedophile and all-around creep. However, she was not at one with killing him, which was not her intent. Stopping him, yes. Stabbing him, if she had to. Killing him, no. This might have to do with how much he bled all over her. It was gruesome. And perhaps as an unknown-at-the-time but definitely therapeutic measure, she detailed precisely how gruesome it was in her journal. His attack on her didn't help. She felt unclean. And unworthy of a man as good as Charlie."

Understanding and compassion suffused his face.

"So she begged off," he surmised.

"She did," I confirmed. The tears hit my eyes, and I picked up the last letter in the stack. "But apparently, she wrote him another letter, a few years after the trauma. However, by that time, he'd met and become engaged to my great-grandmother. His response was loving and kind and of a sort, brokenhearted, even if he was in love again. He'd moved on, and as such, with a good deal of agonized prose, he shared he couldn't start things up again and why, and encouraged her to move on too, like he had. Since he was with Great-Grandma, I can't know for sure, but he'd probably tucked the other letters away, and when that one came, he possibly threw it away so she wouldn't see it. Whatever befell it, it wasn't with her others."

"And the ring?" Battle queried.

I reached for another letter and flourished it. "Right before all of this happened, Charlie was getting impatient. He posted her engagement ring to her. It was right after that, she begged off. Eventually,"—my hand with the letter listed down—"he got angry. Told her to keep the ring, not that she really wanted it, his words. He never was truly hurtful. What he was, was deeply wounded."

I looked down at the ring on my finger and kept talking.

"He thought it wasn't fancy enough. He thought it demonstrated the life she'd be leaving behind to be with him, and she didn't want anything to do with the life he could provide for her. That was the last letter he wrote to her, and she didn't respond, until she approached him again years later."

"But he thought wrong," Battle stated.

I nodded despondently.

Then I slipped an envelope out of one of the journals.

"Apparently, some time later, she wrote him once more. And he wrote back."

"What did he say?"

"She'd obviously been living for years wracked with the idea that he thought she thought he wasn't good enough for her, so she told him all about it. From what I can tell from Charlie's response, she shared everything about Arthur Hughes-Davies."

His head ticked in shock. "Jesus, that was a risk."

I tucked the letter back into the journal. "This might explain why the last two letters are gone from his stash, at least the very last one. I can totally see him destroying it to protect her."

"Yes," Battle agreed.

I kept sharing.

"He was again brokenhearted. And this time, even though years had passed and he was happily married, he was pissed. He was angry she didn't tell him. Angry she didn't trust him. Angry she didn't think he'd love her, no matter what, support her, no matter what she went through. Even so, he was more pissed at Hughes-Davies, and you could tell he still cared for her greatly, because he might have been mad, but he was again, not cruel." I shook my head. "All of it was hard to get through. But somehow, that was the worst. Him sharing what she should have known. That his love was real, and no matter what, he would have stuck by her side if she'd only given him the chance."

Battle traced his knuckles over quiet tears I didn't realize I'd shed.

And it made me feel better, especially when he whispered, "Darling."

"That last bit, honey, was because I had to quit reading her journal around the time they were falling in love. Great-Grandad was right. She *should* have known. She should never have doubted him. The way she described how they fell in love." I swallowed. "Obviously, it was completely different. It still reminded me of you and me."

At that, he leaned forward and kissed my nose.

When he sat back, I told him, "There's good news."

"Please share," he said gently.

"She didn't die a sad spinster. She may have lived nominally in this house, but for the most part, she was partner to a farmer who leased the south field. They had no children, because one of them couldn't conceive. But from the age of thirty-two to his death when he was seventy-four, and he was two years older than her, they lived together and loved each other. She returned to The Downs fully for the next year, after which she died."

"All of that is in those journals?"

Another nod from me. "She didn't write in them as frequently after she met her Clive. Her brother Bishop, apparently, sanctioned this and worked very hard to keep scandal from touching them and making sure they had their privacy. Times were different after he passed away. It wouldn't be as much of a scandal, but even so, Cannon was charged with doing the same." I gave him a soft look. "From Harmony's writings, Bishop reminds me of somebody."

Battle ignored the compliment.

"Why didn't they marry?"

Finally, something made me smile.

"She was somewhat of a forward thinker for her time. She didn't see the point, and Clive agreed. They were committed, that was all they needed. If she'd fallen pregnant, they would have tied the knot so their child wouldn't face scorn and bullies. But she didn't, so they didn't. That said, everyone in the village knew, and everyone loved Harmony as well as Clive, so they just went with it, and they lived happily in their little space in the world for the more than forty years they were together."

His eyes moved through the letters and journals scattered around me, and then to mine.

"So the mystery is solved," he said.

"It is indeed."

Battle looked about as deflated about the whole thing as I felt.

And that was the man I loved.

"Obviously, I won't write about any of this in my book," I assured.

"I appreciate that, love, but we do have to call the authorities."

We did?

"Wait. Why?" I asked.

"There is the matter of a man who's been missing for eighty years."

"The only one who cared was his mother, and it is without a doubt that woman is dead."

"It's likely he still has family."

"He died single and childless."

"That doesn't mean there isn't family."

"Battle, he was a pedophile, and I would hazard to guess, if he has any descendants, they would not want anyone to know that. Now his bones are turning to dust somewhere in an unmarked grave. And good riddance to bad rubbish. He's forgotten. Great-Granddad married a woman he loved, had a family and a long life. Harmony found a man she loved and had a long life with him. Maybe not the happily-ever-after of a romance novel, but even so, they both had their happily-ever-afters. If you tell the police, this will be a huge deal. Way huger than Chelsea's bullshit."

Battle didn't appear convinced.

Therefore, I kept at him.

"If you call the cops, you'll not only bring attention to this house, this family, but also Harmony. She took pains to live a quiet life." I gestured to the letters and journals. "I think we should bury this back in the floorboards, with Harmony's letters to Charlie, and if they don't entirely disintegrate and become one with The Downs, we can let some future generation that happens upon them read about two good people who fell in love, the world conspired against them, but they had their HEAs anyway. And the bad guy got his due."

"HEA?"

"Happily ever after."

His lips tipped up.

"Please don't do that to her," I begged. "Or Saint, Bishop, Flint, those footmen, even Aileen, Unity and Marie. All the people who cared for her in the end and took care of her. Let very dead pedophiles lie where they belong. Missing but forgotten."

"You're right, sweetheart, there's no use dredging it up now."

Yeah.

That was the man I loved.

I pushed up so I could kiss his jaw, sat back and whispered, "Thank you."

"In the end," he began. "We're her family, you included in a way. We should protect her like they protected her."

"I knew you wouldn't let down the side," I replied, and quoted, "Aristocrats are dab hands at holding their secrets."

"Sorry?"

"Something Tempie said."

"Sounds like her." Then, "Are we going to tell the girls?"

"I'll let that be your call."

"I think they'll be glad to know Harmony found happiness after all."

That would be my call.

I just nodded.

"What now?" he asked.

"Well, I can't type. My hands aren't bad, but they feel tight and typing will probably exacerbate it. And I need a shower. I still have rain hair."

No lip tip that time, he smiled full out.

"Rain hair?" he inquired.

"I saw myself in the mirror this morning. I look a fright."

"You look beautiful to me."

And again.

The man I loved.

Still, a girl couldn't have bad hair for long, says me.

"So...for me, shower," I stated. "Then I think I need a nap. After that, I need to fuck a hot duke. And hopefully, that'll bring us to cocktails."

"I hope you know, I will always be up for a fuck, but not with you having an injured knee and palms."

"We just Home-Office-official, unofficially, soon-to-be-officially-official got engaged," I reminded him.

I'd tell him later, as crazy as it was, his official, but unofficial, soon-to-be-officially-official proposal was the *best thing ever*.

"I suppose I could eat you without causing further injury," he mused.

I rolled my eyes.

But my pussy got happy.

He bent and kissed my nose again.

When he sat back, he said, "Shower for you. And nap. We'll play it by ear after."

"Doable," I replied.

He smiled and got up.

He also helped me tidy all Harmony's and Aileen's stuff before he helped pull me out of the sofa.

And more helping, this being me to the bathroom even if I was totally fine to walk.

I didn't share that.

I asked, "Are you okay with Chassie and Christian?"

He heaved a sigh. "I'll always see her as the curly-haired, six-year-old my mother, and essentially my father, left me to raise. I understand she's an adult. That doesn't mean my heart will ever come to terms with it. But my head must, for Chassie."

Man, he was going to be such a good dad.

"Yes, it must, for Chassie," I agreed, feeling all melty, because my guy was so great. "And Christian, because he really is a solid bloke."

He focused on me. "Do you understand half the shit that comes out of his mouth?"

"Not even a quarter of it." I paused, "But Chassie does."

"It's like the skies opened up and dropped the perfect man for her in the gamekeeper's cottage," he noted.

It was just like that.

"Much like they opened so you could walk into my study," he continued.

Aw!

I loved him *so much*!

This made me kiss him.

He let me.

Then he forced me into the shower.

I took a nap and woke to my villainously handsome Battle taking off his glasses, making him look the handsome villain, before he left his laptop on the coffee table between the couches where he was working to join me in bed.

I got magnificent head, which led to an equally magnificent orgasm.

But Battle refused to allow me to return the favor.

Ah well.

It was almost time for cocktails anyway.

EPILOGUE
THE REST

Before we hit the plum parlor, Battle texted the girls to meet us in his room, without Hamish and Christian.

I was lounged in a couch with good hair, a bum knee and a post-orgasm glow as they started parading in.

Prue was first.

Chassie was second.

And Tempie came last, doing it bitching.

"Whatever this is, I'd first like an explanation of why Hamish cannot be here," she demanded.

One could say Tempie had done a total turnabout in the whole arm's length thing with Hamish.

I loved it.

"Did you read the letters, Vivi?" Prue asked before anyone could answer Tempie.

"I did," I answered.

"And considering Vivi uncovered irrefutable evidence a member of the Talyn family committed justifiable homicide, this is the reason why Hamish and Christian aren't here," Battle put in.

Tempie hissed in shock, Prue and Chassie gasped.

But on that intro, they didn't mess around and found seats.

When they did, I told the story.

Battle followed me up with, "And it's been decided we'll not be going to the authorities so they can put the case of the missing viscount to bed. As family, we'll do what Harmony's immediate family did. We're going to protect her secret."

"Of course," Tempie agreed easily.

Prue and Chassie also quickly agreed, though they did it by just nodding.

Battle looked between Tempie and Chassie. "I'll leave it up to you whether you share this with Hamish and Christian. Hamish won't breathe a word, I know." He focused on Chassie, and his voice gentled. "But you and Christian are new. He's rather a straight arrow, so I'd request you please be cautious."

Chassie nodded again.

At this point, I asked her, "How's your ankle?"

"It's totally fine," she answered. "And I knew it was. Christian was overreacting."

So she traded one overprotective man for another.

Good on her.

"Can we get a drink now?" Prue requested. "After that story, I need one."

I was with her on that.

Apparently, so was everyone else, since we all headed out to join Hamish and Christian in the plum parlor.

And get this, I didn't have to walk down the stairs because my unofficially, soon-to-be-official fiancé carried me down them.

Wasn't he the best?

Battle waited until everyone had drinks in their hands and were lounged in the seating area before he announced, "Mum phoned me."

I stared at him because we agreed Sunday lunch.

And this was not Sunday lunch.

Then again, both Hamish and Christian were there, and I knew it was weighing heavily on his mind, so might as well. Especially if he could take that weight off his mind.

"Excuse me?" Tempie asked ominously.

"She'd heard I was in a serious relationship, and she wanted to know, if I were to marry, if she was still able to refer to herself by her title," Battle finished.

No one said anything, except Fitzy, who, in a tight voice, announced, "I need to check on something with Cook."

And then with a stiff body, he strode out.

Just to say, Fitzy and Patsy had been there a long time.

I didn't know precisely how long.

I just knew they held affection, and even love, for the Talyn family. As such, they couldn't miss the four of them had been forced to navigate life essentially without parents.

And he excelled at his job, so being infuriated, he'd take that elsewhere.

Once Fitzy left, Prue queried in a small voice, "That's all she asked?"

I got up and hobbled over to sit beside her on the sofa, where I took her hand.

"Sorry, sweetheart," Battle said when I was in position. "That's all she asked."

Hamish tucked Tempie closer. Christian nabbed Chassie's hand. I held Prue's fast.

Again, there was silence.

"Does anyone have anything they want to say?" Battle invited.

"Or shout," I added.

"She was grasping and vacuous when she was around," Tempie noted. "It's hardly a surprise she hasn't changed."

After Tempie said this, Chassie made a noise then started crying.

Battle began to make a move to go to her but settled when Christian got up, pulled her out of her chair and into his arms.

I watched Battle watching this.

This meant I watched Battle struggle with handing over the reins he'd held so steady and strong for twenty-eight years, providing love, support and protection to his baby sister.

Witnessing this struggle, I wished I was holding his hand.

But for Chassie, no real shocker, her big brother bested it.

Chassie pulled from Christian and cried, "God, she's *such a bitch!*"

She then started sobbing again and Christian tucked her right back to his chest.

"How are you hanging in?" I asked Prue.

"It"—she pulled her shoulders in and released them—"hurts. But it always hurts. I can't say I'm surprised. Except at the level of cruelty it took for her to call Battle to ask that question when she can just Google rules of the peerage and know."

"It's not cruel. It's selfish and thoughtless and lazy, all her, all the time," Tempie stated. "It didn't even occur to her to think how Battle, or any of us, would respond to her call."

This was the sad truth.

The room descended into silence again.

Eventually, Chassie stopped crying, and Christian sat her back in her chair, but he pulled his closer to hers so she could list to the side and rest her head on his shoulder.

"This is what I know," Hamish announced.

Everyone looked to him.

He didn't disappoint.

"For better, or for worse, the challenges life gives us make us who we are." He looked down at Tempie tucked to his side. "If she was not an awful woman, you might not have had to become savvy and strong and able to love with an invisible depth that has no ending."

God, I just loved Hamish for Tempie.

He so *got her*.

Hamish looked to the group. "That woman was a reprehensibly terrible mother. But you four would not have what you have if she wasn't. It doesn't make the flaws in her character right. But it does bring out in stark relief the strength of all of yours."

Jeez.

I so totally liked that guy.

Tempie did too, if her grabbing his beard and pulling his mouth to hers so they could make out hot and heavy on the couch was anything to go by.

As fabulous a moment as that was, it went on a long time.

And Prue got done with it.

"Yuck!" she cried. "Go to your room!"

They broke, and Tempie snuggled up against her hot Scotsman with a smug smile on her face.

"Hamish is right," I said. "I told my sister I felt comfortable here, in this beautiful jewel of a massive house, which could and maybe should be formidable, but it isn't. Because it's so full of love. You four built that. And I'm so honored I was even invited to walk through the front doors to experience it."

"Oh, Vivi," Prue said and gave me a hug.

I hugged her back.

"Shall we metaphorically bury mother like our ancestors buried dead bodies and move on?" Tempie suggested, to Hamish's head jerking and Christian's eyes narrowing on her.

Battle sighed.

I returned to the chair next to him and my drink.

Bartholomew started snoring.

And a loving family in a house filled with love sipped cocktails while they waited on dinner.

The next Monday, when Battle was back in London, and my hands had healed enough I was back in the studio (with electricity and phone line repaired), Prue came out and knocked on the door.

She stuck her head in.

"I know you hate interruptions, but I need to ask you something," she said.

"Girl, I need to stand or my hip flexors are gonna be locked in sit position for the rest of my life." I looked out the windows at the sun shining and suggested, "Wanna take a walk?"

She nodded.

I left the cats snoozing (as was their wont), and we walked out into the sunshine and Chassie's flourishing garden.

"What's up?" I prompted.

"Natalie and I just had a long chat, and I'm accepting an offer for my book."

She then told me the advance, and I stopped dead.

She stopped with me.

"Holy fuck," I whispered.

"Is that a lot?" she asked.

"Uh…*yeah.*"

I was really becoming a master of the English understatement.

Go me!

"Okay, see, I want to publish under a pen name," she declared.

This came as a surprise.

"You don't want to put your name on your books?"

"I don't want to put the Talyn name on the books."

Another surprise.

"But why?" I asked.

"A lot of reasons," she answered, starting to walk again, so I did too. "One, I don't want to do book tours. I don't want to do signings. I want to stay anonymous. I know you all talk about it, really excited about that possibility for me. And I know that sounds ungracious. But, if people, uh…*like* my work, and there are a lot of them. I might get…" —she wagged her head side to side—"you know."

I did know.

Uncomfortable in a crowd and being the center of attention.

"A lot of artists, heck, a lot of people are introverts," I said. "But you don't have to agree to do signings. And just so you know, your publisher probably won't pay for a book tour unless the books become huge successes. So you might not even have to worry about it."

Though, her books would be successes, leading to publishers pressing her to do tours.

She could still say no.

"You're right, but the name Talyn will be on the books."

"Yes," I agreed. "And you're not proud to do that?"

"I would be. Definitely. However, people will know it was me."

"Yes," I repeated.

"And attention will come to me, and maybe our family."

Ah.

The Talyn Privacy Thing.

I didn't remind her I was marrying her brother, and I put my name on my books.

That said, post-unofficial/official engagement, Battle and I had the discussion, and so I could honor Mom and Dad, we agreed, even though I was oh-so going to take the name Talyn when we married, I'd continue to write under Vivienne Dupree.

"I was thinking, if you're okay with it, my pen name could be Harmony Charles," she said.

I stopped dead again as emotion clogged my throat.

Therefore, it was croaky when I pushed out, "Oh, Prue."

"I know they were both happy with other people in the end, but it's still so sad. I want them to be together somehow."

I agreed.

And that was the perfect way to do it.

I wrapped an arm around her shoulders, hers went around my waist, and I set us to walking, saying, "I think that's beautiful."

"Right? I did too."

"And you do you, however you want to. Always. Because you're awesome."

"You are too, Vivi. You know that, right?"

I looked down at her as we made the verdant lawns of the north parkland.

And I smiled.

That Wednesday, I took another break from the book.

I parked the Peugeot in the town centre car park, went to the door by the Boots, punched in the code, got the buzz, walked up the steps and knocked on another door.

Ravenna answered.

"I have the kettle boiled," she said and let me in.

She made tea, and we sat down.

She took a sip, then leaned forward to set the cards on the table in front of me.

"You know I'm not here for a reading," I said.

"Hmm," she replied.

"The cats. The ghosts. The *house*," I prompted. "You saw more in those thirteen cards than you let on. In fact, you knew something was up the minute you saw me. So, please, tell me."

"I can tell you the veil has settled down," she replied.

Ugh.

"Is that all you're going to tell me?" I asked.

"It had to be righted."

Great.

She was going to be all cryptic mystic.

"Can you explain?" I requested.

"It's hard to say what I need to say," she began hesitantly. But luckily, she kept going. "However, since I can tell you want to hear it…"

She paused for me to confirm.

I nodded my head to do that.

She socked it to me. "Your great-grandmother was not the love of your great-grandfather's life. Harmony was."

Even though I suspected this…

Even though this was what actually drove me to The Downs…

Even though her journals and the tone of his letters pretty much screamed it…

I was bummed out for my great grandma.

But I sat silent and listened.

Ravenna, as usual, had it going on.

"What had to be righted is…love. Harmony was the love of Charlie's life. Charlie was the love of Harmony's. Sometimes, this love is so great, it has magical power all on its own. Their love was so great, it had this power. When it was thwarted, it affected the veil."

This was a little hocus-pocus, but it still made sense.

Ravenna kept going.

"Of course, they both went on to find happiness with others, and that's good. But it was not what was meant to be. When what's not meant to be *is*, the veil is disturbed. And it stays that way until what went wrong is righted."

"Battle and me," I deduced.

She nodded.

"Of her blood, of his. Yes. The duke and you." She studied me closely. "Don't mistake the forces we can't explain interfering in this as anything but what it is. The fact your ancestors weren't, has no bearing on the depth of what you and the duke have. Again, the bottom line of it is, you two were meant to be too. What you have with the duke has its own power, and that power is significant. Thus, the veil around The Downs is at peace once again."

This was hocus-pocus too.

But to me, it *totally* made sense.

"So I won't see phantom dancers in the ballroom anymore?" I inquired.

She smiled, sipped her tea and shook her head.

Well, that was a relief.

Also, I totally knew she knew what was going down.

"I have tons more questions," I told her.

"I hope I have answers," she invited me to ask them.

"Okay, you said the last time I was here that the veil was disturbed recently, but just now, that it's been disturbed since Harmony and Charlie were parted. So what's the difference?"

"You."

"Me?"

"It was never right, but in my lifetime, it was all I knew. Until things went haywire, because you arrived at The Downs."

Okay.

Right.

That made sense as well.

"So you saw in the cards that I saw the ghosts in the ballroom," I said.

She just nodded.

I kept going.

"Now, I can understand why I saw the scene from when it was a hospital, since that was about Harmony and Charlie. But I also saw a Regency ball, and there were lights coming from there on a night when I was in danger. And I could swear they were calling to me to get to the house and be safe."

"As they would," she confirmed. "If something happened to you, the veil would have to wait for some other descendent of Charlie's to meet some other descendent of the duke's to make things right. I'm sure it was disturbing to see those scenes, as you call them. But they weren't malevolent. They were needed. Thus, they appeared for a reason."

Again.

Made sense.

Crazy sense, but sense.

"But the Regency ball?" I pushed. "That one scene came out the strongest."

She lifted her shoulders. "Who knows why ghost do what they do? Maybe it's because you're a student of history and the house showed you what it thought you wanted to see. Maybe there's some link to Harmony, or even Charlie, from that period we don't know." She grinned. "Maybe they just wanted to come out and play." Her grin died. "Probably, they were just what the house conjured up to communicate with you. Happy times. Dancing and friends. Girls hoping to make a match and fall in love." She wagged her brows.

"Men hoping for other things. Pretty gowns and sparkling jewels and dapper suits. I know I wouldn't mind seeing that. Much better, more friendly and welcoming than injured men back from the front who would never be the same again."

That made sense too.

Kind of.

"And the cats won't interfere anymore?" I pressed.

"If there was ever a creature at one with the veil, it's the feline. If the veil is at peace, they will be."

Good.

I wasn't a big fan of hitting the deck yet another time.

That done, I asked the million-dollar question.

"How do you know all of this?"

"Blood is blood, luv. Aileen Flannery was my great-grandmother."

Holy shit!

I burst out laughing.

Ravenna did it with me.

It wasn't until we had a long chat about ghosts, familiars and fate, and I was at the door, ready to leave, that she dropped the bomb.

"Would you like to know where the bones are buried?"

I looked down at her in shock. "You know?"

"I have some chops, Vivienne, but even I'm not that good. Great-Gran lived to be ninety-seven. And she liked to tell stories."

Oh boy.

Although I was curious to know where Hughes-Davies was buried, I wasn't sure it was good she knew.

She shook her head. "There are some bones that deserve to go undisturbed. And Great-Gran sensed my abilities, so she didn't tell anyone but me. I'm quite happy that man is dead and buried, a mysterious footnote in history that anyone who took an interest would learn only that he was an ass and not missed by anyone but his mother. So I won't be saying anything."

That was good too.

I thought about her question and made a decision.

"The estate is so beautiful, I don't want to know where he is. I don't want knowing that to mess up my perception of even an inch of that place."

Or Battle's, since I'd obviously have to tell him.

"Saint, Bishop and Flint agreed," Ravenna said. "This is why he wasn't buried on The Downs. Close, but not on duchy property."

"But Harmony said—"

"Harmony was wrong. They didn't tell her because she was true of heart. I think her brothers worried all their lives she'd eventually turn herself in to the police. They corralled Clive into helping them make sure she didn't. And part of looking out for her, they kept that secret to themselves." She shrugged and lifted her hands to her sides. "No body. No murder."

"Justifiable homicide," I corrected.

"Quite," she agreed on an eye twinkle.

"So, where is he?" I asked.

She grinned mischievously. "Where he should be. Under a manure pit on the farm to the south of The Downs."

Buried under shit.

I burst out laughing again.

And so did she.

Later, when I told Battle where Hughes-Davies was, he busted out laughing too.

And since I wasn't done with how awesome I thought Saint, Bishop and Flint's funereal decisions were for that dick, I joined him.

That said, even though all of what Ravenna told me made sense (or a certain kind of it), I wasn't entirely sure all of it was true.

Prue hadn't seen those visions, and the intruder that night followed me, seemingly unaware of the ghost ball, and he couldn't have missed it.

It was safe to say I had an overactive imagination, I was dealing with Mom's death, the challenge of a new book, and experiencing trial by fire as I became a part of a family while falling in love with the man of my dreams.

Not to mention, Chassie's floorboard had been loose for decades so Harmony could hide her things under it. It was likely it would give eventually.

Last, cats were cats.

In the end, it didn't really matter if it was phantasmagorical or real.

The end result was worth it.

It was several weeks later.

On a sunny day.

While Battle and I were watching my very young nephew and niece fail miserably at croquet (I mean, the mallet was taller than Rayray! but she was determined to play, God love her).

That was when he took my hand.

He slid Charlie's ring from my finger, a ring I hadn't taken off since he put it on. He grabbed my other hand and slid it there.

He then reached into the pocket of his jeans and went back to my left hand.

And there, he slid an almost-exact replica of Charlie's ring to Harmony on my finger.

Of course, the diamonds were a whole lot bigger.

But other than that, it was the same.

In other words, it was outlandishly *perfect*.

Just like my fiancé.

He then raised my hand to his lips and kissed the ring, before he pressed my hand flat on his chest.

"Marry me?" he whispered.

I really wasn't sure whether a duke throwing a strop about me leaving the country, exiting the room, coming back, dumping a bunch of rings on the table and telling me to pick one before shoving several on my finger to unofficially officially ask me to marry him was better than doing it standing in a beautiful garden of a beautiful house in the sun with our families close and happy.

But since I got both, who cared?

"Try and stop me," I answered.

He let my hand go, curled both arms around me and kissed me.

The wind drifted through the trees.

The ghosts settled in their graves.

And the world was set to rights.

At least it was at The Downs.

As for all the rest…

Prue's book release went as expected.

It was a phenomenal success.

She immediately signed another deal.

Once the attics had been cleared, the Talyns went to work, and her upstairs studio was created.

It was totally kickass.

Something else expected: not long after her first release, she got a streaming deal.

But not before me.

My book about Elizabeth and Christopher Hatton was optioned and made into a film.

I used part of the million pounds I got from Chelsea's dad, which I'd given to Battle to invest for me, to purchase the fabulous gown I wore to the premiere, and obviously, Battle escorted me.

A gazillion pictures were taken of us.

And seriously, I had no clue how he did it.

But not a single one of them shared more than a partial profile.

Though a few of them got a good shot of my amazing dress.

So that worked for me.

As for those million pounds…

We did a family thing in both Paris and Milan, that being everyone went with us, including Battle, Hamish and Christian.

Prue and Chassie also did their Switzerland thing.

The world opened up for everyone at The Downs.

Even so, it was always there, homebase, so although we all had our adventures…

No one was ever gone for long.

Also about those million pounds…

It took some effort, but it was effort I gleefully expended, filling my part of Battle's and my closet.

I received those sexy nighties, and with my windfall, I bought a lot more.

Truthfully, it was a waste of money. My man was visual, tactile and imaginative, and adding that visual usually meant any sexy nightie I donned ended up on my body for a few minutes and on the floor for a whole lot longer.

That didn't stop me from buying them.

Not at all.

I'd been wrong about François.

He was one hundred percent *not* gay.

Though I was right about one thing.

He was also one hundred percent seriously in love with Prue.

It was just that it was another kind of love altogether.

He confessed this to her when she went to London (by herself!) to tool around some museums and do some shopping. He asked her to dinner, and she went thinking it was some kind of client relations thing.

It was not.

They started dating.

They fell in love.

They got married in the single weirdest wedding I'd ever attended (the theme for the décor was goldfish (don't ask me), even the cake topper was a goldfish with a bow tie and another one wearing a veil—I'll let you fill in the rest, just be sure to do it the weirdest way possible), where she wore a creation designed by her fiancé, which was the single weirdest wedding gown of all time (yes, it was orange).

It was still fantastic, mostly because it was so weird, fascinating and fun.

And they were deliriously happy.

I was one of three bridesmaids.

Battle gave his sister away.

When those two weren't in London, François worked with Prue in what became their studio in the attic.

And oh yeah, he totally moved in.

They had four children.

Two daughters, one named Kahlo, one named O'Keeffe (though, they called her Georgie).

And two sons, one named Matisse, the other was called Basquiat.

Tempie's wedding to Hamish was intimate and elegant and no expense had been spared.

I was honored with standing up for her too.

And obviously, Battle gave her away.

Tempie let go of the flat in London, but if they were there, they stayed in Hamish's.

They also spent quite a bit of time at Hamish's family estate up near Aberdeen.

Even so, they took their places at The Downs and added two children to the menagerie.

Both boys.

Angus and Fergus.

They were borderline hooligans and drove their mother crazy (no, I will not admit to accepting Angus's dare to skateboard through the great hall (but between you and me, I did)).

Even so, she adored them beyond reason.

As did we all.

Chassie and Christian married in the gardens.

Of course.

It was also small, intimate and very casual.

Surprising me, and making me melt into uncontrollable sobs, she asked if I'd accompany Battle when he walked her down the aisle.

Naturally, I agreed.

They started their married life in the gamekeeper's cottage, and I understood that.

Even if the house was huge, they wanted a little bit of privacy.

Then again, not many girls, after their first time with the man they were falling in love with, had their entire families invade her bedroom the very next morning.

So I could see privacy was a thing for those two.

Once they started having babies, however, they moved to the big house.

They had five children.

Two boys, Alder and Rowan.

And three girls, Briar, Flora and Juniper.

Once Christian earned his PhD, the two of them started a niche gardening business where they took clients who were having issues with their gardens. Bugs, disease, irrigation, whatever, Christian would go in and diagnosis it, and Chassie would help him irradicate it, replant (or fully redesign) and get the garden flourishing again.

In no time, they were all over the UK, rehabilitating gardens.

A bit of time after that, they were all over the continent doing the same thing.

They loved living, working and parenting together.

And since the night of Midnight Mayhem, they never spent a night apart.

Not once.

Prue, Chassie and I continued our cooking classes (it won't surprise you, Tempie never joined).

Once Prue got breakfast down, she stopped coming.

But Chassie and I kept it up until she had a good month's worth of recipes she could make (her shepherd's pie was to die for!).

And she made them often, cooking for her guy.

Then, when they were at the big house, helping me with Sunday lunch.

Before all of that happened, while I was writing my book in the studio and Battle worked in his study, Prue and Chassie took off one day, returning to Glastonbury.

They came back with a beautiful, carved wood box.

So, when Tempie and Hamish showed for the weekend, I invited Ravenna over, and everyone went into the ballroom (oh yes, the girls told their men everything).

In there, Battle, Hamish and Christian (this was before the François revelation) carefully disassembled a square of parquetry.

The girls and I put Charlie's letters, Harmony's letters and journals, and Marie's and Aileen's journals, with Aileen's clippings into the box.

I also put the engagement ring Charlie gave Harmony in that box.

Battle and I rested it under the floorboards.

On top of it, Prue put a picture she drew of them, Great-Granddad in his uniform, Harmony in a pretty summer dress, walking together out in the gardens of The Downs.

Chassie placed one of her bouquets on top of that. The bouquet had white lilies (which she shared denoted purity) and red roses (obviously those symbolized love).

On top of the flowers, Ravenna placed a polished rose quartz shaped in a heart with the two-snakes-entwined symbol carved on it that she told us represented two interwoven spirits.

So yeah.

That worked.

Once all of that was laid to rest, the men carefully replaced the parquet square.

And then we all went to the plum parlor for a drink.

We did this leaving Charlie and Harmony in the place where they met, the place where they fell in love…

Resting together for (maybe) eternity.

How did I handle this in my book?

Obviously, I had to get mystical about it.

I left in the happy but sad ending.

I left out the homicide.

I wasn't sure how my editor would take the hints of magic in it, but she loved it.

It sold huge (maybe because word got out I'd fallen in love with the current duke while writing it, not hard since I was wearing his ring and living with him, but I preferred to think it was because the book was good, and Charlie and Harmony's story was compelling).

I sold the option for that too, a single season for streaming.

And at the premiere, I wore another fantastic dress.

But as was Battle's magic, as ever, the photographers went away with essentially nothing.

Battle did not get into Harry and Scotty's shit for not doing what it would be impossible for them to do: somehow intuit danger on a several hundred-acre estate and move to handle it.

He already knew there were vulnerabilities in their security. Namely if someone wanted to take the long trek sidling through the property of one of the attached farms owned by the duchy that didn't have tall fences protecting them from access to the parkland, outbuildings and the big house.

This being what Chelsea's hired stalker did.

What Battle did do was augment the security so there were more cameras monitored by the company he contracted with for the front gate.

He boosted this by getting me my own dog who he left with me at The Downs, and who just stayed at The Downs even if I wasn't there, in order for that pooch to keep alert for whoever Battle loved who was there.

It was an Old English Sheepdog. I allowed Prue to name him.

She chose Crispin.

Don't ask me why.

But Crispie he became.

And I adored him.

We all did.

Including Bartholomew.

Battle also made a change to the studio.

He had curtains added on the windows.

And as I worked on my next book, the one after that, and the one after that (you get me), we utilized them.

Often.

We also put a fair effort into besting his challenge to have sex in every room of The Downs.

But with so many people around, this wasn't easy.

That said, there were so many people around.

And that was awesome.

Rebecca did not contact Battle, or any of them again.

Until years later, when she was dying.

Because they were who they were, all four of them swallowed down their pain and anger and went to Greece to visit and say goodbye.

Obviously, all the partners went with.

She was beautiful, even at the end of her decline.

And I was nice to her face.

But I was glad to take my man home.

Chassie stayed with her the two weeks it took to reach the inevitable end.

And because they were who they were, they buried her next to their father in the family plot.

Atlas would wish this, so there was that.

But Rebecca would feel entitled to it, and quite frankly, that sucked.

Though life was life, you couldn't have everything your way.

I wondered if Rebecca learned that in the end, with only one daughter near her side, and her being there out of duty only.

Regrettably, I doubted it.

As I was in on the whole ceremony to add Harmony and Charlie to the house forever, I got over my fear of the ballroom.

Truth, it wasn't a room that was ever used, outside the weddings we seemed to keep having at the house.

But I never saw the lights or the ghosts again.

Further, the cats never acted weird or tripped me into being where they wanted me to be (though, they did trip me, just because they're cats).

In fact, nothing weird or supernatural happened at all.

And call me crazy.

I was kind of bummed about that.

I used some more of my millions to buy myself some shit-hot riding breeches and boots.

Battle approved, though I thought he approved more of the fact that, after we rode, he got to peel them off me.

I got really good at riding.

So good, Battle and I rode frequently.

Sometimes we did it alone. Sometimes with Tempie and/or Hamish, Prue, Chassie and/or Christian (François didn't ride).

I tried to shoot a shotgun, but that bitch put an angry bruise on my shoulder and nearly knocked me flat on my ass (Battle warned me about the kickback, but *damn*).

That bruise was visible for over a week.

No thank you.

Though, I enjoyed watching my guy decimate the clay pigeons flung through the air.

It was all kinds of hot.

An aside: François might not ride, but the dude was hell on wheels shooting clay pigeons.

It was almost as fun to watch Battle shoot them with the way Prue would cheer and clap every time her hubby hit the mark.

Seriously, they were so cute together.

Battle took me back home to The States repeatedly.

My grandparents loved him.

Solène loved him for me.

Alex thought he was the shit.

And Matty and Rayray absolutely adored their Uncle Battie.

They all came out for Battle's and my wedding.

Another small affair in the gardens.

My gown was gorgeous.

My groom was way more beautiful.

Solène walked me down the aisle.

But Bartholomew went with us.

When the pastor told Battle he could kiss the bride, he did, twice.

First, he kissed my freckles.

And only after that, he kissed my lips.

Prue's wedding present was another abstract portrait.

This one of me.

It was of my profile, my hair pulled back in a soft chignon.

The only thing that was truly distinct was my face.

In my hair, my neck, my bare shoulder, there were cats and dogs and horses, flowers, rings and rolling parkland.

Outside the rings, it looked like The Downs lived under my skin.

Like Battle resided there.

It was perfect.

Battle had it mounted over our bed.

And it was safe to say, he liked it better than me.

I gave Battle three perfect (says me) babies.

Noble, our oldest, a boy.

Archer, our second, also a boy.

And Fury, our last, a girl.

It was good when I finally started pushing them out. One could say my man was at a loss without a whole brood to take care of.

So I didn't mess about in giving him a new one.

It didn't surprise me he was as good of a father to boys (I had no doubts about him being the best girl dad in history) as he was a brother to his sisters.

Then again, Battle Talyn, Duke of Burleigh, was good at everything.

Yeah.

Says me.

Tempie and Hamish and Battle and I shared the south wing with our broods, Prue and François and Chassie and Christian and their broods shared the north.

Cocktails had to be moved to the games room because it was bigger, and as such, fit more people, with more room for babies to crawl, then toddlers to toddle, then tweenies to bop and teenagers to laze.

Fitzy and Patsy stayed with us until they retired to the steward's cottage (the men who eventually replaced Harry and Scotty when they moved on lived in the attic apartments).

They did this rent free and on a generous pension from The Downs.

Though, they weren't there often, since they used their pension to do what they'd always wanted to do: travel the globe.

Fitzy the Second (though we called him Bonzie), Fitzgibbons and Patsy's eldest son, took over with his wife, Connie.

And every night at The Downs, some were there, some might be away, friends would join, or it would be just family.

But always, the dining room table at The Downs was full to bursting.

Just like any house filled to the brim with love…

That was as it should be.

The End

The Manors and Mysteries Series will continue…

SECOND AUTHOR'S NOTE

As you now know, this book tackles sexual assault, bullying and negligent parenting.

If this book has brought up things you need to talk to someone about, I'll offer a few resources here that are there to help.

Bullying: Stomp Out Bullying, stompoutbullying.org

Sexual Assault: RAINN, rainn.org

And I do encourage you to reach out to these organizations, or someone you love and trust, to find support.

This is a love story, in all that entails, and I hope I got the point across that those who love you want to do what they can to be there for you.

If you need that, I urge you to let them.

ACKNOWLEDGMENTS

As you do, I was scrolling through TikTok, and I happened on to this awesome chick who told thorough stories in compelling, informed, contemporary, accessible and sometimes hilarious ways about the Tudor dynasty.

Because her posts are so interesting, I always stop to watch, and doing so, she reminded me of something I forgot about myself.

How much I adore history.

Therefore, a big shout out to Viola Swamp, who, first, helped bring about my Vivienne, and second, if you do TikTok and you want to know all about the Tudors, Shakespeare and anything about that time period, you simply *must* follow her.

Onward from that, if you know my books, you know I sometimes search for inspiration for clothes, rooms, pets, etc. I put all of this on my Pinterest boards.

For this book, I was trying to find inspiration for Prue's artistry and came across this amazing painting that informed the fictional one Prue painted of Battle. This will be on my Pinterest board, but I'm grateful through this research that I discovered Frank Moth. His painting "Roots" is the basis for Prue's painting. If you have an interest in seeing the work of a talented artist, check him out at FrankMoth.com

The Nag's Head in this book is based on a pub of the same name my in-laws used to take us to when we visited them up in Nantwich. I looked this pub up to give them a shout out, and sadly, it seems it's since closed down. Happy times were had there. Memories were made there. And they had great steak dinners. So I guess I have no choice but to shout out to the old Nag's Head for gifting me with all of those treasures.

The only graphic novel I've ever read in my life is Rachel Smythe's *Lore Olympus*, which I cannot recommend highly enough. Indeed, I haven't searched for another one, because I fear nothing can compare to how much I enjoyed Smythe's books. You can grab these in print or read them on Webtoons.

Also, I nicked one of my besties, Beth's, maiden name, Burleigh, to give to my duke. So, thanks for that, Bethie!

Last, I never wish to forget expressing my thanks to all the fabulous women listed below: my team, smart, savvy, talented women who help to make my books all they can be and go as far as they can go.

Kelly Brown
Kimberly Callahan
Marybarb Galeziewski
Tanaka Kangara
Amanda Simpson
Emily Sylvan Kim
Stacey Tardif
Grace Wenk

NEWSLETTER

Would you like advanced notification about Upcoming Releases?
Access to exclusive content? Access to exclusive giveaways? The first
to see a new cover reveal? Sign up for my newsletter to keep up-to-
date with the latest from Kristen Ashley!

Sign up at <u>kristenashley.net</u>

ABOUT THE AUTHOR

Kristen Ashley is the *New York Times* bestselling author of over one
hundred romance novels. She's a hybrid author, publishing titles independently and traditionally, with books translated into fourteen
languages and millions of copies sold.

Kristen's novel, *Law Man*, won the *RT Book Reviews* Reviewer's Choice
Award for best Romantic Suspense, her independently published title,
Hold On, was nominated for *RT Book Reviews* best Independent
Contemporary Romance, and her traditionally published title, *Breathe*,
was nominated for best Contemporary Romance. Her titles *Motorcycle
Man*, *The Will*, *The Hookup* and *Ride Steady* (which won the Reader's
Choice award from *Romance Reviews*) all made the final rounds for
Goodreads Choice Awards in the Romance category.

Although Kristen is super proud of all those accolades, she's just
happy that—after years of writing with no publisher or agent interested in what she did—she now has a loyal readership who, on social
media, she can share recipes with and regale with stories of her bent
toward being a klutz.

Kristen was born in Gary and raised in Brownsburg, Indiana, but since
leaving her home state (Hoosier by birth, Boilermaker by the grace of
God!), she's lived in Denver and the West Country of England. All of

these places were home, and she's put them in her books with all the love she still has for them.

Now, after years of cold, misty days in the UK (that she still misses, along with cream teas, custard and battered sausages), Kristen resides in almost constant sun. She writes at her desk in Phoenix or among the deer and javelina in her little cabin up in the Arizona mountains, regretting often that she forgets to put the sunshade over her windshield, thus her car often doubles as a human oven. Even so, she loves calling all the sun, saguaro and beautiful mountains home.

You can read more about Kristen and her books at KristenAshley.net.

facebook.com/kristenashleybooks
instagram.com/kristenashleybooks
pinterest.com/KristenAshleyBooks
goodreads.com/kristenashleybooks
bookbub.com/authors/kristen-ashley
tiktok.com/@kristenashleybooks

ALSO BY KRISTEN ASHLEY

Rock Chick Series:

Rock Chick

Rock Chick Rescue

Rock Chick Redemption

Rock Chick Renegade

Rock Chick Revenge

Rock Chick Reckoning

Rock Chick Regret

Rock Chick Revolution

Rock Chick Reawakening

Rock Chick Reborn

Rock Chick Rematch

Rock Chick Bonus Tracks

Avenging Angels Series:

Avenging Angel

Avenging Angels: Back in the Saddle

Avenging Angels: Tenderfoot

Avenging Angel: Bad Medicine

The 'Burg Series:

For You

At Peace

Golden Trail

Games of the Heart

The Promise

Hold On

The Chaos Series:

Own the Wind

Fire Inside

Ride Steady

Walk Through Fire

A Christmas to Remember

Rough Ride

Wild Like the Wind

Free

Wild Fire

Wild Wind

The Colorado Mountain Series:

The Gamble

Sweet Dreams

Lady Luck

Breathe

Jagged

Kaleidoscope

Bounty

Dream Man Series:

Mystery Man

Wild Man

Law Man

Motorcycle Man

Quiet Man

Dream Team Series:

Dream Maker

Dream Chaser

Dream Bites Cookbook

Dream Spinner

Dream Keeper

The Fantasyland Series:

Wildest Dreams

The Golden Dynasty

Fantastical

Broken Dove

Midnight Soul

Gossamer in the Darkness

Four Realms Series:

Night's Fall

Ghosts and Reincarnation Series:

Sommersgate House

Lacybourne Manor

Penmort Castle

Fairytale Come Alive

Lucky Stars

The Honey Series:

The Deep End

The Farthest Edge

The Greatest Risk

The Magdalene Series:

The Will

Soaring

The Time in Between

Manor and Mysteries Series:

Too Good to Be True

Perfect in Every Way

Mathilda, SuperWitch:

Mathilda's Book of Shadows

The Rise of the Dark Lord

Misted Pines Series

The Girl in the Mist

The Girl in the Woods

The Woman by the Lake

The Woman Left Behind

Moonlight and Motor Oil Series:

The Hookup

The Slow Burn

The Rising Series:

The Beginning of Everything

The Plan Commences

The Dawn of the End

The Rising

River Rain Series:

After the Climb

After the Climb Special Edition

Chasing Serenity

Taking the Leap

Making the Match

Fighting the Pull

Sharing the Miracle

Embracing the Change

Finding the One

The Three Series:

Until the Sun Falls from the Sky

With Everything I Am

Wild and Free

The Unfinished Hero Series:

Knight

Creed

Raid

Deacon

Sebring

Wild West MC Series:

Still Standing

Smoke and Steel

Smooth Sailing

Other Titles by Kristen Ashley:

Heaven and Hell

Play It Safe

Three Wishes

Complicated

Loose Ends

Fast Lane

Perfect Together

9 781954 680920